I veere

bounced onto the  mystery car appeared out ... the tall pines, eclipsed b ... ed away somewhere ahead

"Why didn't we hear it start?" I asked James.

"It's a hybrid."

"We're in a car chase with a Prius?" A car chase with a Porsche or Ferrari was respectable, but with a battery operated car? All bragging rights vanished.

I shifted into warp speed and surged downhill. Seconds later, we faced the hybrid's rear bumper. The spot for the license plate sat empty.

"He's not getting away," I said.

The hybrid turned and launched up a hill, kicking up pebbles and a dusty haze. It fish-tailed and I nearly nipped it in the rear. I executed a sharp left and ran over something large. And lumpy.

"Stop," James said.

I skidded to a halt, a cloud of dirt trapped in my headlights. The Prius escaped through an open gate and onto La Paz. My eyes cut to the rearview mirror. My tail-lights illuminated the road behind us in an eerie red glow. As I surveyed the scene, not a trace of saliva remained in my mouth.

Kudos for Lida Sideris

Recipient of
2014 Helen McCloy/Mystery Writers of America
scholarship
and the inaugural
Bharti Kirchner/San Francisco Writers' Conference
scholarship

Murder and Other Unnatural Disasters

by

Lida Sideris

This is a work of fiction. Names, characters, places, and incidents are either the product of the author's imagination or are used fictitiously, and any resemblance to actual persons living or dead, business establishments, events, or locales, is entirely coincidental.

Murder and Other Unnatural Disasters

Contact Information: info@thewildrosepress.com

Cover Art by *Debbie Taylor*

The Wild Rose Press, Inc.
PO Box 708
Adams Basin, NY 14410-0708
Visit us at www.thewildrosepress.com

Publishing History
First Mainstream Mystery Edition, 2015
Print ISBN 978-1-5092-0240-9
Digital ISBN 978-1-5092-0241-6

Published in the United States of America

Dedication

To all who have
so generously helped me along the way,
especially Mom V.

Chapter 1
The Night Before the Big Day

Woodchips scattered beneath my pounding feet on the pine-scented trail between Ardmore and Valley. It was ten-thirty on a Sunday night and I needed to burn off some energy. Nervous energy. And satisfy a yen for a sandwich. An ice cream sandwich with a cakey, chocolaty wafer and creamy vanilla packed inside. Pure sweetness. It was only two miles to the store. I'd be back in no time.

A train whistled from the pouch pocket of my pink hoodie. Mom's ringtone. I sent the call to voicemail. I was in no mood for a lecture on serial killers.

"You're not out by yourself, are you?" Mom had asked during my last run. "Think like a wildebeest. They move in packs to avoid predators. How will you fight a serial killer all alone?"

She really needed to lay off reading *National Geographic*. Who's ever really alone in the city anyway? Besides, I carried protection: pepper spray, my psycho glare, and a roll of quarters. Brass knuckles are illegal in California.

I cradled the quarter roll in my fist and breathed in the briny air. A new job awaited me in the morning—a serious job with a serious paycheck. A job that was completely out of my league. I took in another breath and fought back a tidal wave of insecurity.

Think about something else.

My name is Corrie Locke. I'm twenty-six-years-old and I'm not the reckless type. Okay, so my gene for caution is a recessive one, but it's still there. I know what I'm doing.

I turned right onto Pier Avenue and slowed to a brisk stroll down the well-lit Hermosa Beach sidewalk. I paused long enough to give myself a good body shake, wet dog style, to liberate all lingering tension.

Minutes later, I entered the parking lot of a compact convenience store. I gathered my tangle of hair into a ponytail, twisted it, and secured the mid-section with a barrette at the back of my head. My ends stuck out on top like a rooster tail, but I could live with that.

A short, stocky guy stood outside the store entry. He gave me an appraising look, sooty eyes lingering on my chest. I considered chucking him soundly under the chin with my fist, but I didn't need an assault charge on my record. He nodded his approval despite my cave woman updo and lack of makeup. He squatted, picked up a lit cigarette from the pavement, took a quick drag, set it down, and followed me inside.

I shoved the quarter roll into my pocket and headed across the store, past junk food displays and magazine stands. I stopped by the refrigerated section along the back wall. The stocky guy reclaimed his spot behind the counter. He snapped his neck from side-to-side and followed up with a knuckle-cracking marathon. I threw him a look that could shrivel a watermelon.

"Do you mind?" I said.

He shrugged and turned his back to me, watching my every move in a narrow strip of wall-to-wall mirror running along the top of the store. I slid open the glass lid of the freezer case.

"Give me your cash."

I crouched down low and peeked around the corner of the aisle. A man in a black ski mask pointed a gun at the cashier. A semi-automatic pistol. I jerked out of view and reached into my pocket. I pulled out my cell-phone.

"Hey," the robber said. "You think I don't see you?"

My heart beat a wild, tribal tempo.

"Get over here. Now."

I started to rise when, out of a back room, a tall, skinny guy tripped past me. His hands shot up. He flicked a look my way, all blood drained from his face, mouth and eyes gaping. My fingers tightened around my cell-phone. But before I could push 9-1-1, the unthinkable happened. A train whistle escaped.

"What's that?" the robber asked.

I gulped.

"Get your ass out here. Before I shoot my way over to you."

I straightened and stepped out into the open. The robber's eyes and gun darted back and forth between me and the guys behind the counter.

"Move," he said. "And lose the phone."

I bent down, lay my phone on the graying linoleum, and side-stepped over to the others.

"Up with the hands."

My fingers reached for the ceiling. My eyes locked on the thief.

"Open it."

The short guy fumbled with the cash register.

"Quit stalling!" The robber gripped the gun with

both hands and aimed at me. "Give me the money or she's dead meat."

The employees' horrified eyes latched on to mine. I held my breath, my gaze glued to the barrel.

"Hurry."

A trace of orange rimmed the tip of the gun. I squinted. It *was* orange. I was sure of it. How sure? Fairly to pretty damn.

The short guy pushed a side button and the register drawer sprang open.

"Put the money on the counter." The robber waved the gun at me. "You. With the squirrely hair. Give me your wallet."

"What?" I said, my voice sounded squeaky. "Squirrely?"

He stretched out a gloved hand, palm up, and wiggled his fingers. "Now."

"Please don't hurt me. Please. I'm frightened. I've only got some change—"

"Do it!"

I reached inside my pocket and felt the quarter roll. I cupped the solid mass, yanked it out, and smacked it against the barrel of the gun. Air-bound, it bounced off the candy aisle and crashed to the floor.

Meanwhile, the stocky guy grabbed a bottle of beer and knocked it on the side of the robber's head. He hollered and crumpled, moaning.

****

"The orange tip was a dead giveaway," I told the police officer when he arrived. I massaged my aching knuckles. They still throbbed from the impact. "Most of it was cut off, but I know a toy gun when I see one."

"That was no toy, Miss."

“What?” There was that squeak in my voice again.

“Any bullets coming from that baby would have been the real thing. The perp’s girlfriend was sitting outside, in the getaway car. She’d painted the barrel orange last night, to match her sneakers. He had trouble cleaning off the tip.”

“It was real?”

He had no chance to reply. I threw up all over his black leather boots.

“Sorry.” I leaned against the counter, panting from my expulsion. Mom’s train whistle blew again. You’d think we lived nine hundred miles apart instead of only nine.

“You were in a hold up?” She said after I briefed her. “It’s all your father’s fault.”

Everything was his fault. Especially after the divorce.

“You’re not a cop, not a criminologist, not a detective—”

“Private investigator…”

“Or in any kind of law enforcement. You’re not your father. You’re a lawyer.”

“I know.” Truth is I didn’t want to be a lawyer. My parents wanted it for me. I mean, I like unearthing facts buried in ambiguities, which both the law and private investigation offered, but I craved more. The hunting down of missing puzzle pieces, finding them, and joining them together to solve a crime. I missed the mad rush of catching bad guys doing bad things to good people, which is what I used to do with Dad. And which is what I accidentally did tonight. But that chapter of my life was closed. I was just a regular person now.

"I'll see you in two weeks when I get back from New York," Mom said. "And don't be nervous about tomorrow, sweetie. Nervousness can lead to nail biting, panic attacks, projectile vomiting—"

"Okay, I get it."

"Remember to follow directions. The worst thing to do is to take matters into your own hands."

"Right." I understood perfectly. I had to take matters into my own hands. The good news? She never found out about my jogging on the trail alone.

Chapter 2
Unexpected Surveillance

I woke up at four the next morning, alert and on edge, stuck in surveillance mode from the old days when I trailed Dad on his cases. Since my drive from Hermosa to Newport Beach took barely an hour, I arrived early for my first day on the job. It seemed only natural I conduct a little quasi-surveillance while I waited. Just this one last time.

I parked across the street in the lot of a garden-variety warehouse and stepped out into the breezy February morning. Tall, skinny palm trees swayed and shook their leafy heads, letting loose a light, smoky scent. I buttoned my blazer and planted my pumps behind a row of spindly hedges, eyes fixed on a two-story office building. My office building, that is.

Minutes later, a BMW sailed in, followed by a Mercedes. A Porsche revved by next, trailed by a few forgettable imports and domestics that scattered themselves toward the back of the parking area.

While I debated going in early, a blue Aston Martin slid in the lot and stopped, spitting distance from the double glass door entry. The driver's side swung open and a man hopped out. It was Him. CEO Arthur Keith. His coppery hair gave him away. It stuck out like he'd caught his finger in an electric socket. His dark suit fit his executive status, but instead of a briefcase, he carried a black backpack that swung loosely at his side. A red flag unfurled in my mind. Backpacks are useful for carrying all sorts of things: books, food, shoes, overnight stuff. And pressure cooker bombs. I shoved the last thought aside.

Arthur jetted toward the back of the lot and disappeared beneath a clump of tall trees. Moments later, a small, white pickup drove in and idled near the same trees. Arthur reappeared and, with a hand at each end, pushed the backpack into the open window of the passenger side. His indelicate handling convinced me it wasn't ticking. I exhaled.

The truck peeled out of my line of vision and re-emerged in seconds, exiting the same driveway. My eyes fastened on the driver. A red baseball cap squashed the top of his black curly hair and a wide mustache overpowered his upper lip. Meanwhile, Arthur had returned to his Aston Martin. He opened the trunk, grabbed his briefcase, and stared directly my way.

I ducked and squatted behind the hedges.

"Oh, man." I jumped back and landed on my bottom. The sprinklers had streamed on and showered my lower half.

"What do you think you're doing?"

A full-figured security guard stood off to one side, hands on hips.

"I'm getting in a little yoga before work. I got carried away with the standing frog pose."

"I've been watching you. If you're gonna hide out, you ought to know the nearby hazards. Have you looked at your shoes lately? Those are cute by the way."

I sat up, grabbed my ankle, and pulled my black suede pump closer. A pink wad of bubblegum clung to the leather sole. "Oh, dear God. These are my mom's. She's going to kill me."

"Hold on." The guard pulled out a razor blade from the pocket of her light blue poplin shirt, knelt down, and removed every last bit of the sticky mess. She was surprisingly limber considering she stood six feet tall in her rubber soles and was built like Babar the elephant. Her hair was the color of maple syrup and sat piled on top of her head in a neat round bun. Her eyes were as dark as straight espresso.

"You saved my life," I said. "Thank you."

"Wait," the guard said. "I saved your life? Does that mean you owe me?"

"Not exactly." I hauled myself up. "There's an old Chinese saying that when you save someone's life, you're responsible for it."

"I don't think so. I'm pretty sure you owe me."

I dusted off my wounded backside and examined my legs for cuts and scratches. "Well, see you." I walked toward my car.

"Who you hiding from, anyway?" she asked, close at my heels.

"I wasn't hiding. I'm just waiting. It's my first day of work, over there…" I pointed to the mirror-coated building. "At Keith-Ameripictures. I got here a little early."

"You're spying, aren't you? You're spying on your future coworkers. I get that. I had the jitters myself when I got this job."

"I don't have the jitters."

"It's hard to know what to expect. Nothing to be

scared about, honey."

"I'm not scared."

I could change a flat in the dark on the side of the road, shoot a Glock, and reenact an incident at the scene of the crime using just the facts and instinct. All courtesy of Dad. Flat tires, weapons, and crime scenes didn't make me nervous. But new jobs did.

The security guard took out a can of WD-40 from the pocket of her cargo pants and sprayed the remnants of gum on the asphalt. "That's a movie studio over there. You some kind of actress?"

"Lawyer."

Her head snapped toward me. "For real? Me too."

Lawyers popped up faster than weeds these days.

"Well, almost. I'm in law school. At Columbia."

"Columbia?"

"Uh-huh. Columbia California School of Law. I got class tonight. Online. It's one of them schools that come to you. It's somewhere in the Sierra Nevadas."

My eyes cut to my watch. "I'd better go."

"What's your name, anyway?"

"Corrie Locke."

"Nice to meet you," she said. "Gwenaveera Bankhead, at your service. You can call me Veera. I have a feeling we're going to be good friends."

I took a deep breath, slid into my car, and motored away to start my new, crime-free life.

Chapter 3
A Flea Among Butterflies

"I can do this." I pulled into the parking lot of the only movie studio located in Orange County. If I had to practice law, this was the life for me. The glamour, movie premieres, limo rides, and limitless swag appealed to my superficial side.

I parked next to a black Porsche. I had officially arrived.

I swung open my door, stepped out, and stumbled toward my neighbor's side. My hands slapped against the Porsche, breaking my fall. I backed off, but my finger and palm prints lingered on the smooth paint. At least I didn't trip the alarm. I bent over and blew on the prints. I rubbed away, using the sleeve of my jacket as a cleaning cloth, until not a trace remained. I could practically see my reflection. I was off to a good start. I blew out one more time for good measure, and the crazy wailing of the alarm pierced my eardrums. I turned and stumbled toward the office, and hustled through the front door.

Moments later, I stood in the high-ceilinged lobby. No one seemed to notice the alarm. Or me. Worker bees—sales, marketing, mailroom staff, and assorted help—buzzed around down here. Executive offices awaited upstairs. My office. I wiped my damp palms along the top of my skirt.

Keith-Ameripictures wasn't exactly a full-fledged studio. It was a production arm of a giant motion picture octopus. After Arthur turned a picture book, produced on a shoestring budget, into a box office megahit, the studio gods gifted him with a multimillion-dollar Ameripictures contract. Arthur used the funds to open his very own mini-studio, affectionately referred to as the Complex.

"Keith-Ameripictures, would you please hold?" the receptionist rattled on. Short cinnamon hair curled around the band of her headset. She juggled calls with an Irish lilt. After a minute, she turned to me, brows bunched together. "Your significance please?"

"I'm Corrie Locke, here to see Marshall Cooperman. My new boss," I said. "It's my first day."

"I'm Molly. Welcome," she said and rang Marshall. "Up you go."

While the peons barely glanced at me downstairs, scientific scrutiny awaited on the top floor. Fashion and face inspectors examined me from head to toe and all angles. I deflated. My shoes made the cut, but I was underdressed in a gray pinstriped, polyester skirt-suit. A flea among butterflies.

I took a deep breath and made a mental note—raid Mom's closet on the way home. Mom was the senior buyer of European designer collections at Saks Fifth Avenue, which was very convenient, except that I was barred access to her wardrobe. After a healthy dose of begging, she'd lent me her shoes, but that was all. I used to borrow her clothes on the regular, until a padlock appeared on her closet door, thanks to an accidental olive oil spill on a silk blouse. It didn't help that a neighbor's bulldog chewed Mom's Louboutins on my watch. I was certain she'd removed the padlock by now. But I'd bring bolt cutters, just in case.

"Make yourself at home." Lesley, Marshall's assistant appeared behind me. Slim and attractive, with inky hair that flipped upward at her shoulders, she looked no older than me. But she admitted, during my second interview, that she hovered near Marshall's elderly stage of life. He was thirty-eight.

Her almond-shaped eyes rolled over me. "He's going to be a few," she said and left.

"A few" stretched to a half-hour before he cracked open his door. I later learned the first rule of Marshall Law: "Always keep appointments waiting while you watch the cooking channel, check out the Lakers' blog, or relax in the lotus position. Do your thing while waiting visitors become increasingly annoyed and/or anxious. Gives you the edge."

Marshall Cooperman, Vice President, Business Affairs, hired me. For that, I owed him my first-born child and a lifetime of Twitter following. I'd competed with a Harvard Law grad who'd hauled a briefcase to his interview stuffed with contracts he'd drafted while interning at Disney. Yet Marshall chose me.

I was smart, but not genius; attractive, but not flashy; experienced, but in a different field. Plus, I was young, naïve, and unlearned in the ways of business affairs. Therefore, I posed no threat in an industry rife with paranoia and insecurity.

"Traffic okay?" Marshall asked. He could relate to my commute. He drove in from Santa Monica.

"Grand," I said. My overly-early start was a distant memory.

Marshall handed me a stack of contracts, led me to

the doorway, and gently shoved me toward my office. My name sparkled on a silver plaque on the door. Roughly a quarter the size of his, my office made me happy.

He idled in the doorway. “I need you to take a call tomorrow, with Winona from publicity. I’ll get you the deal points. Most of us will be at the funeral.”

I nodded and wondered if I should ask. I was new and it wasn’t my business. Yet Marshall waited. “A funeral?”

“For Claire. She worked in IT. She was only twenty-five. Accidental drug overdose. We’ll talk later.” Marshall exited.

I shook off a light mantle of sadness and sized-up my space. Twin ficus trees with slim braided trunks stashed in shiny black pots flanked the window. A built-in bookshelf lined with the latest DVDs hugged the opposite wall. Movie posters and an LCD TV adorned the remaining wall space. I really had arrived.

I slipped behind my desk and labored until my thighs prickled from lack of motion. I slapped the tops of my legs with my hands and froze, ears perked. Two sets of breaths filled the quiet. Mine and the open-mouth kind. I looked up. The personification of the Cheshire cat occupied the doorway. He lacked the stripes, but honed the rascally grin and round face, complete with the promise of mischief.

“Well, hello, *hello*,” he said. “I expect to see a lot of you around here.”

My heart nearly escaped from its rib cage. It was the boy wonder up-close, Arthur Keith. The man with the coppery, stand-up hair who’d stared at me this morning when I was hiding in the bushes. Well, not exactly hiding. Waiting.

"I'm..." This was no time to be tongue tied. "...happening to meese you."

His grin widened at my fumble. "Not as happening as 'meese.'"

He breezed out, and I wilted into my seat. Why? A simple smile would have been so effective. Look what it did for the Mona Lisa. Instead, I appeared a complete idiot.

I ended up staying until eight that night.

"How was your day?" Lesley leaned a shoulder against the doorframe to my office.

"Solid," I said. "How was yours?"

"Well, I measure my days by the number of homicidal thoughts I have. I only had two today. So it must have been good."

I wasn't sure whether to laugh or call 9-1-1.

"See you tomorrow."

She left and I closed up my briefcase. I'd almost made it to the door when I heard voices outside my office. I flattened my back against the wall.

"You must go."

I recognized the receptionist's Irish lilt.

"Not just for Claire. For Druby," she said. "He'd want you to be there."

"My funeral card's all filled up for the year," Lesley said. "And I haven't gotten over Druby."

"He was such a kind soul."

"All I know is he was too young to die."

"But so was Claire. That's why you should go tomorrow."

"Forget it, Molly," Lesley said.

I peeked through the doorway. They parted ways.

Two unexpected deaths so close in time? How's that possible? I ran a fact check on Druby using my phone and found an *Orange County Tribune* article on him. He was the assistant head of security at Keith-Ameripictures until six weeks ago when his car was found at the bottom of Lake Aliso Niguel. With him in it. Cause of death to be determined, but the coroner leaned toward suicide. I'd only worked here for one day and found his death disturbing. I couldn't imagine what the others felt. Too depressing to ponder for long, I headed out.

Most of the lot was empty when I reached my car, including both spots next to me. It wasn't until I sat inside that I saw the note beneath my windshield wiper. I stepped back out and grabbed it. Someone had scribbled,

I'll be watching you.

Chapter 4
Confrontation Alert

I arrived at the Complex early and marched straight in the next morning, ready for my first meeting with the executives. My official coming-in party.

When Marshall and I entered the conference room, everyone but Arthur and Bryce Bachman, the Executive VP, was assembled. Between introductions, I marveled at my surroundings. The whole building was done up in a modern style, but this traveled beyond, into alien territory. As in Martians. Gravity-defying, neon orange chairs scattered along a glass-top table that burst out in a ledge around a white plastic base. The furniture was made in Germany, Marshall told me. Way before all of our times, except Marshall's, and the even older head of marketing, Rob Root. His abundant, pepper-speckled hair matched his goatee. He stared at me briefly before tossing a look of dismissal my way. The kind reserved for stray paperclips.

Minutes later, Arthur rushed in, a human jet ski. He skidded to a halt, happy grin etched on his jolly face. I blushed when I recalled yesterday's interchange. His pale blue eyes intercepted mine, and I hoped his memory was short.

My attention was diverted to the man behind him. He eclipsed Arthur both in height and looks. In strode Arthur's number two in a gray suit, eyes hidden behind aviator shades. Despite the green-tinged lenses, I recognized Bryce Bachman from his pictures in *Variety*. He looked so hot, his suit practically sizzled. I tore my gaze away and focused on steadying my pounding heart.

Arthur took his throne. Praise and flattery flowed while he snacked on cinnamon rolls and sticky buns. When he stopped chewing and spoke, cheers and applause filled the space.

"Let's do a film on that talking toilet series," Arthur said.

"Brilliant." "Why didn't I think of that?" "These sticky buns are dope."

Toward the end of the meeting, Marshall introduced me. I offered a few words of gratitude and dedication to my new job. I didn't falter, but no one noticed except the Vice President of Accounting, Stefon Bellendorf. His full lips turned up into a smile. He gave me two thumbs up.

"Nicely done," he said.

The rest packed up, checked smart phones, and slid to the edges of their space-age chairs to prepare for blast-off.

After the meeting, Rob Root pushed past me in the hallway. "Watch out, sweetheart."

I trailed him to his office. "Did I do something to upset you?"

His assistant wedged his wiry self between us.

"Yeah," Rob said. "You parked your car next to mine."

My eyes glanced off the bank of windows behind his massive desk. Rob's empty chair swiveled away from me, positioned for a sweeping view of the parking lot. Binoculars rested on the broad interior ledge. It didn't take an Einstein to figure out that he drove the Porsche that I landed on yesterday. He'd left the note on my windshield.

"It was an accident," I said. "I tripped. I examined your car for scratches. There were none."

"You touched my passenger door," he said. His assistant shared his look of pain.

"I gently rubbed against it. Did you find any marks?" I asked with all the patient concern of a nurse in the terminal ward.

His face turned red. "If I did, you think I'd be this calm?"

His assistant nodded in agreement.

"Sorry," I said. "It won't happen again."

"Pat!"

The assistant slid closer to Rob and they locked heads, absorbing themselves in an open red folder. I fled to my office to scream in peace.

Lesley waited by my door. "You're wanted in the principal's office." She jerked her thumb behind her toward Marshall's domain.

I found him poring over a batch of documents sitting on the mahogany plane of his pedestal desk. "Heard you made friends with Rob today," he said.

When did he hear? Only a minute had passed since I'd left Rob's office. "Yes. We're besties now."

Marshall handed me a memo and folded his school-girlish hands. "That's for today's call. Jake Arnon's a friend of mine. The deal points are all there."

"Are we willing to give in on any of them?"

"He represents a small production company out of Thailand. They're not going to ask for much." Marshall slipped his narrow shoulders into his black jacket. "We'll talk when I get back. And remember, work with Winona on this one. She's in publicity. She'll help. And be sure to stroke Jake."

Second Rule of Marshall Law: "To treat the right people the right way, 'stroke' them."

Stroking Jake sounded unappealing, phone wise or otherwise, but I'd do my best.

I returned to my office, called Winona, and left her a message to meet earlier. I reviewed Marshall's memo until my stomach growled strongly enough to measure 6.9 on a Richter scale, had one been handy. At least I looked presentable. I'd raided Mom's closet last night and borrowed a few outfits. I wore her lawn green pencil skirt and black wrap-top. I was dressed for battle. The bolt cutters did the job.

Giggles and laughter drifted in from the hallway. The non-funeral goers had loosened their ties and kicked off their heels. I grabbed my purse and surfaced outside into welcoming rays of sunlight. Temperatures were pegged at sixty-four and partly cloudy, but it felt like spring had hit, full force. I whipped out my sunglasses and used my phone to guide me to the nearest deli. I found one on MacArthur.

My heels clicked along the pavement and I pictured my lunch—the ice cream sandwich I'd missed yesterday and—my ears sharpened. A steady clack-clack plodded along behind me. The sound of shorter, clunkier heels, keeping time with mine. I turned my head to one side and brushed my shoulder off with my fingers. My eyes rolled over a pudgy guy with curly black hair, jeans, and a white dress shirt. Scuffed up cowboy boots completed his lower half and a wide black mustache accentuated the top. It was yesterday's man. The one who took Arthur's backpack.

I jaywalked across Von Karman, halting and skipping between speeding cars, honking horns be damned. Smoky exhaust vapor invaded my nostrils and I coughed, gasping for fresh air. I glanced behind me. My pursuer mimicked my reckless maneuver and was nearly plowed over by an SUV. Expletives flew behind my back from all sides. At least my crossing had been dignified.

I continued to MacArthur. He did the same, the distance between us shrinking with his every step. I stopped, sank onto a bus bench, and fiddled with my phone. My pulse quickened. My eyes flicked toward him. He shoved his hands in the pockets of his jeans and walked head down, into an office building.

Was he following me or not? Had I lost my touch? When I shadowed Dad on his cases, I could spot a pursuer, blindfolded, using just my sense of hearing. The pattern of the footsteps is a dead giveaway. Anxious, determined, hurried. Keeping perfect time with the target. Like the guy behind me.

I entered the deli and sniffed newly cooked, deep-fried potatoes. My stomach grumbled again. I ordered a chicken and avocado sandwich and headed toward the freezer. I opened the heavy glass door and stuttered at the blurry reflection. The man with the mustache sat on a white resin chair in the patio area, a newspaper open wide in his hands. I turned and stared at him. His eyes locked onto mine.

I paid for my food and headed outside. He shot up, the hastily folded newspaper crackling with agitation.

I stopped in front of him. "Why are you—"

"Put your hands behind your back." A security guard grabbed the guy's arms and twisted them behind him.

"You again," I said.

Veera flashed a smile while she slapped a set of cuffs on the guy. "Hello, Corrie. How are you today?"

"Why are you cuffing him?"

"I noticed he was harassing you. Was it harassment of a sexual nature or of a staring nature?"

"Staring isn't harassment," the man said. "Ow."

She'd kicked him in the shin. "You're lucky I'm wearing my guard boots today and not my stilettos. Those pack a damn sharp kick." She turned to me. "I'm on my lunch break." Her eyes dropped to the bag in my hand. "What did you order?"

"He isn't harassing me. He was following me. Why?" I asked the guy.

"I need to talk to you," he said. "It's real important."

"Who are you?"

"Billy Soto. Chief Director of Security Operations at Keith-Ameripictures."

"For real?" Veera's brows shot up. "I arrested one of my own? How about that?"

"You're a security guard," I said. "You have no authority to arrest anyone."

"Truth," Veera said. "But there seems to be corruption among the ranks."

"Were you tailing him? Or me?" I asked her.

"I saw you leave for lunch, and I was hurrying to join-up when I observed this guy following you." She turned to him. "You were harassing her."

"I wasn't," he said.

“Remove the cuffs, please,” I said. “And he’s right, staring isn’t harassment.”

“Oh, I beg to differ.” Veera unlocked the cuffs and slipped them into the pocket of her navy blue bomber jacket. “The US Court of Appeals for the First Circuit found that staring alone can constitute triable jury issues of sexual harassment.”

“That’s only if there were prior acts of harassment. I’ve never seen this guy before. Let alone been harassed by him.”

Veera squinted and regarded me with a hand on her hip. “You’re good.”

Billy rubbed his wrists and set his eyes on mine. “Can we go somewhere private?”

“There’re some nice tables around the corner,” Veera said.

“Not you. Her. This is serious. It’s confidential company business.”

“Stalking is not part of company business. Besides, I know too much. You don’t want me going to your bosses, blabbing on how you were nearly run down—”

“You know nothing. I saw the cars…”

I slipped away while they argued and ate the ice cream sandwich on my walk. I’d squished the last of the chocolate wafer and sweet vanilla between my tongue and the roof of my mouth before they caught up. They were still arguing.

“If you had any brains,” Billy said. “You would’ve noticed I wasn’t trying to hide.”

“Well, you should have been. We wouldn’t be talking now if you weren’t so incompetent.”

“I need her. It’s important—”

“Enough!” My eyes cut to Billy. “You have five

minutes to explain your business before I go back to my office. And you…" I turned to Veera. "Impressive recall on the sexual harassment case."

Veera beamed. "Why, thank you. Guess I'll get back to work. Nothing much happening here anyway." She crossed the street and disappeared into the parking lot where we'd met.

I turned to Billy. "What's your story?"

"There's this issue—"

"Legal issues go to Marshall first. I'm pretty new at this lawyer stuff—"

"I don't need a lawyer." He threw a hand at me. "Forget it. You wouldn't believe me anyway. No one does." Billy stomped toward the Complex.

Curiosity dragged me along the heels of his cowboy boots. "What is it I won't believe?"

"I thought you could help, but I was wrong." He turned his head my way. "But you should help. You owe me."

What was with the "you owe me" factor? Was it a security guard thing? "I met you what? Ten minutes ago? And you haven't exactly done me any favors."

"Yes, I have. But you don't know it. There's a lot you don't know." He turned his back to me and stormed away.

I trotted after him. Not easy in four-inch heels. "Wait a minute."

Billy froze. His head dropped and his shoulders sagged.

I walked around to face him. "It was your assistant that killed himself."

"He didn't. I know," Billy said, in a choked voice. "I know what really happened."

Uh-oh. I was standing on the brink of a sky-high cliff and this guy was about to go over the edge. And maybe take me with him. I had to make sure my hair, limbs, and billowy bits of clothing were out of his reach.

He sniffled, moved closer, and dropped his voice to a whisper. “He wouldn’t do that. He was level headed. Me and Druby, we had no secrets. He was my brother, here…” Billy pounded a fist over his heart. “…where it counts.”

“Sorry, but how is it that I owe you?”

“I switched your record with the Harvard guy’s.”

“What record?”

“Your criminal record.”

“I don’t have a criminal record.”

“Burglary.”

“Oh, that doesn’t really count. I was caught with a few crowbars, slim jims, and screwdrivers. And a pair of pliers. I never actually broke in anywhere and the DA was mad at my fath…it was a possession thing.”

“You wouldn’t have been hired, if they knew,” Billy said. “So I made the Harvard lawyer the criminal instead.”

“What?”

“I gave him your record. And gave you his clean background check.”

I really did owe this guy. “I’m not a criminal,” I said. “Those were just handy tools I carry around.”

“You got them now?”

“No,” I said. Although I did have a couple of other questionable objects in my trunk.

“Then you’ll help me,” Billy said.

It wasn’t a question. It was an assumption with a

mild threat woven inside. I couldn't afford to lose my job. My rent cut out a sizeable chunk of my paycheck. "What kind of help are you talking about?" I asked and checked my watch. It was almost conference call time.

"Can you look into it?" Billy moved closer and wrung his hands.

"Look into what?" I took a step back.

"Druby's death."

"I'm sure the police examined—"

"They were quick and careless. They said it could be suicide, but it can't."

"I'm a lawyer, Billy," I said stiffly. "Not a private investigator."

He moved in even closer. "You and your dad—"

"Keep him out of this." I winced. My heart tried to punch its way out. Was I always going to be known as Monty Locke's daughter? "I've got a meeting." I turned and bolted into the Complex. His stare seared a hole through my back. I didn't have to help. What was Billy going to do? If he fessed up to fooling around with the background check, he'd get into trouble. And I would be canned.

Inside the hushed building, the reception desk flew on automatic pilot. Not a suit or skirt in sight. The tap, tap of my heels echoed up the stone staircase. I escaped into my office and hurled my purse beneath my desk. I folded into my chair and took a deep breath.

Before I'd finished exhaling, Billy poked in his head. "I'll be back later, with evidence."

"Evidence of what?"

He left before I'd finished speaking.

****

I'd barely finished reviewing Marshall's deal

memo when a grinning woman, my age or so, poked her head through the doorway. She spoke in a high-pitched voice, “May I come in?”

“Of course.”

She fluttered inside. “I’m Winona, the publicity director.” She pumped her shoulders up and down. Her fair skin flushed pink and she pointed to a chair.

I nodded.

She squealed and took the seat. “Isn’t it exciting?”

“You mean the phone call?”

“Life.”

Flat-ironed, champagne blonde hair swept her shoulders. She wore a beige cashmere sweater dress and sensible, low heels that purred in comfort causing a pang of envy to hit between my toes.

“I’ll just observe today,” she said. She held her arms straight out in front of her, twisted them together, and took up the shoulder action again.

“Have you talked to today’s caller before?” I asked.

“Jake’s a sweetie.”

I waited for elaboration on that helpful remark, but Winona stared right back. “This isn’t your first deal with him?” I asked.

“No.”

Thankfully, the phone rang. I answered and placed the caller on speaker.

“Jake Arnon here,” he said.

“This is—”

“Whas-up, hubbzz?” Winona said in a throaty voice.

“Winona?” he asked.

“That’s right. The girl you tried to seduce with

your ridiculously black hair and British accent." Winona rose to her feet.

"Um, I don't speak British—"

"Jake, Corrie Locke here," I said. "We have deal points to discuss."

"Where were you last night, J-Ar?" Winona leaned her upper body toward the phone.

"At home." Jake sounded annoyed. "Watching college ball."

"Lost track of time, eh? I stayed up until two—"

"Let's start with the advance—" I tried again.

"I haven't seen you since that night in Vegas," Jake said. "Six months ago."

"We're soul mates!" Winona slapped a hand on my desk. "You must have realized that. We could spend a lifetime together."

"Yeah, and I could grow six more arms and crawl the ocean floor at night."

"I need closure."

"The advance." My palms hit the desk.

"I've got this…" Winona whispered to me.

I shot up and whispered back through clenched teeth, "If I hear one more word, I'm going to shove this stapler—"

"You want to discuss the contract or not?" Jake asked.

The moment Winona opened her mouth, I sat atop the desk, slid across, pivoted, and landed on the other side, standing nose-to-forehead. My nose, that is. I dared her to continue. I spoke to Jake, "The issue is the advance."

Jake cleared his throat. "The high interest rate for payback is offensive."

“I need you—” Winona said.

“To take this deal.” I raised my voice and ran my index finger across my throat. “The interest rate is standard in all of our agreements,” I said. I had no idea if this was true, but it sure sounded serious. “Maybe your client would rather negotiate elsewhere.” I felt my temperature rise in all the sensitive areas. I was about to make or break a deal. Could I crawl back to Jake if he hung up on me? Marshall said he represented a small company, right? My pulse struggled to keep up with my pounding heart. My stare never left Winona’s. She waited, open-mouthed, for Jake’s reply.

“They won’t have a problem with it,” he said.

I breathed again and returned to my side of the desk.

Winona said, “Yes, but we—”

“WE’LL get all use of names and likenesses—” I said.

“Fine,” Jake agreed and was equally conciliatory with the rest of the deal points.

“I’ll draft the contract and send it to your office,” I said. “Anything else?” My finger hovered over the “end call” button.

“There is,” Jake said. “One other thing.”

I wondered where I could get my hands on a paper bag, in case I had a panic attack. Maybe this wasn’t going to work after all.

Jake’s next words spilled out, “I like to seal my deals in person. Dinner tonight, Corrie?”

Winona bobbed her head and mouthed, “Me. I’ll go.”

“Thanks Jake,” I said. “But not necessary.” I hung up before Winona could protest.

"That's exactly what happened to me. Only I couldn't say no. He and I are going to have to talk about this eventually."

"On your own time."

She brought back her smile. "It was lovely to meet you."

Winona left, and I struggled to regain my focus.

****

The funeral goers trickled in minutes after the support staff regrouped and put on the usual stressed-out front. Marshall paid me a visit. Content that his buddy, Jake, accepted the deal terms, Marshall offered this compliment, "He usually gives me a hard time. What did you do?"

"I told him we'd give him fifty grand under the table if he agreed to our terms."

Marshall stared at my straight face in horror, waiting for me to crack.

"Imagine if we offered that to everyone." I waited for the wan smile. And waited. I finally said, "I'm kidding."

"I know. I talked to Jake." For the first time, I heard Marshall laugh. It was more like a series of hisses. "Sss, sss, ssssss, ss ss ss ss." Dysfunctional teapot style. The jokester.

"About Winona," I said. "She was a distraction."

"That was the plan. To add pressure on Jake. It's basic psychology. She threw him off balance and you cornered him."

"You knew she'd act—"

"Insane? Look, instead of trying to predict your opponent's behavior, take command. Create an unpredictable environment. One in which they can't possibly survive. Or at least can't think clearly. Distract them. That's what we did to Jake."

Marshall Law Rule Number Three: "Have a lunatic present when negotiating. Or act like one yourself."

I spent the next few hours struggling over a talent contract. I might as well have tried to fry an egg on water. I fought the urge to crack my knuckles. In fact, I battled against cracking all the bones in my body and the bones of everyone on the second floor. Especially Marshall's for this impossible assignment.

"I hope you don't mind this interruption."

A woman stood in my doorway. She was petite, except for her bust size which could have used a six inch shelf to rest on. An expert makeup job spruced up her plain-Jane face. She cradled a rectangular chrome vase that displayed an array of orchids, mums, and gerbera daisies.

"These are for you." She placed the vase on my desk.

"They're beautiful. Thank you."

She took a seat. "I'm Mandy Keith."

It took me a moment to realize she was the boss's wife. I'd heard she was a little older and smarter than Arthur. He was thirty-two and had never gotten off the merry-go-round. This woman looked older, serious, and smarter. "Nice to meet you."

"We needed a female executive."

Right then I would have scrubbed all the tile on the second floor with a makeup sponge if she'd asked me. I liked being called an executive.

"If you find yourself trying to get something accomplished and it's not happening, let me know. I sleep with the head honcho."

Mandy's somber face broke into a laugh. I giggled right along with her. She stood and laughed her way out the door. She threw me a backward wave.

And on that high note, I finished up my contract the best I could and grabbed my purse and briefcase. I entered the quiet hallway. Most of the office was gone, giving me the chance to escape without any run-ins.

"Corrie."

I heard a loud whisper from behind. I tottered at the edge of the staircase and turned.

"I brought it," Billy said.

A yellow caution sign flashed brightly in my head. "I'm in a huge rush…"

He held out a black backpack. I blinked. It resembled the one passed on to him by Arthur. If it was and I accepted it, I could become party or accessory to whatever illegal activity he and Arthur were involved in. I gulped.

"I can't." I inched my way down the stairs.

"It's the evidence. It was Druby's."

"What?" The backpack was Druby's? Why did Arthur have it? And why did he give it to Billy? I longed to race home, change into sweats and warm fuzzy socks, and collapse onto my futon with a trivial fashion magazine. I was so done with the risky stuff. I did not want to turn out like my father. "Billy—"

"Take it." He shoved the backpack toward me.

"Why?"

"Because." Billy stepped closer. "Your dad was that detective."

"Private investigator." Detectives are on the police force. Dad was a P.I. How come no one got that?

"You worked with him. You're the one who found

the bloody shoelace. When the basketball player was accused of murder. You and your dad figured it all out."

"Talk to Marshall." I scooted down the stairs.

"But I helped you get this job."

I stopped midway. Right now, I needed help keeping this job.

Billy bounded down to me. "Inside is Druby's book. Take a look and tell me what you think. Give it back if you believe he killed himself."

"A book?" A book was harmless, right?

I grabbed the backpack and skipped down the stairs as fast as I dared without tumbling headfirst and creating a messy, potentially embarrassing scene. I'd store the book overnight and return it tomorrow.

"Thank you," Billy called after me.

Sucker, cried a voice in my head.

Chapter 5
The Man in the Picture

I finished my second lemon yogurt and microwaved popcorn for dinner. Fruit and veggies. A balanced meal. I could paint my walls with the rich scent of hot butter.

The phone rang and I glanced at the number. I debated answering it.

"Hello," I said in the most noncommittal tone I could muster.

"Hi," he said cheerfully. Hopefully.

There was a time, months ago, when his calls made me melt like candle wax over a fire pit. Or at least made me smile. Now I wanted to hurl the phone against the wall.

"How are you?" he asked.

"Tired. I'm going to bed…"

"Wish I was there with you."

I pressed my lips together. He didn't know about my new job and I planned to keep it that way. He thought I still volunteered at the Legal Aid, where I'd headed after law school. I badly wanted to tell him never to contact me again. And to move to another part of the country. Or to Zimbabwe. But I didn't. I wouldn't. We worked in the same industry and could cross paths again. The beginning of a career is not the time to make enemies. But I had a valid excuse for never wanting to see him again.

"How's your wife, Clayton?"

I loved how easy it was to hit him below the belt with that four letter word.

After a steady dose of silence, he asked, "Can we talk?"

"No."

"I miss you. I've got incredible news to share."

"Share it with your wife." I ended the call and ignored his repeated attempts to reach me. I headed into my bedroom.

I lived in a cozy bootleg unit a few blocks from the beach. My landlord was a client of Mom's and owed her a favor. She'd agreed that I pay her after my first paycheck came in, which meant I lacked funds for the finer things in life. Like furniture and a TV. But I had an airbed and a swell DVD collection of old movies I'd inherited from Dad, which I popped into my laptop when the mood struck. Right now, I was in the mood for Cary Grant. I was about to insert *Charade* when I remembered Billy. I debated visiting the garage to retrieve the backpack from my car. Cary or Billy? I would scan the book and watch Cary afterward.

Within minutes, I returned to my airbed and lay on my side, the book wide open beside me. Before I could take a look, my cell phone chimed a series of text messages. I grabbed it to tell Clayton to stop harassing me once and for all, except it wasn't him. It was an unknown number. The texts read,

Call me. Now. I need you. Please.

Instinct told me it was Clayton trying to outsmart me by using a different number.

He sent another message.

Have you forgotten me, Corrie? It's urgent.

That's it. I'd let him have it.

It's me. Ty.

"Ty?"

Ty Calvin was one of Dad's earlier cases. The first one we'd solved together, the one with the bloody shoelace.

I placed the call. An instant blur of noise greeted me from the other end.

"Damn, Corrie. Why'd you take so long?"

"I didn't recognize your number."

"You know I've got to keep changing it. How've you been?"

Ty Calvin was a basketball legend, all 6'8" of him. "Fine, thanks."

"Can you come over? To the Center?"

"Tomorrow—"

"Now."

"I've got to work in the morning. Don't you have a game tonight?"

"Shoot, I can't play anymore."

"I'm no good at offering basketball tips—"

"I don't need any tips. I need your Dad."

"He can't—"

"I know," he said softly. I heard the roar of the crowd. "Georgie's missing."

Who the heck was Georgie? Ty's brother? Personal trainer? Pastry chef? "Have you called the police?" I asked.

"No Five-0!" He lowered his voice. "It's a little embarrassing."

I heard the shrill blow of a whistle, followed by applause. The crowd noise grew louder.

"Be at my house in the morning," he said over the din. "Six a.m." He disconnected.

Uneasiness swept over me. Who was Georgie? And why was Ty embarrassed? A Google search on Georgie's identity came up empty. I texted Ty and confirmed I'd be there, first thing. After all, we had a history together.

Wide awake, I returned to Druby's book. Keith-Ameripictures was known for turning picture books into movies. Druby Valdez had created his own picture book, perhaps with that idea in mind. A cheery creation with expert drawings of a happy-faced little boy who sailed the world with his bearded pet goat, adding passengers from different nations. Each page was fastened in place with a plastic sheet, photo album style. In the end, the sailor boy found a little girl to travel with him. Her name was Claire.

Okay, so Claire was the name of the girl whose funeral everyone attended today. And Druby had a thing for her. So what? So they both had died within weeks of each other.

I closed the book and tossed it onto the floor. Almost on cue, something slipped out right before landing. I jumped off the bed and picked up a photo of a sleek yacht named *King Arthur*. I retrieved the book and opened it again. Empty pages followed the story's end, but the last few exhibited photos taken on Arthur's yacht. The yacht filled with partying people. I spotted Marshall in two of the shots, stiffly hanging out in his suit and tie. More photos of the yacht, Arthur and Mandy, and a shot of Arthur surrounded by a group of scantily clad men and women eagerly embracing the good or, in reality, the moneyed life.

My conclusion: Druby was a talented artist and photographer who liked Claire. Billy wasted his time giving the book to me. I closed it, only to reopen it seconds later. One photo demanded my attention: Arthur stood at the front of the boat with four men, one of whom was Clayton.

Chapter 6
Early Morning Revelations

I slept terribly that night. I tossed and turned on my airbed, a tangle of sheets wrapped around my waist and legs. I woke up at four.

I sat up and replayed the previous day's events: How was I going to finish that last contract? Could I have done better on the conference call? Was Winona insane? Did Marshall use her insanity to clinch the deal? What was Clayton doing with Arthur? Should I wear my leopard print, cashmere sweater to work? Trivial thoughts, like what I was going to wear, relaxed me. I gave up on sleep and got ready for my meeting with Ty.

****

Ten foot high, wrought-iron gates sporting spiked tops and bars as thick as a sumo wrestler's wrist secured Ty's Mediterranean style mansion. I stepped onto the brick driveway and caught a whiff of damp grass. I pressed the intercom button again and again. No response. I dialed and redialed Ty's cell phone. Maybe this was a hoax. Could I break the lock? Not with a horde of security cameras capturing my every move. A nomadic wind swept through my thin sweater and I retreated toward the warmth of my car.

I'd almost made it when I heard quick, padded footsteps approaching from behind. I turned.

"Put that thing down, Corrie. Sheez. It's me."

I lowered my stun gun. Ty was all legs and arms and feet, in indigo blue basketball shorts, a red sweatshirt, and rocking horse size running shoes.

"Sorry I'm late. I was out looking for Georgie." His long arms wrapped around me.

"What happened to him?"

Ty pulled away. "He's gone missing. Two days now."

As I tried to recall if Ty had kids, a white sedan ambled by carrying two females wearing funky headgear, turban-style. The driver nodded to us when they passed.

"I see those two every morning," Ty said, following the car with his eyes. "Georgie and I left the house early. We walked to the gate together, like we always do. We'd meet up an hour later and share croissants and milk and shit. But he didn't come back."

"Do you have a photo of Georgie?" I asked.

Ty handed me his cell phone. "That's my boy."

It was a portrait of them on his phone's home screen. Georgie had large blue eyes, big ears, and wore a rebellious expression. He was a Siamese cat.

"Sheez, I played my game like a snowman last night," Ty said. "The ball kept slipping and sliding out of my fingers. I couldn't get a grip. Corrie, I need him. Georgie's my lucky charm." He fought a sob.

I could see how this could get embarrassing. "Male cats hear the song of the siren sometimes, Ty. They wander off."

"This is Bel-Air. We don't hear sirens. And he doesn't wander."

"You're probably right."

"You can still find him, even if he did wander, can't you?"

"I'll find him." I promised to return the next morning.

****

A little over an hour later, I exited MacArthur Boulevard and wound my way to Von Karmen, toward the Complex. I admired the row of full-headed palm trees along the road and inhaled the crisp, melodic breeze sifting in through my open window. Life in Newport was bliss. A direct contrast to the, "Me-me-me" bustle and "Hurry up" mentality of Los Angeles.

I closed in on the Complex and spied a mustached man standing on the sidewalk. He waved his arms above his head, vying for my attention. I pulled over and rolled down my window.

Billy lowered his face to the opening. "What did you think?"

I reached into the backseat and picked up the backpack. I zipped it up and held it out to him. "Druby's drawings were excellent."

"No!"

The unexpectedness of Billy's quiet yell made me recoil. He snatched the backpack out of my hands.

"You didn't look right," he said. "That book was Druby's diary. In pictures. The cops think he killed himself. But he didn't. He was too happy. The book shows that. Besides, the goat story was going to be Arthur's next movie. He made a deal with Druby. See? Druby had too much good stuff going on."

I sighed and looked straight ahead for a moment before returning my gaze to him. "I'm sorry Druby died."

"He didn't kill himself."

"You don't think it was suicide?" A chill trickled down my spine.

"I know it wasn't."

"How do you know?"

"I just do."

"And you want me to know it too?"

Billy nodded. Hope glimmered in his eyes.

"Did he have any enemies?"

"Everybody liked him." Billy shook his head. "Even Rob Root, most of the time."

Well, that said a lot about Druby. "I wouldn't know where to begin. There must have been a police detective assigned to the case. Check with him or her. I'm a lawyer."

He dropped his chin to his chest. "No one believes me. Druby was special."

I recalled the remarks of friends and neighbors of serial killers. They'd shake their heads in wonder and say, "He was such a charming dinner companion."

"Sometimes," I said. "We don't know people as well as we think."

"I know one thing. People choose suicide because they think they'll be happier dead. They can't stand living. But Druby was happy, alive."

He talked sense. All other human instincts are subservient to the instinct of seeking happiness. Still, I said, "I can't help you."

"Fine. I won't bother you anymore." He turned and stormed away.

Guilt jabbed at me, like the beginnings of a hang nail in too tight running shoes. What was I supposed to do?

"Is he bugging you again?" Veera shouted from across the street.

I waved my hand. "No, we're good."

In a few quick, long strides, she stood in the street by my open window. She wore her hair straight today, parted down the middle, eyes rimmed with charcoal liner, lips bathed in coral gloss. "You know, I've been thinking. That security guy…"

"Billy."

"Yeah, him. He seemed real troubled yesterday and thought you were some kind of superhero who could help. I know you aren't, but maybe I can help you, help him."

"I have a job already, thank you very much, which I won't have much longer, if I don't get in there—"

"You and me, we'd make a good team. You're the brains. I'm the street smarts. What's his problem anyway? A cheating wife? He owe somebody big bucks?"

"I'm not pursuing this." I rolled up my window and turned into the lot. I parked and got out.

"These are the facts." Veera leaned against the trunk of my car. "I'm kind of bored over there." She pitched her chin across the street. "I need more stimulating work."

I made a dash for the front door. "Maybe you should find another job," I said over my shoulder. The entrance was a few yards away.

"Or maybe we should help the little guy." She was close on my heels. "Something good might come out of this. Something good always comes outta helping. Karma, you know? One good turn leads to another."

"No," I said, my hand stretched out, ready to push

open the glass door. "That's one good turn deserves another. When he does a good turn, I'll be sure and pay him back." I opened the door and stopped midway. Billy had done a good turn. He gave the Harvard guy a criminal record. My record. That was good, right? Good for me anyway. Harvard could pick up another job in an instant. He probably already had.

Veera moved closer. "You're seeing the light, aren't you?"

The guilt now corkscrewed its way into my conscience, leaving an emptiness that could swell with regret. Just when everything was dandy. I liked working here. This job was mine. I got it almost fair and square. Okay, I'd check out Billy's claim as payback. Veera could do the legwork. I swallowed and said, "Meet me tonight. In the parking lot. Seven-fifteen."

Chapter 7
Afternoon Storm

That afternoon, Marshall requested changes to the draft I'd submitted. I buckled up and hammered away again on the talent agreement from hell. Lesley gave me a few pointers and I barely came up for air. After a couple of hours, a prayer or two, and Lesley swigging from a flask over my shoulder, my creation was done.

The contract was with a television actor who'd agreed to narrate a series of animated movies for kids about four caterpillars struggling to survive in the big city. *Insects and the City* it was called. The list of the actor's demands rivaled instructions on how to fly a space shuttle. The studio would pay for entourage costs, including the actor's personal magician to keep up his temperamental spirits. And the actor insisted on his personal set of sponsors whose products he wanted mentioned in the movie. Child-unfriendly products like Quik-lax for constipation and Harry O's Irish malt liquor.

Marshall asked me to contact the actor's agent, Norm White, about this last point. I should have been suspicious that Marshall trusted me to make the call after barely three days on the job.

I left Norm a voice message. Minutes later, Lesley put through Norm's call. I answered, and before I finished saying "hello," irate yells, shouts, and screams exploded from the other end.

"Who the fuck do you think you are? What do you think you're fucking doing? My fucking client refuses to be any part of this fucking deal. That'll be the fucking day…"

This tango with the "f" word tirelessly continued. No sentence was spared. My option was to freak out or zone out. My over-heated mid-section told me I was freaked.

Norm paused to take a breath and I quickly inserted, "Since we've never spoken, I'm guessing you're mad at someone else. Who?"

"Benson May. That dorky, stupid jackass."

He continued with profanity galore, and I wondered if someone had written a book of synonyms for swear words. Norm sure could use one. I placed the call on hold and looked up Benson's name on the company roster. He was one of our marketing directors. I left a voicemail for Benson and returned to Norm. There was silence.

"Since this is a children's movie based on a picture book," I said, "we'd like to find your client new sponsors that kids and parents alike would appreciate a little more than laxatives and malt liquor. Like an ice cream or candy company. We'll get your client some sweet deals."

I listened carefully to see if I could hear a trace of a chortle.

His response was gruff, but expletive free. "Call me when sponsorship is firmed."

Where was I going to find new sponsors?

A guy wandered in moments later dressed in head-to-toe black from his T-shirt to his motorcycle boots.

His sandy hair was slicked back into a thin, low ponytail that slid down his spine. He flopped into a chair and entwined his slim arms behind his head, knees spread apart.

"If I'd known you were such a hottie," he said. "I would have come a whole lot sooner."

"Benson," I said.

His bloodshot baby browns gave me a once over, followed with a raunchy grin. I linked my fingers to keep from slapping him.

"What did you say to Norm White?" I asked.

"Good old Norm. Not much because we didn't talk. I'm super busy."

He looked more like a slacker than industrious worker. "I need you to find two, kid-friendly sponsors for *Insects and the City*."

"Yeah. Sure." He shot up, shoved his hands in his pockets, and shuffled out.

I waited only a moment before heading toward the back staircase. I sought solace in the Complex theater and slipped inside the dimly lit space. I made my way over to one of many cushy leather chairs that dotted the room, each the width of a love seat. Accenting the seats were polished chrome side tables perfect for holding snacks, drinks, dinner, or even a small, boisterous child. A respectable-size stage graced the front of the screen for when Arthur or other notable wanted to introduce a film.

"Spectacular, isn't it?"

I nearly jumped out of my heels. I turned.

"I never gave you a proper welcome," Bryce said. He wore a navy pin-striped suit over a charcoal turtle-neck. Not a popular combination, but he pulled it off.

He reached for my hand and shook it firmly in both of his.

"Unbelievable." I experienced a floating sensation. An out-of-body moment. He let go of my hand and I sputtered a small cough and came crashing back down. Get a grip. This was the Executive VP I was talking to. "This theater. It's unbelievable."

He studied my face with a concentration reserved for concert pianists. I studied him back. Ocean blue eyes danced beneath sun-kissed brows. I smiled amid a bumpy silence.

The double doors swung open and Lesley burst inside. She paused, almond eyes darting back and forth between us. To me she said, "Marshall would like a word."

I said a quick goodbye and followed Lesley up the stairs. She whispered over her shoulder, "Watch it. He has a crazy jealous girlfriend. And she has spies everywhere."

"Her spies can report we chatted for a whole minute. I plan to avoid him."

"Smart move. She's a real witch."

Marshall reigned behind his desk when I entered. Rob Root had installed himself across from him. He scowled and tapped his fingers on the armrest. Marshall motioned for me to sit.

"Heard you met with Ben May," he said.

Before I could reply, Rob said, "Nobody tells my people what to do. Nobody, but me!"

"I didn't ask Benson to come to my office," I said. "He managed to fit me into his busy schedule all by himself."

"You told him to find more sponsors."

Marshall leaned off to one side, thoroughly enjoying the theatrics. This was a man who required non-stop action to make up for his static personality. "I told Norm we couldn't use the current sponsors," I said. "As I was instructed." I looked at Marshall.

"Here's how things work," Marshall said before Rob detonated or I located lighter fluid to jumpstart his incineration. "When we need something done in marketing, we ask Rob. He takes care of it. Switching sponsors is too big a decision for you."

"But…"

"You were asked to tell Norm we needed new sponsors, not to tell Ben to go out and find them."

"I see." I quieted down. Initiative was not part of my job.

At that moment, I could have strangled Marshall's chicken neck with one bare hand while pummeling Rob with the other. Then there would be two more funerals for the staff to attend. But if I continued in this fashion, I'd be fired. "Sorry. Next time, I'll run it past you," I told Marshall. I turned to Rob and meant to say, "It won't happen again," but instead this came out, "It wouldn't hurt Benson to return his calls promptly."

"We'll talk." Marshall dismissed me.

I marched out of his office, turned, and tripped over a body on all fours, just outside his door. "What the—"

A woman jumped to her feet and placed a finger against her ample mouth. "Shhh." She waved for me to follow her and tiptoed into my office. She turned to face me.

"I wasn't doing what you thought I was doing," she said.

A skeletal woman stood before me in a fitted, red twill sheath dress. Her face belonged on a farm next to a pitchfork, but her California blonde hair was super-model worthy.

"What did I think you were doing?" I asked.

"Listening to what was going on in Marshall's office."

"You weren't?"

"How could you think such a thing?" Her small eyes widened and scanned my room. "This used to be my office. Right next to Marshall's. We were so close…" She put out a manicured hand. "I'm Caitlyn Rose, Human Resources Director."

"Do you usually crawl around outside people's doors?" I asked, giving her hand a quick shake.

She laughed. "Crawl? You make me sound like I'm a newborn."

"Newborns don't crawl."

"Okay, let's quit playing games, shall we?"

"What?"

"I saw you go into Marshall's office and I didn't know who you were. Lesley wasn't around so I had to find out for myself."

"If you're in HR, shouldn't you have known who I was?"

"I haven't finished reading through the stacks of paperwork on my desk yet. I've been too busy."

Was "busy" a synonym for loafing and crawling around?

"Anyway, I'm glad Marshall hired you. When we were at dinner the other night, I told him it was about time he got some help."

Just how closely did she work with Marshall?

"When he woke up this morning, he swore this would free him up so we could have some real fun." Her smile widened until the corners nearly tickled her ears.

So Marshall's commute wasn't all that bad. How did I know she lived in Orange County? She wore her plastic surgery, displayed so famously at Fashion Island, like a Girl Scout merit badge. Caitlyn's nose was pinched at the tip and her breasts sat too high and too round on her stick figure, clearly the work of a novice or possibly distracted plastic surgeon.

"Before I forget." She glanced toward my open door. "We don't tolerate gossip here. This entire building is a gossip-free zone. The same goes for the parking lot and the sidewalks surrounding the Complex. Marshall and I are strict about this. And believe me, there's a lot to gossip about."

I felt certain every Complex ear was pressed to my walls.

"For instance, Stefon, in accounting, is having an affair with Winona, in publicity. Who I thought was a deaf-mute 'cause I've barely heard her say a word, and Arthur was talking about hiring some handicapped people." Caitlyn placed a hand on a bony hip and shook her head. Then she raised her voice a notch and smiled. "Holler if you need anything." She whirled out the door.

I needed a break. Again. I walked down the stairs, barely acknowledging the other office dwellers and entered the parking lot. I slunk inside my car to be alone. And maybe cry a little. Before I could squeeze out any tears, Arthur and Bryce bounded out of the building. Thankfully, my car sat toward the back of the lot, so I wasn't spotted staring. But I slouched down low, just in case.

"Hey." Billy tapped on my window.

I clamped shut my mouth and stared straight ahead. He rapped again, a little harder.

I aimed my lips toward the top of the window and rolled it down an inch. "I need alone time." I whisked it up.

"I want to tell you something. It's real serious."

I shook my head. Billy motioned a hand for me to roll down the window. I held fast, but his pleading eyes convinced me to oblige. I emitted a huff and opened the top. Billy ducked. I looked around. Marshall, Rob, and Stefon had joined the other executives. They departed in an exotic car caravan. A Ferrari revved its engine and exited the lot, followed by a Mercedes and Rob's Porsche.

After they'd gone, Billy leaned down and stuck his lips up to the gap in my window. "Someone stole it."

I shrugged and shook my head. I had no idea what he meant.

"The backpack," he said. "The one you took home. It's gone."

Chapter 8
The Security Zone

Billy's words flared through my head like a comet, from ear to ear.

"You don't need to make up stories," I said. "I'm not interested."

"What do you mean?" He raised his voice and bushy brows. "I'm not kidding. I left the backpack under my seat, went to lunch, and drove to Druby's house afterward, to return it to his mama. I parked and it wasn't there." He paused for effect. "I searched every place." Billy kicked out a black, surplus store army boot and dislodged a piece of asphalt. He looked frantic. Desperate, in fact.

I stopped in my mental tracks. Despite the media madness surrounding his last cases, Dad excelled in finding proof after everyone else had quit. But I wasn't my father.

I opened the car door and stepped out. I shut it and leaned against the smooth metal, arms crossed over my chest, fingers rapping against my biceps. "Why would anyone want to steal that book?"

Billy shook his head. "How do I know? Maybe you took it, so I won't bother you anymore."

"Tempting as that now sounds, I could have said I'd lost it and not returned it."

Billy's brows scrunched together. He eyed the

rough asphalt.

"Who knew you had the book?" I asked. "Besides me?"

"Druby's mama." Billy scratched the back of his head. "That's it."

I had him now. "What about Arthur?"

"Who?"

"The big guy. He gave you the backpack."

"He didn't…"

"I need the truth, Billy."

He squatted and sat cross-legged on the ground. He cradled his cheek with his palm, like a man with a toothache. "Druby gave the backpack to Arthur before he…before what happened. I only took it from Arthur to return it to Druby's mama."

Truth is always somewhere in the middle. "Arthur and Druby had a business deal, that's what you said before."

Billy shrugged a shoulder. "I didn't know much about it."

"Who else knew about the book?"

"No one. No one cared."

What if someone did care that Billy showed me the book? And saw him hand it over. Would Arthur care? What if I jumped into my car and high-tailed it out of Orange County, back to the rapid-fire, now oddly comforting craziness of LA? Here, lunacy hit periodically, unexpectedly, just when I'd found a spot of sanity. I considered taking up knitting. I'd read somewhere that the stretching, distorting, and manipulating of yarn was intoxicating. I would try knitting. Either that or heroin.

I scanned the parking area. A camera hovered

above the entrance to the Complex. Three more were positioned around the lot. "Who has access to the security tapes? Besides you."

Billy looked around. "Molly in reception has a key to the security office."

"Where do you usually park your car?"

"By the back door."

"Perfect."

He hauled himself up. "But today, I parked on the street."

I might as well try to unionize a communist sweat shop in China. "Show me."

Billy led the way. We stopped on the sidewalk. He pointed out his white pickup, parallel parked a few car lengths from the driveway. A place where no Complex security cameras pointed.

"I've got to get back to work," I said. "I'll give this some thought."

I returned to the building with an idea. I summoned up a downtrodden expression Dickens would have loved and stopped at reception. "Hi, Molly."

"Hallo, Corrie."

"I have a problem." I was no stranger to creating false pretenses to get information, even though I wasn't, and never would be, a private investigator.

Molly let the phones transfer to voice mail and listened to my plight.

"I'm missing my favorite blue sweater, the one knitted by Great Aunt Selma days before her passing," I said. "I think someone broke in and took it out of my car."

She banged a fist on the desk. "What is this world coming to? Did you check with Billy? He's good at finding things."

"He's busy," I replied. *Seriously Molly?* "But Billy mentioned you had a key to the security office. I'd like to rewind today's tapes to see who went near my car."

"Brilliant." She dug around in a drawer and came up with a key, which she handed to me. "Security is just past editing. Everything's on the computer."

"Thanks." I took off toward security.

"Good luck," she called after me. "Bring it back when you're done."

I'd watch the tape to see if someone walked out the driveway, in the direction of Billy's truck. It was a long shot, but I was curious. I bolted down the corridor, past the bustle of the marketing, telecommunications, and sales departments; past editing, and there it was—a closed door marked "Security."

I knocked. No one answered. I unlocked the door and paused in the threshold. It smelled slightly of paint thinner. I held my breath. A small white fan whirred and rotated on the white tile floor.

In a new place, familiarize yourself with your surroundings before heading inside. And always look up, Dad had said.

I stopped and scrutinized. Two computers sat atop a white desk, along the wall facing me. Positioned on shelves, at the summit of the other two walls, sat a half-dozen monitors. Just before I stepped inside, I glanced up. A small camera in one corner pointed at the desk. Anyone sitting at the computer monitor would be taped.

I needed a Plan B. I backed away, and ran smack into a bulky, red-faced man in a black suit and flat cap.

"Sorry," I said, tilting back my head. He smelled of thick, peppery cigar smoke.

He peered down through watery blue eyes framed by black-rimmed glasses. Had the big guy followed me? He stepped into the security office and I hurried back to Molly. I returned the key. Fortunately, she was on a call and asked no questions.

Paranoia gripped me in full force by the time I reached my office. I performed a hasty search for bugs. Under my desk, around the planters, the phone, and the wall décor. Nothing. Anyone could enter the security zone because everyone would know about it. I didn't want anyone to know about what I shouldn't be doing. What next?

My contemplation was interrupted moments later when Caitlyn waltzed in. She carried a dozen long-stemmed roses in her arms. "They're from Stan. My new guy. Don't tell Marshall."

"I wouldn't think of it."

"You look frazzled. Are you okay? How about a girls' night out? Tonight. We'll go to Poppy's. It'll be fun."

I'm a "no" person, which means the first word that automatically exits my mouth is "no." So no one was more surprised when I heard myself say, "Why not?"

Chapter 9
A Short But Eventful Evening

Poppy's sleek, polished interior attracted the sophisticated, under thirty crowd like no U-2 concert ever could. Shiny metal countertops and lots of glass and mirrors gave the place a fantasy feel. This was for the young, professional, and mostly civilized patron who appreciated dim recessed lighting and surrealist artwork. The drastic ocean view didn't hurt either.

I spotted Caitlyn and Winona, leaning against a glossy black, high-top table, sucking on straws in tall, shapely glasses. I joined them and ordered a pomtini while Caitlyn gushed about her man.

"Marshall has a waterbed. And he turns the temperature way up when we're naked." She waved her hands up and down and fluttered her eyes to feign ecstasy. I half expected her head to start spinning.

Winona smiled from ear to ear, glowing like a firefly luring prey. She pumped her shoulders up and down and clapped her hands in glee.

"What are you so excited about?" Caitlyn asked her, flipping back her blonde locks.

Winona's smile took a hike. She straightened her spine, pressed her lips together, and turned her back to Caitlyn. My drink arrived and Winona leaned toward me. "How is it?"

I took a sip. "Tasty."

"Excuse me." Winona flagged a server. "May I have one?" She pointed to my pomtini.

"Me too," Veera said and joined us. I'd included her last minute. "Except skip the red stuff. I want gin, gin, and more gin. With a splash of vermouth. And don't forget the olive. I love me some olives."

The server flitted away.

"Listen, Queen Latifah," Caitlyn told her. "This is a private party."

"I know." Veera turned to me. "Thanks for inviting me." She turned back to Caitlyn. "And thanks for the compliment. I love Queen Latifah."

"Oh, so do I." Winona flapped her elbows against her sides.

I made the introductions, but Caitlyn wasn't interested. She squinted at Winona. "Who is he? Your latest."

Winona stood erect. Her lips recoiled inside her mouth. She blinked in succession and tossed her head a few times, but remained silent.

The moment Caitlyn opened her mouth, I cornered her with, "How do you like working at the Complex?"

She downed most of her drink and grabbed a server. "Brandy and sparkling wine. Fast." She turned to me. "It can be either super exhilarating or downright depressing." She scoured the room like a torpedo pilot zeroing in on the target.

My gaze shifted to Winona. Her head swayed to the drone of chatter and pop music. Fashionably attired in a snake print, mesh dress with gold heels, she fit the role of skank tonight.

"You really should finish one drink before ordering another," Veera was telling Caitlyn.

"Why? This is more efficient." Caitlyn adjusted the plunging neckline of her tight-fitting dress downward, while hiking up her skirt. The psychedelic print was enough to induce vertigo in a catatonic dog. She leaned toward me, eyes flitting around the room. "I could eat Marshall up. He's so deliciously sexy."

I eased away as spit sputters sprinkled my cashmere top.

"Who is this guy Marshall? I want me some," Veera said, and Winona went hysterical.

Caitlyn shot them dirty looks. Her second drink arrived, and she leaned over to sputter onto a guy at the next table. His wash and wear cotton shirt easily withstood the onslaught of saliva.

"It's been so upsetting working at the Complex lately," Winona blurted.

"What do you mean?" I asked. Veera leaned in closer to hear.

"Arthur's under a lot of pressure to make money and our numbers are dismal."

"I heard that he and Druby were working on a project together." I threw that tidbit out to see what she knew.

Winona nodded. "Arthur brings in a lot of questionable acquaintances to produce silly projects that shouldn't be green-lighted. Box office bombs like *The Five-Year-Old Peels An Onion*." She burst out laughing.

Veera shot me a "this girl is seriously loony" look.

Winona turned somber again. "But Druby's project was different. It had potential. He died, recently."

"I am so sorry." Veera rubbed Winona's arm.

"Did Druby pitch an idea?" I asked.

Winona nodded, more weakly this time. “He was so sweet, so easy to talk to…”

“What are you gossiping about?” Caitlyn turned her attention back to us.

I considered gathering all of our cocktail napkins into a wad and stuffing it into her oversize mouth. Winona clamped her lips together again.

“See the two guys in the corner?” Caitlyn asked. “I’m going to reel the blond one in. Watch and learn, ladies.” Caitlyn tilted her chin downward, opened her mouth and started panting slowly, eyes half open. She stared across the room at a guy leaning against the bar.

“Is she having a seizure?” Veera asked.

Caitlyn turned toward her. “Don’t poke a hole in my hot girl aura. Now I’ve gotta start all over again. Wait. He’s coming. Yes!” She ended with a fist pump.

The blond headed in our direction.

“I don’t believe it,” Veera said.

Just before Blondie reached our table, another guy cut in and said to me, “Your drink’s almost finished. I’ll buy you another.”

Blondie switched direction and my heartbeat topped the charts. Bryce leaned in close to me, deep blue eyes glued to mine. My internal danger sign flashed wildly.

“Come to mama, baby.” Veera checked out Bryce.

“What are you doing?” Caitlyn asked our new visitor.

“Trying to have a good time. Just like you.”

Caitlyn swore and took off after the blond. “Wait!”

“How about joining me?” Bryce leaned in closer.

Oh so tempting. I mentally slapped my cheek. This was not just about having drinks with a hot co-worker, but with the number two executive in the Complex who could dictate the direction of my career and encourage bad choices. “Thanks, but I’m done here. I’ve got a long drive home.” I hoped he’d go quietly.

“Your drive could be a lot shorter tonight.”

Whoa, whoa, whoa. How was I going to gracefully get out of this one? “I…”

“Let’s get out of here.” Caitlyn straggled back. “I don’t feel so good. I think I’m going to puke.” She turned toward Bryce, and held her mouth. Her torso jerked forward.

“Maybe next time,” Bryce said to me and strode away.

Ah, the sweet rush of relief. “Thank goodness.”

“That guy was *sexay*,” Veera said. “He work with you?”

“He’s the executive VP,” I said.

“Well, then,” Veera said. “That was a close call. You don’t want to date co-workers, isn’t that right, Caity?”

Caitlyn tilted her head sideways and watched him walk away. “If only Bryce didn’t have such a whack job of a girlfriend. But he really cramped my style right then.”

“You mean you don’t feel sick?” I asked.

“Well, I sure could use a doctor,” Caitlyn said. “One who’s single, preferably an orphan so I don’t have to deal with in-laws, carries a heaping wad of cash, and worships the earth beneath my Jimmy Choo knock-offs.” And with that, Caitlyn threw back her head and laughed. Then she sobered and looked at me. “Why doesn’t Marshall return my calls?”

I shrugged. “Maybe he’s busy or tied up with the

latest project or—"

"Seeing someone else? Is it you?"

"Hell, no. I don't form relationships that quickly and certainly not with my boss. Calm down, woman." I took a deep breath. "Thanks for getting rid of Bryce."

"I didn't do it for you. He ruined what could have been a perfect evening for me."

"What about the guy who sent the flowers?" I asked.

She chewed on the end of a toothpick, eyes darting from side-to-side.

"The red roses," Winona whispered to me.

"The one who sent the roses," I said.

"Oh, him," Caitlyn said. She plucked up the appetizer menu and looked it over. "Stan did take me to La Mirage for dinner, which was somewhat extravagant." Her eyes skimmed over us. "Pull your minds out of the gutter, ladies. I didn't sleep with him. Until after dinner. What does that say about me?"

"You need a full tank before the key goes in the ignition," Veera said.

"I need another martini." Caitlyn flagged down a server.

"Let's go," I said. "Bryce is by the door, watching. And I don't want another run-in."

We escorted Caitlyn and her dragging feet back to Winona's Audi and stuffed her inside.

Afterward, Winona lingered. Her eyes cut to Veera, looming beside us, then to me. "Can we talk?"

"You can speak freely in front of me, honey," Veera said. "Corrie and I are partners."

Winona's eyes widened. "Like domestic partners? You make a cute couple."

"We're helping…"

"Veera's in law school and I'm mentoring her," I said. I glanced at Caitlyn in the car. Her head lolled off to one side, her mouth wide open. She was snoozing. "What's up?"

Winona moved closer to me and whispered, "I know someone who could use your assistance."

I cringed. "Why me?" Did I really want to hear the answer?

"Your father—"

"I know all about him." First Billy and now her. Why did everyone bring up Dad? Living in his shadow dimmed the world I was trying to create for myself. When did this Mother Teresa phase of my life begin without my noticing? "Is this a legal issue?"

"You could say that."

Finally.

"Druby's mother, Hilda, owns a small cafe and is stuck with a huge credit card bill. They shared a card, and he ran up almost twenty thousand dollars weeks before he died. She can't pay it." She blinked back tears. "She makes the best tamales."

"Don't you fret. We'll take care of it," Veera said and whispered to me, "I think this one's bipolar." Louder she added, "Won't we, Corrie?"

I shot Veera a scathing look. "Ask Hilda to call me Friday, at five."

"Goody!" Winona clapped her hands. Her smile rushed back.

"I heard that Druby may have…well…" I stopped. Why was I asking? I was a lawyer with an identity crisis.

She leaned toward me. "He didn't kill himself."

Chapter 10
What About Billy?

"How do you know Druby didn't kill himself?" I asked Winona.

Her face clouded. "Who drives to a park at night, breaks in, and plunges his car into a lake? Too complicated for a suicide. Druby was not a complicated person."

"But isn't suicide by definition complicated?"

"Think about it." Winona reached for the handle of her car door.

"Wait."

She turned, light brows lifted.

"You haven't said a word to Caitlyn all night," I said. "Why?"

"I don't speak to anyone whose man I'm sleeping with," she whispered and got in the Audi.

"That girl's got issues." Veera watched her drive off, and then turned to me. "What about Billy?"

I brought her up to speed on Billy and the Druby business.

"What are we going to do?" she asked.

I thought for a moment. "Gather facts and weigh the evidence." Lawyers did that. But so did P.I.s.

"Like what a judge or jury does. I might as well skip law school. I learn more with you. What law school did you say you went to?"

"I didn't." And I didn't want to say. I started off at UCLA, but I was expelled after my second year, thanks to a prank by another student that was blamed on me. I was framed. She was mad after my father busted her dad's home-based marijuana dispensary. I ended up at a night school—North Glendale School of Law. The Humpty Dumpty School of Law is what it should have been called. This was all right before Dad…

"It's okay. The school you go to isn't important anyhow. It's what you do with whatever degree you got that counts."

"What year are you in anyway?"

"One L."

"Only a first year?"

"Well, first month is more like it. I started three weeks ago."

"Oh dear."

"What was Winona saying about your dad?"

I took a deep breath. "He was a private investigator."

A button nearly popped off her metallic cardigan. "You…Monty Locke's kid?"

I nodded.

"I remember now. It was all over the papers. Didn't he—"

"I don't want to talk about it."

"Sorry about your dad." She placed a hand on my shoulder. "But, hot damn. I got myself a real life crime fighting partner. What's my first move, boss?"

"I'm no crime-fighter. We're just…checking things out. As legal people." This was true, right? "Talk to Billy. Find out when, where, and how Druby died. But keep in mind, this probably was just a suicide."

"Maybe. But I hope he was taken out."

I shot her a look that said, "really?"

"For the first time, I feel part of something. Like I could make a difference. It's not like the Peace Corps or *Extreme Makeover*, but it's giving people relief in a way, you know?"

I knew very well from years spent investigating with Dad. The people who'd hired him were grateful when Dad closed a case. "We'll talk tomorrow."

I jumped into my car and nailed it. What Veera didn't know was that unresolved cases kept you up at night. And when you were lucky enough to fall asleep, they cut away like sharp scissors, snipping your insides to pieces. Maybe that's what Druby's death was doing to Billy.

Chapter 11
The Man in the Tree

My flashlight pierced through the darkness. What clues would a cat leave? A crushed flower petal where he miscalculated a leap? An unappetizing mouse tail? As I debated what to do, the white sedan from yesterday floated past Ty's place. The two ladies wore tan hoods over their heads today. I sprinted after them and followed the lumbering car into the driveway. I stopped and caught my breath.

The two had pulled into the service entrance of a mansion, four castle-size doors down from Ty's. The younger woman stepped out of the car and kept a healthy distance. The other nodded my way. They resembled nuns in their austerity and plain clothes.

"What brings you here, sister?" the older one quietly asked.

"A cat. Siamese. Seen him? Wears a lavender and gold collar."

The younger girl's eyes briefly flickered. She glanced at the older woman who said, "I've seen him. At the tall man's house."

"When?"

"Two days ago."

"He's missing."

"Cats go off. They come back."

She brimmed with wisdom. I turned to the younger

woman. "What about you?"

She shook her head and scurried inside.

"Tish doesn't talk much," the older one said.

"Or see much, apparently. What's your name?"

"Trish."

"Tish and Trish?"

She nodded.

"What do you do here?"

"Bake bread. Mend clothes. Hoe the garden."

I waited for her to add "plow the field," but she didn't. After scribbling my cell phone number on the back, I handed her my business card. "Call if you see the cat."

I left and reported back to a low key Ty, after which I headed to the Complex. I pictured the two women. Curiosity is the typical reaction of bystanders. Tish avoided me, making her the prime suspect. Trish played dumb, making her in the know. Now I needed evidence. I'd return tomorrow and keep my eyes open for hairballs and mouse guts.

****

Early the next morning, I stood behind a brocade of manicured shrubbery across from Ty's place and watched him exit his gates in a slow jog, down lush, tree-lined Mapleton Drive. I'd researched my subject on my laptop. Even neutered cats are territorial, so my guess was Georgie didn't wander off, but was unwillingly removed or worse. Ty's call, late last night, didn't help.

"Helicopters keep circling overhead, Corrie, ever since it got dark," he'd said. "It's a war zone over here. The Homeowners' Association says a coyote was spotted on Stone Canyon. Entered a residence through a four inch gap in the gate. They said to keep pets and small children inside. How am I going to keep Georgie safe?"

I didn't think a coyote crossed Sunset Boulevard and made it down to Ty's street. Plus, a war-zone? In Bel Air? "Keep the faith, Ty. Georgie's too smart for a coyote."

I could only hope this was true.

Meanwhile, I decided to play like a cat and figure out where I'd go in case I had a hankering for adventure. I treaded the strip of grass that ran curbside and shined my light up each tree. All were empty except for an elm on the corner of Charing Cross and Mapleton. A sturdy branch sagged, thanks to a grown man sitting dead center, legs dangling. He cradled a long snouted camera in his lap. We regarded each other.

"You've blown my cover," he said.

"Define cover."

"I'm watching that place." His eyes shot toward the Playboy mansion. He flashed a badge. "I'm with *The Herald*. Why are you looking up trees? Somebody lose a monkey?"

I considered whether to question him about Georgie. Tree man would not be interested in a cat. Unless he knew who it belonged to. "I was hired to root out stray reporters. You'd be smart to leave."

I left the tree sitter to ponder that remark and continued my search and stroll operation. Not a cat or dog in sight. I retraced my steps and found the reporter on solid ground near the same tree.

"*The Star* send you?" he asked. He'd pegged me for a rival. Before I could reply, he said, "This is my turf. Is that clear?"

"Crystal," I answered and walked away, pegging him for a tabloid reporter. Probably with the *National Chatterer*.

Chapter 12
The Worst Part of the Morning

I arrived at the Complex and entered the bustling lobby. It was overrun with the early morning crowd, nearly all of whom clutched hot paper cups teeming with complex blends of coffee. Arthur had e-mailed a memo requesting premature arrival by all. He had an announcement to share.

I scanned the caffeinated faces. Not an executive in sight. Meanwhile, restless minds speculated,

"I hear Arthur's partnering with Disney for a *Star Wars* picture book series," and "I'm betting Art's building his own amusement park."

Clearly these were readers of the *National Chatterer*, which incidentally, offers a smidgen of truth to its stories now and then. So I was told by an ex-girlfriend of Brad Pitt's cousin while we waited in the same dental office a few months back.

A commotion arose at the top of the stairs and the bright-eyed executives trickled down the upper portion. The main guys stared down upon us from the landing. I pictured myself up there, standing next to Arthur, or Art as he's known to the execs. My eyes skimmed the top row. Arthur stood in the center, flanked by Bryce, Marshall, Stefon, Rob and—Holy…

"Morning, everyone." Arthur cracked his usual grin.

Nausea struck me in full force. My first impulse was to run off and hope I wouldn't be spotted. But I stopped myself. After all, I did nothing wrong. I didn't know he was married. He told me he and his toilet paper heiress wife were separated. How was I supposed to know they not only still lived under the same roof, but that she was pregnant? It was awful. I wish I felt indifferent, but I hated Clayton. More than my hatred for him, I hated myself. For being blind when I should have seen.

What was Arthur babbling about?

"What did Arthur say?" I asked Winona, who flittered by.

"That's Clayton Pott." She pointed, jumping up and down. "Between Arthur and Marshall. Isn't he adorable? Clayton's heading the new Creative Affairs unit. He's from Universal."

"He's working here?"

"Yes."

My jaw hit the floor. Now I knew why Clayton appeared in the photo with Arthur, in Druby's book.

"But he'll be in the LA office."

"Thank God."

She threw me her wide-eyed, open mouth look.

"It's imperative we expand our LA presence," I said.

Her chin bounced and she clapped her hands.

No one bothered mentioning that Clayton had worked five jobs in five different production companies in the past six years. He blinded everyone with his heavy-handed charm and black Irish good looks. Did I mention that I hated him? The other night I felt nothing. But now he was too close and I didn't need a constant reminder of my mistake.

Arthur paused and everyone applauded. Clayton's gaze roved the room. I slouched and hid behind the group in front of me. I peeked over a shoulder. I took tiny steps backward, hoping to end up in Editing or Purgatory.

The executives finally departed, and we mingled a few minutes before returning to our desks. Unsure of how to handle the situation, I needed to talk to someone. Or find another job.

Minutes later, I hovered at the threshold to Marshall's office. He sat at his desk, flossing his teeth. I rapped on his open door. He turned toward me and offered his signature wan smile, floss dangling from his twiggy fingers. I knew exactly what his thoughts contained. How would the hiring of Clayton affect him? And if Clayton could work out of the LA office, so could Marshall.

"Come in." He waved me inside.

I closed the door, which he found intriguing. How did I know? He arched a sparse brow and threw out the floss. His lips parted and turned up at the corners. The brow raising was no small feat on his part, and I'd yet to see him smile without his lips compressed.

"I've already met Clayton Pott." I chickened out. I couldn't tell him the whole truth. "He made a pass at me."

This was the first and possibly only time I saw Marshall stretch his mouth into a full-blown smirk. His beady eyes lit up. "So, you feel uncomfortable…"

"Yes." I squirmed, thankful I hadn't admitted more.

"You should take the bull by the horns and

confront him."

I didn't tell him that my true inclination was to plant a stick of dynamite in Clayton's car.

"Let him know you're here," Marshall said. "Show him it doesn't matter."

I nodded and left. I would do just that.

I walked into the ladies room and stopped in front of the mirror. I regarded my yellow-tweed skirt and porcelain colored silk top with the high, ruffled collar. Courtesy of Mom's closet. I loosened the keyhole neckline. It was vain of me, but I wanted to look decent before confronting Clayton. To prove that not all attractive women succumbed to his charms. At least not twice in a row.

The door swung open and Winona entered. She clapped her hands. "You look stunning. Can I borrow that top?"

I looked at her and wondered. I was five-foot-seven in my bare feet. She was four inches shorter and bustier. "It's my mom's and she doesn't know I'm wearing it."

"Sneaky. I love it." She put up her hand for a high-five.

I obliged. Guilt nudged me in the ribs. I would tell Mom. Next week. Or after. I'd be more settled in by then. "Do you know where I can find Mr. Pott?" I asked.

"Who? Oh, you mean Clayton. I saw him leave with Arthur."

I nearly put up my palm for another high-five.

"Thank you again for helping Hilda."

I must have looked baffled because she elaborated, "Druby's mom."

I'd nearly forgotten. "No worries."

I walked into my office and breathed easier, knowing that Clayton was out of the building. Before I had a chance to fully recover, my phone rang.

"I have a date with your partner tomorrow night. We're meeting for pizza."

It took a moment to recognize Billy's voice. "Veera's not my partner. She's—never mind. I have some news for you. I'm speaking with Druby's mother later."

"Oh yeah?" Billy said. "Don't tell her about the book."

"I won't. Are you in security right now?"

"I'm in the parking lot. I've gotta go pick up a painting for Bryce."

"When you're done, please check the security tapes. See if you can view someone walking toward your car. Or anywhere near it."

"Okey dokey."

I disconnected. Arthur lingered in my office doorway with his usual enthusiastic, nearly salivating smile. My heart commenced its river dance. How much had he heard?

"I had a dream about you last night," he said.

Just how does one respond to that statement politely?

"If I tell you about it, you'll slap me."

I swear he wouldn't have minded being slapped one bit. He smiled broadly and left. Wait, if Arthur was back, where was Clayton?

I reached into the bottom of my tote and pulled out my cell phone, then tossed it back inside. I'd use the company phone. He was an employee, after all. I dialed Clayton's number. This was no time to be passive.

Sooner or later, we'd run into each other and I didn't want to shrink each time.

Yes! I nearly cried out after the fourth ring. Voicemail here I come.

"Clayton Pott," he answered in the nick.

I fought the urge to disconnect. I swallowed. "It's Corrie." I heard nothing at the other end. "Corrie Locke."

"I wasn't expecting you."

And I wasn't expecting him to be married. Or hired by Keith-Ameripictures. "Guess where I'm working these days?"

"I don't know. PBS? Nickelodeon?"

I didn't like the edge in his voice. Or the public TV and children's network jabs. He was miffed that I didn't respond favorably the other night. "Close, but not close enough," I said. "Keith-Ameripictures."

Silence.

I showed him. I added, feeling a little bolder, "I saw you this morning with Arthur, and when I came by later to say hello, you'd already left the Complex."

"Actually, I'm still in the building. I'm in Marshall Cooperman's office."

And I thought I was so smart.

Chapter 13
A Turquoise Afternoon

Bucketsful of annoyance drenched me after my talk with Clayton and although I told him in my most sincere voice that I'd stop by later, I didn't. I'd avoided physical, in-person contact with him for nearly two months, and I planned to keep it that way. I holed up in my office and tiptoed out only twice. Once to use the ladies' room and much later to determine if the potential threat to my sanity had vacated. Lesley assured me that Clayton had returned to Los Angeles. I was rid of him, for now.

Just as I recovered, Marshall strolled in.

"I need you to draft a director agreement. Here's the memo." He handed me a piece of paper with the name and contact info. "Claude Rupert is the director."

"When do you need this done?"

"Let's say by Wednesday at five."

"Okay."

"Leave the monetary amounts blank for now. Term is one year with extensions. Put in an exclusivity provision, name and likeness, and include a sentence or two about our approval rights over editing. In fact, we should choose the editor. That's vital."

"Of course."

He stared at me a moment and left.

I'd start on the contract first thing in the morning.

I finished up another agreement and noticed a new email message in my inbox.

This will confirm our conversation this date wherein you advised me that the agreement with Claude Rupert will be completed no later than noon, Monday. Marshall

There was a "cc" to Arthur.

Why did he change the due date so quickly? I sighed heavily enough to nearly lift the stapler off the top of my desk. My stomach grew hot. Marshall was no slouch. But like everyone else that crossed my path at the Complex, he was demented. Time to depart.

When I approached the double glass doors, I remembered my phone appointment with Druby's mom. But my feet refused to turn. I'd call her later.

I exited into the lot and spotted a small, neatly dressed woman in her late forties, weaving through the cars, turning her head in all directions, as if searching for something she'd lost. She clutched a cell phone in one hand. Her jerky movements caused the phone to drop and discard a piece or two. She bent to retrieve it.

I neared and heard her muttering in Spanish. I guessed her identity. "Hilda?"

She shot up, head snapping in my direction. "*¡Dios mío*!" A hand pressed over her chest and tears trickled down her cheeks. "You are the one I supposed to talk to? I no want to call. I come instead."

"Let's walk to my car." I steered her toward my mobile office and we sat inside.

"I keep…especting my…my son to be here," Hilda said.

"I'm so sorry." My heart swelled to the size of a cantaloupe.

"You know my Druby?"

"We never met. But everyone says wonderful things about him."

"He was so kind. So good. He make beautiful books."

"I read the one about the sailor boy. It was excellent. *Excelente*." My Español was not the greatest.

"Thank you." She blew her nose and wrestled with her hands. "My son, he never use credit cards. He so careful. Our card was for emergency only." She took a moment to contain herself. "After—he is gone, I get bills. Mucho bills. What happened? I want to know."

"Credit card tampering or fraud, maybe?"

She removed a large envelope from her handbag.

"Are those copies of the statements?" I asked.

Hilda nodded.

I gently took them from her and reviewed the paperwork. The bill amounted to just under twenty thousand dollars. "Did you call the company and explain?"

"They no believe me. They say I must pay."

"I'm sorry to ask, but when did Druby pass away?"

"January tenth. Seis weeks and one day ago. I never forget."

I scanned the invoice and receipt. The transaction was dated three weeks before Druby's death. Almost nineteen thousand was dropped at Depuis Jewelers in Newport Beach for a sapphire ring. Druby ran up the bill this high? As security assistant? And what did he do with the ring? A gift for Claire?

Hilda held a tissue to her nose. "I no have the ring. I look everywhere. He would have told me about it. He no kill himself. It is a sin."

The Complex appeared to be a hotbed for flings, sudden appearances, and unnatural disasters waiting to happen.

"I know." I held up the statement. "May I keep this?"

Hilda nodded and opened the door. "You call me?"

"Yes."

She walked unsteadily away. How overwhelming it must be to lose a child and learn that he had a potentially damaging side. I contemplated visiting the jewelry store. Then I almost kicked myself. What was I doing? I was a lawyer and not a very experienced one. Why was I involved in a case that was considered a suicide? I could lose my job. I could become homeless. Or worse. I'd have to move in with Mom.

I was in the middle of reversing my car when Molly tumbled out of the Complex in her purple, ankle-high boots. She halted in the middle of the lot and glanced around. She placed a clenched fist at her waist and stamped a stiletto.

I rolled down my window and drove over to where she stood. "Do you need a ride?"

"No, bloody hell. I mean, thank you, but I should have left ages ago. I have a date tonight, and I'm stuck here."

She stood, hands on hips, with shimmery turquoise nail polished fingers. Molly radiated the trapped animal look. Her zebra print top only enhanced the image.

"Can I help?"

"Not unless you know where Billy is. I can't find him."

"What does your staying have to do with him?"

"He left to pick up Bryce's half million dollar

Picasso etching from San Pedro at noon. And hasn't been seen or heard from since."

Chapter 14
The Better Part of the Day

I awoke in darkness with questions swirling in my head. What happened to Billy? Why didn't he return to work? I thought of Bryce. What kind of salary enabled him to afford a Picasso etching? Or did the company pay for it? How long did Molly wait for the police to arrive? And did any of the execs ever show up? As I contemplated wearing turquoise nail polish, I fell back asleep.

****

I called Veera first thing in the morning and told her about Billy going MIA.

"What do you mean he's missing?" Veera asked. "I was gonna wear this gold, strapless, spandex mini that would force any man to confess to anything. But I've been thinking, what if Billy offed Druby and is trying to act all innocent-like…"

"What happened to Billy needs help and getting good karma?"

"That was before. I've toughened up some since."

"Well, tough or not, it's on hold for now."

"Crap."

"Let me know if you hear from him." I disconnected and hoped someone heard from him soon.

****

I drove beneath the mottled shade of the tree

canopy on Beverly Glen and turned onto Charing Cross, toward Ty's place. The Playboy Mansion must have hosted some shindig the night before. Plastic cups, empty wine bottles, and other assorted party debris littered the street. I slowed when I passed Ty's. All was quiet, with no cats in sight.

I left the neighborhood and parked nearby. That is, on the nearest street that allowed parking by uninvited, non-homeowner vehicles. Street parking was strictly forbidden on Mapleton Drive.

I devoured a strawberry pop tart and made my way to Ty's. The perfect lawns were likely mowed on a daily basis. I inhaled the scent of fresh cut grass and heard an engine rumble behind me. Trish and Tish drifted by in the white sedan. Tish turned back to offer a long stare, and they disappeared down their driveway.

Before I could budge, a blue van pushed past and parked one mansion away from me. *Logan Valley Dairy* was printed on the back. I jogged over. A guy, dressed in white from head to toe, loaded glass bottles into a metal crate.

"Good morning, Tommy," I read the embroidered name on his shirt.

"Hey," he said, clinking bottle necks.

"You deliver once a week?"

"Twice."

"You ever see him around?" I flashed a Georgie photo that Ty had given me.

"That monster!" Tommy dropped a crate, bottles clanging. "I used to wear shorts and T-shirts until he clawed up my arms and legs. Now I wear long sleeves and pants. Even in the blistering summer."

"This isn't the Mojave desert."

"Yeah, well I get hot and sweaty in this outfit, but what can I do? I like having scar-free skin."

So Georgie had enemies and was clawed and dangerous. "What did you do with the cat?"

"Avoided him. He's evil. He acts all innocent, sitting by the gate, licking a paw. But when I get close, he hisses and attacks my legs. I like my legs."

"When was the last time you saw him?"

"Over the weekend. Hanging around the gate. Waiting for me."

"See anyone else?"

"Are you kidding? I keep my eyes on that cat the whole time I make deliveries on this street. Why are you asking?"

"He's missing."

"Hallelujah. Don't get me wrong. I hated him, but not enough to hurt him. If that fiend's around, you'll know. He meowed like he wore a mic. That was one loud-mouth cat."

I left Tommy and walked the strip of grass, up and down the block, listening. No meows. And yesterday's man-occupied tree sat vacant. I leaned against an English style street lamp and questioned a few neighbors and workers. None were fond of Georgie. None admitted seeing or hearing him lately. I gave up and headed home.

****

An unfamiliar, but wildly attractive car sat in my driveway. I pulled over and jumped out to inspect the BMW M3, previous model, in the stunning shade of imola red. Not one ding, speck of dust, or blemish desecrated the body. The tires were fat, the rims were black. No one I knew drove that car. Clayton was a miser who plodded around in an age-old, dent happy, silver Jaguar sedan, despite the fact that he'd married a toilet paper heiress. Besides, Clayton never visited my place and never would.

"Yoo-hoo. Up here."

My gaze shifted to the top of the staircase that led to my unit. Leaning over the wooden balustrade outside my front door smiled a very welcome face. "Michael!" I took the stairs up two at a time. "You didn't tell me you were in town."

Michael Parris and I had been pals since junior high school. A couple years older, he'd helped me through homework, and I'd helped him color coordinate his clothes. After high school, Michael veered off to Princeton for his bachelor's and master's degrees, after which Stanford rewarded him with a Ph.D. in computer science. Meanwhile, I stayed local. No sense of adventure.

I was happy to see him, in person, and out of email, text, and phone modes. I gave him a big hug. "Are you on a break from teaching?"

"Sort of a permanent break."

"You resigned? Wait, come in and tell me." I unlocked my door.

"I'm not here to chat," he said. "I'm here 'cause your car's been crying out for help. It must be so embarrassing to drive around with that thick layer of dirt and grime. What color was it again?"

"I forget."

In the old days, Michael, who had a thing for clean vehicles, stopped by and washed my car. It was a nerdy thing. I helped sometimes, but cleaning wasn't one of my passions in life.

“I finally got the job I wanted, Corrie,” he said. “Just like you.”

I looked up at six feet of boy-next-door, good-natured looks. He beamed and I beamed right back. “Congratulations,” I said. “Why didn’t you tell me about your new job or your sweet ride?”

“I wanted to surprise and impress you in person. And you didn’t want to deprive me of witnessing the distinct look of pleasure of seeing your oldest—” He moved in closer.

“And mostly absent—”

“Best friend, who’s here to stay and will make it up to you. Besides, my job was confirmed yesterday.” He threw up his hands. “I’m ecstatic. It’s heady and amazing and heady. And I didn’t want to seem superficial about my super fine ride.”

My laugh tickled me all the way down to my toes. I’d hoped Michael would return someday soon. He’d been pining for an LA job since before the birth of the iPad. Appointed co-associate dean at a top-tier, private tech college in Pasadena, he’d made the move. And made me proud. I told him so.

He grinned and shot me a glance. “Shucks, well, you know, when you’re brilliant, things kind of fall into your lap, after getting rejected forty-six times. So how do you like your new job?”

“Besides the fact that I work with a deranged bunch, I love it.”

I hauled out a fold-up chair from the garage and planted it nearby. I lounged and we chatted about our jobs while he coaxed a sparkle out of my twelve-year-old three-series. My car was ancient, but it was a BMW. Since the fuel pump, brakes and radiator were replaced, it's been a dream to drive. I barely heard the creaks and groans anymore. And the tires had a few good miles left before going completely bald.

Michael tackled the back seat with leather cleaner and a baby's-bottom-soft cheesecloth, both of which he stored in his trunk. He carried cleaning supplies. I carried illegal weaponry. We made a good team. He wiped down the seats and reached deep beneath the passenger side. I hoped he didn't find too many popcorn kernels from yesterday's drive home.

"Hey, what's this?" he asked.

"I was starving."

It wasn't stale popcorn in his hands.

Chapter 15
Mid-Afternoon Disturbance

Michael gripped a photograph in each hand. They must have slipped out from Druby's book and taken refuge beneath the passenger seat.

"Friends of yours?" he asked.

I stood behind him on tippy toes and rested my chin on his shoulder. I scrutinized the pictures. "That's Arthur—head honcho." I pointed. "Marshall—my boss. Bryce—executive VP, and..." I hadn't told Michael about the thorn in my heart. "...Clay Pott. He recently joined the company."

"Clay Pott? As in terra cotta? Like in gardening, planting..."

"And cooking a variety of sauces and stews in. Yes."

"That name could give a guy an inanimate object complex."

"More like a Casanova complex." I studied the next photo. Arthur's arm was slung upward around an unfamiliar man, a large specimen with a shaved head and round, black-rimmed glasses. He looked slightly away from the lens and stood next to Bryce, along with a frumpy woman with breasts yearning to burst out of a low cut halter top. "That's Arthur and his wife." Mandy wore a thin-lipped smile. "That's Bryce next to her, and I'm not sure about the big guy."

I briefed Michael about Druby and Billy while we searched my car for more photos, but only the two surfaced.

"The book's missing?" Michael asked. "And Billy who gave you the book is missing? And the owner of the book is dead of an apparent suicide?"

I nodded.

"And, Miss Corrina Locke, you don't think anything's wrong?"

"I don't want anything to be wrong. And I don't want to get involved."

"The photos in your car make you involved. And the fact that you've spoken to Billy and Druby's mother makes you involved too."

I never liked that Michael was so rational. When I was in the tenth grade and he was a senior, he'd asked another senior to the prom, instead of me.

"This is Beth's last chance to go, and I'm pretty sure no one else will ask her," he'd said. "But you'll have plenty of opportunities."

The prom didn't interest me, but it would have been kind of nice accompanying a senior. Plus, Michael should have at least asked. Why did we stay pals for so long? Because when I turned eighteen, he told my chum of the moment that I was the type who'd only grow prettier and prettier the older I got. Who could abandon such a visionary?

"You should find out if anyone's heard from Billy," Michael said.

"You don't have to tell me what to do. I planned to call him today." I really did.

Michael smiled. "I know. Billy probably took the scenic route back to the office or got sidetracked and fell asleep under a banyan tree. Right? Let's have lunch and you can call him after. What's your mom got cooking?"

"She's in New York, but I have to stop by and do some closet shopping, so we'll check out her fridge."

"Isn't her closet padlocked?"

"I'm not sure." I didn't tell him about my bolt cutters. It was no big deal. I'd clean and return everything I'd borrowed before Mom got back. And we'd all live happily ever after.

Before we could budge, my cell phone rang. It sat squarely on the seat of my beach chair. We looked at it simultaneously. It was Clayton.

Chapter 16
The Afternoon Field Trip

I refused to answer Clayton's phone call.

"Isn't that the guy from your work?" Michael asked. "Maybe he's found Billy."

"Clayton's new. He doesn't know anything."

"Then why's he calling? Don't you want to know?"

"No."

And that was the end of that. Clayton didn't leave a message.

We took Michael's car and stuffed ourselves with melt-in-your-mouth, delicious Greek spinach pie sitting in Mom's freezer. Afterward, I tried Billy's cell phone, but got no answer.

"What was the name of the jeweler in Newport Beach?" Michael put away the last of the dishes. "Where Druby made his big purchase."

"Depuis."

"I haven't been to Newport in a long time."

"I'll show you around."

****

We arrived at Fashion Island over an hour later. The slight delay was because Michael drove at speed limit, in the slow lane, and wasn't much for using the gas pedal. He'd always been a stickler to rules and never gotten a traffic ticket in his driving career, unlike yours truly, for whom it was, at least, an annual event.

When we entered the gold toned, rather spectacular, dome-shaped Depuis, Michael whistled in awe. “Druby had good taste.”

Walls were faux finished in hues of gold. Sconces sat on columns, adjacent to cheery floor-to-ceiling windows, and radiated soft beams of light upward toward a magnificent circular ceiling mural, some twenty feet high. Michelangelo-like angels floated above, strumming harps, to ensure all purchases were made in heaven. Large bronze pots hosted regal white orchids. This font of luxury certainly didn’t fit the gentle, down-to-earth Druby I’d imagined.

While I planned how to approach a salesperson, I heard a voice from behind ask, “How may we be of assistance today?”

We turned to face an attractive, chestnut-haired woman in a lemon hued, lace dress. She smelled of jasmine and looked as if her only purpose in life was to wait on us.

“We need information,” Michael replied.

I placed a hand on Michael’s forearm. “We’re shopping for an engagement ring and heard of this beautiful store. My heart’s set on a sapphire. Preferably the size of Catalina Island.”

“You came to the right place. I’m Bette, the assistant manager. Please follow me.”

Michael grinned, glad to turn over the reins.

Encouraged, I said, “I know exactly which one I’d like.”

“You do?” Bette looked interested.

“A friend bought a ring here for his fiancée, last December. December twentieth, to be exact, if that helps." I recalled the date on Hilda's bill.

Bette consulted a nearby computer screen and, while we waited, I oohed and aahed over the exquisite jewelry.

"May I ask your friend's name?" Bette peered at the screen.

"Druby. He said he spent around nineteen thousand."

I prayed she didn't ask for Druby's last name because I'd conveniently forgotten.

"He spent that much?" Michael chimed in, probably realizing I needed assistance. I was grateful for his distraction. "You didn't tell me that, honey lamb."

I slapped him on the arm and said to Bette, "He's kidding. Aren't you, baby cakes?"

Bette smiled politely. "You're lucky you knew the date. A cornflower blue, sapphire and diamond ring, with the sapphire weighing in at 4.2 carats, was sold to Eduardo Druby Valdez on December twentieth for a little over eighteen thousand. It was an enchanting piece."

"Wasn't—isn't Druby amazing?" I said to Michael. I hoped to glean more information from the helpful Bette.

"I remember that sale because it was unusual," she said.

Michael and I waited. She was quiet, so Michael asked, "Well, Druby was—he is an unusual guy. Was he wearing that white cowboy hat and the alligator boots?"

"He was eccentric all right," I added.

"Then his way of conducting business makes

sense, I suppose," Bette said. "Let me show you a similar ring."

She walked away, and Michael and I exchanged glances. We quickly followed.

"Druby loves to crack off-color jokes." I hoped a clue would be sent my way. "Did he tell you the one about the angry vegan and the pony? Or was it the vegan pony that was angry?"

Bette laughed sweetly. "I never met him. Mr. Valdez didn't come in himself."

Michael's eyes cut from me to Bette. "How did he know which ring to purchase?"

Bette reached into a gleaming glass case and removed a sapphire and diamond cluster ring. It was all I could do to force myself to listen to the conversation.

"He'd been in before," she said. "He was familiar with what we carried. He ordered and paid via fax."

"You take orders like that?" Michael asked in mild disbelief while I drooled over the ring. "When so much money is involved?"

Bette's smile wandered off. "Mr. Valdez is a personal friend of one of our best customers."

"Of course." I shook myself out of my sapphire and diamond trance. "You mean Arthur Keith."

"Yes. Mr. and Mrs. Keith are regulars. What's your name?"

I didn't miss a beat. "Caitlyn Rose." I smiled innocently.

I don't enjoy lying one bit. But I simply could not provide my real name while conducting an investigation. Even though I was not a private investigator and should not have been involved in an investigation in the first place. Meanwhile, Michael experienced issues with Bette's lack of authenticating the identity of the true buyer of the ring. It clashed with his sense of propriety and ethics. My lying, however, didn't disturb him.

"How did you verify that Druby knew Arthur? Did you confirm the credit card belonged to him?" Michael insisted, again dampening Bette's smile.

"Credit must be approved prior to purchase," she replied stiffly. "It was, and we proceeded with the sale." She turned to me, smile in place. "You like?"

"It's magnificent." The ring twinkled on my finger. "Is that what made this an unusual sale? The fact that it was done by fax?"

"Not at all," Bette said. "We have a very elite clientele that often conducts business via telephone, fax, or email. What was unusual was the person who picked up the ring."

I could tell she had no plans to elaborate. "Was it Druby's fiancée? She is a bit pushy."

"It was a messenger."

"What's so unusual about a messenger?" Michael asked. "Many busy executives send messengers."

Bette's smile hit the road yet again. She'd had enough of Michael. I sensed Bette was about to clam up completely. "Get your credit card, sugar lips." I knew very well that he carried no wallet on him. The pockets of his jeans and T-shirt were empty. Jeans and a T-shirt that looked mighty fine on him. To Bette, I said, "This is the most beautiful ring I've ever seen. But that's so unlike Druby. To send a messenger, I mean. He lives and works close by."

"Well, as your fiancé stated." She shot a glance at Michael that would have caused all the spines to fall off the back of the stoutest porcupine. “The messenger was not unusual. Many send representatives or underlings to pick up items. But in this case…” Bette’s gaze scraped sharply against Michael. He bristled and obligingly moved away to view another display case. She leaned toward me. “The messenger said another messenger paid him to pick up the ring. He had no contact with Mr. Valdez.”

Michael was close enough to hear. He and I swapped puzzled looks. Then I said to him, “You didn’t bring your wallet, did you, pumpkin?”

“I knew I left something important at home. You’re going to have to pick up the tab for this one.”

“He may look hot,” I told Bette and put a finger to my temple. “But it’s empty upstairs. Thanks so much. We’ll be back.”

We stepped out into the toasty Orange County sunshine and shot questions back and forth. “What was that about?” “Who called under Druby’s name?” “Why go to such trouble?”

“Did you bring your wallet?” I asked.

“Of course,” Michael said. “That’s like asking if I left my ear at home. I was just playing along. It’s in the glove compartment. You think I’m hot?”

“What?” I slowed my pace and eyed the parking lot. A familiar figure appeared in front of us. A brawny man in a flat, black cap. He leaned against a brass rail, in a spot reserved for valets, next to a black SUV limousine. I grabbed Michael’s arm and pulled him sideways to a clump of well-tended banana trees. I hid behind a sprawling bird of paradise next to the trees. But not before I caught the eye of a nearby security guard who threw me a disapproving look.

"It's him," I whispered.

"Druby?"

I glanced at Michael. Afraid that I'd finally sent him over the edge with my crazy, half-baked, impromptu legal-investigative work, I patted his arm. "No. Not Druby."

Michael looked at me searchingly. My face grew warm. He had such lovely hazel eyes. "It's…"

Before I could finish, the limo driver, cell phone pressed to an ear, advanced in our direction. I turned my back to the approaching man. "I literally ran into that big guy when I left the security office in the Complex last week. I'll tell you about that later."

I inserted myself deeper into the trees and the driver whisked by. My phone chose that moment to blow out a train whistle. I rapidly answered.

"Someone broke into my closet," Mom said. "Looks like the work of an expert. Or the daughter of one."

We never had a conversation where Dad didn't come up. "Sorry. It was an emergency. I promise to return everything."

"Just because I'm in New York doesn't mean you have unlimited access to my wardrobe."

"Okay, Mom," I said. "But I'm busy right now. Can I call you later?"

"You're not doing any detective work, are you?"

"You mean private investigation? Absolutely not."

Michael dabbed at my forehead with a tissue. Sweat flowed freely when I lied to Mom.

"Talk to you later." I ended the call and took a deep breath. "Thank you, Michael."

He smiled. "No worries. Oh, and the guy went

inside that boutique."

"Depuis?"

"No, some ladies' clothing place."

"Wait a minute," I said.

"What?"

"How did Mom know I'd broken into her closet?"

"You broke in?"

I felt a tap on my shoulder. I turned and faced the security guard.

"Step out of the shrubbery, Miss."

"I'm hiding from my father. He doesn't approve of him." I pointed to Michael. Fashion Island seemed to bring out my lying side. I returned to the pavement.

The guard gave Michael the once over and said, "You should listen to your dad." He turned and walked away.

"Hey," Michael called out. "I'm not a bad guy. In fact, I'm good. Dads really like me."

"Michael, we're playing a part here, remember? And you are good."

We waited and watched the front door of the shop from a more discreet spot - the patio of a cafe. Michael sipped an espresso while I downed a peach iced tea and pictured myself in my mother's closet. It was a large walk-in, with clothes hung according to color on either side, shoes neatly aligned in a row along a long shelf on top, and an antique dresser at the back end. A full length mirror graced the inside of the door. A small, round vanity mirror sat on the dresser. Somewhere a wireless camera was hidden, likely activated by a motion detector.

"Do you have a date tonight?" Michael said.

"No." I had to figure out a way to get in Mom's

closet without getting busted.

“How about a movie?”

“You trying to make up for the ring you didn’t buy?”

“And I thought I was being subtle. Who’s that?”

I turned to where Michael stared. The big guy had exited the shop with a woman. I knew her.

Chapter 17
Espionage in the Afternoon

Mandy Keith pranced in front of the chauffeur. She headed for the limo. The big guy followed, gripping numerous shopping bags in his large hands. Michael dogged my footsteps and we pursued our targets.

"Looks like your everyday, humdrum entertainment mogul's wife and her gigantic chauffeur," Michael said.

"I bumped into him after I left the security office last week."

"He doesn't appear too sketchy, if you ignore the deep-set eyes and the long, C-shaped scar on his left cheek."

My head snapped toward Michael.

"I'm joking," he said. "But it's a coincidence that we happened to see them."

"Maybe Arthur's making merry somewhere and wants to make sure his wife is occupied."

"You've only been at your job for a week? Most people don't see this much action in a year."

"The entertainment industry has its own time zone. Everything moves faster."

Before Mandy entered the limo, a young woman trotted up to the car door. I half expected the big guy to tackle her, but he didn't budge. Mandy gave her a quick embrace. The woman pumped her shoulders up and down. What was she doing here?

Winona wore dark shades, a brown fedora, and a coral colored trench coat. She looked like she'd popped out of a parody of *Mission Impossible*. She twisted her hands together and spoke to Mandy. The boss's wife turned to the chauffeur, using shooing motions to tell the big guy to get lost. He hesitated, reluctant to leave. She put out her palms in an irritated, "What are you waiting for?" stance. He walked to the front of the limo, crossed his arms and turned his back to the ladies. They strolled across the lot and escaped from our line of vision. At least Winona wasn't sleeping with Arthur.

"Any idea of what's going on?" Michael asked.

"That's Winona, publicity director. Maybe they're just friends, enjoying a little shopping."

"Or planning their next hit."

"Maybe I should follow and sort of bump into them." I started to move forward.

"Wait." Michael hooked a finger onto the back pocket of my jeans. "If you do, you could disrupt something that's supposed to happen. Something big, something that might blow this thing wide open."

"What thing?"

"Whatever this is."

"It's not like I'm going back in time and disturbing someone's fate. I want to know what they're up to. I'm going in." Before I could budge, Mandy returned, alone. The chauffeur opened a back door, she slid in, and the limo disappeared through the lot.

"Now what?" Michael asked.

"Let's go back to my place. I need to see those photos again."

****

Michael drove in the slow lane the entire way and used turn signals when passing. Turn signals are taboo in Southern California. Especially in Los Angeles where they elicit the exact opposite response from most Angelenos whose knee jerk reaction is to hit the gas. It took us extra-long to reach home. Annoyed tailgaters were our constant rear-end, horn-honking, finger-flipping companions.

"Why do you drive a sports car, Michael?"

"For looks. And in case the day comes when I need that extra power boost."

"Like when you're driving the getaway car in a bank robbery?"

"More like when I need to move out from behind a semi to avoid rocks the size of potatoes from cracking my windshield and blinding the eye of my beautiful passenger."

"Thank you, Michael."

"For what?"

"Reminding me to relax and enjoy the ride."

****

Michael's slow pace and the steady hum of traffic really did help me relax. My eyelids drooped and thoughts of Dad drifted into my head.

Dad's sleuthing career was born two decades ago during his day job at UCLA. He was a professor of Motion Picture History who helped a fellow academic find his missing wife, presumed dead. Dad discovered she'd run off to Ecuador (where the cost of living is much lower) with a local tax assessor. After that, my father embarked on a life-changing hobby. Mom had issues with the hobby. My parents divorced when I was eleven, which meant Dad spent more time sleuthing than he did with me.

On occasions when I hung out with my father, I mostly sat in his office and studied his every move. He pored over his cases and classwork, occasionally tossing philosophical gems my way.

"Remember, we're not here, in this life, for small victories or compromise. We're here for total victory," and "Don't underestimate the power of your feminine wiles. Things are never so bad, they can't be made worse."

Cryptic and politically incorrect stuff. That was the norm for Dad. Mom blamed his sleuthing on his addiction to Bogart films and Perry Mason.

Our bonding occurred in spurts, usually over a cup of coffee. We'd walk from his place in Brentwood, up Bundy to San Vicente, where we'd sit and sip in a mom and pop style coffee shop with dark wood floors and walls and matching furnishings. I can still smell the burnt sugar, toasted nut scents. He'd order a hand-crafted Ethiopian blend with a hint of blueberry, and pour a little of the hot liquid for me in the bottom of an oversize porcelain cup. He filled the rest with cream and a smattering of brown sugar crystals.

"Your mother doesn't need to know about our coffee breaks, sweetheart."

I agreed. This bittersweet feast for my senses of taste and smell belonged to me alone. Regular coffee never tasted the same after that.

Once I got to high school, he supplemented our coffee-sipping afternoons. Instead of going to the movies or riding bikes together like other fathers and daughters, Dad and I practiced target shooting using a silencer and steel plate racks. Knife throwing contests were commonplace in the guest room of his condo, which made perfect sense because he never had any guests. Mom thought we were taking art history classes at the Getty Museum.

"Your mother doesn't need to know about the weapons, sweetheart."

I learned a thing or two from Dad, especially about shuriken, better known as Japanese throwing stars.

"Move the body along with the wrist," Dad would say. "Let the blade slip out of your hand, at exactly the right moment."

It got so my shuriken always hit the target. Never mind that shuriken are illegal in California.

"It's a weapon of distraction, not destruction," Dad said. "To give you time to escape."

He gifted me with a belt that hid a shuriken inside the star shaped buckle. It was my version of a Wonder Woman belt. Except mine was black with a six-point gold star spread out in a silver circle. I wore it whenever we were together.

I helped with the Ty Calvin case and became, if not Dad's right hand, perhaps a pocket in his favorite jacket. He left UCLA, after my freshman year, to become a full-time private investigator.

My bobbing head knocked sideways against the car window and I jolted upright. I blinked a few times. I was surprised to find Michael pulling into my driveway.

"It's in the small mirror on the antique dresser," I said.

"What is?"

"Never mind." I'd figured out where Mom had hidden the video cam in her closet.

Michael turned off the car and beamed. “If you think my driving skills are relaxing, wait until you try my Shiatsu massage.”

“Isn’t that a type of dog?”

“Funny. Ha-ha. You’ll see what I mean one day.”

I shook off all remnants of sleep and slipped out of the car. “Follow me.” I climbed the stairs, unlocked the door, and stepped inside.

“Love what you’ve done with the place,” Michael said, his gaze wandering the living room.

“I don’t like clutter.”

A white futon sat near the window next to a hexagonal shaped, oak coffee table, which also functioned as a dinette, lamp and gaming table, handy foot stool, and magazine stand. The airbed, an armchair, and a two drawer dresser graced my bedroom. A roughed-up dart board decorated the living room wall. Another gift from Dad.

I strolled to a kitchen drawer, lifted the utensil tray, and pulled out the photos we’d discovered in my car. I showed Michael the one with Arthur, Bryce, Mandy, and the stranger. Only he wasn’t so strange anymore.

“That’s him.” I pointed to the big guy sporting black-rimmed glasses, a shaved head, and Arthur’s hand on a brawny shoulder. “The chauffeur.” I hadn’t recognized him at first. The short sleeve dress shirt, cargo shorts, and penny loafers threw me off. Plus, he looked off to one side, as if something had captured his attention.

Michael scrutinized the photo. “Holy moly, that is him.”

I popped a frozen cheese pizza in the oven and Michael tossed a salad. He also whipped up a tasty vinaigrette dressing.

"Michael," I said. "I'm not a private investigator. And I don't want to be." My mom would've burst with joy if she'd heard me utter those words. "We wasted our time going to Newport today."

"We're going to crack this case, and it won't be all that hard."

"We're on a case?"

"We sure are." Michael crunched on a Persian cucumber. "You're the perfect Nancy Drew. And you've got that Wonder Woman belt, right?"

"You mean the one no one's supposed to know about? And who are you, anyway? A Hardy boy? Hercule Poirot?"

"More like Encyclopedia Brown."

I smiled and thought of my father again. "I helped Dad with his cases, mostly by accident."

Michael moved closer, knife in one hand, tomato in the other. "You're trying to assist someone who has nowhere to turn. Your dad would be proud. He had a knack for solving hidden crimes, cases with clever and cunning perps, and you'll find you do too."

"You think so?" Michael's belief astonished me. Could there actually be a crime? "Druby might have committed suicide after feeling distraught over…something," I said.

Michael scooped up some salad and dropped it on a plate. "Maybe. But that ring purchase was calculated. Something's rotten in your humble little fishing village."

My cell phone rang. I glanced at the number. Clayton again. Michael's eyes shot to me. "No," I replied to his telepathic query about my answering it.

The coward didn't leave a message.

****

We went to the movies and watched a cringe-worthy film. I had to cover my eyes for long stretches because of the gore, and the holes in the plot were big enough to make a gopher writhe with envy. I think Michael enjoyed giving me the green light when I could open my eyes again. In real life, I had no problem wielding a weapon and using it if I had to, but Michael wouldn't even carry a stun gun for fear of an accidental Tasing. Go figure.

When we pulled into my driveway, I felt awkward and tongue-tied. This was date night for most.

"Let's go for a walk, along the greenbelt path," Michael said.

"Excellent idea."

My feet had swollen to the size of ripe pomegranates in about-to-burst pressure chambers cleverly disguised in a pair of T-strap sandals. I longed to slip into sweats and walking shoes.

Michael followed me up the stairs and gazed skyward. He inhaled deeply. "I actually missed the singeing scent of oil refinery fumes." He exhaled and coughed. "I think it got my nostril hairs." He rubbed his nose.

"Enjoy. I'll be right back." I hustled inside to my bedroom to change. My arm reached out to the light-switch, but I never made contact. I was shoved back, slammed against the wall, a stun gun pressed against my shoulder. My body went rigid. All motor skills abandoned me. I folded and crash-landed. A dark, hooded figure raced out of the room. I wasn't sure if my lips were moving, but my mouth turned into an expletive factory. My eyes teared from the agony and my whole body cramped.

Michael bounded in. "I heard a thud. What the…?"

This was the part where Michael gave me the massage he'd bragged about. The one named after a dog. He propped my shoulder against the wall and used his fingers, knuckles, palms, and elbows. Then he took off his socks and black Chuck Taylors. Too limp to protest, I lay in a quasi-catatonic state while Michael's bare toes looped along my back. I struggled and finally opened my mouth.

"Michael!" I stumbled up, ready for action. My body tingled, not from lingering pain, but from newfound energy.

"Did I not tell you?" he asked smugly. Then his brows furrowed. "You okay? Did you get a look at your attacker?"

"It happened too fast."

"Did he take anything?" Michael turned on the light switch. I inventoried my room. Dresser doors hung open, lopsided and exposed. The bedding was ripped off and the airbed askew. I flipped open a small, floral, heart-shaped box made of sturdy cardboard.

"My jewelry's still here." Most of it was faux, so I could see why. "How'd he get in?"

Michael swept out of the room. I shadowed him into the kitchenette and found him staring at the slightly ajar, back door.

"The doorknob's broken off," he said. "Let's call the police."

"Nothing's missing. Who would I press charges against? If the police come, they make a report and leave. What would be the point?"

"You think it's the photos? Druby's pictures? It has to be. I'm staying here tonight."

"That makes no sense."

"True, I'm no good with weapons, but I've got a yell that can be heard as far as the Santa Monica Pier. I'll sleep on the futon."

"I mean the photos. Who would want those?"

"Where are they?"

I put a finger to my lips. Being a P.I.'s daughter, I should know better. The intruder could have deposited a listening device. I grabbed a notepad and wrote: *Photos are in my purse.*

"The DA's office has them," I said out loud, and, putting my mouth up to his ear, I whispered, "Someone must have seen Billy hand me the book. Whoever has it now noticed the missing photos. Someone who'd seen it before. Someone at the Complex."

We searched my place for bugs.

"You know," Michael spoke up. "The DA's office will take this very seriously. I'm going to tell my good buddy, the ADA. That's 'Assistant District Attorney.' He'll pass it on to the FBI. That's the Federal Bureau of Investigation."

"Good idea."

"They check everything these days to make sure there's no threat to Homeland Security."

I whispered, "Homeland Security?"

Michael whispered back, "In case we have an audience."

"I know." I cracked a grin.

We continued, but uncovered nothing. The ringing of my cell phone interrupted our fruitless search. We raced to the kitchen where my phone lay on the counter.

"It's from the same person," Michael said.

I blew out a sigh and clenched my fists. This time Clayton left a message:

"I had an interesting conversation with Marshall today. You told him a bunch of crap about me, which I don't appreciate. You may think I've got a lot to lose, but so do you. I carry a ton of weight with Arthur. He really likes me. If you want to keep your job, you'd better shut up."

"Dammit." I couldn't delete the phone message fast enough. What did Marshall say to him?

Michael stepped closer to me. He placed a hand on each side of my face and lifted it up so our eyes met. "What's wrong?"

"Did I mention that I work with bitches, bastards, and overall asses?"

Chapter 18
I Come Clean About Clayton

Michael phoned his old friend, James Zachary, to figure out what to do about the break-in. An assistant DA in North Orange County, James strategically picked his cases, taking only those that made him look remarkable. He bragged a ninety-seven percent conviction rate. How does anyone achieve that without a streak of corruption?

James said since nothing valuable was removed, local law enforcement wouldn't bother taking prints. They'd fill out a basic report to be filed in a cobweb-laden drawer. We didn't call the police. We called the locksmith.

After the locksmith came and went, Michael and I took our walk on the wood-chip path between Ardmore and Valley Drive, using his cell phone as a flashlight. A lively ocean breeze put a skip in our steps along the pine-scented trail. Dirt and small leaves were whipped into dusty, mini-cyclones that whirled in front of our feet. Multi-geographical greenery encircled us—lost cacti, stocky palms and pines, and an abundance of ice plants.

"I love the different scents," I said over the drone of passing cars. "They're kind of spicy."

"Plants are most fragrant when crushed. An aromatic execution. It's from people stepping on them."

"How thoughtless."

"Thought takes too much effort."

"Yet, you were thoughtful enough to offer to stay with me tonight. I'm glad you'll be here."

Michael threw me a sidelong glance, and I repaid him by spilling out everything about Clayton during our stroll. How I met him six months ago at an Entertainment Law Symposium at USC, where I'd gone hoping to find a paying legal job. Clayton was a co-writer on a one-hour drama at Universal that lasted all of two episodes.

A doe-eyed Clayton had informed me that he and his wife had split. He'd met Bonnie Pearlman, toilet paper heiress, in college, and they'd married, only to find they shared little in common. She focused on the material benefits of life, while he preferred humanitarian pursuits. What he meant was womanitarian pursuits. They'd navigated marriage counseling and his and her therapists, to no avail. This is the part where the term "sucker" should be engraved on my forehead. I'm surprised I didn't open my mouth and allow him to slip the hook into my upper lip. That's how easy a catch I was. If I wasn't blinded by his charms, I might have saved myself a lot of shame. In my defense, Clayton resembled the type of man displayed on the cover of a *Harlequin* romance, complete with the physique and cinder-block chin. Yet, a stronger woman could have exercised self-control, right?

I remained encased in infatuation, until I Googled Clayton and discovered that he and Bonnie attended a fundraiser for a political candidate, days after we'd met. Her strapless, black satin number was accessorized with a prominent baby bump.

I saw him one last time, at a bar, long enough for me to throw, “How could you?” at him. My guilt enveloped me so tightly, I could have been shipped to Iceland in an open cockpit without a rip or tear. I was practically a home-wrecker.

Clayton still called after that, expecting our liaison to continue.

“We all make mistakes, Corrie,” Michael said.

It made me wonder what mistakes he’d made, if any.

Before we hit our respective sacks, we paid a visit to my garage. I unearthed a few items that belonged to Dad, and shared with Michael the importance of carrying a tactical, serrated folding knife on one’s person at all times, especially when involved in shady situations. My father never left home without one. I gave Michael a three-inch knife.

“Keep it on you. In your pocket, on your belt, wherever you’ll have easy access,” I said. “That’s the kind used by law enforcement and the military. It’s fast opening. You’ll find it handy.”

“Sure, when I want to cut an apple in a hurry or a stubborn piece of beef jerky…”

“I’m not joking.”

We practiced throwing our folding knives to the target: my weathered, red, white, and black dartboard. He learned surprisingly fast. I practiced throwing my shuriken, just for fun.

“That is so ninja,” Michael said.

The shuriken didn’t work for him. He couldn’t quite get the flick of the wrist down. His star landed mostly on the floor and ceiling.

An hour later, I lay down on my airbed and looked forward to a decent night's sleep. The moment I nodded off, the phone rang. I hoped it was Clayton. Yelling would be so liberating. But it wasn't.

Chapter 19
An Unexpected Call

"Billy? Are you okay?" I sat up.

"Yeah, mostly. Just sore in the head."

"What's wrong with your head? What happened?"

"I went to the Port in San Pedro to pick up Bryce's artwork. I was walking to the container terminal to get the picture, and I was jumped and knocked out with a piece of wood. In the back of my skull. I woke up in the hospital."

"Are you all right?"

"My head aches, but yeah. They took my wallet. And left me for dead."

"Thank goodness you're not."

"No. Thank goodness Bryce's picture is okay. I would have been in big trouble."

"Did the police catch the guys?"

"No. They won't. I never saw them. But that's not why I'm calling."

I waited, knowing it had something to do with Druby.

"You think I'm crazy?" he asked.

"Well…"

"You wouldn't think I was if you knew me before. Before Druby died."

"Maybe you're—"

"A little crazy? It's because I know something's

not right. But I can't figure it out. I need help. Oh boy, do I need help."

My impatience, combined with a hefty dose of weariness, bubbled over. It didn't help that paranoia kicked in again. No bugs in my place, but still, a conversation between cell phones could be picked up by someone hovering nearby.

I said, a little louder than planned, "I can't help you."

"But…"

"Goodnight." I disconnected and waited for the dreaded wave of paranoia to pass. But if I had a carrier pigeon, I'd send Billy a message about how I really felt—that he was on to something.

Chapter 20
Georgie Is Heard

Michael accompanied me to the stakeout at Ty's the next morning. I updated him on Georgie's disappearance while I drove, until I got hungry. I parked the car in Westwood, on Weyburn.

"Why are you stopping?" Michael bounced a knee up and down. "You were just getting to the good part about the milkman."

I exited the car and headed for Stan's Donuts, with Michael at my heels. "I've got needs, Michael."

I ordered two sugar jellies and milk. I got some for Michael too. Nothing was left by the time we returned to the car except for a dusting of powdered sugar on Michael's chin. I stifled the urge to lick it off and wiped it with my fingers instead. There's nothing quite like a sugar high first thing in the morning.

Ten minutes later, I backed in at the street end of Ty's driveway. We lounged inside while I finished telling Michael about Tommy the milkman. My eyes scanned the street. Residents were likely sleeping off alcohol-drenched soirees. Not a soul or vehicle in sight.

"The Amish ladies should have passed us by now," I said. "Unless they don't work on the Sabbath."

"What kind of car do they drive?"

"That kind." I pointed to the white sedan lumbering by with Trish behind the wheel.

"Should we bring them in for questioning?"

"Since this is not a police investigation and we're not officers, no."

"Let's go chat with them."

Before we could budge, a white bath-robed Ty opened his iron gates. He ushered us inside and into an elegant, feast laden banquet room. Our donut consumption didn't hamper our appetites. Michael filled his plate with Belgian waffles and whipped cream while I sampled the blueberry blintzes. Ty had no appetite.

"Georgie and I always share breakfast." He sank down into an armchair. "That's his place over there." Ty pitched his chin toward an empty chair where a booster seat sat.

"Don't you have practice today?" Michael asked.

"What's the point? My game's gone."

"Georgie would want you to continue in his absence," I said.

"My heart's not in it. I'll just mess up."

"Could you pass the lemon custard please? It looks delicious," Michael said.

"That's G.G's favorite," Ty said. "That and the artisanal cheese platter. He's crazy about the triple crème brie."

"I'll have some of that too." Michael reached for it.

"We're going to find him." I slapped Michael's hand. "Come on."

****

"Man, he's under a lot of pressure," Michael said. "Georgie must be some cat."

"That's what everyone says."

We ransacked the streets looking for signs of the

missing feline. After an hour, we took a break and drove toward Sunset Boulevard.

"Hey," Michael said. "What's going on?"

The blare of a horn split the quiet into pieces.

I slammed on the gas and turned a corner. I glanced in my rear view mirror. A big, blue delivery van swerved behind us in hot pursuit, honking madly.

"Must be road rage," Michael said.

I hooked a quick U-turn to avoid being rear-ended and pulled over by the curb.

"What are you doing?"

"It's the milkman."

We jumped out and so did Tommy the milkman. He barreled toward us, panting. "I found him."

****

Tommy delivered chocolate milk on Sundays. When he'd left bottles on the doorstep of the Tish and Trish house, he'd heard Georgie's "eardrum shattering" meow.

"I really hate that cat," Tommy said. "I know he's in that house."

After he departed, Michael asked, "Should we pay the owner a visit?"

Five minutes later, we stood on a cobblestone driveway, in front of the Tish and Trish mansion. A large wooden gate, surrounded by elaborate stonework, stood between us and the front door. We tried the service entrance intercom, but it didn't work. The front gate intercom did.

"WHAT?" A gruff voice answered.

"We're looking for a Siamese cat," I said. "He was spotted here."

"Preposterous."

"Don't make us come back with a warrant," Michael said.

"Beat it." The intercom shut off.

Our repeated attempts were fruitless.

"Let's get Ty. He'll kick their asses," Michael said.

"We're not even sure Georgie's in there."

"Let's stick around and listen."

We stood outside the place and utilized our sharp hearing skills for the next twenty minutes.

"Do you hear a siren?" I asked Michael.

"I don't hear anything. Wait." Michael tilted his head, straining to listen. "No."

We heard a woman before we saw her. She was power-walking and speaking into her cell phone, "*Khak bahr saresh…*"

"Sounds Hebrew or Arabic," Michael said.

"It's Farsi. She's swearing."

"How can you tell?"

"I've learned a thing or two along the way."

"Like?"

"It would be prudent to require potential dinner dates to take a lie detector test before agreeing to meet." I felt satisfied with my common sense approach.

"You don't need that, Corrie. You're wiser now. If you find out where the date lives, we'll break in, and do a complete search. You'll learn a lot that way."

My eyes glanced off his face. "When was the last time you broke in and entered anywhere?"

"Maybe I've learned a thing or two along the way."

Soon after, Michael's stomach commenced grumbling loudly enough to scare off a flock of bickering crows roosting in a nearby elm tree. We wouldn't hear Georgie if he meowed on my shoulder.

"The way I see it," Michael said. "We have a few options."

"Such as?"

"Continue listening—"

"Which means do nothing."

"Doctor a search warrant and get inside—"

"Which means our possible arrest and incarceration."

"Come back tomorrow with ammo."

"I like that."

"I thought you would."

We left.

Chapter 21
Are You There, Georgie?

Although I carried a Taser, a handgun, a couple of knives, paperclips and binoculars, we left the weaponry, break-in device and long distance viewer in the trunk of my BMW when we spied Ty standing curbside in front of his estate the next morning.

"I'm coming with." He wore shorts and a sweatshirt and jogged lightly in place.

"What for?" Michael asked.

"If G.G. senses I'm close by, he'll let me know."

"Has it occurred to you that maybe G.G. needs some alone time? Give him some space, man. He'll come back when he's ready."

It was too dark for Michael to see the killer look I sent him. But I punched him soundly on the upper arm.

"You got a cat?" Ty stopped moving.

"No."

"Then shut up."

"Walk four houses down, Ty, to the place with the stone wall," I said. "We'll meet you at the gate."

We drove off and I said to Michael, "What were you thinking?"

"I saw the photos in Ty's house. He smothered that cat."

"This is no time for Freudian pet analysis."

Ty joined us outside the grounds of the Trish-Tish

house. The white sedan floated in moments later. Trish paused, stuck out an arm, and punched in the gate code. I speed-walked toward her and memorized the numbers.

She stepped out. "Sister, you are jeopardizing our livelihood."

"Yeah," Ty said. "Well my livelihood's on the line too, sista."

"Is there a cat in this house?" I asked.

"We have no animals," Trish replied. "Fat man has allergies."

"Have his allergies been troubling him lately?"

"Fat man does not talk to servants."

"Georgie," Ty shouted out. "You here, baby? Papa misses you. G.G.?"

A balcony door opened and a tanned, rotund man, with a shock of white hair appeared, wearing a thin, cobalt blue satin robe and an enormous belly. "Shut the eff up. I'm trying to sleep here." He peered down. "You that basketball player?"

"I'm looking for my cat."

"You should be looking for your game. It sucks."

"You got my cat up there?"

"Get lost before I call the cops." He slammed the door.

"Where's Georgie, Corrie?" Ty hung his head, his shoulders sagged.

"Come on, Ty." I placed my hand on his arm.

Tish and Trish hurried into the house. I tossed my keys to Michael. "Take the car to Ty's. I'll meet you there." I turned to Ty. "You should go to practice today. Act as if all is well and it will be." I sounded more Zen than I'd intended. "We'll get Georgie back."

Ty nodded. He periodically shouted, "Georgie!"

during our trek to his house.

Michael barely made it there before us. I'd like to think he took a detour, but it was just his driving.

"Take this." Michael held out a business card to Ty. "If you ever need to talk, I'm here for you, bro."

Ty nodded and they gently bumped fists. We promised Ty we'd return soon and drove away.

I dropped Michael off at my place and headed to the Complex. After Ty's problem was handled, I would be done. No more P.I. work for me. My life would be dedicated to practicing law and only law. The high-profit kind. No more helping people because of Dad. All I had to do was convince Billy to let Druby rest in peace. Or the next blow to Billy could be fatal.

****

I arrived at the Complex extra early Monday morning. Seven sixteen to be exact, in an effort to irritate Marshall. Always first in and last out to display his devotion and justify his paycheck, according to Lesley. But I had a solid excuse for my targeted irritating. Marshall had no right to turn on me and reveal all I'd said to him, in confidence, about Clayton, *to* Clayton. And adding more to it, by the sound of Clayton's voice.

I neared Marshall's office and heard the squeak of his swivel chair. He cleared his throat long and loudly. It sounded more like the cranking up of a Model T. Next, he yanked open drawers and slapped folders against his desktop. That way no one would miss his sacrificial early arrival.

I coughed like a gorilla with a petrified banana stuck in its throat when I passed by his quarters. It was all I could do to keep from pounding on my chest. I pictured myself marching up to him, solidly landing my clenched fist onto his brittle left cheek, and knocking him over, stunned to the ground. If someone walked by and noticed me gritting my teeth, that would be why.

I slipped behind my desk and tackled the director contract Marshall assigned to me. Halfway through, Lesley raced in, followed by an unfamiliar woman, about my age, dressed in what resembled the decade old uniform of a flight attendant on a mid-size airline. Her brown pixie cut was home-highlighted in pronounced, bleached stripes. Large blue eyes, shot about in all directions, like they were out of order.

"Corrie," Lesley said. "This is Penny, your new assistant."

She didn't look like anyone Marshall or Lesley would select. "Thanks for finding Penny for me."

"Thank Caitlyn. She hired her."

That made sense. She was a front for Caitlyn's eyes and ears. "Penny, please come back in an hour."

I sent Penny away when she popped in later, so I could finish the draft, which I finally did just before noon. Less than ten minutes after I pressed send, Marshall summoned me to his office.

He rested his chin on his knuckles and didn't say a word when I entered. His glittering crow-like eyes followed me to the chair across from his desk. I sat.

"Why did you include a paragraph about editing?" he asked.

"You asked that we have approval over editing and that we choose the editor."

"I said the opposite."

"Where in the world would I come up with that on my own?" I said. "I've never drafted a director agreement before."

"There's another contract with Claude Rupert in the files," Marshall said. "Did you review it?"

"No," I answered, angry that I hadn't thought to do that and annoyed that Marshall neglected to direct me to the agreement. How was I supposed to know? I'd clearly failed the course in elementary telepathy. If anyone should be annoyed, it should be me.

"Listen, if you're in over your head, I need to know. Claude was angry…"

"I thought you were going to inspect the contract," I said. "Before sending it to him."

"I'm too busy to look over every piece of paper that crosses my desk."

This was hardly a "piece of paper" if this conversation meant anything. But loser was my name in this game, no matter what I said or did. "I can redraft and resend it so it's more to Claude's liking," I said. "I could—"

"Done," Marshall said.

"What?" That one word actually came out quite civilly, as I hovered near hollering. We'd engaged in a battle that had already been resolved.

"I'm sure you learned a valuable lesson from this experience," Marshall said.

I stormed away without waiting for further commentary or permission.

Before I sat down, Lesley trudged in. Penny trotted so close to her heels, she nearly smacked into her when she stopped. Lesley said, "You're wanted in the principal's office again." Then she turned to Penny. "Go finish the filing." After she left, Lesley leaned toward me. "Marshall's a world class bastard. One time

I followed him up the stairs and watched him step into a pile of dog doodie. He went hysterical."

"How did dog doodie get on the steps—?"

"No one ever found out who put it there. Only a devious mind could sneak dog poo in a sealed container, have a can of air freshener ready to block out the stink, time it right to get Marshall up the stairs, make sure he planted his shoe in the exact spot and bam. Could have been anyone. Let's go. You don't need to get into more trouble."

Like any good yo-yo, I followed her back to Marshall's office. He motioned for me to sit. I did.

"The legal department will be moving to the Los Angeles lot," he said. "In a few months."

I stifled my urge to shrug and look utterly bored in order to hide my irritation. I nodded to indicate I listened raptly. On the upside, this was good news. My commute would be shorter. I could go home for lunch—or to Rodeo Drive.

"But you won't be moving." Marshall fiddled with some papers on his desk.

I shoved my hands under my butt. If I strangled him, could I argue excessive provocation?

"Not to LA anyway. You'll move to a new site, a few miles from here. Your office will be bigger."

How could I explain that it wasn't about size? This was likely a man whose own shortcoming rivaled a well-used grammar school eraser. "Isn't there room for me on the lot?" I asked. "Maybe a cupboard under the stairs?"

"Art doesn't want to be without legal counsel close by."

I refrained from chortling. Marshall and I were the

division's "legal counsel." But Arthur had a local firm comprised of forty-two Newport Beach attorneys at his disposal. They did the hard stuff, like go to court and crack down on copyright violators. Marshall and I negotiated and drafted contracts. When we were given proper information, that is.

"I'll get you on the lot after I'm settled. And…" He practically oozed empathy and understanding. "Clayton Pott." Marshall paused to look at his computer screen. An emergency email, no doubt. Perhaps from a terrorist organization or a Gaddafi offspring. Marshall wanted to see me sweat.

My heart thudded fiercely at the mention of Clayton's name, but I appeared calm and collected. I blotted a pearl of sweat from my forehead with my pinky.

"He'll be in the LA office too."

Praise the Lord, I wanted to shout. But instead I nodded primly. No more letting this man in on any of my personal stuff. I stifled a scream and stood. The moment he turned back to his computer screen, I left.

Lesley sat at her desk, but the area set up for Penny was empty.

"Where's Penny?" I asked.

Lesley frowned and peered around. "Want me to hunt her down?"

"No, thanks. She'll show up."

I returned to my office and called Winona to ask her about Fashion Island and Mandy Keith. An unfamiliar voice answered and said she was out sick. Before I could ponder her absence, a bandaged head poked into my office. Not a head I expected to see. Billy stood at the threshold, carrying a large recyclable cloth bag in one hand. He entered without fanfare and walked over to my desk. He opened the bag so I could look inside. Curious, I took a peek. It housed a smaller plastic bag filled with oranges.

I gazed up at him. “Shouldn’t you be in the hospital?”

“The doctor said I could go home. My head’s pretty hard.”

“I believe it.”

He opened the bag wider and gestured for me to look in again.

“I drank my OJ this morning.”

Billy put his hand inside the bag and shuffled around. Then he gave me a nod to look again. It wasn’t fruit he wanted me to see.

Chapter 22
Missing Pieces

"You found it?" I reached inside and extracted Druby's missing photo book. I looked up at Billy. He gave a slow nod. He appeared a paler version of his usual self, hollowed out and worried. "You should be at home, resting."

"It was in my office," he whispered. "Right here." His thumb flipped downward.

Billy crumpled into a chair and started to speak. Only I wasn't listening. The familiar wave of paranoia deadened my senses. This is why I fit so perfectly in the entertainment industry, with the rampant fear that someone better, younger, with thicker hair and a higher end wardrobe would slip right in and take over a coveted job. But my paranoia involved bad guys. What if the villain was in this building? Now?

I strolled out of my office and motioned for Billy to follow. He trailed me down the main staircase and into the parking lot.

"Let's go for a walk. To my car," I said.

I unlocked the door and opened the hood, in case we were being watched. After all, Rob Root was always an audience member. Billy didn't say a word. I leaned in and stretched my torso over the engine. "Where did you find the book?"

"Behind the desk in security. I must have put it on

top, and it fell back there. Today, a pencil rolled off. I looked for it and found the book and the backpack."

"Had you checked there before?"

Billy looked me in the eyes. "I got down on my knees and searched. It wasn't there. I'm sure of it."

Was he just plain crazy? Bryce entrusted him to go to the port in San Pedro to pick up a valuable piece of artwork. Arthur appointed him head of security. Billy frequently ran errands for all of the executives. They wouldn't tolerate irrational, bizarre behavior. Unless, of course, they themselves were irrational and bizarre.

"Please, I won't ask for your help again," he said. "I just wanted you to know that I found it." He turned and shuffled toward the building.

I closed my hood and locked my doors. I caught up to him. "Did you check the security tape to see if there's any sign of someone walking toward your car on that day?"

He turned to me. "You don't think it fell behind the desk?"

"No."

Billy stared and blinked a few times.

"I believe there's a possibility someone may have killed Druby," I said. "And faked his suicide."

Billy's mouth hung open.

"I believe you."

He cracked a small grin. "That's good. Because I don't even believe me anymore."

"You survived the port attack, but we can't go on like this. Next time—"

"Yo!" A voice called from across the street.

We both turned to see Veera waving our way. She jogged up to us. "I got something you need to see."

Chapter 23
More Missing Pieces

"Do you have it or not?" I asked.

"Don't get so excited. I got this," Veera said.

"You have access to the security tape. From across the street?"

Veera nodded. "I sure do. Just not yet." To Billy, she said, "You stood me up."

"Not exactly." I told her what happened.

"You still owe me dinner," Veera said to Billy. "How you doing by the way?"

"It's good to be alive," he said.

"Amen."

"And you owe *me* dinner."

"I don't owe you—"

"So when can we see the tape?" I asked.

"Well, here's the thing." Veera shifted from one rubber sole to another. "I gotta sweet talk the in-house surveillance engineer into letting me take a look."

"Yeah, sure," Billy said.

"I bet I'll have a clue about your friend's case before she does. Even if she is the daughter of…"

I slipped away while they argued and returned to my desk.

****

A statuesque woman floated into my office, excess Botox superglued a small smile onto her Chagall-like face. A nose job shrieked for attention as did enhanced cheekbones. In a breathless voice, she announced, “I’m Alana, Assistant to the Executive Vice President.”

I felt a slight draft along my palm. My eyes flicked downward. Her fingertips brushed past my open grasp. Her hand retreated to her chest and caressed the strap of her blue cross-body bag.

“Bryce would like you to meet him in the parking lot at five,” she uttered in one breath.

I panicked when she turned to leave. Was this about Billy and me talking by my open hood? Or me and Hilda? Or me and Veera?

“Wait.” I dampened her exit. “May I ask why?”

With eyes that looked like she wanted to stab me in the heart with a jagged tooth dagger, Alana stroked her cross-body bag. “To tour the new office with him.”

Precious relief greeted me. “Nice, thank you.”

She left and minutes later, the cell phone buzzed in my green tote. This was a welcome interruption.

“Good timing,” I answered Michael’s call.

“Hey, I’m the forest that starts the fire. Can I come over later?”

“Eightish?”

“I’ll be there.”

I disconnected. My new assistant wandered in.

“Were you looking for me?” She carried an unprofessional, dreamy look in her eyes. She may have addressed me, but mentally, her low heeled wedges tramped another frontier.

“I need an agreement red-lined. Do you know how to do that?”

“I think so. What’s a ‘red-line’?”

“Patty—”

"Penny."

I held out a document. "Compare the new agreement to the old and mark in red all changes. I need this contract returned to me in twenty minutes."

She reached for the agreement. "Don't you have trouble concentrating? There are so many cute guys around here."

I gripped the contract, not allowing her to pull it from my grasp. "Mark the revised content in red, so I can view the changes. Understand? The draft is in your email."

Penny blinked her eyes twice and left. I took that as a yes.

When I stepped outside to check on her fifteen minutes later, her neck was cranked behind her, parrot style. Bryce had bent over a neighboring desk. Penny's eyes fluttered at his derriere and I thought I heard purring.

I snapped my fingers in front of her face. "Penny."

"Yeah?"

"Are you done yet?"

"You said twenty minutes."

I held out my right hand. She placed hers in mine in a limp handshake. I snatched back my hand and grabbed the document from her desk. I marched into Caitlyn's office. Caitlyn leaned back in her chair, a bare foot rested atop her desk.

"I have an emergency situation that needs immediate attention," I said.

Caitlyn sat up. "A situation with Marshall?"

"With Penny. I don't think she has the attention span to do a good job."

"Give her time. What's it been, like five minutes?"

Caitlyn twirled a yellow highlighter in her crimson tipped fingers.

A fresh batch of antique roses rested in a glass vase on her desk. “Are those from Stan?” I tried to perk her up so she’d focus on my problem.

She barely gave them a glance and nodded.

“I’m not happy with Penny,” I spoke louder and was still ignored. “She’s too busy trying to land a man to be any good to me.”

“What? Which man?”

“She’s not picky. She’ll take the first one that turns her way. I think she was headed into Marshall’s office.”

Caitlyn shot up. “That’s the last straw. She’s got to go.”

True to her word, Caitlyn terminated Penny and agreed that I’d personally interview the next batch of assistant candidates.

Thirty minutes later, I skipped downstairs to meet Bryce. While I waited in front of the entrance, a car raced in at top speed and screeched to a halt, steps away. The occupant abandoned it and hurried my way. It was the King himself: Arthur.

Chapter 24
Bryce Makes a Move

Arthur zipped toward me with his usual Cheshire cat grin. The motor of his Aston Martin idled in a rough roar, driver door wide open. Eminem rapped from his radio.

"Have you been to the LA lot yet?" He scratched the back of his head. His unkempt hair resembled tall fescue grass in its thickness and erratic nature, as in golf course rough, probably drought resistant too. I half expected a grasshopper to jump out.

"No," I replied.

A buff college student dashed full-speed across the lot from somewhere behind the building and dove into Arthur's car. He peeled off and parked it ten feet away.

"Let me know when you want to go. We'll ride in my helicopter."

"Sure."

He practically tap danced into the building. The Great Flood could cover all the land, right up to the tallest skyscraper, and I would not get into a helicopter with him. Or into any closed space where I couldn't exit in three seconds. Arthur made me nervous. It wasn't just his unpredictability. He reminded me of a kid who was incapable of following directions, impossible to control, and who would not keep his hands to himself.

Bryce drove up nearly twenty minutes later. Benson May got out of the passenger side. He donned straight-leg denim with a white dress shirt. He tossed me a quick grin. Rapid onset amnesia had conveniently erased the memory of our run-in last week.

"Good to see you." He shook my hand tightly and leaned in to peck my cheek.

I sniffed cigarettes and spearmint gum.

"Are you free for lunch this week?" he asked.

"Uh…" I waited. He's going to forget this conversation in three, two…

"Gotta run. I've a meeting with Rob. Later." Benson disappeared into the Complex.

"Let's take my car." Bryce leaned his head toward me from the driver's seat.

"I'll follow you," I said. "I'm leaving directly after."

He gave me a nod. I hurried to my car, flung my handbag in the backseat and started the engine. I mashed my foot on the accelerator. Bryce had rocketed off. I viewed his tail-end flying around the corner. He tore through the intersection as if world domination depended on it. I broke several laws to catch up to him.

Ten minutes later, Bryce turned onto Newport Center Drive and into a parking lot belonging to a white, three story building. A bright, grill like exterior bordered tall, blackened glass. The best part? Not the limo tinted, abundant windows, but the walking distance to Fashion Island.

I stepped out into a prickly breeze and inhaled the mingled scents of jasmine and seaweed. Sweet and salty. Bushy jasmine sat in a neat row in front of the place. The ocean glimmered nearby.

"Is this the Complex, the sequel?" I asked when I caught up to him.

"It's the Complex, the final frontier. Only the executives will be housed here."

"You and Arthur?"

"Eventually."

"The VPs?"

"Soon."

We climbed a wide, cement staircase to reach the reinforced glass entry doors. Bryce unlocked and opened them, barely stepping aside for me to enter. I brushed past him and into an empty, high ceilinged lobby that welcomed us to the tune of rapidly rushing water cascading down rough-hewn granite. The story-high waterfall, surrounded by lush, tropical greenery, commandeered one wall; a bank of gleaming elevators awaited orders on the other side. Bryce strolled over to the elevators and pushed the "up" button.

"Who's in here now?" I felt uneasy sharing an uninhabited building with him. It was like wearing a blindfold in close quarters with a snake that could be carrying a rattle at the end of its tail.

Bryce smiled a dazzling smile. I flashed him the same, just because I could.

"A few marketing directors are on the first floor," he said.

Yet there were no cars in the lot.

He read my mind. "Their stuff is here, but they officially relocate in two weeks." He held open the elevator door, blue eyes glinting. "Don't worry. I won't bite. Not too hard anyway."

I reminded myself not to turn my back on him and side-stepped into the closed space. We leaned against opposite walls. He fixed his eyes on me. I managed a few seconds of the same before I refocused on the stainless steel bumper rail that lined the three walls.

"Nice hardware," I said.

"So what do you think?"

"Of this building?"

"No."

This wasn't going to be easy. I had to take control. "Oh. You mean Keith-Ameripictures. I love it."

His phone vibrated constantly from his pant pocket, but he glanced at it only once, which gave me a chance to admire his nicely tailored, navy/gray shadow plaid suit. His sky blue dress shirt winningly complemented his eyes. The overall effect was stunning. But I was totally unaffected. I wiped my sweaty palms on the wall behind me.

"We're big." He held open the door to the second floor. "But you haven't seen anything yet. We're in major expansion mode."

I whisked past him. He leaned down toward my head, practically burying his nose in my hair.

"Do you mind?" I squirmed.

"You smell good."

"So does hot chocolate, but you don't nosedive into that, do you?"

"I might. I love hot chocolate."

My eyes scanned the area for the stairwell. Or any fast escape route. Huge, potted trees framed our entry. Twin hallways rested on either side of a black top reception desk. Recessed lighting enhanced the natural indoor brightness, thanks to the multitude of windows displaying a spectacular ocean view. But no escape hatch in sight.

"Is there a stairwell? In case of fire?" I asked.

"The building's fireproof."

Clever, but unhelpful. I followed him into the foyer.

"I brought you here for a reason." He turned to face me.

Oh dear. "To show me the new digs?"

"That's only part of it."

I flexed my thumbs, ready to push hard against his eyeballs.

"I'd like to apologize for Rob's rudeness last week. It was inexcusable."

I relaxed my fingers. I forgot that words traveled at light speed throughout the Complex. "You could have apologized at the office."

"And I'm sorry if I appeared aggressive the other night. At Poppy's."

"Do you go there often?" I walked down the sun bleached hallway. He kept pace.

"I overheard Caitlyn tell Alana you'd be there."

I peeked into an office. "These are really spacious."

"I want to change things, between us."

"So you offered to buy me a drink?" I looked at him.

"I thought that's what you wanted. It usually works. That was before I realized you're not like other women."

"I don't do office romance, Bryce."

He smiled. "I'm flattered. You're very attractive, but I'm in a relationship." He stepped closer. "I want…"

I stepped back, glad that I carried a revolver in my

handbag. Wait. Where was my handbag? Dammit. I'd left it in my backseat.

"I want us to be friends."

I studied his face. He rivaled Abe Lincoln in the sincerity category. "What kind of friends?"

"Most people at the Complex don't feel they can talk to me. There's a disconnect. But you can. Any time." His hand latched onto the top of my arm.

"Good to know." My shoulder shimmied away.

His hand retreated. "Let's look at your suite."

If all he wanted was to be work friends, that was fine. But was that all?

"Coming?" He turned into an office toward the end of the corridor.

I joined him and peeked into the empty room. It bragged a wall of windows with the same uninterrupted ocean view.

Bryce flashed his signature dazzling smile. "How's this?"

I took a deep breath. "Perfect."

"So be it."

I half expected a clap of thunder and accompanying lightning. But all remained quiet. Bryce followed up with a quick tour of the rest of the floor before we headed back to the parking lot.

"What are you doing tonight?" Bryce asked when we reached my car.

"Meeting a friend."

"I'm going to stay home. And think about you," he said. "How to make you happy at the Complex."

Oh brother, I thought. His overactive charm poured out like a lone drainage pipe after a flash flood. "I'd better head home—"

"It's been hard lately." He stared out at the magenta tinged horizon and shook his head. "So much has happened. Unpleasant things. The assistant head of security, Druby—he died unexpectedly. He…"

I was riveted.

"…seemed to have this sixth sense." Bryce blinked and turned to me. "I'd be in my office, at a loss about what to do about some problem, and I'd hear a knock on my door. Druby would be standing there, ready to listen. He had a special sensitivity to the needs of others. I'd tell him my problems and feel like a burden had lifted. I don't have anyone like that anymore."

What could be troubling a man who seemed to have it all? "Do you want to talk?"

His blue eyes flitted back and forth between mine.

A moment later, a silver Porsche screeched into the parking lot and slammed to a halt, one arm's length away. A darkened window rolled down to reveal a woman wearing oversize black shades. A pink silk scarf covered her head. Her full red lips forced a smile.

"Bryce," she said. "Paprika needs you. Now."

"I'll see you tomorrow." I darted to my car. I shoved my key in the ignition and watched Bryce get into her Porsche. She peeled away. Was she the girlfriend? Was he another two-timer? Or did he just take odd pleasure in initiating a series of awkward moments?

I eased toward the exit and stepped on the gas. My eyes cut to the brightly lit lobby. Just before my wheels hit the street, a lone figure stepped outside of the building.

Chapter 25
Near Disaster

Thanks to an overdose of freeway traffic, I didn't get home until nearly eight. Hunger pangs sent me into Mr. Hyde mode by the time I crossed the threshold. Thankfully, Mom kept my freezer stocked with homemade frozen dinners so I didn't wither away from lack of proper nutrition or perish from excess junk food. I tossed my purse onto the futon, kicked off my heels, and heated an Italian beef stew with tomatoes, wine, and mushrooms.

While it warmed in the pot, I leaned over the stove for a taste. A heaping spoonful dripped down my chin and splattered onto my clothes. Correction: onto Mom's red and white silk wraparound dress.

"Oh dear God."

I'd like to say that by Michael's arrival, peace permeated the atmosphere. I'd like to, but I can't.

I raced to the door, yanked it open, and flew back to the kitchen where I rubbed the stain with a wet paper towel. "Michael!"

"Did you eat anything yet?"

"I'm in the middle of a catastrophe."

Michael ran in. "Another break-in?"

"Worse."

He spotted the scarlet stain. "Holy moly."

"What do I do?"

"I hope you're not using hot water."

I gulped.

"Get me some glycerin. Quick."

"What?"

"Just give me your dress."

"Turn around."

An emergency is no time for modesty, but Michael brings out my straight-laced side. I slipped out of the dress, handed it to him, and sprinted from the kitchen in my bra and panties.

I emerged in sweats and found Michael laboring over the sullied dress. He tapped and stroked the spot with a small toothbrush. Then he flushed it with some kind of solvent. He pressed a clear mixture onto the stain with a dish rag.

"There's a small chance we can save this," he said. "Let it dry, and if the stain remains, we'll resort to alcohol."

"I'll need straight-up scotch when I tell Mom—"

"Rubbing alcohol. For the stain. But don't worry. I think we got to it in time." The corners of his lips turned upward. "I don't get to see you in damsel-in-distress mode too often. Or in your bra and underwear."

"I'm no damsel. Except when it comes to cooking and cleaning."

"And that's where I fit in. How was your day?" He followed me into the living room.

I sank onto the futon and told him about Billy, the new office, and my encounter with Bryce. "The way he talked about Druby…it was a side of him I didn't know existed. He seemed so vulnerable."

"Vulnerability is overrated. It's like wearing running shorts in a basketball game. What's the big deal?"

"Why are we talking about basketball?" I asked. "What about Billy?"

"What about him?"

"I'm certain his attack at the dock was a message. To back off the Druby matter."

"You're right. Billy's probably been asking questions. I'd do the same if I were him. Of course, it doesn't hurt that I have a primo connection in the DA's office. James gets me inside info. Billy doesn't have that luxury."

"And that's why we've been checking things out."

"Right on. And to show my commitment, I've obtained a copy of the police report on Druby's suicide, with a little help from James."

I truly admired Michael. He was always on the ball despite his geriatric driving skills. Why didn't I, the lawyer and daughter of a renowned private investigator, think of getting the police report? "And you kept this from me because?"

"It wasn't clear how involved we should get."

I hid my exasperation the best I could. "Dammit, Michael. Don't I have a right to know? What did you learn, anyway?"

He ambled toward the front of the room and peered out the open mini blinds. "It was early Sunday morning when the manager spotted Druby's car in Aliso Niguel Park."

I stood and followed him. He moved from window to window, pulling shut the cords to keep out the night. He used his fingers to brush away lingering dust on the blades. I handed him a damp rag.

"Where was the car?" I asked.

"At the bottom of the lake." He ran the rag slowly along a blade.

"How did he spot it there?"

"Once a month, the manager and a few workers practice scuba diving, remove lake debris, hunt for buried treasure, and search for their own Loch Ness monster. On that particular Sunday, they found Druby's body, trapped in his car. According to the report, the vehicle broke through a chain-link fence, careened down a dirt road, and accelerated into the lake. All costs for damages were covered by Arthur Keith."

"Sounds cut and dry."

"That's why there was barely any investigation."

"Anything else?"

"Yes. Have these blinds ever been cleaned?"

"Let's stick to the case."

"Right. Druby lived with his mom. And all reports of him were glowing, from his pastor, neighbors, relatives, friends, and most coworkers."

"What do you mean 'most'?"

"An investigating officer interviewed a Complex employee who claimed Druby dinged his car doors. Regularly."

"That particular character witness is big on over-reacting."

"Well, there may have been two sides to Druby."

"A serial, door-dinging side?"

"A fast, high-life loving side. I can't even contemplate the other." Michael gazed down at the dark wood floors. They would not have passed a white glove test. I half expected him to pull out a wet mop.

"It's hard to believe someone who created such a sweet picture book had a dark side," I said.

"Even children's book authors can have a wild side. And there was a suicide note."

If you wondered whether I had an analytical mind, that question was now answered. Never did I ask Billy about a suicide note, nor did I consider the existence of one.

"Don't knock yourself for not asking Billy or Druby's mom or anyone else about a note." Michael dragged the rag alongside the edge of a dust-strewn wall. "You have a lot on your mind." He regarded me with the patience of a seasoned Tibetan monk. Possibly the Buddha himself.

"I didn't think of it because I'm not a private investigator. And we shouldn't be having this conversation." I sat on the edge of the hexagonal table. "Was there a handwriting analysis?"

"The note was typed. All it said was, 'I'm sorry.' It was in a sealed plastic bag in the glove compartment."

Someone wanted it to stay intact. "Was it signed?"

"No. It was printed from his laptop."

"So, before he killed himself, he took the time to print out two words from his computer?"

"People aren't thinking clearly when they're contemplating suicide," Michael said. "There's no way to make sense of his actions."

"Or maybe the killer left the note in Druby's car. To complete the picture."

Michael walked over to me. "Motive?"

"Druby knew too much about something out of his league. Or possessed something someone wanted. Or maybe it was a nighttime fishing spree gone wrong."

"Oh yes. The perils of carp fishing in the dark. James said there's no basis to reopen the investigation—"

"Unless there's new evidence. I know. Billy came to me because I'd helped Dad on the Ty Calvin case. But that was ten years ago."

"You found the evidence to convict Joey Powell and set Ty free."

"By accident."

"Accident or not, you placed the right person in prison. Not to mention the other cases you and your dad solved."

"Yes, but we worked together. Finding the shoelace…" Even I wasn't sure how I happened upon it. "Was a fluke."

When I was a junior in high school, I tagged along on Dad's interview of basketball great Ty Calvin, accused of murdering his fiancée. Strangulation via shoelace. Michael had left for college by then. I spent a lot of time alone. Mom decided Dad should keep an eye on me.

Over the Thanksgiving holiday I spent with my father, Ty Calvin hired him. Or more accurately, Dad was hired by one of Ty's high-powered attorneys who anticipated Ty's arrest for murder. He had no alibi and, during his last encounter with the victim, they'd fought, leaving Ty with a bloody nose. She'd accused him of cheating on her. But she'd been the cheat.

Dad questioned Ty poolside at his Bel Air home. I couldn't repeat the content of his replies, but Ty left me with an impression. Not the kind one leaves after sitting on a pillow for any length, but more like a slightly smudged fingerprint. A feeling of what he was like. A simple, forthright man with a soft side no killer could ever possess.

That evening, Ty sent us to a party where we bonded with his teammates. The hyped-up, tall people only gathering was a prime spot to meet Ty's pals who'd vouch for his character. Hardly a place for an impressionable teen. But Dad didn't notice. He questioned Ty's teammates and I kept out of the way. I ignored everyone, except Joey Powell. A young giant, new to the group, he was the only one drafted straight out of high school.

"Hey, you got a booger sticking out of your nose," he'd said to me.

My hand shot to my booger-free face. His body shook with laughter.

Dad interviewed Joey on a blue stone terrace overlooking a brightly lit and energized downtown Los Angeles. Joey had assembled his gangly self and stilt-like legs into a wooden director's chair. He prattled nonstop. If he suspected anyone within earshot wasn't listening, he'd yell out or, if close enough, he'd punch the person in the arm. I wore an ugly, dark red and purple bruise for a week afterward. At nineteen, he wasn't much older than me, but he carried around a sense of urgency, as if life could end at any moment.

"Ya'll gotta see me dance on the court, you hear? When the ball's in my hands, I own it. I recorded the deed. You see me play last night? I was balling."

My impression of him was that he beat-up prostitutes in sleazy motels.

Early the next day, on a hazy Southern California morning, my father and I spent quality time at the crime scene, in an alley in a revamped section of Glendale. Thanksgiving Thursday meant few people milled about. Dad poked around while I thought about Ty. Soft-spoken and serious, there existed a sloth-like slowness about him.

I'd called Michael. "Ty doesn't seem capable of racing around the court."

"You're right, but he's an incredibly effective player. He's not quick, but he'll turn and make a spectacular basket from wherever. He's extraordinary that way."

Just as I'd thought. I couldn't imagine Ty killing his fiancée and running off. Even if he did kill her, he'd stick around and wait to be caught or confess, first chance.

In the deserted alley, Dad talked to Hamid, the shop owner who'd found the body. I pretended to be Joey, the hotshot, ego-heavy giant. If Joey took out the fiancée, what would he do? Shove the body into the nearest trash bin and tear out. I looked around. There was a rusty, metal bin sitting across from me. I hustled over, followed by Dad and Hamid.

"I came to dump my rubbish here," Hamid spoke with a heavy Middle-Eastern accent. He was a small, wiry guy in an oversize red polo shirt and baggy black pants. He looked like his body had shrunk beneath the clothes. "I opened the lid. Like this." He lifted the creaky top. The stench of wet coffee grinds and discarded vegetable parts escaped. "And I saw a lady's purse sitting on the side, buried. A very nice purse."

We peered inside.

Hamid shuddered. "It lay here, underneath smelly garbage, with one edge sticking out. And I thought, 'my gosh! Someone threw away this fine handbag?' I cleaned it and took it home for my wife." He turned to us. "It was a Louis Vuitton. Inside, I found the wallet. I looked up the name on the driver's license and called the number. No one answered, but I left a message. The police came the next day. They searched inside this container. Near the bottom lay the body of the young girl. So very sad."

Bitter bile filled my throat and I'd gagged. A profound disturbance had washed over me, stinging my skin like wet wool. I managed to breathe and spurt away, the biting stench of decaying trash and stale food trapped in my nostrils. What would Joey have done after dumping the body?

I'd forced my mind away from the scene and envisioned the good-time loving Joey, in the alley, racing away. I broke into a run and dodged a short pile of bricks that sat adjacent to a building. I stubbed the toe of my tennis shoe on a second pile, and tripped and turned down a narrow walkway marked "private." Two tall, windowless structures buffered the path, while hard cement, cracked and uneven, jolted my soles. The walkway led to a deserted Brand Boulevard, normally filled with the rapid back and forth of traffic and cars jockeying for a parking space. Just before I reached the path's end, I saw a couple stroll the sidewalk. I pressed my back to the building. A chill tarried down my spine. I was certain Joey's back had touched the same wall. That's when I noticed the shoelace.

It was thick and round and white, smattered in dark red at one end. It lay hidden beneath an empty, long-neck beer bottle in a small, opaque plastic bag. I turned and ran back to my father.

Dad tried to shield me from the public eye. He told the cops he'd found the shoelace, but Hamid lived to talk. He thought special skills led me to locate the incriminating evidence. It was just chance and a knack for reenacting the crime. The press had a field day with the sixteen-year-old that solved a high profile murder. I even testified in court. The blood evidence matched Joey's, and Ty was cleared.

After that, Dad spent less time with me. It wasn't until my sophomore year at UCLA when he gave in to my pestering. Fascination for his unconventional career path had grabbed hold of me. I shadowed Dad on his cases.

I took a deep breath and shifted gears, picturing what I'd wear to work tomorrow. A belted, short sleeve, emerald-colored dress with a pencil skirt. Thanks, Mom.

"What now?" I asked.

"Simple," Michael said. "We either treat this as a closed case, per the police report, which we're not going to do, or as a possible homicide and investigate quietly. We can question witnesses, dust for fingerprints, eat more jelly donuts…"

"When I left the parking lot of the new Complex tonight, someone came out of the lobby."

"And?"

"I thought Bryce and I were the only ones in the building. But there was this guy. He looked like Benson, who works at the Complex, but it wasn't him. I saw Benson, maybe thirty minutes earlier, running off to a meeting."

"So? The meeting was cancelled, and he decided to join you."

"Maybe. Except, Benson had changed his clothes. He wore jeans before and later, a black hoodie and track pants. And his hair was shorter. A lot shorter."

"Did he have enough time to change and drive there?"

"Yes. But no time for a haircut."

"Maybe it was a wig. Or maybe he stopped at a drive-thru barbershop."

"Funny." I exhaled so deeply, I was certain I'd emptied my body of all air. "This is insanity, Michael. A week ago, I was as close to happy as I'd been in a long while. I'd started a new job with a solid paycheck and now, I'm losing my mind. I can't do my hair and makeup if I'm wearing a straitjacket. And I can't risk losing this job. I have to tell Billy I'm done with this. Or things will erupt, with me dead center."

Michael stood beside me. "Eruption means destruction and major clean-up afterward. You're not so good at clean-up. Let's think this through. But first, I'm hungry."

"There's some stew left."

"Allow me." Michael stepped past me and into the kitchen. He reheated the stew and dug into his jean pocket to fish out his ringing cell phone. "It's Jimmy Z., as I refer to him nowadays. Actually, that just started right now. Don't tell James." He moved away to talk to James.

I hadn't seen James in a long time. I sucked in a wad of air. A warm jet stream shot through my chest. Was he still incredibly attractive? Did it matter? I shivered and shoved visions of him aside. I pictured my life without a murder or suicide investigation. I'd pay more attention to drafting contracts, plan clever conversations to toss at Arthur the next time he popped into my office, devise a way to keep sticky notes pressed to the top of my desk from curling up…

Michael darted over. “Druby wasn’t alone when he drove his car into the lake.”

Chapter 26
Early Morning Adventure

James, a workhorse by nature, had returned home from the office and, after speaking to Michael, conducted his own mini-investigation into the Druby matter. Unsatisfied with the results, he'd contacted the detective-in-charge, Marcia Delgado, and arranged to meet-up early tomorrow at the lake. Michael and I would be joining him.

Ty wasn't happy when I told him I couldn't make it to his place in the morning.

"What if I never see G.G. again?" he asked.

"You will."

"You know what's extra special about the little guy?"

"His cattitude?"

"The way he follows me around, but never wants anything. He makes no demands. I mean, yeah, he gets feisty and once, he scratched up my leg so bad, I needed eight stitches. He loves me for who I am. Do you get that?"

"I do. We'll find him."

****

Michael drove us to the lake. He said he planned to spend the day around Orange County after he dropped me off at work.

"What are you going to do?" I asked.

“Visit Disneyland. I hear they sped up Space Mountain.”

“You may have to sell your car to pay for admission.”

“Well then, I’ll just walk the perimeter, jump up every few feet, and sneak peeks inside whenever I can.”

I knew exactly what Michael had planned. He’d poke around the Druby case, using whatever clues James uncovered. My insides fluttered again at the thought of seeing James. I took a deep breath and blew out a long exhale.

When we entered the lake’s parking lot, I switched from heels to ballet flats for the hike in the park. But Mom’s form-fitting emerald dress wasn’t going to make trekking around easy. The good news? Yesterday’s wraparound silk had been salvaged, thanks to Michael, which meant my trips to Mom’s wardrobe would continue despite the video cam. I dug a hand into my purse and pulled out some grub.

“Want a Larabar?” I asked.

“What flavor?”

“Apple pie or lemon.”

“Apple.”

“Good deal. Lemon’s my favorite.” I handed it to him. He was done in three bites.

We exited the car and meandered down a hill to the lake. Detective Delgado arrived minutes after we did. Around forty or so, with dull, black hair and cracked lips, she was small, but tough, like a hedgehog. Her pleasant enough smile hid the toughness, but when it vanished, sharp-edged bristles appeared. It was miraculous how much a smile transformed a person.

“Top of the morning to you,” she said and plodded

down the small hill in a manly brown pantsuit and Doc Martens. She ignored the existing dirt path and carved her own, trampling many a plant and errant weed. An unmarked blue folder was tucked under one arm.

After introductions, she pointed to the folder. “The ADA asked me to share this. But I’ve got to warn you.” At this juncture, she looked only at me. “The photos aren’t pretty.”

Visions of open flesh wounds and dismembered body parts skidded through my mind. I glanced at Michael. He’d paled and his breath burst out in short spurts.

The detective slapped me on the back with the folder and cracked a lopsided grin. “Kidding.”

I nodded, relieved. I caught Michael’s gaze. He breathed normally again. My stomach chose that moment to grumble like a newborn bear cub. I ripped open the wrapper of my Larabar.

Before we could review the crime scene shots, a tall, rugged, and handsome guy in a dark gray suit joined us. I felt a chamber of my heart pop wide open. My knees wobbled and I mentally kicked myself.

“Hey.” Michael gave him a nod.

“James Zachary,” I said. “Fancy meeting you here.” I could have used a quick soak in the lake right about then.

James grunted and gave me a peppy squeeze. He smelled of lemon and warm spices and a green forest. The kind I wouldn’t mind getting lost in.

“I’ve missed you,” he said. “Like I’d miss a pebble in my sock.”

I pulled away.

His eyes roamed over my face and hair. I fought an

urge to punch him in the stomach. I didn't handle overt stares gracefully. Fortunately for all, he turned to Detective Delgado and shook her hand. She blushed and batted her short, mascara-free lashes.

"Did Valdez die of drowning?" he asked, his eyes skimmed the lake. "That question may appear superfluous since his body was found in a car, fifteen feet underwater. But is it?"

"Well, there's the suicide note," Michael said.

James said to the detective, "You skipped the autopsy. Why?"

"Homicide was ruled out." She sounded apologetic. "The medical examiner is working on whether it was suicide or accidental death."

My stomach grumbled again. I bit into my Larabar.

"Breaking through a chain-link fence, accelerating down a hill, and diving head-on into a lake? Come on. That's about as accidental as—" James snatched the bar out of my hands and ate it in one bite. I think he swallowed it whole. "Lemon. My favorite."

Michael laughed nervously, and I shot him a gaze that raked right through him. He wiped away his smile and shifted his weight from one sneaker to the other. James may be an ADA, but he hadn't changed over the years. I tried to cringe inwardly only, but it wasn't easy. I took a deep breath and asked Delgado, "Does it typically take so long to confirm a suicide?"

"With budget cuts and—"

"A moron for an ME, yes, it takes too long," James said. "What clues were found on-site?"

"There's evidence that someone else might have been here that night." Detective Delgado crossed her arms over her chest. "But I was the only one who believed that. No one backed me."

"Do tell," James said.

She lowered her voice. "The gardening crew showed up early on the day of discovery, before we did, and tampered with possible physical evidence. If any traces existed of a secondary character, we didn't find them."

"Gardeners? That never happens in the movies," Michael said.

"Any evidence in the vehicle?" I asked the detective.

"Only personal effects and an empty plastic bag."

"How large?"

"Pillow case size."

"Well, someone planned for a seamless escape. They knew the gardeners would be here. The plastic bag could have been filled with ice or something equally heavy that dissolves easily in water. Someone could have thrown it onto the accelerator to propel the car into the lake." All eyes turned to me.

"There's no proof of that," James said.

"That's what makes this murder so brilliant," I said.

"Far-fetched, since ice floats, but it's a possibility." James turned to Delgado. "Since the investigators failed to find a worthwhile lead, the conclusion was that Valdez died of a suicide."

"Detective, what about Druby's cell phone?" Michael asked. "Any unusual calls that day?"

I threw an approving look at Michael, who returned my smile. James scowled at both of us.

"There was no phone on him," she said. "Or in the vehicle. And the phone bill didn't indicate any out of the ordinary calls."

"Any chance of an autopsy now?" I asked. "The ME—"

"Has the IQ of a horsefly," James said and shot off, zig-zag fashion. He paused at the top to say, "Delightful to see you, Corrie." He disappeared over the hill.

"That's to show he has manners," Michael said.

"Since when are you his interpreter?" I said. "He has the manners of a baboon."

"Yes, but we need this baboon right now. Powder pink, calloused butt and all."

"Butt out." Guilt ridden, I added, "Pun intended."

"Hard to tell who's the craziest of all sometimes," Michael said.

"Focus, kids," Delgado said. She opened the folder. "Valdez's mother reported he came home at nine-fifty-three that night. He'd been out bowling. He texted her habitually when he arrived home. His car was spotted the following morning at about six. Death was pegged around three a.m. See here." She removed a photo from her folder. A close-up of what must have been Druby's hand. "The wrinkling of the fingers caused by water immersion is slight. No washer-woman hands for this boy. Which means he wasn't in the water all that long."

"So he left the house after returning home," Michael said. "To drive here and kill himself, when only a little earlier he'd texted his mom as usual that he was home?"

"That's right." The detective stepped back and away, as if to better observe the scene. "The coroner…she's not that alert. Her findings weren't exactly coherent. A wrong body was taken from the hospital under her watch, and in another case, despite evidence of a beating, she ruled out foul play."

"Why didn't anyone confront her?" Michael asked.

Detective Delgado hesitated. "Her brother's the presiding judge in the county."

"That explains James' flipping out," Michael said. "Not that he doesn't flip out often, but he's had run-ins with that judge, and a few others."

"What's your theory?" I asked the detective. It was a question I recalled my father asking. An investigator's gut feelings were particularly helpful when the detective had been at her job a while. Delgado carried the cynical expression of a weary veteran.

"I wouldn't be here if I believed suicide was the conclusive answer. No signs of depression, drugs, illness, or any mental disorder. He seemed to have everything going for him."

"You mentioned the possibility of someone else being present," I said.

Delgado stared at the dirt beneath her feet. I could have run back and forth to the lake's edge two times before she opened her mouth again.

"There was a witness, but he was questionable. A homeless man, Tom John, slept in those bushes that night, so he said." She nodded toward a clump of parched shrubbery. "The noise and bright lights woke him. He watched a car hurdle down that dirt road…" She paused to point. "And land at the lake's edge. Everything went dark. Then he heard a car door open. Then another. He lost track of the number of times. The trunk opened and shut, the vehicle jolted forward, and there was a splash. Tom John blacked out soon after. We found him later."

"Druby went in and out of the car before going into

the lake?" Michael asked.

"Here's the thing: Tom John heard noises up there, before and after the car plunged in." She pointed toward the street. "Shuffling noises and a man talking."

"What did the man say?" I asked.

The detective looked through the file. "Sounded like, 'so sweet,' or something like that."

"Why didn't you use this witness?" Michael said.

"He's got credibility issues. Last summer we found him with gashes on his hands and forearms. He went into the park convenience store to get napkins to wipe the blood. He said he was attacked."

Michael and I swapped glances. "Who attacked him?" I asked.

"Bigfoot," she replied. "On the night of the Valdez incident, Tom John claimed that he looked up at the top of the hill, toward the street, and car headlights illuminated the scene. He saw someone standing there."

"Bigfoot again?" Michael asked.

She shook her head. "The pope."

Chapter 27
Close Encounters of the Worst Kind

"Michael?" I wouldn't have minded playing hooky and hanging out with him today. "You know what's strange?"

"Yes. That there are people out there who eat wasabi ice cream." He turned the steering wheel and his upper body toward the Complex. Another old lady driving trait.

"That the time I spent with Dad brought me to this point in my life."

"The real question: where's it going to take us?"

"Us" was a big word. One I was happy to embrace. I stared at his cheery profile and felt a warm glow inside.

Twenty minutes later, he pulled into the Complex. I grabbed my purse and briefcase. "Come up and see my office."

"Later."

What happened to the "us" part? What kind of best friend was he anyway? He'd rather investigate something we shouldn't be investigating than hang with me? He turned and smiled. A film of guilt washed over me. I leaned over and kissed his cheek. His skin felt warm and smooth beneath my lips. "Thank you for being here."

His brows shot up and he blinked his eyes. "Thank

you for thanking me, for being here. But, do me a favor? Keep your distance from potential murderers."

"That would mean practically everyone in the building." I slipped outside.

"I'm serious."

"So am I." I watched his car glide away.

I'd barely entered the Complex when I heard. "Today's the day." Caitlyn waved from the top of the stairs.

"That's nice." I slowed my upward climb.

"It's what you've been waiting for."

I've been waiting for a few things: my lottery ticket to win and my hair to look like it belonged at a fashion shoot. But I was certain Caitlyn meant neither of those things. "What?" I asked when I reached the landing. I took her bait. My stomach grumbled, no thanks to James, and hunger weakened my resolve.

"You've got appointments starting at one-thirty and every twenty minutes thereafter, until five, to interview legal assistants." The words spilled out while she applied pink lip gloss and smacked her lips. "We're going to find that right someone, just for you. You get a ten minute break at three-fifteen."

"Righteous. I'll just cram all my work into that convenient little slot."

Caitlyn laughed hysterically, as if I'd unleashed the ultimate joke. "No worries. I've talked to Marshall and we're good."

I had trouble believing her, so I went straight to Marshall's office. Caitlyn tripped behind me in anticipation.

"She told me." Marshall tossed a cavalier smile toward Caitlyn, who twinkled back. "We'll work around your appointments."

They'd likely spent the night together or engaged in illicit activity that very morning. The thought made me long for a blindfold.

Caitlyn whispered in my ear before I could escape. "Your boyfriend's smokin'."

I gave her an exasperated look and returned to my office. Michael was not my boyfriend. I knew women ogled him, and I was okay with that, as long as they didn't do it around me.

"Yes. It's true." Caitlyn wandered in during my self-absorption. "Marshall and I had a…"

And here's where it got gross. She licked the lips around her ample mouth and rolled her eyes upward in a freaky effort to look ecstatic. I knew that look. I'd worn a similar expression after twenty minutes of walking around a city block in a pair of four-inch pumps. The shoes—gorgeous. The pain—unbearable.

"A lovefest last night."

"What happened to the guy who sent the roses?" I tossed my purse and briefcase beneath my desk.

Caitlyn waved a bony hand. "Stan? He's the in-between kind. Filler. Like that icky Styrofoam popcorn stuffing in boxes. He's no Marshall." Again, she zoned out into Marshall waters I would never charter.

"I've got to work."

"You can't," she said. "Bryce wants you. In his office."

Oh no, I thought. Could he fire me over last night? "Why?"

"Maybe he wants a 'lovefest' with you. I saw him leering at you in Poppy's. Even though he destroyed my night. But watch out for his girlfriend. Paprika's a witch."

Caitlyn left, and I dragged my heels toward the back of the building and Bryce's office. I stopped when I spied a blonde heading toward the stairs. "Winona," I called after her.

She turned and gave me a finger wave. "Hi, how are you? Isn't a gorgeous day?"

"Hello, fine, and yes," I replied. "I heard you were sick yesterday."

"Oh, I had a terrible migraine. But I'm much better now."

We walked down the stairs together. "I saw you at Fashion Island on Saturday," I said. "Talking to a woman in a limo."

"Saturday?" Her eyes darted off and parked on one side before returning to me. "Yes. How did you know? You are the sly one." She giggled and suddenly stopped. She dropped her voice and whispered, "That was Mandy, Arthur's wife. It's all on the down-low."

As if I didn't know. "She seems easy to talk to."

"She's scary smart. Mandy's the brains behind Arthur's success."

"You happened to run into her on Saturday?"

"We get together now and then. To talk. She knows I have access to certain VIPs around here."

Winona was a regular Mata Hari.

"We meet," Winona said. "Whenever I have… information."

"About Arthur?"

We reached the bottom of the staircase and Winona dropped her whisper another notch. "She wants to know about finances. How much money we're making. Income and expenses. Profit and loss. Details."

"Doesn't Arthur fill her in?"

"Ha! He's not exactly the responsible type, is he? She wants behind the scenes, up-to-date news. Which I get straight from the top." She twisted her arms in front of her and smiled broadly. Caitlyn was right about Winona sleeping with the accounting VP. "We'll chat later, okay?" Winona trotted away.

Was this Mandy's way of keeping track of Winona? She obviously had an insatiable appetite for men at work.

I raced back upstairs to meet Bryce. I couldn't deny my attraction to him. But logical reasons kept me at bay. His girlfriend, his executive status, his coming on to me at Poppy's. Then again, would a one nighter be such a bad thing? *Yes!* I couldn't tell whether the voice in my head belonged to my conscience or Michael.

Alana stood guard in front of Bryce's door. Platform pumps put her at six foot two. We eyed each other. I kept thinking she'd mention that Bryce awaited my arrival, but it occurred to me that speech could mar her carefully painted crimson lips.

"Bryce asked for me?" I tried to encourage her to speak.

Alana adjusted her brown patent leather cross-body bag and swept past me. My eyes fixed on Bryce's closed door and, although my feet yearned to make a run for it, I forced myself forward and knocked. All was quiet, until the office door cracked open.

****

I heard the airy swish of a backside sink into a leather chair. I pushed the door open wider and stepped inside.

Bryce did not sit facing me. Instead, an attractive woman reigned behind his glass top desk. Tanned and athletically toned, she sat rigid in a sleeveless, sand colored silk dress that draped over her body and fell in a low V-neckline. A nearly empty glass of champagne bubbled in front of her. A half-full bottle kept it company.

"I hear you've developed an unhealthy interest in the object of my affection," she said.

"Guilty as charged, if the object is beautiful silk dresses."

Her hair was the color of mocha, the ends were dipped in burnished gold. She raised her chin and flipped long waves behind her shoulders. "You know exactly what I mean."

I recognized the full, pouty red lips. It was the jealous girlfriend. "Your informants failed to tell you that my interests lie elsewhere."

She grasped the glass and took a swig. "Champagne?"

"I'm working."

"Right. Gin then."

A bottle of gin materialized next to her on the desk. She rested her left hand on top of the bottle. My eyes flicked to her third finger. An enormous sapphire ring roosted there. She caught me inspecting the ring, stood, and advanced closer. The overpowering scent of tea-rose wafted toward me.

"Surprisingly, I like you." She tried flattery on for size, while she circled as if looking for a place to land. She was petite despite her six-inch heels. Perhaps this power play was to compensate for her deficiency in height.

I fought an urge to kick off my shoes to even the playing field. "I was told Bryce wanted to see me." The activities of the Complex amounted to one big game show. "Am I in the right place?"

"Are any of us ever in the right place?"

"Tell Bryce to call if he wants to talk." I exited and realized that there was my office, and there was the rest of this joint, which resembled a psych ward, except instead of straitjackets, these patients donned designer wear.

I marched to Caitlyn's quarters. Her office sat empty. I heard a rustle behind me. Caitlyn raced in, palm resting over her heart. She was panting.

"Is it Marshall?" she asked.

"What? No." Talk about a one-track mind. "What did Bryce say to you this morning?"

"What do you mean?"

"You said Bryce asked to see me."

Her small eyes widened to the size of pearl onions. "That's right." She reached inside a waste basket beside her desk, rummaged through, and pulled out a note. She read it: "*Send woman lawyer to my office when she gets in. Bryce.* It was sitting on my desk when I got here."

"Bryce knows my name. Who's the female in his office? And I don't mean Alana."

Caitlyn shrugged. She'd lost interest now that Marshall wasn't involved. She angled behind her desk and opened a bottle of purple nail polish. She painted a nail. "What did she look like?"

"Brown, wavy hair. Slim. Same height as a leprechaun."

"Was she wearing a dress that looked like it could fall off any minute?"

"Yes."

"That's Paprika. Girlfriend and sometime fiancée." Her eyes cut to mine. "Stay. Away. From her. She is the office terrorist. So where's Marshall?"

"I saw him trailing Arthur."

Caitlyn threw back her head and laughed. Then she stood, came over, and placed a skeletal arm around my shoulders. I wrinkled my nose and hacked my way to the door. I'd caught a whiff of the piercing odor of nail polish.

"Let's get together again," she called after me. "How about tonight?"

Before I could part my lips to reply, she put up a hand. "Wait. Can't. I have plans already. Only Marshall doesn't know it yet." She mumbled something about what to wear for her date that night, beneath her clothes. I left in a hurry and vowed to bolt my office door the moment I got inside.

I viewed Lesley's back through my open doorway. She was speaking to someone in my office. She turned toward me when I entered.

"I couldn't get rid of the bitch," she said.

On my desk sat the wench with the perpetually falling dress. I longed to toss her out my window so I could get a breath of much needed fresh air. But, I exercised self-control. Paprika stood and moved past me toward the threshold.

"You'd better not make a play for Bryce," she said.

A high-pitched, nervous voice answered from behind me. "Are you kidding me? Have you seen Corrie's guy? Smokin'." It was Caitlyn to the rescue. She did, after all, always lurk around Marshall's corner of the world.

Another head poked in my office, behind Caitlyn. “What’s going on?” Marshall’s eyes glittered.

“Marshall,” Paprika squealed, wiggled toward him, reached up, and wrapped her arms around his scrawny neck.

Caitlyn looked as if she might burst if a sharp object brushed against her.

“Why wasn’t I invited?” Arthur had a bloodhound’s nose for a party.

“People,” I said. More bodies slunk in and the noise level rocketed. A bottle of wine appeared, and streamers. I had to reclaim my space. I climbed up on my desk. “This is a touching reunion, but I’ve got work to do. Please hug on your own time and in your own space.” I derived a distinct satisfaction from being bossy. “Out.”

Within a few minutes, they’d vacated. I shut my door and sank into my chair. I longed to creep beneath my desk and hide until Michael arrived to fish me out. I’d be perfectly content there, sheltered from the insanity. Instead, I reached into my handbag and grabbed the cell phone. I’d missed two calls from Michael. I started to dial his number when the man of the hour entered, without knocking.

“Heard you hosted a gala in here,” Bryce said.

“In your honor. Too bad you missed it.” I felt increasingly cocky. Must have been the visit to the murder scene. Or was it suicide?

“Paprika can be territorial. Can you blame her?”

“I like to place blame where blame is due.” Once again, I teetered on the tensioned high wire that could lead to my termination.

He turned to leave.

"Bryce," I said. The stress of the job, the death of a person I'd never even met, and lacking funds to shop in a favorite department store for far too long had taken a toll on me. I didn't want to be fired. And I didn't want to be the enemy of the number two executive in the Complex. "I'm sorry. It's been a stressful morning."

Bryce edged closer. He placed a finger under my chin, lifted it, and forced me to look at him. "You're forgiven." His eyes moved to my lips.

I managed a sickly smile and blurted, "That's a beautiful sapphire ring on Paprika's finger."

Bryce regarded me. He almost dared me to go on.

"I saw a similar one at Depuis, in Fashion Island."

He lifted a brow and made his exit. I closed the door after him. He didn't confirm or deny that his purchase came from Depuis. Did he have something to do with Druby's death?

Just before I'd made it to my desk, the door opened. Bryce strode in again. He closed in on me and stood a breath away. I met his gaze, swallowed, and sniffed. He smelled good, a masculine blend of lavender and cinnamon.

"You don't know me at all, do you?" His gaze pierced through mine.

I held my breath. What should I do?

Before I could determine, he strode out the door and I stumbled to my chair. My forehead sank into my palm. I needed to talk to someone. I pulled out my cell-phone and called Michael.

"I was just going to call you," he said.

"You won't believe what happened."

"You won't believe what I found."

"What?" I asked.

"The homeless man who witnessed Druby's death."

Chapter 28
Close Call

Michael had returned to Aliso Niguel Park after dropping me off at work. He nosed around and found himself spread eagle on the dirt. He'd tripped over a tattered sneaker emanating from a clump of rosemary bushes near the spot where Druby's car became lake-bound. Michael had stumbled across the questionable witness.

"The guy who fingered the pope?" I asked.

"The same. And he wasn't all that incoherent."

"How did he know it wasn't Bigfoot that night?"

"The guy Tom John saw resembled the pope more than Sasquatch. You see, way before he started living in bushes, Tom John was Thomas Jonathan O'Hara, former altar-boy and cub scout. His mom died when he was twelve. That's when his world cracked and he fell in."

"Did he hallucinate the pope?"

"Not quite. Last year, when the pope was in Saint Peter's Square, Tom John caught him on TV in the local pub. But what really captured his attention was the pope's saturno."

I patiently waited for Michael to explain. I tapped my foot in rapid succession. "Turn what?"

"A hat resembling the planet Saturn, with a wide, circular brim, and rounded top. Saturno are a favorite of the top Catholic clergy. The pope wears one with gold cords. That's how Tom John recognized him."

"Is that what he told the police?"

"He ID'd the pope because the guy wore white. Tom John says they never got around to the red hat."

"The pope wore a red hat?" What kind of fashion statement was that?

"Tom John's guy wore white clothing and a red saturno hat, so Tom John assumed it was the pope."

"An honest mistake."

"How did you get him to talk?"

"I plowed him with alcohol."

"That's not like you, Michael. Playing on someone's weakness to get information," I said. "That sounds more like me."

"I bought a bottle of vodka, emptied it out 'til there was less than an inch of the stuff at the bottom and filled the rest with water. About five proof, I expect."

"He fell for it?"

"He complained, but drank most of it."

"I also bought him a burger, fries and a strawberry milk shake. He was happy."

"A regular fairy tale ending. Tell me the rest later. I've already missed three calls."

"Wait, you uncovered something today."

"Bryce's girlfriend wears a sapphire ring like the one at Depuis."

"No way," Michael said. "Do me a solid and stay away from him."

"A solid? Are you reading *Urban Dictionary* again?"

"Just stay away."

"I will. See you later." I disconnected.

It was possible, assuming Tom John wasn't making it up or hallucinating, was sober and actually in a shrub near the lake just before Druby's demise, that he witnessed it all. But someone dressed like the pope? Too bizarre. And what about Paprika's ring?

****

I checked my watch. I'd met assistant candidates all afternoon and had my fill. The first one wore enough cologne to suffocate the town of Harmony, California, population eighteen. The next one asked if we allowed pets because her hamster didn't do well alone at home. The rest were equally deficient. My last appointment was due at any moment.

"Hello."

I looked up at a smiling Veera. She wore black slacks and peep toe pumps with a red sweater. Her earlobes sported gold hoop earrings that could fit around my wrist. Her hair was pulled back in a ponytail. "What are you doing here?" I asked.

"I'm your new assistant."

"Excuse me?"

"If you're smart, like I know you are, you'll hire me."

"Why would I do that?"

"Because I look good, do spreadsheets, file stuff, type fast and you know I got a legal mind. I can even speak Latin for the complex cases. 'E pluribus unum.' And no one would dare cross you with me around."

"Don't you have a job?"

"I quit."

"They canned you?"

"It was a mutual decision. Besides, over here, I can really watch your back instead of craning my neck from across the street all the time." She rubbed her neck. "Ouch."

"Isn't this perfect?" Caitlyn popped in. "You're already buds and Veera quit her job just to work for you."

My eyes cut to Veera's. Her brows were slightly lifted, her smile slimmed down and the possibility of disappointment registered in her dark eyes. I really didn't want to interview anyone else. "I'll give you a two week trial period."

"One week and it's a deal," Veera said.

"Ten days."

She stuck out a hand and we shook. "Thank you, Corrie Locke." She leaned in closer. "Didn't I say we're gonna be good friends?" She hustled out with Caitlyn in her wake.

I was happy Caitlyn had brought her in. She came through this time. Wait. Maybe she could again. I jumped up and ran to the door. "Caitlyn."

She reappeared in an instant.

"Do you know where Bryce bought that beautiful sapphire ring for Paprika?" I asked.

"Why? Who wants to know?"

"Me. It's spectacular."

"Did Marshall put you up to this?" Her eyes fluttered.

"Well…" I started, it was cruel, I know, but she could possibly uncover valuable information.

"I'll check with Alana." Caitlyn darted out.

I returned to work again and opened a folder. My alone time lasted all of two minutes.

"I've not acted like a friend and I apologize." Bryce swooped in like a bat in a tailwind. "Let me take you to dinner tonight, to make amends."

I had to admit he looked breathtaking when he wore his sincerity suit, in a nerve-wracking sort of way.

"I'd love to," I said with zero self-control. A vision of Michael flashed in my mind. I returned my eyes to the open folder. "But I have plans."

Bryce perched at the edge of my desk and gazed at me over his shoulder. "Break them."

Was Bryce capable of firing me? Yes. And if he had something to do with the Druby matter, he could do a lot more than fire me. "Remember the run-in I had with Paprika this morning? I don't want that to happen again. But I appreciate the invitation."

He continued perching. "About Paprika and the ring—"

"Corrie!" Caitlyn skidded to a stop when she saw Bryce. "Oh." She froze, mouth open long enough to invite a few flies in, had any been buzzing around. "I need to talk to Corrie."

"So be it," he said. "Enjoy your evening, ladies." And he left.

"What is it?" I'd been so close to getting information.

"Doesn't Bryce look scrumptious?"

"Why did you interrupt us?"

"I knew you'd want to be the first to know. Marshall's coming over to my place later. We're going to have us some fun." She danced a quick two-step and left.

Just what kind of mixed messages was I sending these people? I stood, packed up my briefcase, grabbed my handbag, and bolted out the door.

By the time I hit the sidewalk, the day sagged and

dimmed. A pang of sadness jabbed me. Not for any sins I'd committed, but for things I hadn't done yet. What if I never did? My father chose a risky business and it destroyed him. I took a deep breath and steered myself in the direction from which I expected Michael.

A small, white pickup rumbled my way and pulled over next to the curb. The passenger window rolled down. "What's the hurry?" Billy asked.

I stopped and regarded him. So much had happened since we spoke yesterday. "I'm waiting for my ride. You okay?"

"I'm more than okay. I only worked a few hours, nobody's pestering me, and I'm alive. It's all *bueno*."

I smiled and turned to leave.

"I got something to tell you."

I heard the click of heels approaching from behind. Veera grinded to a halt next to Billy. "Corrie, I got news."

"How do you two do that?" I asked.

"I was in the middle of telling her something," Billy said to Veera. "It's real important."

"Mine's a life-changer." Veera placed a large hand on a large hip. "You know I got a friend who works in-house security, at my old job across the street."

"You got sacked?" Billy asked.

Veera's brows scrunched together. "We came to a mutual understanding."

"Would you hurry up?" I asked. "I've got an appointment."

"I'm getting the tape," Veera said.

"He's gonna give me the tape," Billy said. "The one that shows who broke into my car."

"He's playing you, boy. It's got my name all over

it."

"When?" I asked, my eyes flicked between them. "When are you getting it?"

"Tomorrow," they both said.

"Wait. One of you do this. Okay? Don't mess up."

Veera narrowed her eyes at Billy and bunched her lips. "You take care of it. I got more important work to do now anyway, working for a busy executive and all." She turned to me. "See you later, boss." Veera sauntered off.

I sure liked being called an executive. I'd like it more if I really was one. "Let me know what happens," I said to Billy. "And be careful."

"Don't worry. I'm like a cat with nine lives." He motored off.

I hoped Georgie hadn't used up all of his nine lives, for Ty's sake. My cell phone interrupted my thoughts. I dropped everything I carried on the sidewalk and began my frenzied rummaging through my purse. On days when I practiced calm awareness, my phone loyally sat in a zippered pocket inside. On days when I resided in a hazy bubble of crazed activity, my phone constantly shifted positions. Today had been a shifty day. I finally located the slippery phone, too late. The missed call came from the District Attorney's office. James left a brief message, asking me to call. Maybe I would later. Or never.

I threw out my anchor at the corner, eyes scanning the street for Michael's red BMW. This apparently wasn't to be an early pick-up day. Maybe he'd stopped at a railroad crossing in anticipation of a train. If he even suspected a yellow light, he'd slow down and wait until the light finally turned. His little old lady driving skills mystified and annoyed me. And now a hint of worry whispered around my ears. He was unusually late.

Ten minutes later, I spied him approaching. I dropped my tote and briefcase and waved. Michael whipped around the bend and barreled toward my building. How could he have missed me? I'd stared right at him, but his gaze had focused ahead, in automatic pilot mode. He wouldn't have seen Big Foot or the pope in his red hat, even if they'd stood together.

I lugged my stuff back to the Complex. Not easy in high heels that nestled my feet so comfortably until noon. And turned into a bed of nails by two. I cradled my phone in my hand and waited for it to ring, but it maintained a monastic silence. I tried calling Michael, but it went to voice mail. I marched into the building. Reception sat empty.

I stepped back outside and surveyed the parking area. A silver Porsche Boxster veered past to within inches of my person. Paprika's head barely made it past the top of the steering wheel. To my credit, I hardly flinched, but a vein pecked violently against my left temple. That didn't stop me from spitting on her trunk before she sped off. It was a whopper too.

I continued my hunt for Michael and finally spotted his red car, parked in a far-off corner. I trudged through the lot, and found him, hunched over by the trunk. He panted and stared at the ground.

"Michael?"

Chapter 29
Evening Emergency

"He'll be fine," the emergency room doctor informed me. "It was a small amount, enough to give him a stomach and headache."

"Will he have any side effects?"

"Give the boy a day or two, and he'll be good as new."

I'd found Michael, pale and vomiting behind his car. He'd suffered abdominal pain and I drove him straight to the ER. The physician on duty believed Michael ingested cleaning fluid or household poison. He carried a bottle of cleaner in his trunk. Was it possible he accidentally drank some? About as possible as my joining an ant colony. That's why he'd missed me standing on the corner. And why he'd driven like a typical guy.

"How do you think he ingested the toxin?" I asked James when he arrived.

"Mikey can be such an idiot." We walked toward Michael's room. "He forgot to lock the doors while he played Inspector Gadget. Anyone could have entered the car and tampered with his water bottle. I'm taking it to a lab for testing."

"It's my fault." I tried not to let the full weight of my guilt open the flood gates of my tear ducts. "I got him mixed up in this. I keep thinking I'm going to drop this, but I don't. What is my problem?"

"Corrie." He grabbed my shoulders. I wouldn't blame him if he shook me senseless. "I blame myself." James withdrew his hands and dropped them by his sides. "I thought you were dealing with amateurs. The break-in at your place indicated as much. I revisited the case thinking if I could prove murder, it would be another feather in my cap. I like feathers. A lot. I don't want to be an ADA forever, you know."

I'd regarded him as arrogant in the past, but this was not arrogance.

James' lips turned upward in a small smile. It was enough to loosen his solid exoskeleton, leaving me a bit flustered at the sudden change in a day riddled with sudden changes. I felt certain I'd have to seek therapy after this.

"Tell me you didn't talk to Mikey on your cell today," he said quietly. His face clouded. "About our visit to the lake."

My head shake turned into a reluctant nod.

"Cell phone conversations are easy to pick-up. But you know that already." He frowned and planted his hands on his hips. "You rode with Mikey, right? Take his car home. I'll drive him to his folks' place and get it later."

"I'm staying. Until I'm sure he's okay."

"What do you plan to accomplish by sticking around?"

I clenched my fists. "It's called a show of support. It's what friends do. But how could you know anything about that?"

James and Michael had been pals since kindergarten. I couldn't figure out why. Where Michael was squarish, a bookworm, absentminded, a rule stickler, and a natural behind an apron, James was molten lava hot with a matching temper, a man's man and a woman's dream kind of guy, every six foot four inch, two hundred pounds of him. I'd had a huge crush on James my senior year in high school, the kind that turned my insides to mush and drove me to a mirror every thirty seconds. But all he did was make fun of my skinny arms.

"They're like hot dogs pinned to your shoulders," he'd said.

And he wasn't fond of my unruly hair.

"You belong on the wall of a prehistoric cave, next to pictures of wooly mammoths."

The final straw came one afternoon at Michael's twenty-first birthday bash. James and I were alone in the kitchen. He planted a kiss right where he shouldn't. On my mouth. A frightening, rousing, breath-defying kiss. I'd slugged him and my crush evaporated like a drop of water under a heat lamp.

"Let's go tell him you're leaving." James held out his palm.

I slapped the back of his hand and stormed away.

James tailed me. "Make up your mind, Corrie. Do you want to be friends or not?"

There it was again. What was it with hot guys and friendship? I stopped and faced him. "Truce."

"Truce."

James' expression was unreadable. He rolled up the sleeves of his blue checked shirt. I admired his casually styled hair and bursting-at-the-seams biceps. I felt certain all female jurors automatically sided with him. Well, not this female. I sucked in my breath and continued toward Michael's room.

When I told a groggy Michael goodbye, he motioned for me to bend down closer. I lowered my ear to his mouth.

"I see a bright light at the end of a tunnel. I haven't much time. Promise you'll nail my killer after I'm gone."

"What are you talking about?"

"Don't you know? I've been poisoned. Get yourself that German Shepherd you've always wanted and name him after me. That way you'll always have Parris."

"Cut the cornball," James told him.

"James." My gaze shifted upward. "Can't you see he's in pain?" I returned to Michael. "You're going to be fine."

"The light…"

James grabbed a passing nurse. "Will you tone down the fluorescent lights already? They're killing this patient."

She scurried to the light control, and the room went dim.

"Corrie," Michael said. I bent down closer. "Don't do anything without me. Don't be contumacious."

"There's no such word."

"Yes, there is."

"What does it mean?"

"Stubbornly disobedient."

"There's no such word. I'll see you soon." I squeezed his hand and walked out to the parking lot.

"Wait," James said. He jogged toward me. "Mikey's dad is on his way. He'll take him home. I'll follow you."

"For what reason?"

"Where do you live?"

How far would arguing get me? "The bottle tampering was to send us a warning. Why would they go to my place and finish me off?"

"You think psycho killers are predictable? They may want to make sure you got the message. In case you're dense. Or contumacious. Now, where do you live?"

"I'm no damsel."

"I know you're not."

I'd been enough of a troublemaker. "Longfellow, Hermosa Beach. 600 block."

Nearly two hours later, James followed me inside my place.

"Nice artwork." James strolled over and peered at my tattered dartboard. "Why don't I see any darts? Or holes that look like they were made by darts? What are you throwing?"

"Oh, you know. Knitting needles, butter knives, nail files." I left him to admire my décor and slipped into the bedroom. My shuriken were well hidden in a locked metal cash box in the garage. Since they were illegal in California, I didn't need an ADA finding them. I changed into a lavender T-shirt and black leggings, and pulled my hair into a loose bun. I applied rose-tinted lip gloss and returned to the living room. I found James rummaging around the futon. "Find anything interesting?" I asked.

He held a wrinkly popcorn kernel between his thumb and forefinger, and a pink sock in the other hand. "I left you a message earlier because I want to give you something. For the short term." James reached into an inside pocket of his jacket and pulled out a black Taser, slightly larger than my cell phone. I shuddered and recalled my recent stun gun incident. “It’s okay,” he said. “You’ll need something to protect yourself.”

I grabbed my handbag and reached inside. “You mean like this?” I held out a Ruger GP-100 revolver, another gift from Dad.

“You know how to use it?”

“I wouldn’t have it if I didn’t.”

James nodded, his lips slightly upturned. “I underestimated you.”

“It’s not the first time.”

He turned to leave and stopped, his hand clutching the knob of my front door. “You’re dropping this, right?”

“I am.” I’d turned the corner into dangerous. “I’m done.” Someone else could get hurt. More seriously next time.

James turned to face me. As I wondered what he’d say or do, he left without a word.

Chapter 30
The Catnapping of Georgie

Ty was eager to join in the hunt for Georgie the next morning, but I convinced him not to. "Stay home and prepare for his return."

I got into my car and turned the key. Nothing happened.

"You need a new battery, girl." Ty shook his head. "No. You need a new car. This one's hurtin'. What is it, five or six years old?"

"Twelve, and it's fine." I turned the key again. Dead air.

"It's going to break down when you need it most. What if you're in East LA when that happens?"

"I'll just call on my favorite friendly giant to come get me."

"My mechanic'll fix it while you go find G.G."

****

I stood outside Ty's gates and waited. I zipped up my lightweight winter jacket and jogged in place. The turbaned ladies drifted by at a quarter past six. I high-tailed it to their mansion, using the vigorous run to simultaneously warm and tone me. Breaking into a sweat before going into work in the morning was a good way to keep undesirables away. And murder suspects.

The service entrance was closed. I punched in the

gate code that I'd watched Trish use. The tall, wooden gates barely swung open before I squeezed inside. I hustled to a side door and knocked. Trish opened it.

"Mind if I come in?" I flashed a silver badge that hung inside my jacket. I held my breath. Dad had used this badge occasionally. He'd taken it off a fallen cop, and I'd inherited it. If I got busted, my legal career would be done. Pressing my luck had become routine.

Trish backed away. I stepped through the open door and into a Tuscan style kitchen with a massive stone hearth.

"Do you want to talk here or outside?" I asked. What was I looking for anyway? Cat toys? Catnip? A litter box?

"I'm kneading bread." She showed me her floury hands.

"Okay. We'll chat here. Where's Tish?"

Like London fog, Tish appeared. She'd likely been listening, close by. Both ladies wore black T-shirts and sweat pants.

"You two need to return the cat," I said.

"No cat here," Trish responded.

"Are those chocolate chip cookies?" I asked.

A fresh baked batch rested atop a white porcelain dish on a wooden kitchen table.

"They are vegan," Trish said.

"I'm an equal opportunity dessert lover." I took one and bit into it. "Delicious."

Trish fiercely punched a doughy lump lounging on a white marbled countertop.

"Ty Calvin is a powerful man," I said. "He wants his cat back."

"Is there a reward?" Tish asked.

I wandered the room before answering. I admired the shiny collection of copper pans in varying sizes, hanging along one wall. Their turbaned heads followed my movements. I considered taking another cookie. The sad part? I wasn't even hungry. "The reward is in doing the right thing," I said.

"I see no cat. You see a cat?" Trish asked.

"No. But I see cat fur. All over Tish's clothes."

Trish stopped kneading. "Come back later."

"What's wrong with now? You don't want a kidnapping charge. That would mean being buried alive in a frigid, body fluid populated tomb. That's what LA jail is like. How would you make bail?" Melodramatic, I know, but I was in that kind of mood.

"I know where he is," Tish said. "I'll show you."

"No." Trish's head snapped toward Tish.

"I'm not going to a slimy jail. Come on." Tish waved a hand.

I followed her through French doors that led to an expansive, grassy area. Beyond it sat a free-form pool outlined by shrimp colored travertine. Trimmed palm trees of varying sizes fanned out around the stone. At one end of the pool, an elaborate rock waterfall cascaded before a grotto. The rush of tumbling water drowned out all noise except for a hideous yowling that sounded like an enraged Donald Duck.

"The fat man does not swim," Tish said.

"That's no surprise."

"He never uses the pool house."

Which made it a perfect spot to stash the kidnap victim.

"Ow!" I felt a swat on the back of my head. A tomato fell off to my side. I ducked behind a poolside boulder.

Trish advanced my way, one hand clutching a basket full of pseudo projectiles in the form of tomatoes, apples, and oranges. Even a pineapple. Now that would hurt. I don't mind a reasonable amount of trouble, but fruit projectiles?

"Ma," Tish said. "Stop it."

"No, you stop."

"There's no reason to massacre perfectly good produce." I stood and stepped toward her. I peered in the basket. "Is that a honeydew melon?"

"I need to work."

I understood only too well. "You won't lose your job. I promise. The fat man did a bad thing, and we can make it right." I wrested the basket from her hand. "Now go back inside."

She stormed away, throwing us backward glares every few feet until she disappeared into the kitchen.

I set down the basket. Tish and I hot-footed it to the waterfall and slipped between the liquid slats, and into an empty concrete space that reeked of chlorine. She pushed open a door in the wall. It opened into a glimmering gold and marble infused, windowless room with a chaise lounge, vanity, and oversize bathroom. Tiny, white feathers from ripped decorative pillows lay scattered across the white marbled floor. Georgie had wrestled the pillows and won. He sidled up to me, yowling like a maladjusted two-year-old in the middle of a monumental tantrum. I longed for ear-plugs. This was one furious cat.

Tish shut the door behind us. "He's mean."

"You would be too if you were holed up in here. It's torture for a cat used to freedom and sumptuous breakfast buffets."

"Every morning, Georgie comes outside with Ty Calvin. I watched the cat rubbing against Ty's ankles, looking up at him, purring. He doesn't look at me that way. He hates me."

"You took him away from his home. What did you expect?"

Tish burst out crying. "He forced me. He makes me hold Georgie down every morning. Look at my arms. They hurt!" She rolled up her sleeves. Long, fresh scratches crisscrossed her forearms.

"Who makes you?" I asked.

"Fat Joe."

"Fat Who?"

"The boss, Joseph Mankowitz. Fat Joe is his nickname."

"Your boss made you kidnap the cat?"

"He's borrowing him. The gardener said Ty Calvin rubs Georgie's head before every game and wins. Fat Joe wanted to win too. "

"Isn't he too pudgy to play basketball?"

"At the horse races."

"Has he been winning?"

Tish nodded. "Fat Joe rubs the cat's head and picks the winner. Every time."

"Really?" I considered rubbing the feline menace's head and running out and buying a lottery ticket. My thick sleeves would protect my arms, but what about my face?

"Fat Joe won't be happy if you take Georgie," Tish said.

"You can't keep something that belongs to someone else without permission. Open the door."

She did, and Georgie wasted no time. He scampered out, tail arched and bristled.

"How are you going to catch him?" Tish asked.

"I'm not. If he's so smart and so physical, he can find his own way home."

"What about me? I'll get in trouble."

"We'll see." I exited and texted Ty. I asked him to wait in front of his house and yell out Georgie's name.

Meanwhile, I trekked down the driveway. Before I reached the end, I turned and faced the house. I placed my thumb and index finger in a U-shape between my lips and whistled loudly. A hulky bodyguard and two Dobermans galloped to the gate across the street.

The rotund catnapper stepped out and hollered from his balcony, "Hey, what are you doing?"

"Borrowing a cup of sugar," I said.

"Get the hell out. Before I call the cops."

"Go ahead. Call. I'll tell them all about your definition of borrowing. Ty Calvin would love to hear where his cat's been stashed the past few days."

"Ooooh, I'm scared. Like I'll serve prison time for borrowin' a stupid cat."

"You think that's how the court will view it? Under California Penal Code Section 487g, a person who steals or maliciously takes away any animal of another for commercial use, in this case, for an illicit gambling operation, is guilty of a public offense punishable by imprisonment. And don't forget the mental distress you caused Ty, along with the threat to his lucrative and highly publicized livelihood." I let that sink in. "You'd better be nice to your help too. They'd be great on the witness stand." I'd learned a thing or two in law school, after all.

With a fast-beating heart, I jogged over to Ty's, following the obnoxious wail of Georgie's meows. The milkman was right about the built-in microphone.

I arrived in time to view the happy reunion. Ty cradled the furry sparkplug. Georgie clawed at all the loose parts of Ty's extra, extra, extra large T-shirt. I hoped G.G. wouldn't go for the face.

Ty waved, blood dripping off a fresh scratch on his chin. "Thank you, Corrie. Come watch me play Saturday, you hear? I've got my game back, girl. I owe you."

It was heartwarming.

Chapter 31
Morning Headache

I should have felt chipper when I arrived at the Complex. My best friend was safe. Ty's game was restored. Marshall was nowhere to be seen. And my hair was under control. But I didn't. All because of a man I'd never met and whose death had opened up narrow slots of danger. The trouble was I liked danger. Risky outcomes thrilled me. So did the possibility of overcoming fear and uncertainty. Was that so wrong?

Lesley poked in her head. "Bastard alert. Line one."

"Thanks." I picked up the phone. Where was Marshall calling from? "This is Corrie."

Marshall's muffled voice came from a great distance and with a nasty echo. He sounded like he was on a speaker phone after falling in the bottom of a giant toilet bowl. "We need to discuss the Earl deal," he said.

I responded James style. With silence. Veera poked her head in to say, "Great dress." while I wrote down a "to-do" list for the day.

"Hello?" Marshall picked up the receiver.

"I'm here." I'd made progress.

"Check your e-mail. I'm sending a deal memo regarding Ronald Earl, one of our producer-directors." Now he spoke quietly into the phone as if he sat in a law school library in the heat of final exams. "Ronnie

Earl is on *Variety's* 'Producers to Watch' list. Draft a production agreement between Keith-Ameripictures and Ronnie. Have it done by noon tomorrow."

I turned to my computer and started typing an e-mail. "Any deal points unique to this contract and unspecified in the memo?"

"Good, you're learning to be alert," he said. "Earl gets his fee, sixty percent upfront, a limo, and five thousand per week in expenditures."

"What kind of expenditures and for how long?"

"Expenses for his protégé, the foot masseuse, and fresh floral arrangements, excluding any flowers used in juvenile science experiments. And three months tops."

"I'll get on it." And with that as my good bye, I disconnected and hit the send button on the e-mail to Marshall, which read like this:

> *This will confirm our conversation wherein you advised me to draft a production agreement with Ronald Earl, based entirely on the deal memo and telephone discussion of this date as follows:*
>
> - *fee payable to Producer 60% upon execution;*
> - *limo at Producer's disposal for up to three months from execution of contract along with a personal assistant, masseuse and fresh flowers (excluding carnations) during the aforementioned time period;*
> - *$5000 per week in expenditures for a period not to exceed three months from execution of the contract;*
>
> *Said draft shall be completed by noon*

tomorrow.

I had to restrain my hands to keep from patting myself on the back.

Moments later, I received this response from Marshall:

Send agreement by 4 p.m. today. This supersedes all previous communications.

Why'd he change the deadline in a span of two minutes? I e-mailed him with one word: *Why?*

Lava poured through my veins, but I forced myself to calm down. If anger succeeded in leading me astray, the return to reason could take a while. Who knows what I'd do or say once my reason abandoned me? My oversize handbag always carried some form of weaponry.

I glowered at the tile floor. I leaned closer. Barely perceptible coffee stains spattered the area by my chair-leg. Since alcohol was the drink of choice for Bryce's deranged girlfriend, she didn't spill the java. I hadn't seen Veera drinking coffee either. I bent down and scrutinized the floor.

"Corrie!"

I jerked up my head and bumped it hard on the edge of the desk. That's when I saw it.

Chapter 32
Morning Oddity

A little bigger than a quarter and rectangular shaped, the listening device created a pimple beneath the otherwise smooth surface of my desk. A new addition since the last time I checked. And very amateurish compared to my father's equipment. My first impulse was to pry the interloper off, but then my eavesdropper would know that I knew. Instead, I took a picture with my cell phone and sent it to James.

The top of my head smarted from a small bump and Marshall's yell. His reaction to my e-mail was to march into my office and shout out my name.

"Why did you ask me 'why?'" he asked.

"I didn't understand the rationale for the sudden deadline change." I smoothed back my hair over the painful spot.

"To make a good impression on Ronnie. The faster the better. Treat him like he's our only client," Marshall said. "We need to…"

The next words came out simultaneously from both of our mouths, although mine contained a sarcastic bite.

"…stroke him."

Surprisingly, Marshall cracked a dwarfish grin. There was still hope for me. He left. I longed to call Michael, but I had to exercise caution.

While I debated what to do, Veera popped in. "You

got a real weirdo waiting to see you. Says he's a producer. Looks more like one of those mad scientists. Charlie O'Keefe is his name. Want me to get rid of him?"

Marshall's draft awaited me, but I could use the distraction. "I'll talk to him."

Moments later, a strange apparition appeared. He circled my height and age. His dirt-colored hair lay flat on his head and was combed off to one side, pasted to his head. Thick glasses sat like framed ice cubes, balancing on top of each eye, magnifying his eyes to the size of egg yolks. A red and green checked sport shirt covered the upper body, and khaki pants with ripped-at-the-edges cuffs monopolized the lower portion.

"I'm Corrie Locke."

He chuckled and blinked in slow motion. He sat.

"You're one of our producers?" I asked.

Charlie nodded and handed me his card. "I want to talk to you about a project."

"Why me?"

He stared at the floor. I could almost see the thought-waves bouncing around in his head. "Can I tell you why over lunch?"

"How about now?"

"I don't feel relaxed here."

"You don't?" Did he suspect the bug in my office?

He wiped his forehead with a white handkerchief. It was drenched. He moved it down to his neck, the backs of his hands, his palms…

"Do you mind?" he asked.

I observed in disturbed fascination. "By all means."

"Can you drive us?"

"Where?" I suddenly felt suspicious of this sweaty fellow. "Think about it, and I'll be right back." I raced out of the office and over to Lesley who fidgeted behind her computer. I whispered, "Who is Charlie O'Keefe and why is he in my office?"

Lesley whispered back, "Small-time producer, and one of Arthur's BFFs."

"Does Arthur have a lot of BFFs?"

"Gobs and gobs. And a few of them land production deals. Charlie's stuff is too small for the big guys. He has no credits anywhere."

"How embarrassing."

"Tell me about it. But Arthur's behind him a hundred percent. Maybe Charlie's thinking you're the one to make it happen."

"Can I tell him to go away?"

"You can. But he may go cry babyin' to Arthur. Can you handle that?"

I thought it over. "What are the possible ramifications?"

"Arthur goes to Marshall. Marshall comes to you and says, 'Handle it.'"

"Thank you." I flipped a U-ey and returned to my office. Charlie remained seated, only now his feet were bare and he wiggled his toes. His wet socks were drying on the arm of his chair. I looked outside. No sign of rain or flash floods.

"I'll meet you at noon," I said. "Downstairs."

Charlie nodded, slipped into his loafers and left. He forgot his socks.

****

Two hours had lapsed and I hadn't heard from James. I hoped he had the resources to identify the device beneath my desk. I didn't want to bother Michael who'd texted me twice already to see how *I* was doing. His thoughtfulness was heroic. I planned to complete Marshall's agreement by noon, go to lunch, return, provide final touches, and send it off. Unfortunately, I sat on a slippery slope.

"Do you smell smoke?" I heard a voice outside my office ask.

I listened and sniffed at the same time. No stampede or smoke odor. I was willing to bet that if there was a fire, Marshall would be the first one out of the building. Not for safety reasons, but because Marshall always came first. I stayed put. I had a contract to finish.

Moments later, a scream sounded in the distance, followed by the fire alarm. When I reached the parking lot, Marshall was already there.

Chapter 33
Insanity Before Lunch

"Every single person who works here is insane." Lesley folded her arms across her chest. "Except you and me."

Smoke had infiltrated the second floor from the conference room. Pat, Rob's wiry assistant, had started a bonfire in the conference room wastebasket. Not because it was too cold in the Complex. We had state-of-the-art heating. But because of a piece of malfunctioning office equipment. Rob's paper shredder stubbornly refused to shred that morning, contradicting Rob's passion for shredding all things paper. Pat, in a panic, took the discards into the conference room, tossed them in the metal wastebasket, and lit a match. Wastepaper basket fires are of the fast-burning variety and, before Pat could move after lighting the paper, the sleeve of his lavender, fancy stripe, dress shirt with barrel cuffs, caught fire. Pat screamed, wrapped himself snugly in the colorful Tabriz carpet in the entry of the conference room, and rolled along toward the main staircase, creating quite a spectacle. The video was already playing on YouTube.

"Did anything else catch on fire?" I asked.

"I don't think so," Lesley said. "But what about smoke damage to Arthur's artwork? What about that gorgeous Persian rug? And how are they going to get this smoky smell out of my hair?"

All very practical questions. I didn't spot Arthur anywhere. For now, comment was plentiful and punishment readily meted out for Pat.

"Pat could have killed us" and "Throw him in the slammer" and "Working for Rob would make me start a fire too. With Rob in it."

Medics carted Pat away. Caitlyn volunteered to sit with him in the ambulance, probably because Marshall, astonishingly, offered to follow Pat to the hospital. Rob was nowhere to be seen.

"Ready for our lunch?" Charlie, of the carelessly dressed and messy hair Charlies, stood before me. He'd changed into a blue and yellow checked shirt with navy slacks. He sported pale yellow socks with his penny loafers. The parking lot crowd didn't faze him.

"You left your socks in my office," I said, relieved for a break from the frenzy which I called work.

He nodded.

After a few moments of silence, we headed toward my car.

Chapter 34
Insanity During Lunch

Some people don't need a pickaxe to plant the seed of impatience in me. Exhibit A: Charlie. Partly because of his penchant for speaking in riddles, but mostly because of his eraser-proof smile. It wasn't the Cheshire cat grin that belonged to Arthur or Alana's surgically implanted smirk. It wasn't even the pasted-on, nervous smile popular among the employees. Charlie's was more of a jack o'lantern grin, wide and freshly cut, friendly, but in a creepy way.

Once we were seated, I labored to pry conversation out of him, practically cross-examining him to discover the reason for our meeting.

"Isn't it true you're seeking to produce a movie based on an existing children's book?" I asked.

He nodded wildly like I'd hit the jackpot, but replied, "No."

I waited and when he failed to elaborate, I prodded, "Is it an original script?"

He shook his head no, smile growing wilder.

Lunch was served and we'd made no progress. So I ignored him and scanned the bustling restaurant. Two familiar faces sat across the high-ceilinged room. Bryce and Benson, who looked like he'd lost weight. His hair hung looser, darker around his gaunt face. It could be that he was ill, wore wigs, and lost weight as a result of his illness.

I slid my chair sideways, turning my back to the Bryce/Benson duo and returned to the leering Charlie. I casually asked the half-crazed, quasi-movie producer, “So is it a book that’s yet to be published?”

“No.”

I like playing games like *Scrabble* and chess, even *Hangman* in the right circumstances. This was none of the above. I gave up and dug into my beet salad. Charlie tore his gaze from me and attacked his Fettuccine Alfredo.

“I heard you’re buds with Arthur,” I said between bites. “How did you two meet?”

Charlie slurped up a long piece of fettuccine through pursed lips. He replied a minute later, as if I’d just asked. Perhaps the lengthy fettuccini had made its final slide down his throat. “We lived next door to each other when we were kids.”

That meant he knew things about Arthur no one else would know.

“Pepto Bismol,” he said.

“No, thank you.”

“Your salad dressing. It looks like Pepto Bismol.”

My fork froze midway to my mouth. I eyed the raspberry vinaigrette. He was right. I dropped my fork and returned to utilizing my Sherlock Holmes type skills to uncover the purpose of our lunch. After several attempts, I hit bulls-eye.

“You want to produce a movie based on an adult tale watered down to appeal to kids.”

Charlie’s head bobbed up and down. “Based on an H.G. Wells book.”

“Like *The Time Machine*?”

"Yes, but not *The Time Machine*."

It turned out to be a little known, Wells' short story, *The Magic Shop*. "Who's going to prepare your script?" I transferred my gaze over my shoulder to search for Bryce and Benson. They no longer sat at the table where I'd spotted them.

"We are," Charlie said.

I glanced at him to confirm that "we" meant him and me.

It was my turn to nod in agreement. Arguing would be futile. Taking everything in stride would help me keep my wits. Never mind that I had no writing experience. Where did Shakespeare learn to write, anyway? Or Jane Austen? And the really beautiful part? Charlie didn't even ask if I had experience. "What does Benson May do at the Complex?" I asked.

Charlie stared at his empty china plate. Faint swirls of butter and cream trimmed the dish. Charlie licked his lips. Was he thinking of how much he'd enjoyed his meal or contemplating licking the plate clean? He put a hand on each side of the dish.

"Benson works in marketing." Charlie had no chance to lick. The server yanked away the plate and scowled at Charlie. "When do we start?"

Not only was he defeating my attempts at snooping, he harbored very high hopes. Besides my legal job and my moonlighting as private investigator (when I shouldn't be) on a possible homicide and catnapping, I was going to be a scriptwriter? I never cared much for sleep anyway.

"I'll get back to you on that," I said.

Minutes later, we sat in my car, ready to return to the Complex. I aimed the BMW toward the driveway and my eyes flicked to the rearview mirror. Bryce and Benson stood near a black Suburban. I braked with gusto.

"Did Benson look different to you today?" I turned to Charlie. "He was in the restaurant."

"I didn't see him."

"He's standing behind us right now."

Charlie tore his stare away from me, turned, and scanned the area behind him.

"I don't see him."

I looked over my shoulder. Benson stood talking to Bryce. I pointed. "There he is."

Charlie shook his head. "That's not Benson."

I sighed. Why did I attract these types? Men with major peculiarities. "Yes, it is. Talking to Bryce. Or is that not Bryce either?"

"That is Bryce. But, that's not Benson. It's Dom. Benson's twin brother."

"Dom May?" It wasn't Benson I saw at the other Complex, it was Dom. "What does he do?"

"I'm not sure."

"Can you introduce us?" I wasn't insane after all. But Charlie was.

"I've never met Dom," he said.

Now I felt thoroughly puzzled by the oddity that sat in my car. "How did you know who he was?"

"I've seen Dom and Ben at the Complex. And at Artie's house. I'm observant. For instance, you spent a lot of time watching Bryce and Dom at lunch. Then you took your eyes away for a minute and they were gone. They knew you were watching."

"How do you know?"

"They saw you first."

This guy was creepy, yet intriguing.

"What else did you notice?"

"You wanted to ask for more lemon in your water because you smelled chlorine, but you got sidetracked by Bryce and Dom."

"And how do you know that?"

"You frowned after taking a sip and sniffed the glass. Then you stared at the lemon slices on the table of the couple sitting next to us."

"Not bad." I gazed in semi-admiration at Charlie. "What am I thinking now?"

"You wish you could find a pair of fashionable work shoes, comfortable enough to sleep in. Preferably in an animal print."

This guy was scary. "You are good." I glanced in my rearview mirror. Dom and Bryce had disappeared again.

"They drove off while we chatted," Charlie said.

I plunged deeper. "Did you know Druby?"

Charlie hesitated before nodding.

"Do you think he killed himself?"

He removed his eyeglasses and rubbed them on a sleeve. When he turned toward me, he no longer resembled an animated character from *South Park.* His grin had faded. "Arthur didn't do it."

Chapter 35
Suspects in the Afternoon

I maneuvered out of the parking lot and headed toward the office. I hadn't considered Arthur a suspect, had I a list of suspects, which I didn't. After Charlie's last statement, he stared straight ahead, sans glasses or smile. I had a strong feeling he was watching me from his peripheral vision, so I kept my expression bland. I even suppressed a sneeze.

"Interesting. About Arthur being a suspect," I finally said.

"Anyone that believes Druby didn't kill himself counts Arthur as a suspect."

I turned to face Charlie and nearly missed the off-ramp. I swerved and squeezed between two cement trucks in order to exit the freeway. He didn't say another word. I wasn't sure if it was because he'd said enough already or because he feared I'd get into an accident.

"What's Arthur's motive?" I asked when I neared the Complex. "For those who believe."

"Why do you ask?"

"I can't help myself. My father was a private investigator." I came clean pretty quickly this time. "It's in my genes."

"They were business partners. Druby's project was important to Art."

"Financially important?"

He shrugged and bit into a large slice of silence the rest of the way.

We reached the parking lot before I spoke again. "If you want to talk more about Arthur and Druby…"

Charlie shook his head and left.

My phone vibrated from the backseat. I dove a hand into my handbag and retrieved it. Two missed calls from James and one message. I listened and heard James say,

"It's a cheap, amateurish listening device that anyone can buy off eBay. Small-time, which is a good thing. Don't tamper with it. Call me."

The second message was from Michael. I didn't listen to it. Instead, I called him, remembering mid-dial that I had a contract to finish.

"Hel—hel—hel—lo?" Michael's barely audible voice cracked.

"Are you all right?" My stomach turned. He sounded terrible. The heck with Marshall's contract. Michael needed me.

Laughter interrupted my thoughts. Michael's chortles. "You didn't listen to my message, did you? I knew it. I told you I was feeling better."

"Michael!" I slapped my hand against my thigh, angry that he'd toyed with me regarding something so serious and that he found me so predictable. "I was worried, but obviously I wasted my energy on you." I got out of the car and walked across the street. Away from the Complex.

"Sorry." He mopped away his laughter. "I'm stir crazy from being cooped up at Mom and Dad's. Where were you?"

"At lunch. Did you talk to James?"

"No. Why?"

I briefed him on Ty and Georgie, my lunch, Benson and Dom, and the device under my desk.

"I can't believe I've missed all the action," Michael said. "Can you lock yourself in a closet or something? Until I get my sea legs back."

"If only. Talk soon."

I entered the Complex, walked up to my office, and angled in behind my computer screen. I was psyched to complete the contract, when I noticed an e-mail from a "TJ321@hotmail.com," with the subject: "Meet me."

It took a full minute for me to realize the sender was the homeless guy who witnessed the Druby drowning. I read:

I know something you don't. 6:30 tonight. Aliso Niguel Park. Leave your car in the top lot. I'll be at the lake. No Police. Don't reply. Just be there. Tom John."

Questions spun around in my mind.

Was it really him? Was he sober? Should I go? Alone? Was the Pepto Bismol salad dressing laced with MSG? A mind-numbing headache held me hostage.

I took two aspirin and forwarded the e-mail to James. I was about to press "send" when I froze. What if my e-mail wasn't secure? I raced out of the building, heels and all, in what had to be *Guinness World Records'* time. I threw myself into the BMW, drove a few miles to a residential neighborhood, whipped out my phone and sent the message, via my personal G-mail, to James.

Back at the office, I immersed myself in the contract and completed it just before four. I hit "send" and requested Marshall review it before forwarding.

"How's Charlie?" Marshall strolled in minutes later.

If the building suddenly filled with dry brush and a wildfire blazed, it wouldn't spread nearly as fast as the gossip that flowed so freely around here.

"Fine."

"Your hair looks messy." He displayed a lopsided grin and left.

Smoke and wind had infiltrated my decent morning hair so that it now resembled a halfway house for brooms that didn't make the cut. I felt mildly offended.

Minutes later, I received a response, both from Marshall and James.

Marshall informed me that the Earl deal went sour, and the agreement was no longer needed. How long had he known? I looked at the bright side. He didn't find any mistakes this time.

I hesitated before opening James' response and my eyes shifted to my shoes. My feet were killing me. I could almost see the bunions sprouting, thanks to my gorgeous black pumps. I couldn't chance opening James's e-mail in the Complex. I was willing to bet the air vents had eyes and ears. I grabbed my purse and phone and raced downstairs, pain be damned.

Certain that my exit was monitored, I strolled across the street and out of view. I read James' e-mail:

I'm going alone tonight. Will tell you what happens.

I dialed his phone. He picked up on the first ring.

"I'm coming with you for two reasons," I said. "First, to watch your back. I don't want any friend of Michael's getting hurt, even if it is you. Second, Tom John contacted me, not you. And I have P.I.

experience."

"Do you not understand how suspicious this is? This scene has shifted to very dangerous. I'm taking Delgado," James said. "And you gave me three reasons."

"Tom John's met her before, remember? He might clam up if I don't show. And the third reason was thrown in because I'm feeling spontaneous."

"As in combustion?"

I did sort of feel like exploding.

"Remember what happened to Mikey? You're done with this stuff," he said. "You said so yourself. You're not coming."

"I have to." Druby's death was a boomerang that kept landing in my lap. Tossing it aside was no good. I'd have to hold on until I was done with it. If there was a killer out there, he was all mine. I gritted my teeth.

James wasted no more time. "I checked the email ISP. It came from the Aliso Viejo Public Library, earlier today. I'm there now. One of the librarians told me a grungy looking guy hobbled in, first thing, reeking of Eau de Whiskey, and asked to use the computer. He gave his name as Tom John, but I couldn't verify."

"Where should we meet?" A familiar rush washed over me. Like sitting at the peak of a hill in a roller coaster, anticipating the downhill thrill.

"There's a Laguna shopping center about five miles from the lake," James said. "Be there at six. Park by the south mall entrance." He disconnected.

I strolled back to the Complex and headed to my office. But first I stopped to see Caitlyn. She lounged behind her desk.

"How's Pat doing?" I interrupted her thumbing

through *The Hollywood Reporter*.

"Marshall and I are going to check in on him tonight."

"I'm surprised that Marshall was so helpful."

Caitlyn's eyes crawled upwards and glazed over. "Marshall is so compassionate. He's a real humanitarian. That's what he is. Yup."

I'd apparently missed that self-sacrificing side of him. "Was Rob there too?" I asked.

Caitlyn busily blinked her eyes, perhaps to encourage a teardrop to fall, but in fact, one of her false eyelashes had loosened and threatened to float away. Her head bobbed once. "Marshall was such a comfort to Rob. He gave him a great big man-hug…" Caitlyn shivered at either the tenderness of the memory or a sudden gust of wind.

"Talk to you later, Caitlyn." I raced out before she got graphic.

"Heard you and Charlie got together today," Arthur said as he sailed by. He did a fist pump. "Whoo-hoo." He disappeared before I could even process his statement. All neighboring eyes fastened on me.

"Yes, I had lunch with Charlie today," I said. "So what?"

Lesley grabbed my arm. "You look like you could use some hair spray. Let's go to the ladies room."

I followed her inside. She turned to face me.

"You're not going to like this," she said.

Chapter 36
A Hairy Afternoon

"This isn't about my hair? That's a relief," I said. Lesley and I talked to our reflections in the mirror of the upstairs ladies room.

"It's the miserable bastard. He's telling everyone you and Charlie are having an affair."

"After one lunch?"

A moment ago, Marshall was hailed as a humanitarian and now a slanderer?

"I overheard him telling Arthur," she said. "Marshall knew you and Charlie met today and he tossed you in the gutter like a sack of sludge. You know how the minds of some guys work."

I knew how lesser minds worked.

"I don't blame you for being enraged."

I stared at my reflection. I looked a little irked, but enraged?

"Want to slash his tires later?" Lesley asked.

I could derive satisfaction from that. I shrugged.

"Let me know." Lesley patted me on the shoulder. "There's a steak knife in the kitchen that would be perfect."

Moments later, I returned to my office, finished up my work, and paid Marshall a visit. I took a deep breath and sauntered in.

He shot up and slipped into his suit jacket to leave.

"Marshall." I stood before his desk. "We need to talk. I'm enraged."

He froze, one arm mid-reach to his briefcase. Now I had him. Any display of emotion grabbed his attention, especially emotions of the negative variety.

His squinty eyes flicked to mine. "About?"

"Haven't you heard?"

Marshall broke into a slight grin, eerily resembling Charlie. "Heard?"

"I'm having an affair."

"Really?" His small grin expanded. His beady eyes glittered.

"With Charlie. Whom I only met today. Can you believe it? All the hot guys in this place and some moron matched me up with Charlie."

The dysfunctional teapot giggles escaped his lips. What had I expected? That he'd fess up? "That's hysterical," he said and loosened the knot of his tie.

I smacked a fist into a palm. "Any idea of who's inane enough to start that rumor?"

Marshall shook his head at the reckless rumor monger. "Do you?"

"I have a strong suspicion." I let that sink in. I hoped he'd feel the need to watch his back.

His eyes narrowed and shot to the door. Was he going to make a run for it? Should I tackle him if he did? Visions of standing in the unemployment line, holding an empty soup can, dashed through my head. I'd gone far enough today.

"I heard you're going to pay Pat another visit tonight," I said. "That's thoughtful."

Marshall turned somber. "It's important he think we care to avoid any potential liability."

So the appearance of humanitarianism stemmed out of his role as legal counsel. “But Pat took the initiative of starting a fire in the conference room.”

“All he has to do is claim it was under Rob’s directive.”

Lawyers can be a cynical bunch. It stems from the training, ever focusing on the worst case scenario. I had a sudden impulse to ask Marshall something.

“There’s a lot of talk about Druby,” I said. “What did you think of him?”

“He was a good guy.”

“Yes, but what did you think of his being Arthur’s business partner?”

“Artie did that transaction himself. I wasn’t involved. Remember that. Stay out of anything that’s not necessarily compatible with company business. That’s how we keep our jobs.”

“In case something illegitimate goes down?”

He narrowed his eyes. “In case it’s anything but a square deal.”

I nodded. It would be in my best interest to avoid Arthur. I left the office. It was nearly time for my meeting with James.

Chapter 37
Finding an Opening

While I waited for James to show up, I phoned Michael and told him I'd finished work for the day. I didn't elaborate on my evening plans.

"I'll be sitting behind my laptop all night," he said.

Translation: Come over.

"I'd love to stop by, but I'd arrive kind of late. I've got a few errands to run," I said. "How about tomorrow? I'll leave early and come visit."

"Sure," he said quietly.

Translation: That sucks.

"Call me later and tell me what happened today," Michael said. "I want to hear more about the catnapping."

Translation: If you don't call when you get home, we're done.

"Okay."

After the fact, I'd tell him about tonight's meeting. We disconnected and I thought about Tom John. I didn't expect much. He was probably aiming to get cash for incidental information he'd forgotten to tell Michael. The meeting would likely last all of ten minutes. Maybe I'd surprise Michael and pay him a visit after all.

James opened the passenger door and slid inside. "What do you think this guy wants?"

"What most people want." I drove out of the lot. "Dough."

"You still watching Bogart movies?"

I turned my head toward him. James' smile caught me by surprise. Damn, he looked good. "Too often, it's about money."

He nodded and pulled out his phone. He texted with one hand and fidgeted with a small black flashlight in the other. "The gates at the lake are locked every day at five-thirty," James said. "How are we getting in?"

"Tom John practically lives in the bush. Maybe he has his own key," I said, aware that my unsound logic would rankle James.

He gave me a sidelong scowl. "That's the most idiotic thing I've ever heard."

His joking mood had evaporated to match his somber courtroom attire. I caught my breath while I gave him the evil eye. Even at the end of the day, he showed no signs of wear and tear. His complexion was flawless and without benefit of makeup, no less. But, I reminded myself, he was totally devoid of kindness. I refocused.

"Tom John must be an expert at breaking in the park," I said. "I'm guessing tonight's all about show and tell. He's going to show or tell us something."

"Such as?"

I shrugged. "More evidence that the pope was involved. A catfish he caught with his bare hands. How should I know?"

James grunted.

I'd annoyed him again. He turned quiet the rest of the ride.

Minutes later, I idled at the section of La Paz Road

that hosted the park. "Have you ever looked around this place during the day?" I asked.

"Why would I?"

I drove the perimeter, Michael style, at ten miles per hour. I motored so close to the curb, my front tire scraped. After which I ran over the next curb. James shot me dirty looks both times. From our vantage point, an uninterrupted chain link fence surrounded the park.

"I should have brought wire cutters," James said.

"I've got some in my trunk." I stopped the car. "But we're missing something." I rested my chin on the steering wheel and thought for a moment. "There must be a service entrance around here somewhere." I lifted my head. It hit me, the way to get in. I hooked a U-turn, went to the start of the park, and drove south again, past the front entrance.

"What do you think you're doing?" James asked, one eye on the road and the other on me.

I stopped next to a closed, chain-link gate which led to a dirt driveway. "See if it's open."

"It's obviously shut."

"How do you know it's locked?"

He shook his head, left the car and jogged over to the gate.

I couldn't see what he was doing. The street lights were dim and his back faced me, but he tugged at something. Nothing happened. He returned.

"It's locked." He sank back onto the seat. "Let's get the wire cutters."

"Not so fast." I nailed it and drove farther south. Just before we reached the end of the park, we spotted another gate. This one was wooden with no peep areas between the slats. James got out and went through the motions. He struggled with the gate and moments later, slid it off to one side.

"Jackpot." I advanced onto the worn and cracked asphalt lot.

While James snooped around with the flashlight, I considered backing my car into a spot. Dad always backed in, in case a quick getaway was in order. Before I could move, James halted and snapped his head toward the lake. I slipped into the first spot, tail first, next to an old pickup truck with questionable running capabilities. I jumped out.

"What is it?" I asked.

"I heard something. Down there." James pointed to the lake area.

"Let's go."

Only the faintest outline of trees and shrubs appeared around us. The moon hoarded its sliver of light behind a screen of slow-drifting clouds. We stumbled down a dirt path that wound its way downward and lakeside, James' flashlight in the lead. I took in the night scents of pine and candy-sweet shrubbery and stuck close to James.

"What's that?" He pitched his chin toward a large boulder near the edge of the lake.

I strained to focus and saw it. I nearly jumped out of my shoes. The silhouette of a figure. Someone sat on the boulder.

Chapter 38
Dead or Alive?

James' flashlight formed a large, dim circle on the ground, slightly ahead of our feet.

"He's not moving," I whispered and stopped in my tracks. The shadowy figure sat motionless, hunched over. One firm pat on the back would send him reeling forward. "Is he…?"

"Probably wasted." James sounded more hopeful than certain. He called out, "Tom John?"

James waited a beat, then quick-stepped in front of the figure, one hand behind him, under his jacket. I reached under my jacket as well. But what good's a gun if all you have for company is a dead guy? James shined the light on the figure and illuminated a khaki colored raincoat with the hood pulled over the head. Something protruded out of a top corner of the hood. I inched over to where James stood.

"What the…?" I said.

We stared at an oversize stuffed animal, a big Mickey Mouse, complete with round yellow feet, white gloves, and red shorts. A mouse ear stuck out at the top edge. It didn't fit beneath the hood.

"The joke's on us," I said.

"Nobody makes a fool out of James Herbert Zachary."

"Did you just talk in the third person?"

"Shhh." James turned toward the street.

"Let's call in big Mickey," I said. "He's evidence."

Before either of us could budge, we heard a fracas behind us, from the parking lot.

"Now what?" James took off at a run.

We raced upward. I tripped along the dirt road behind him. Just before we reached the top, we heard clicking noises, a creaking sound, and a car door slam.

We reached the lot. My chest tightened like all the oxygen had been sucked out. No sign of human or stuffed animal life. No other car besides mine and the dilapidated pickup.

"Do you think he got into the old truck?" I whispered.

"Wait here." James moved toward the vehicle, crouching as if ready to take cover. He held a revolver in one hand and the flashlight in the other. Meanwhile, I edged toward my car. I couldn't remember if I'd locked it in the rush of events. Was anyone residing inside? Did I live in denial of possible danger? It sure looked that way. I approached the BMW and dared a peek.

"Damn," James said. "It's empty."

I jumped a foot and gave a muffled screech at the sound of James' voice.

"What the hell are you doing?" he asked.

"Sightseeing. What do you think? I was checking my car for unwanted borders, okay?"

"It's not okay. I told you to wait—"

"Just because you're an ADA…"

Behind him, the shadows shifted and parted ways. A dark object launched toward us. I opened my mouth, but the words ran away.

James spun around. "Start the car." He pointed his

gun at the lightless vehicle headed our way. "Now."

I dove into the BMW and stuffed the key in the ignition. James' shot rang out. The loud clang split open the night. The oncoming vehicle shot straight for James. He dove off to one side. The vehicle swerved and turned down the dirt road, toward the lake. I hit the gas, barely stopping for James to scramble inside.

I veered out of the parking lot and bounced onto the cavity-ridden dirt road. The mystery car appeared out of nowhere from beneath the tall pines, eclipsed by the darkness. Now it raced away somewhere ahead.

"Why didn't we hear it start?" I asked James.

"It's a hybrid."

"We're in a car chase with a Prius?" A car chase with a Porsche or Ferrari was respectable, but with a battery operated car? All bragging rights vanished.

I shifted into warp speed and surged downhill. Seconds later, we faced the hybrid's rear bumper. The spot for the license plate sat empty.

"He's not getting away," I said.

The hybrid turned and launched up a hill, kicking up pebbles and a dusty haze. It fish-tailed and I nearly nipped it in the rear. I executed a sharp left and ran over something large. And lumpy.

"Stop," James said.

I skidded to a halt, a cloud of dirt trapped in my headlights. The Prius escaped through an open gate and onto La Paz. My eyes cut to the rearview mirror. My tail lights illuminated the road behind us in an eerie red glow. As I surveyed the scene, not a trace of saliva remained in my mouth.

Chapter 39
Homicide in the Evening

"I killed him." My knees shook and wobbled. I was surprised I was still standing.

We abandoned the car and staggered over to the lump that I'd trampled. Sprawled on the dirt, in front of my car, lay the body of a man.

"Tom John?" I said.

"He can't hear you, Corrie." James bent over the inert form.

"I was talking to you." Even during an emergency, he rattled my shaky nerves.

James checked for signs of life. I squeezed my eyes shut to block out the dreadful sight. God, please let him be alive.

"No pulse." James straightened and faced me. "The hybrid ran over him first." He swiped his palm with the fingers of his other hand.

"How do you know? The Prius could have knocked him down. And I finished him off."

"Hold on." James shined the flashlight onto his palm. He crouched back down, by the body. I joined him. James shifted the light onto Tom John. Like James' hand, the body was covered with small hairs. So was the surrounding dirt.

"What's this?" James said.

I patted the ground with my hands while James

sifted through the dirt around us. Bits and pieces of human hair fluttered on and encircled the body.

"This guy's been dipped in a barrel full of hair clippings," he said.

"How—"

"This was staged. It's a DNA carnival. Someone dropped him off here, or what was left of him, and went to a ton of trouble planting excess evidence. Someone bent on covering his tracks."

"Like in the jewelry store. Two messengers made the purchase."

James straightened and took out his cell phone. "I'm going to call the police. We'll tell them I was behind the wheel."

"Why?"

He ignored me and reported the body.

When he finished, I asked him why again.

"There'll be questions. Lots of them." His eyes were glued to mine. "I don't want you mixed up in this any more than you are already."

"I can handle questions. Besides, you only got involved because of me."

"Come on," James said. We hustled up the dirt road. "Here's the story: we drove here together, but you waited in the parking lot while I investigated. I heard a noise, came back to the lot, and took the car when the hybrid showed up. You saw nothing. You know nothing."

"James…" I felt a warm glow trickle up my arm. He'd slipped his hand into mine.

"Let's wait up on the street," he said.

"I can't let you do this. Why would you?" I pulled my hand away. I couldn't figure him out. Why get himself into trouble?

He stopped and spoke calmly, "Don't speak to anyone about what happened."

"Not even Michael?" In my bewildered state, I still waxed practical. "I tell him everything."

"'These aren't the droids you're looking for.'"

The Jedi knight mind trick had no effect on me.

"Hand me the keys," James said.

I gave them to him.

"You don't have anything incriminating in your car, do you? Illegal contraband, open container of alcohol, machine gun?"

I shook my head. "Why would the killer arrange this meeting?"

"To force us to stop looking into this matter—"

"By getting us seemingly more involved. We can't investigate when we're under investigation. Why didn't you say so?"

"You knew it all the time," James said. "That's why I want you kept out of this mess. You'll be free to forge ahead. If you want to."

I wanted to, all right. I gulped and tried to slow down my breath. "Nobility doesn't suit you, James."

"Don't worry. I'll take off this suit of armor as soon as we're done. It's making me all itchy anyway." James shot me a glance. "You're no quitter, Corrie."

That last comment smacked me between the eyes and nearly sent me reeling. He was wrong. I am a quitter. I never found my father's killer. We waited wordlessly on the street until the police arrived.

Chapter 40
My Expulsion

I pulled over just before I got on the 405 freeway and threw up. I grabbed a sturdy plastic bag from the back seat in the nick of time, so my car's interior remained unaffected by my expulsion.

I arrived home after midnight, dragged myself up the stairs, unlocked the door, and crashed onto the futon, a throbbing head and dry mouth my unwelcome companions. Sleep was long in coming and short in staying. When I awoke, my head no longer hurt, but my mind relentlessly replayed the previous night's happenings.

I'd never witnessed a crime scene investigation, not even with Dad. We'd typically arrived after the fact. Or left before. But tonight was different.

The police filtered throughout the scene. The ghastly green glow of chemical light sticks illuminated the borders of the dirt road. Tom John's battered body lay in an ugly sprawl, highlighted by potent, portable lights. Two detectives zeroed in on James and me. The younger one sported a hook nose that only a wicked witch could love. An unforgivably long-stranded comb-over stretched across the older guy's scalp.

James remained cool during his grilling. No one questioned his replies. I spoke only when addressed and offered curt answers. The younger detective glowered at me with narrowed eyes. If he had his way, I'd be behind bars, possibly in solitary confinement or lockdown because of my reluctance to talk.

"The car plates were removed. I never saw the driver, and elected not to follow the car, once I realized I'd run over something," James said.

When the senior detective pulled James aside, the other one focused on me.

"What are you packing?" he asked.

"A Glock 26. How did you know?"

"Your jacket's bulky in the wrong place. I noticed when you raised your arm to play with your hair."

I bet Charlie would also have noticed, as well as the fact that I carried a smaller, rainbow colored Sig pistol in my handbag.

"You know what the penalty is for carrying a concealed weapon?" he asked.

"Three-to-nine years on top of whatever crime you're convicted of committing."

The detective nodded. "You expect me to keep quiet?"

"I expect nothing. The real question is: what do you expect?" Once again, my cockiness reared its obnoxious head, this time out of exhaustion and anxiety. Out of the corner of my eye, I saw James heading our way.

"What's going on?" he asked.

"Possible CCW," the detective said.

"Why are you assuming she doesn't have a permit?"

"Does she?"

I reached for my wallet and pulled out a permit that could have passed for a credit card. My father had drilled into my skull the necessity of proof. I never carried a gun without it.

"Sorry." The detective shuffled away.

James grinned. "I didn't know you had that."

"Tonight's chock-full of surprises."

James tried to get the detectives to allow me to leave. He finally succeeded around eleven o'clock. One of them agreed to drive James to his car, but first James walked me to the BMW. It had been photographed, brushed, scoured, and ransacked to provide samples to the CSI unit. I reached the car door, but before I could open it, James grabbed my arm.

"You okay?"

I nodded, nauseated by a throbbing headache. I could have puked at any moment. Too much excitement jostled my stomach acids. I swallowed and opened the door. I slipped inside.

"The crime scene investigator believes Tom John's been dead a while," James said quietly. "There's no fresh blood. No way to know how long until the ME provides her report. But the temperature of the body is the same as the surrounding environment, and it's taken on a greenish-blue hue. That generally indicates the passing of a twenty-four hour period."

I breathed again and the saliva began to flow. It was comforting to know I wasn't an accidental homicidal maniac.

James kneeled beside my open window. "You sure you're okay?"

"Fairly to pretty damn." His skin, so close to mine, radiated a warmth that blossomed in the cold night. His hand reached out and smoothed rogue hairs away from my face. My heart somersaulted.

"Go to work tomorrow and act like nothing happened," he was saying. "Stay calm and keep your head. We're going to outsmart whoever's behind this."

"Whomever."

"What?" He scowled, straightened up, and retreated.

Good thing. Calm was foreign with him so close. My head tipped back against the head-rest. Dad was ever the cool thinker. Ever the out-smarter. I could be calm and cool, right? I took a deep breath. How did a simple request by a stranger escalate into a full-blown, double murder investigation with me on center stage?

Eyes closed, I grabbed my pillow and stumbled to my bed. On the bright side, at least the Ty matter was solved and I could sleep in tomorrow. I eventually dozed off, only to be awakened by the doorbell a short time later.

Chapter 41
The Ungodly Part of the Morning

Despite my grogginess and pounding heart, I managed to pull on a sweatshirt, grab pepper spray, and scramble to the entry. I flipped on the outside light switch and peered through the peep hole. No sign of life. I cracked open the door and poked my head out into the damp morning. It smelled of cold, steamy wetness. I slammed the door before my hair frizzed, rattling a few windows in the wake. I slunk back to bed, obscenities rolling off my tongue like chestnuts on a park slide.

My head didn't even touch the pillow before the doorbell rang again. This time I grabbed my Sig. I would plead insanity.

I viewed the back of a heather gray hoodie through the peep hole. I yanked open the door, gun at my side. "This better be a matter of life or death or lottery winnings."

He turned to face me. Outfitted in low-riding baggy jeans, oversize white T-shirt, and hood over a black baseball cap, the intruder raised his stubbly chin. White sneakers and black shades accented the street-wise look, as did the thirty pound silver crucifix hanging around his neck. "Yo," he said. "You don't need that." His thumb flicked to my pistol.

"I'll decide if I do or I don't."

"Can I come in?"

"No." Before I could slam the door, an oversize sneaker jammed itself at the bottom. My gun took aim.

"Yo," he said. "You talk to Ty?"

"What about?"

"My problem. Check your phone, woman."

There was something familiar about this pseudo-slum dweller. His mouth formed a crooked line that turned down at the ends. He cocked his head sideways and I shut the door. I fished out my cell phone from my handbag. Ty had left a voicemail message earlier. What was with these ungodly hours?

"Corrie, I'm sending Fo over, okay?" Ty said. "You did good for me and Georgie. I know you'll help Fo out too."

I returned to the front door and opened it. "Take off your sunglasses."

He lowered them enough for me to see his pale blue eyes.

"Fo O'Five?"

He nodded once.

"Where's you whip?" I talked his talk, so he'd feel more at home. After all, before me slouched one of the best-selling hip hop artists of the 2000s.

"My boy's circling around 'til I'm done. Now can I come in?"

I caught my reflection in his black shades when he tripped inside. I glimpsed the crazy outline of my temperamental tangle of hair and nearly cried out. Even worse, I still wore yesterday's clothes beneath my sweatshirt.

"Excuse me." I hurled myself into my room and narrowly avoided a tantrum when I viewed my face in the bathroom mirror. Globs of black eyeliner and mascara smattered around my eyes, pro-football player style. My skin had puffed up below my left eye making it sit higher than the other. If I auditioned for the part of Quasimodo, I'd be a shoo-in.

I washed up, combed out my knotty strands, applied fresh makeup and changed into a T-shirt and leggings. I casually side-stepped into the living room, allowing Fo to view only my right profile.

I didn't have to worry. He was busy rummaging through my refrigerator, shades off, hoodie intact.

"Why'd you run off after ringing my doorbell the first time?" I asked.

"I thought I heard someone coming."

"That was me, answering the door. Do you always get up so early?"

"Who's getting up? I ain't been to sleep yet. You got anything with caffeine?"

I handed him a Green & Blacks, eighty-five percent organic dark chocolate bar. He took it and bit into it, wrapper and all.

"Ty said you always up early." He spit up paper.

"I got up early as a favor to him. And because I have a regular job."

He blinked and stared at me blankly.

"I work in an office during the day."

"Sucks for you." He sank onto the futon. "My problem, it's…embarrassing. Ty said you're good with that kinda crap."

"I'm a lawyer, Fo. That's what I'm good at," I said in an effort to convince myself.

"I don't need no suit. I need a Sherlock. A badass Sherlock. One who won't talk to no one who don't need to know nothing."

"I'm no badass, but I'm good at keeping quiet."

"Two days ago. There was an abduction."

I'd become an expert on petnappings, thanks to Georgie. "Which one of your animals was kidnapped?" I stifled a yawn.

"It weren't no animal. It was me."

Chapter 42
Investigation of Fo's Abduction

I changed into a gray lace pencil skirt, cobalt blue top and matching wedges, and tagged after Fo's black Rolls to Serra Road in Malibu. It was all freeways, billboards, and mid-rise buildings until we hit the Coast Highway. The road yawned and stretched along the drowsy ocean, and a saffron sunrise lit up a glorious sky. If there was a piano handy, I would have banged out a few notes in appreciation.

We stopped in front of an oversize wooden gate and idled in front of Fo's walled-in compound. The gate slid open to reveal a long, winding driveway. Gravel crunched and crackled beneath my tires and I wound my way up, flanked by compact lavender bushes with pinecone shaped blooms. Behind another set of identical gates reigned Fo's pad, a boxy, concrete structure, half-hidden behind a row of tall, well-tended sycamores standing in salute.

I parked and got out. Round, concrete stepping stones ran alongside the home. They led us through the morning mist to acres of freshly mowed lawn that rivaled that of the White House. The moist grassy scent tinted the cool air. I fought the urge to roll around on the immaculate greenery.

"See what I'm talking about?" Fo said.

"It's magnificent. Did you grow this from seed or

sod…" I stopped. A hideous circle, measuring about thirty feet in diameter, was burnt into a portion of the perfect lawn. "Who did this to you?"

"Aliens."

"What? WHAT?"

"Two nights ago, I sat over there." Fo pointed out a row of black cushioned, chaise lounges. "I fell asleep and woke up on my back on this hard-ass table, blinded by freaky lights. I was poked with a metal stick, right here." His middle finger landed on his chest. "Someone was talking. In a language I didn't get. Found this circle the next morning."

"No way," I blurted out before I could stop myself. "I mean, are you sure you weren't dreaming?"

"Did I dream this?" He yanked down the neck of his hoodie and shirt to expose a shoulder with wall-to-wall tattoos.

"Is that a naked Bart Simpson popping out of a wedding cake?"

"Over here." Fo tapped the top of his shoulder with his fingers. "You're the first human being laying eyes on this. Besides me."

Concentric circles sat in the only space devoid of tattoos. A series of tiny, brown circles gave way to larger ones, in a simple, geometric design burned into his skin in a formation resembling a bulls-eye.

"That ain't no bulls-eye," Fo said.

I made a mental note to ask him later where he took elementary telepathy class. "What is it?"

"Crop circles, like in Stonewall."

"You mean Stonehenge. May I take a photo?"

"No." His head jutted out toward me.

This guy was perpetually crabby. "I want to

research the artwork," I said. "I won't show it to anyone."

"Hold up." He sauntered away.

Apparently, he thought a few feet's distance would prevent my hearing his conversation. It didn't. He called Ty to complain about my questions and ask if I could be trusted. Major hand gestures and sideways stares were sent in my direction.

Fo disconnected and sauntered back. "You good."

I took photos of his arm and the burned circle with my phone, and texted Ty:

Does Fo have drug or alcohol problems? Or is he insane?

Ty texted me back moments later: *Used to be a meth addict. Still drinks some. He's crazy, but give him a chance, Corrie. Like you did for me.*

"Last night. I saw red lights. Four of them. Hovering up there." Fo's pale eyes shot skyward. "They disappeared, one at a time. They were watching Me." He blew out the last word in one breath.

"Anyone else see this?"

"Wiggins!" His shriek was high-pitched and ear-splitting. It pierced through my chest and echoed in the nearby hills.

We both turned toward padded footsteps approaching from behind. The driver joined us. Stocky and short, with a pencil thin mustache, he looked old, fifty even. Shoe polish black hair lay perfectly parted on one side atop a high forehead. He focused on me, unblinking, brows raised as if bored or arrogant.

"Wiggins is a Brit," Fo offered as an introduction. "Used to be MI5."

Wiggins spoke in a low monotone. "British internal

counter-intelligence. Circa 1990."

"Why doesn't Wiggins investigate?" I asked Fo.

"Unidentified flying objects and extraterrestrials hardly fall in my realm of expertise," Wiggins said.

This was beyond my capacity as well. "Sorry, I can't help. Like I said, I've got another job."

"I'll pay you double what Ty paid," Fo said.

Interesting since Ty didn't pay me anything. I'd considered it a favor. Fo reached into a pocket and waved some bills.

"Whoa." I gasped at all the Benjamins.

"I can't go to the po-po. They'll think I'm all cow-shit crazy. Word'll leak, and the paparazzi'll be all over Me." Again, he spat out the last word in one breath. "I need help." Fo regarded me with one eye shut and head cocked.

I could smell the Benjamins from where I stood, a faint mix of tobacco, cheap cologne, and shoe-worn city sidewalks. They'd pay my rent and then some. "Are your grounds secure?" I asked.

Fo pitched his chin toward Wiggins, who confirmed, "Like the Masada in Israel. The Alamut in Iran."

"I'll take that as a yes." I handed Fo my card. "Send me names of everyone who worked here the night of the abduction. Or had access. Including security and household help."

"Whaddaya mean, send?"

"E-mail."

"You going somewhere?"

"My day job." I noted his skeptical look. "I solved Ty's case the same way. I work by day and investigate during my off hours."

Fo stuck out his lower lip. "I'm not down with that."

"Okay, find someone else." I turned to leave.

"Wait, I got issues."

"I noticed."

"Please."

A courteous plea is my undoing. "How long did your abduction last?"

"About an hour, earth time."

"How do you know?"

Fo pulled up one sleeve. An oversize, black Casio with a cracked face decorated his wrist. "See? It broke when the aliens took me. It stopped at nine-forty-five. I figure it's about an hour."

"Get me a list of names. I'll be in touch." I headed to my car, Wiggins at my heels. "You see or hear anything unusual?" I asked him. "Like the lights in the sky?"

"To refer to the Master as phobic is entirely appropriate."

"I don't understand."

"He imagines vividly. And regularly. He sees clowns and turtles and oddities, such as UFOs."

"No turtles or clowns around here?"

"Last week, he requested my presence to confirm the sighting of a turtle on a rock. I saw none. He has an unnatural fear of hard shell creatures. No crustaceans are permitted in the kitchen. Then, a few nights ago, he rang for me, about four a.m., to disperse a clown in his quarters. I made haste and discovered nothing. I spent the remainder of the night calming down Miss Flavia."

"Miss who?"

"His current, significant female."

"She didn't see the clown either?"

"She was satisfying her penchant for a peanut butter and Raisinets sandwich in the kitchen. I'm afraid Mr. Fivie is freaking out."

"Mr. who?"

"Fo was Forrest Orson Fivie before he was Fo O'Five."

"What's your full name?"

"Albert Lord Wiggins," he replied with a slight bow of the head. "Lord was my mother's maiden name."

I handed him my card and asked him to call should more strangeness arise.

"You mean like Fo seeing zombies or Johnny Cash?"

"Exactly."

Chapter 43
A Surprise in my Office

I parked the car at the Complex and checked my phone. A missed call from James triggered a recent memory. "Oh-oh."

An early morning dream flashed through my mind. In my brief state of slumber last night, I'd dreamed about James. An "R-rated" dream. A tingling sensation rustled up unwanted feelings in the middle of my chest, like a whirling dervish was trapped inside. My dislike for James had shifted to something else. In my dream it was passion. In real life, it was more like tolerance. Maybe I felt a passionate tolerance. And gratitude. I was grateful he'd stepped in to help. Without being asked. Grateful to have survived my first, nearly two weeks as business affairs associate and covert, temporary, amateur homicide, kidnapping, UFO abduction investigator, and future screenwriter. Just grateful.

I'd nearly made it to the top of the Complex stairs when Billy blocked my path.

"A body was found at the lake last night," he whispered, wide-eyed. "Where Druby was killed."

How did he know?

"Another murder at the lake. Do you believe it? Someone should open a funeral parlor across the street. Hello?"

"Sorry. Who told you about the body?"

"What body?" Veera joined us. We formed a circle of three, heads bowed toward the center.

"The local news," Billy said. "Two joggers saw it in the park. Real late last night. A homeless guy was killed. Drowned maybe."

"What's this homeless body gotta do with us?" Veera asked.

"He was found at the lake where Druby died," I said. "How did they spot it?" I asked Billy.

"From the sidewalk, with a flashlight. Early this morning."

So that was the story. Vague and shadowy. Like the identity of the killer.

"What should we do?"

"We should contact the police," Veera said. "Seek out similarities. Right?"

Two sets of dark eyes stared at me. I turned to Billy. "What about the security tape? From across the street. You have it yet?"

"Well…"

"Shoot. I could have had a batch of tapes if I'd done it myself," Veera said. "What's wrong with you?"

"You said you couldn't. That's why I got stuck…"

I slipped away. They were in the throes of arguing and didn't notice. I wasn't sure what to do next. I'd nearly made it to my office when a text came in from James. He wanted to know how I was. His consideration mystified me. I took a deep breath. My head pounded from too little sleep, and my temple throbbed like a hammer tapped against it from the inside. Which meant I appreciated the surprise in my office about as much as I'd appreciate building a full size igloo with bare hands in the dead of winter.

A visitor stood by my window, eyes fixed on the doorway. Eyes that brimmed with pleasure when I walked in. Or was it lust? Or heartburn? I fervently hoped for the latter.

Charm trickled off his tongue and fell in tiny star-shapes around my desk. I tightened my lips and slipped into my desk chair. Invisible hands slapped over my ears, closing them to his words. Unfortunately, I'd forgotten my blinders. He slowly removed his black leather jacket, eyes fastened to mine. He sported a thin, blue, Italian T-shirt with short, form-fitting sleeves, to better display his flex-happy biceps and rippling abs in an attempt to recapture my faltering attention. I averted my gaze, pulled open a desk drawer, and feverishly searched for a staple remover.

"Corinna," Clayton spoke softly. His voice strummed my heart strings. "I miss you. You're the best thing that ever happened to me. You're intelligent, beautiful, and astoundingly kind."

Okay. The "intelligent and beautiful" part slightly weakened my resolve. But with "astoundingly kind," I mentally sharpened my double-edge butterfly knife. I'd found a pair in one of Dad's storage boxes that morning. Clayton had forgotten that I'd kneed him in the groin in my attempt to keep him away when I found out he was married. Maybe he considered that "astoundingly kind?" Perhaps his other flings threatened to cut off choice body parts with a machete.

"Have you seen my letter opener?" I tossed my red leather tote to the side of my desk. It landed with a thud. "It's pearl handled and piranha tooth sharp. During the dry season, a single piranha can take down a grazing cow, unwary fisherman, or serial philanderer."

A few months ago, I would have run off with Clayton to Timbuktu. Or at least as far as Santa Barbara. Now I merely wondered what my eavesdroppers thought of the excess sugar water pouring into my office. It really wasn't sugar water, but Sweet N Eat or some other phony substitute.

Clayton moved in and brushed the top of my arm with the back of his fingers. I squirmed and yanked open a desk drawer. I pulled out a file, leaned forward, and slapped the fully loaded folder on top of my desk in order to obliterate a weak bodied fly and maybe scare Clayton into making his exit. I missed on both accounts. He continued stroking my arm. I considered smacking him on the side of the head with the folder.

"I can't be alone in missing what we had," Clayton whispered, I think, in English.

"You are alone and we had nothing, Clay."

He shot up. "Don't call me that. You don't know how I've suffered. Being called Clay Pott most of my life. 'He's oh so incredibly attractive, but empty inside.' I'm as deep as they get and have a lot to offer."

"So make your offerings to your wife."

He regarded me somberly. "I was loyal to Bonnie, until I met you."

"Why are you here?" I was eager to kick him out. In fact, one foot flung out in anticipation, banging on the inside of my desk. "Get out."

In a few moments, his entire demeanor changed. He went from Don Juan to Don Corleone. I wouldn't be surprised if a horse's head popped up in my bed tonight.

"Why are you so bitchy?" he asked. "I feel so used.

You used me to get this job."

"Really?"

"You know how influential I am. I know the right people. What did you do? Drop my name during the interview?"

I grabbed a file and turned my back to him. In two strides, he was beside me.

"Can't you see I want us to get along?" he said. "To see each other now and then, alone, preferably in a romantic setting with some fine wine and tapas, without all hell breaking loose? What's wrong with that? You used to like my company. I'm in pain. Don't you care? You have no feelings."

I turned to Clayton. "We're done."

"Oh no, we're not."

"Oh yes, you are, if I got anything to say about it." Veera had joined us.

"Who are you?" Clayton's eyes rolled over her.

"I'm the one who's gonna take you down. I'm gonna take you down to Chinatown, if you don't get out." Her neck bent from side to side and she cracked her knuckles. "Now instead of later is a good idea."

He glanced from Veera to me. "I'm going to report you. Both of you. You'd better start looking for another job. I warned you, Corrie. I'm pretty powerful. You'll see." He stomped out.

Veera stared after him. "Does he mean business powerful? Or like he's good at lifting weights and shit? 'Cause he does have some fine muscles."

"He does. But I'm not worried. I have seniority. Sort of."

"So what do we do, Boss?"

"Get a copy of that videotape."

"That's what I came in to tell you. I'm all over it." She raced out.

Alone at last. I texted James, told him I was fine, and shifted my attention to the memos sitting on my desk. A narrow red light flashed on my phone, warning that calls needed to be returned. I breathed deeply and checked my e-mail.

"Oh no," I said and read this:

Dear Artie, Bryce, and Rob:

As Vice President, Business Affairs, I strongly advise we forgo making any kind of deal with Ronnie Earl. Entering into a contract with him would be disastrous. I communicated with Ronnie, but he was self-serving and demanding. Frankly, I am shocked Corinna Locke considered such a deal. However, inasmuch as she is still relatively new here, she will not be held accountable. I favor terminating this relationship.

Very truly yours, Marshall Cooperman

cc: Marvin Mason, CEO, Ameripictures

I realized I'd held my breath while reading. My ears perked and sharpened, straining to hear a stampede of executives advancing in my direction. He did mean terminating the relationship with Ronnie Earl, right? I still had a job, right? How could Marshall blame me for this deal? The upside? Clayton wasn't copied on the e-mail. While I tried to focus on the positive (my hair looked decent) and avoid a panic attack, Lesley poked in her head. She looked her usual slightly distressed self.

Before she spoke, I said, "Marshall?"

She nodded.

"I really should work out of his office," I said. "It

would be much more efficient."

"I could set up a little fold-out desk and plastic chair in the corner. Facing the windows so you don't have to look at the bas—"

"Basically, I'm in trouble again." I followed Lesley out the door.

Just when I felt certain nothing could be worse, I entered Marshall's office and discovered it could. Facing a firing squad would have been preferable. Marshall and Clayton sat laughing like old bowling buddies. I was surprised they weren't wearing matching jerseys. Marshall hissed his giggles and Clayton threw back his head, emitting belly laughs. I heaved aside a tidal wave of insecurity.

"What's the joke?" I hoped my fierce frown would extinguish their mirth. "Or did you guys just finish a tickling marathon?"

Marshall's hisses dissolved. He motioned for me to sit while Clayton oozed warmth. He even stood as I entered and held out a chair for me. Our previous encounter had entered the annals of history. I sat down.

"I'm amazed," Marshall said.

"I didn't—" I started.

He held up his hand.

"There's backstory you don't know about," Clayton said.

"Excuse me?" I wanted to say, "didn't you just get this job?"

"Marshall had a fling with Ronnie's ex-wife. Ronnie harbors a grudge," Clayton said.

I relaxed a little. It wasn't about me.

"It was a very serious fling," Marshall added.

"Ronnie and I had a long talk this morning,"

Clayton said. "We came to an understanding."

So Ronnie was his bud?

"Listen," Marshall said. "Ron's a powerful guy in this industry, and we wanted him. We thought the deal was over, but Clayton saved the day."

Clayton sat up in the chair, his head slowly swelled to the size of the planet Neptune, that gas giant. "Bonnie and Ronnie are old pals," he said. "They were classmates at Harvard Westlake. She called him, and he came right over. We're good to go."

"The deal's moving forward?" My skin broke out in an infectious rash.

"There's always a way to skate around obstacles, you know what I mean?" Marshall said. "It's all fine now. Next time, follow-up, Corrie. Talk to me. Talk to Clayton. That way you'll be one of the first to know what's going on, and you won't have to grope blindly or be blindsided."

I'm not a groper, nor blind, but all I said was, "Yes, Marshall." I stood and moved toward the door. I heard Clayton say,

"Bye, Corrie."

I chose rudeness over bothering with a reply, however, not being rude by nature, I threw a small wave and left.

I returned to my office only to find another surprise waiting.

Chapter 44
Michael's on the Job

Michael leaned against the edge of my desk. He shot up when I entered my office. "I had to see you.

I closed the door and wrapped my arms around him. I squeezed tightly and backed off. Why was I the one always doing the hugging? I walked rigidly to my side of the desk. "How do you feel?"

He reached a hand behind him, removed a knife and flung it at the wall behind me. It landed squarely in the middle. "Like an action figure."

"Get a little target practice in while you were bedridden?" How would I explain the cleft in the wall? It was a small slit, but a sharp eye would notice.

He strolled over to the wall and pulled out the dagger. "Does wonders for a speedy recovery."

I stared down at a new addition on my desk. The metal vase of flowers from Mandy had been replaced by a tall glass cylinder holding a batch of yellow and pink roses. "Michael, they're gorgeous. Thank you."

Michael's brows met in the middle. "They're not from me."

"What?" A small white envelope stuck out from between the stems. I opened it. "It's from Bryce. 'As the sun makes ice melt, your understanding gives me peace of mind.'"

Michael folded his arms across his chest. "What a

bunch of cr—"

"Crazy sweet, right? I shouldn't have any doubts about him."

"Doubt is a necessary part of life, Corrie." Michael stood tall, hands on hips. "Never leave home without it."

"What?"

"You should be zeroing in on a suspect and it might be him."

"It's not Bryce. He has no motive."

"Maybe you just don't know what it is."

"And you do?"

"I'll come up with something. But first, let's eat."

"I've got a ton..." I stopped myself and remembered the bug beneath my desk. "Of contracts to finish, but I can spare an hour."

"Walk me to my car?"

Work was clearly out of the question.

We swept out of the upstairs lobby and breezed past Bryce and Clayton. Their conversation stalled and gave way to open stares at Michael and me. Michael's gaze narrowed and he channeled a lethal glare. I grabbed his arm and led him away.

"This whole place is infested with murder suspects," he said when we stepped outside.

"And philanderers."

We stopped by his BMW. "We need to talk," he said.

Had James briefed Michael about Tom John? "About last night?"

"About Fo."

****

Fo threw an epic tantrum after my departure and

phoned Ty to whine that I wasn't up to the task. Ty calmed him by promising my partner's services. After Ty called Michael and filled him in, Michael drove straight to Fo's pad.

He entered the compound and parked in the driveway next to a matte white Lamborghini Aventador. And spent the next twenty minutes mesmerized by the fine Italian automobile. Fo spotted him on the security cam, gently cleaning the car's exterior with virgin sheepskin chamois. Michael sprinkled bottled water to wet the cloth and added mild geranium scented dish soap to the wash bucket.

"Anything else would have been too harsh," he said.

"You never use bottled water on my car," I said.

"I will when you get a Lamborghini."

"Did you examine the imprint in the grass?"

"I did. Looks like the work of a blow torch. Poor Fo. He seemed exhausted from the alien capture."

"But he was only gone an hour or so."

"Aliens don't follow our method of keeping time, Corrie."

"Seriously?"

"If we want to help him, we have to believe. Believing doesn't necessarily mean it's true. You know, like in Santa or *Doctor Who*."

His argument actually carried an iota of sense. "Go on."

"Flavia, Fo's lady friend, or his 'Flavia of the month'." Michael grinned. "Explained that before the abduction, Fo knew swear words in eight different languages and was a terrific short order cook. Now the guy can't even hard-boil an egg, let alone swear in

Hungarian."

"Did you happen to see aliens too, Michael?"

"Keep an open mind. *Wiki* confirmed that Fo swears in many tongues."

"Did you talk to Wiggins?"

"The manservant had to finish up my car cleaning job. But I investigated alibis. Flavia was on a girls' night out, and Smiley, Fo's best bud, was asleep. The help had solid alibis."

"We'll have to question everyone more thoroughly."

"I've gone one step better. You'll be proud of me. I think." Michael ran a hand through his dark waves. "But possibly a little annoyed too. Try to focus on the reasons to be proud."

I contemplated screaming right then and there. The glass-shattering variety of scream, like Fay Wray's while ascending the Empire State Building in the grasp of everyone's favorite giant ape, King Kong.

"Before I visited Fo," Michael said. "I stopped by your place and borrowed one of your dad's listening devices from your arsenal."

"You don't have a key to my place."

"True. But remember when I said I know a little something about breaking and entering? I forgot the key to my last apartment so many times, I'm a break-in expert."

"You're right. I am annoyed."

"I planted a bug on Fo. I put my hand on his shoulder and presto! He's bugged."

I thought I had surprises for Michael, but he was jam-packed with them.

"I'll let you know what I find out. See you in an

hour," he said and shuffled away.

I returned to my desk and bustled through the rest of the morning. I jumped ship just before noon and found Michael pacing outside the entrance.

"I've got it," he said. "I have intel on the alien landing."

Chapter 45
Lunch Time Encounter

"Fo's gardener got mad over a hole in the lawn?" I asked Michael. We'd stepped out into the pale winter sunshine that lit up the outside world. Fluorescent lighting is so anti-rosy complexion. "Who cares about one hole in acres of grass?"

"You have to understand. Shaka mows once a week and there's not a rock, twig, or imperfection in that lawn, let alone an earwig or spider. Each blade is the same size and height. The 'devil's circle,' those are his words, had already set him off. So when he found 'a puncture wound'—those are his words too—about a quarter inch in diameter and four inches deep, surrounded by missing blades, he went ballistic."

"That's a cruise ship full of crazy. Who, in Fo's inner circle, would like to see him declared insane?"

"Can't say. Once Fo switched outfits, I couldn't hear anymore."

"Well, good work, Michael."

He followed me to the passenger side door of his car and opened it, ever the gentleman.

"We have a lot of catching up to do," I said.

"I know."

The moment he hit the driver's seat, I talked nonstop until he pulled into the parking lot of a local eatery. We planted ourselves in a red vinyl booth and I only paused long enough to order nachos and cheese. Meanwhile, the details of last night's meeting, car chase, and crime scene investigation poured out of my mouth like fresh cement, nonstop and thick on specifics. I brought Michael completely up-to-date.

"You know what this means?" he asked.

"Yes." I attacked the tortilla chips when they arrived. "It means next time, I'd better shoot out the tires of the car I'm chasing."

"It means we've got to solve this in the next two days."

"Why?"

"So you can return to a normal, or at least, semi-normal life at work, which you've yet to experience, and I can start my new job in peace."

"Aren't you going to miss the intrigue? The trips to the ER?"

"Yeah, but I could use a short break. A man can't live by intrigue alone."

We locked eyes for a prolonged moment and my face grew warm.

"The chip bits look very becoming on you," he said.

"What?"

He reached out and picked off a tortilla chip piece stranded in my hair. How embarrassing is that? I blinked and turned to stare at my reflection in the window. Bits peacefully intermingled with my hair. My gaze drifted past the chips to the parking lot.

"Michael," I whispered. "Look."

He followed my stare. "What's he doing here?"

The towering chauffeur loomed outside, hands shoved in his front pant pockets, brown derby shoes spread apart.

Michael slapped some money on the table and stood. “Come on.”

“Where are we going?”

“To have a little conversation. How’ll we close this case quickly if we don’t take action? Besides you’ve only ten minutes left for lunch.”

We hurried out to the big guy. A short, fat cigar stuck out of his mouth. He didn’t budge when we approached.

“Hey.” Michael cleared his throat. “I’m Michael Parris and this is Corrie Locke. You already know her, don’t you?”

“Hi.” I smiled and stuck out my hand. I received a bone crushing handshake. It was brief, but my aching hand could have used physical therapy. I massaged it to jumpstart the blood back into circulation.

The chauffeur’s ham-shaped chin dropped and he eyeballed me. Was he going to pull out a weapon? Or force us into his car? Which, at the moment, was Arthur’s Aston Martin. At least we’d be kidnapped in style.

“Are you meeting someone here?” Michael asked. “Or soaking up some rays…”

The chauffeur’s gaze bounced off Michael. “Getting food.”

I realized I’d yet to hear his voice, which sounded as deep as an oil well and gravelly, like a beetle that discovered its vocal chords, thanks to modern science.

“You’re here to pick up food?” Michael said. “Come on. Or is it to—”

I grabbed Michael’s arm so our backs faced the chauffeur. “Don’t be so abrupt. We need to—”

"He's not here to get food. Guaranteed."

"Here's your order, Sir." A server held out a large paper bag in front of the chauffeur.

He took it and handed the guy a bill. "Keep it."

"Thanks." The happy waiter skipped away.

I flicked an "I told you so" look at Michael and glanced up at the chauffeur. "I'm looking forward to moving into the new office building. Will you be in there too?"

He shook his head and grunted. "Upstairs."

"Where?"

"Marshall's office."

"What?" This was a news flash. "When?"

"Monday."

"And he's going to…?"

"LA."

"I see." When was Marshall planning on breaking it to me?

"Hey," Michael said to him. "I hear you're doing a fantastic job at the Complex, man."

The chauffeur snorted.

Oh no, I thought. In Michael's mind, he's throwing this guy off the scent because he's going to ask…

"What do you think about Druby's death?" Michael wasted no time.

Two deep grooves formed a V-shaped crevice between the chauffeur's feathery brows. "It was a shame."

"Yeah? Well, it wasn't a suicide," Michael prompted, clearly on a roll. "Where were you the night of—"

"With Artie."

"Doing what?"

"Talking."

Now that was suspicious. This guy talked about as much as a tree stump.

"What about?" Michael asked.

The chauffeur squeezed his lips together. Despite serving up a hefty dose of silence, Michael didn't let up on the grilling. A narrow ridge arose along the chauffeur's temple and began to pulsate wildly. I was afraid the vein would burst any moment.

I grabbed Michael's arm. "I look forward to seeing more of you at the Complex." I yanked Michael away to the car.

"What are you doing?" Michael said. "I was about to pop the question."

"What question?"

"You know, 'did you kill Druby?' Now we got nothing."

"Au contraire. We learned a lot. Marshall's moving out sooner than I expected, thanks very much for telling me. And the chauffeur doesn't believe Druby killed himself." I thought for a moment and added, "He had nothing to do with the murder."

"How do you know?"

"His reaction. He genuinely seemed to care about Druby."

"I didn't exactly witness an outpouring of love."

"No, but he softened up. Leave him to me."

Michael bit his bottom lip. We got into his car and motored toward my office. "What next?"

"I have no idea."

"Well, I do. You're going to find out the chauffeur's name and get it to James. He'll tell us if the guy has priors."

"Good call."

"When you get back, send me a list of Complex suspects."

"Right."

"But not from your computer."

"I wouldn't consider it."

"And never discuss anything remotely connected to Druby inside your office."

"Not remotely."

Michael turned into my street. "You're making fun of me."

"Not true. I'm grateful you and James stepped in to help, without being asked."

Michael grinned, faced forward, and slowed. "What's going on?"

The chauffeur dominated the middle of the Complex driveway.

Chapter 46
The Unintended Limo Ride

Michael parked his car, and we met-up with the chauffeur. He tipped his head sideways and tossed a curt nod toward the limo which was parked on the street, next to the driveway. We switched direction, heading toward the blackened Lincoln. But the chauffeur blocked our path with his Mack truck-like body.

"Make up your mind," Michael said.

"Not you. Her."

"That's not happening,"

"It's okay," I said and asked the chauffeur, "Am I going somewhere?"

He nodded once.

"Where?"

"For a ride."

"Why?"

"To talk."

I was intrigued. "How about if he follows in his car?" I placed my hand on Michael's arm. "You can't blame him for feeling anxious." Which is exactly how I was feeling at the moment. But my curiosity was stronger.

His head dipped downward and Michael backed off. The chauffeur strode toward the limo, and I hustled behind him. He opened the door leading to the back end and stuck out a large hand to indicate I should get moving. No smile. No small talk. He had all the charm of an army tanker.

Just before I slid inside, I realized I wouldn't be riding alone. I'd feared this very scenario.

The Cheshire cat sprawled along one end, smile fully stretched across the lower half of his face. Hard to swallow his surprising box office success. He didn't look genius. In fact, he was a dead ringer for a short-legged toad whose long, sticky tongue unrolled and flipped out to take in whatever he fancied. I hesitated.

Arthur raised a ginger brow. "Get in. We're going to drive around and chat."

If talking was all that transpired, I was fine. But I had my doubts.

I planted myself in a far corner of the oversize compartment and took in the smooth charcoal gray leather seats, the rosewood stained bar, and the fiber optic star-like lighting on the ceiling. I could get used to this. The limo eased away from the curb.

I craned my neck to check behind us. Michael followed.

"Boyfriend?" Arthur asked.

I nodded. Explaining about Michael had no place in whatever conversation we were going to have.

"Finally." Arthur's brows jumped up and down. "We can consummate our relationship."

"I beg your pardon?" I watched far too many old movies.

"Why do you think you were hired?"

"Because you needed another lawyer?"

"Guess again." Arthur opened a nearby cabinet. He grabbed a bag of gourmet popcorn with one hand and a large teakwood bowl with the other. He ripped open the bag and poured in the popcorn. "Want some?"

My fingers skimmed the edge of the bowl. I picked up a few morsels.

"Billy told me about you," Arthur said. "And why you needed to be hired. Your father—"

"Was a private investigator, I know." I finished his sentence. The mystery of how I beat the other candidates was revealed.

"And together you cracked impossible-to-solve cases."

"'Together.' That's the key word."

"You must have learned something from him."

"Is that why I was hired?"

"Not exactly. You're a decent lawyer, sweet on the eyes, and you were in Marshall's top twenty choices."

My ego shrank to the size of a split pea.

"Relax. So far you're doing great." He licked the tips of his fingers. "You arrived at the right time. Employee morale is down, thanks to Druby dying on us. The police aren't interested. And I don't want Mandy to know I've hired a detective."

"Investigator."

"This way no one will suspect you're my snoop."

"That's investigator. Which I'm not. I'm a lawyer."

Arthur launched more popcorn down his throat. "The ink was barely dry on our partnership contract when Druby was taken down, and I admit it was a one-sided deal. I got the lion's share and I shouldn't have signed it, but I did. I'm greedy, but I'm not ruthless. And a ruthless bastard killed Druby." Arthur closed his eyes and placed a hand against his forehead.

"You don't believe the suicide theory?" I asked.

He opened one eye. Then the other. “You like your job?”

“I do.”

“You know what I like? Fame and fortune. I love it. The downside?” He crammed a fistful of popcorn in his mouth. “I don’t know who my friends are anymore. I don’t know who I can trust.” He spit out popcorn bits.

I expected the grin to fade, but it didn’t. “That doesn’t upset you?”

“Why should it? I’m having the time of my life.” He put aside the bowl and reached into the depths of the cabinet. He extracted a pink cardboard bakery box and propped it on his lap. He pried it open and snapped up a small, lacey Florentine cookie. He tucked it in his mouth. “Have one,” he said, his mouth crammed with sweetness.

I plucked a cookie out of the box. It was delicious. “Why’d you ask if I liked my job?”

“You’ve been poking around Druby’s death. I know all about it. And I heard about the homeless guy. Last night, at the lake where Druby’s car went in.”

“Did you have lunch today?” I needed to know.

“Yeah, but Mandy was with me, so I had a spinach salad. Tadpole food. She’s always feeding me salads.” He shuddered and ended with a head shake. “A man’s gotta eat.” He continued ravaging the cookies.

I wondered if his voracious appetite ever quit.

“The homeless guy. He witnessed Druby’s murder.”

“How do you know?” I asked. “And how do you know it wasn’t suicide?”

“Same way you do.” He licked his fingers with gusto. “I’ve got connections. There’s talk around the

Complex that Druby was murdered. That it was an inside job. I won't have that. And I won't have anyone thinking I did it. We're going to put this behind us, with your help."

"I can't."

"Can't or won't?" He jammed another cookie in his mouth.

"I can't do it without my father."

"You helped him crack four cases in a row. Cases that baffled the police." He continued feasting and eyeing me while he chewed, complete with irritating, lip smacking sound effects. "You'll do it, and you'll get a bonus for it."

"I'm not my father."

"That's where Francois comes in."

"Who?"

Arthur turned around and rapped his knuckles on the privacy glass. "Hey, Frannie. You're going to be assisting our investigator. Meet Francois Dupree."

"Frannie" ignored us and turned south onto Coast Highway.

"I'm going to make this easy for you," Arthur said.

"How?"

"By giving you a clue. One that you and Frannie and your boy-wonder…" He jerked his thumb back at Michael who followed closely. "…can use to solve this mess."

"Why don't you tell the detectives about it yourself?"

"Because." He tossed the mangled pink box off to one side. He rummaged through the cabinet for more grub. "You're going to keep me out of this. Whatever we talk about, it's attorney-client privilege. I've gotta come out clean. Understand? To maintain my credibility."

More like incredibility, I thought. He pulled out a box of cereal, tore open the top, grabbed a large ceramic bowl, and poured in sugar-coated, frosted flakes. Some hit the target, while the rest scattered on the plush gray carpet. He offered the bowl to me first. I politely declined. He wasted no time plunging in his paw.

"What if I don't solve this case?" I asked.

"I hear the Harvard boy is still looking for a job."

Icicles formed on the limo's ceiling.

"About the homeless guy and what he saw that night." Arthur pulled out a photo from a manila envelope and handed it to me. "How's that for an excellent clue?"

"Too obvious."

"Great discoveries usually are."

Chapter 47
Arthur's Plan

Frannie pulled into a parking lot across from the ocean side of Coast Highway. He parked in the red zone in front of a gelato shop in a newer, crowded-to-the-brim, mini shopping center. Arthur must have depleted his food supply. He stretched an arm over his head, reached back, and rapped his knuckles on the privacy glass. It slid open before he finished knocking.

"Di Asporto," he said to Fran and translated for me, "It means to go. Wanna gelato?"

"No, thanks." I had one heel dangling out the door.

"One chocolate gelato topped with raspberry sorbetto for me. Get your usual," he told Fran and slid shut the privacy glass. "He likes the blood orange sorbet. Disgusting, right?" He opened the glass and said, "Get one like mine, for Corrie's boyfriend."

"He's—" I said.

"Going to love it. Maybe he'll let you try some." Arthur did the jumping brow thing again. He leaned toward me. I simultaneously leaned back. We heard a rapping on a side window.

Michael's face was inches from the glass. He peered through the dark tint. "How's it going in there? Hello?"

A window rolled down an inch and Arthur said, "She'll be out momentarily." It rolled back up.

Michael's car was parked a few spaces away. Escape was in my cards. But I had two questions for Arthur. "This photo's all you've got?"

"It's more than you have. I'll also give you a list of suspects."

"And this list is based on…?"

"My gut."

Since his gut was usually full, I couldn't imagine any room remaining for hunches. But I nodded and asked a burning question, "Where did the Complex get its name?"

"I thought it up. There's something James Bondish about it. A place filled with intrigue, deception, secrets, and beautiful people. And now we've got our very own villain. Fits perfectly, doesn't it?"

Too perfectly, I thought.

Chapter 48
A List of Suspects

"Was that Arthur in there?" Michael asked.

I sat in the passenger seat of his car and nodded. I pointed to his open window. It framed a large, hairy hand holding a waffle cone jammed with dark chocolate gelato. A red plastic spoon sat on one side.

"Hey, nice to see you again, bro." Michael took the gelato.

The chauffeur retreated. Seconds later, Arthur and the limo streaked down Highway 1.

"What's this?" Michael stared at the cone.

"Compliments of Arthur. For making you follow us around, I suppose."

"Thoughtful. I am getting hungry."

I showed him the photo. Michael studied the picture between spoonfuls and licks.

"Crikey," he said. "I've always wanted to say that. This is incredible. Wait, who's this? The pope in the red robe and saturno? Is this a costume party? Harsh looking for a holy man, isn't he?"

"That's Rob Root, vice president of marketing. Arthur thinks he killed Druby. Because of that costume. Rob wears the pope get-up every Halloween."

Michael scrutinized the picture. "This guy has 'killer' written all over him."

"Arthur believes the photo makes it an open and

shut case. I disagreed, but I'm wondering, Rob is pure emotion, of the mostly volatile kind."

"Any motive ideas?" Michael dug into the dessert.

My mouth began to water. "Maybe Rob wanted to partner with Arthur, and Druby got in the way."

"How do you know Arthur didn't plan the whole thing? God, this is good."

"I don't. Aren't you going to offer me any?"

"Sorry." Michael turned the gelato over and maneuvered out of the lot. "What else? Jealous lover?"

I took a taste. "This is delicious." Arthur had impeccable taste buds. "Maybe it was some private masquerade party gone wrong. Except Druby wasn't in costume when his body was found."

"I'll ask James whether Rob's got priors." Michael turned to me and I handed him the gelato. "We're all caught up now," he said.

"Yes, but the minute we part, there'll be new developments. Like a BBC miniseries. There's something else. Arthur said I was hired over more qualified applicants because he expected me to solve the Druby case."

"He's joking."

I was silent.

"What happens if you don't?"

"Hasta la vista, baby."

"He'll fire you?"

"Oh, Michael."

"You won't be fired. You can't be. We'll crack this. I'm pretty sure. Well, mostly sure."

"We'd better." I grabbed a hank of my hair and scrunched it between my fingers. I had rent to pay, car payments, shoe shopping, food—I sure liked eating.

Living near the beach was nice too. I couldn't part with the scent of seaweed. I gulped.

Ten minutes later, Michael dropped me off at the office and I hauled myself inside the Complex.

Lesley blocked my path at the top of the stairs. "Marshall's been asking for you. He's mad. He wanted to know where you were. You'd better go in. And put up your hackles."

How would I explain my extra-long lunch?

Marshall leaned toward his widescreen TV when I entered, chin resting on a fist, eyes glued to a detergent commercial.

"You wanted to see me?" I said.

He stared at the screen for another ten seconds and turned it off. He focused on me. "Where were you?"

Before I could part my lips to reply, Francois stomped inside. He held out a green folder. "From Arthur," he said to me.

I took it. He threw Marshall a nod and left.

Marshall's maidenly brows shot up to his hairline. "What was that about?"

"When I returned from lunch, Arthur requested a meeting. I drove with him and Francois to get a gelato."

"I've had gelato with Art before." He bumped his fingertips together in a pyramid and stared at the folder in my hands. "What's that?"

"I'm not sure." I flipped it open and held it up, so Marshall only viewed the outside. Arthur had scribbled down names of suspects. "It's a list. Of everyone that's relocating to the other building." Time for a distraction. "You're on here. Hey, you're moving to LA. Starting Monday?"

Marshall coughed up a tepid smile. "I got

confirmation this morning. You'll join me soon." He thumbed through some papers. "Clayton's wining and dining Ronnie Earl at his home. The deal is firm."

"Excellent." Maybe Clayton's charm worked on the male gender as well. "Our efforts weren't wasted."

"Good to see you're getting situated here. It's a big deal for Arthur to hang out with an associate. I hope it was time well spent."

I didn't want to think about the implications of this last statement or say something I'd regret, so I said, "Absolutely. Back to work."

Just before I reached my office, I heard my cell phone ringing from the depths of my handbag. I dug in and unearthed the phone. It was Hilda.

"I so upset," Hilda said in a quivery voice.

"What happened?" Here it was, I thought. Druby's dark side.

"My boy, you know, everybody like him." Her voice cracked.

"Take your time." I headed toward the back staircase.

"I call Billy and he say to tell you."

"Hold on." I plowed down the stairs and outside. I hurried away from the building. "Yes?"

"It is a note," she whispered. "I find in Druby's closet."

My mind raced. Another suicide note? A love note? A musical note?

"It's from…" She sobbed. "Rob Root. Is terrible."

Hilda quieted down enough to read it to me. Druby had picked up Rob's dry cleaning and Rob found a stain on one of his freshly laundered shirts, which he blamed on Druby. "Rob say he 'hate' my son," she said. "What kind of person hates? He kill my boy. I know."

True. It didn't look good for Rob, what with the pope outfit and now the hate note. But was he a murderer? I promised to get to the bottom of Druby's death.

I'd barely disconnected when Michael called to say he was meeting James at the Medical Examiner's lab at four-thirty. He gave me directions and asked me to join them. I said I would. But to leave early without irking Marshall, I had to strategize.

"One more thing," Michael said. "A weird thing. After I dropped you off today, a woman stopped me at the driveway. She asked if I was your boyfriend."

"Must have been Caitlyn."

"She said her name was Paprika."

"What?"

"She said it was a good thing you had me because she'd hate to lose her fiancé."

"Bryce is not the loyal type."

"Neither is she. She asked for my phone number, so I gave it to her. I got hers too."

That did not sit well. "Why?"

"I thought it might come in handy."

"Michael, she's insane. Maybe a sociopath."

"I know, but sociopaths might be helpful."

"What if she's psycho as well? Will that be helpful?"

"She asked me to join her for drinks later."

"And you said?"

"Corrie would kill me."

Damn straight. "Good boy. See you soon." Was it revenge on Paprika's part stemming from twisted thoughts about Bryce and me? I shoved her aside and concentrated on tracking down Arthur. I couldn't locate him or Fran. Finally one of Arthur's cheap hussy assistants offered a direct hotline to reach him.

Once she got Arthur on the line, she handed me the phone and pinned her eyes to mine, crackling and snapping her chewing gum against perfect teeth that resembled a row of glossy pearls.

"Scram," I said.

"You're interrupting his training." She flipped her hair and wiggled away.

Arthur panted at his end. I'd caught him on his exercise bike. He told his trainer to get out and I heard a door slam.

"You find the killer?" he asked.

He was munching on something crispy. I guessed, by the sound of the crunch, that Arthur opened a bag of potato chips the moment the trainer left.

"Not yet. I need to leave early today to meet with forensics."

"Go, go, go!" Arthur was so ecstatic at that prospect, I thought he was going to ask to accompany me. But he evidently had some self-control. "Go and tell me all about it after."

"How do I explain my absence to Marshall?" I'd reached my fib quota. "He wasn't too happy about my extended lunch today."

"Yeah, but Frannie took care of you. Leave Marshall to me." Arthur crunched more loudly. "I'm going to tell him to drive to the LA lot right now."

"To do what? Decorate his new suite?"

"Brilliant. We make a great team." Arthur disconnected and I returned to my office.

Minutes later, Lesley popped in to say Marshall

had left, and she was doing the same. “You look stressed,” she said. “Maybe you should go home too. Or we could do something constructive, like booby trap the bastard’s office. You know, with invisible string so he trips all over the place and maybe bumps his head and gets a concussion. Or lapses into a coma. That would work. Or we could remove the screws out of his chair so he falls hard on his ass—”

“Ask me another time.” She sounded more destructive than constructive.

“I will.” She left.

I was ready to go when I realized I hadn’t seen Veera in a while. I scribbled a note on a Post-it and told her I was leaving. I stuck it to her chair and headed outside.

“Wait.” Billy’s voice rang out behind me the moment I hit the asphalt. He caught up and said, “Can I walk you to your car?”

“Sure.” He realized I didn’t talk indoors.

“Hilda tell you about the note?” he asked. “Rob didn’t mean anything. He hates everybody.”

“I meant to ask, what does Dom May do?”

“I don’t know.”

“You’re in security. You know about everyone who works here.”

“He doesn’t work here. So I don’t know.”

“Hold up.” Veera catapulted over from across the street. She clip-clopped fast and unsteady in platform pumps with skinny wooden heels. “I got news.” She put on the brakes. “I talked to Freddy.”

“Who?” I asked.

“Alfred Chan. The guy who does security across the street. Where I used to work.” She jerked her thumb over her shoulder toward the warehouse.

"What do they do again?"

Veera lowered her voice and turned her back to the building. "It's Allied C Corp. They're a bunch of Chinese running it. They make computers, women's hosiery, and reproductions of antique Ming vases."

"Really?" I was impressed with the variety.

"I got the goods." Veera opened her white jacket to show me a box stashed under one arm. "The videotape."

"Of the break-in?" Billy's eyes grew round. "Of my truck?"

"That's right. I got talent. Besides, Freddy owes me for attesting to his sound morals when he became a US citizen. I was his character witness."

"Did he have a green card?" I asked. "You don't need a witness with a green card."

"Yeah, but Freddy didn't know that."

"Am I in the tape?" Billy asked.

"No and you won't be," Veera said. "We'll be looking at your pickup."

"Oh yeah." He clasped his hands in front of his chest. "Let's see it."

I hesitated. Michael was waiting for me. "Now?"

"Uh-huh," Veera said. Her eyes cut to Billy. "Hop to it."

"Let's go to the security office," Billy said.

I followed them back inside through a side door that led to security. Billy popped the tape into a machine while I texted Michael and told him I'd be late.

"Press fast forward," Veera said, eyes glued to the screen. "Wait for it. Wait…there."

The camera was affixed to a corner of the second story and pointed downward, taking aim at all that entered and exited the premises. It ably taped a portion of the action across the street at the Complex as well. We viewed the side, front end of Billy's white truck, down to the lower section of the driver's door.

"This doesn't tell us much," I said. "Other than Billy parked in that spot."

"Hold on, hold on, that's what's up."

A figure appeared from the waist down. Black sweats and sneakers took quick, short strides to the driver's side. The intruder's black gloved hand opened the driver's door and closed it moments later, running back the way he came. He cradled the backpack in his hands.

"I am good." Veera screwed up her face and unleashed a fist pump.

"There's no way we can ID that person. It could be Marshall for all we know," I said.

"It's not Marshall." Billy shook his head. "You know what this means? Someone went into my car. Someone really did."

"Was your door unlocked?"

"I never lock it. I got nothing worth stealing."

"Did I say I was good?" Veera said.

"Concentrate," I told her. To Billy, I asked, "Any idea who it could be?"

Billy closed the door. "It's Mrs. Keith. Mandy."

"Why would you think that?"

"The clothing. That's what she mostly wears, sweatpants and sweatshirts."

"Guess what, Billy? If you drop by my house, you'll notice I'm fond of sweats too."

"Besides, she doesn't like me."

"Not good enough. That would make Rob the killer since he hated Druby. Plus, I don't like Rob, but you won't catch me going into his car any time soon. "

"You just scratch up the outside," Billy said.

"What?"

"That's what he said."

I remembered the file with Arthur's list that Fran handed me today. I'd forgotten the names. "May I take this tape with me?"

"Why?"

"I know someone in the DA's office. He can zoom in. I might see something important. It's good to have friends in high places."

"It's good to have friends in low places too," said Veera. "It's good to have friends, period."

I took the tape and opened the door. "Gotta go. I forgot something."

I climbed the backstairs two at a time and stopped in front of my door. It was shut. I'd left it open. I turned the handle. It didn't budge. It was locked nightly, so this wasn't unusual, but it was too early. My ears perked. I heard someone's high-pitched humming inside. I whipped out my key, shoved it in the lock, opened it, and stepped through the doorway.

"Oh, hello," Winona said in a shrill voice. She sat in my chair. Behind my desk.

"Explain," I said.

"I was passing by and ducked in for some privacy. All I've got is that flimsy cubicle downstairs, and it is so noisy. I didn't think you'd mind."

"Oh, but I do mind. This is not a community office."

"I thought I saw a memo about doubling up." She stood, pushing the swivel chair away with the back of her knees. She took baby steps toward the door. "You can use my cubicle."

My eyes fell upon the green folder on my desk. The one Fran had given me earlier. It sat wide open. And empty. In two quick steps, I blocked Winona's path. "Where's the list?"

"List?" She blinked while her hands clutched her chest. She tried to make a dash for the door, but I grabbed her by a sleeve. My fingers dove into the cleavage of her pink cotton blouse and plucked out Arthur's list. My eyes cut to the piece of paper. The word "SUSPECTS" ran prominently across the top. Winona threw me a shocked look. "How did that—I mean I was…"

"Doing Marshall's bidding? You could have taken a photo of the list with your phone or memorized the names."

A hand shot to her open mouth. "I didn't think of that."

"Now the question is how to silence you."

"I promise—"

I put up a hand and called Veera on my cell phone. "Would you…"

Veera popped in before I finished speaking. "You rang?"

"I've got to run to a meeting and I need someone to convince Winona to keep quiet."

Veera shot Winona a death glare and snatched the paper out of my hand. "What's this?"

"A joke that I don't want anyone to take seriously." I snatched it back.

"Got it." Veera upped her glare a notch. She towered over the trembling Winona. "You shut your mouth, you hear? If you even whisper a word, I'm going to dislocate all of your limbs. Then I'm gonna pour Kool-Aid all over your sorry ass and plant it in an ant's nest. Not just any ant, but the Argentinian. Those tiny bastards are known for loving sweet things. Like your Kool-Aidey butt. They've got an evil bite."

I had to hand it to Veera. Her method of torture sure was original. I left a whimpering Winona to Veera. I had to find a way to stop Marshall from nosing into other people's lives. But first, I was late for my appointment.

Chapter 49
Late Afternoon With The Medical Examiner

The medical examiner's office sat in downtown Santa Ana, fourteen miles east of the Complex. That's not far, unless you're running late and all of Orange County traffic is squeezed onto the freeway, including a tour bus that's sightseeing in the fast lane. I inched forward. I considered parking my car and sprinting the distance, but the gridlock cleared in the nick of time.

"We're closing," a gruff security guard told me. He leaned back in his desk chair and chewed a round lump inside his left cheek. I wasn't sure if it was his cud, tobacco, or an oversize tongue. His name tag read, 'Gordo' and he sported a bushy unibrow that could house a family of quail.

"Hello Gordo. I'm here to meet Assistant DA Zachary in the DNA lab." When I use my firm voice, it's impossible to deny me anything.

"You could be here to see the President of these U-nited States. But we close in two minutes. You can't go in."

My voice grew firmer and combined with my unyielding mental prowess, I might as well have been Obi-Wan. "Tell the medical examiner and ADA Zachary that Corrie Locke is here. This is a matter of top level importance."

"I don't care what level—"

"Tell them."

We faced each other in a visual stand-off. Well, he was sitting, but looked menacing nonetheless. That's how Michael found me.

"Corrie?" Michael said. "What are you doing? Let's go."

"She's not going anywhere." Gordo rose, blocking out the remaining rays of sunlight from the dirt-streaked, office grade window behind him.

I glowered at him until a fire alarm went off, and so did Gordo.

"Quit screwing around and get over here." James stood behind us.

I stared at James and knew. He'd activated the alarm.

Michael and I hotfooted behind him down a stark white corridor.

"Tom John died of poisoning about eighteen hours before you ran over him," James said.

"Poison?" I froze in my tracks. My heart hit the cold, hard, mercilessly scrubbed floor and scattered a chill up my spine like a blast from an icy fountain. The gleaming white tiles glowed eerily from the fluorescent lights above. My father's last cup of coffee had been laced with ricin. "What kind of poison?"

Michael slowed and faced me while striding backward. "Sodium azide."

I swallowed. For a second, I thought that my father's assassin was at work, killing others using the same poison that killed Dad.

"Move, people," James said.

We resumed our advance.

"What were the results of the toxin found in your

drinking water?" I asked Michael. I jogged to keep up with him.

"Oh that," Michael said. "It was antifreeze. Ethylene glycol. Sounds like the name of a southern belle, doesn't it? Just enough to cause dizziness, blur my vision, and encourage me to lose the contents of my stomach."

"Thank God it wasn't worse."

James shot a gaze over his shoulder. "Whoever dumped the hair cuttings over the body did a first-rate job confusing the CSI team. There was a variety of hairspray and gel residue on the clippings. Barbershop or beauty parlor remains." He pushed open a heavy metal door with one hand and stepped inside.

Michael stopped and held it open for me. "What kind of person thinks to do that?"

"The kind with an eye for detail," I said.

We entered a brightly lit room that reeked of ammonia. Fluorescent lights possessed most of the ceiling. Five stainless steel tables on large wheels stood at regular intervals along one side. Round, gray rubber trash containers, lined with orange plastic bags, buffered the end of each table. Metal sinks, pans, and medical tools sat on a long shelf on the other end. In the center stood a matronly woman wearing a white smock, cherry red lipstick, and short hair.

"She did the autopsy on Tom John today," Michael whispered.

I nodded, grateful that Tom John was nowhere to be found. I moved forward and stuck out a hand. "I'm Corrie Locke."

"Dr. Tizzard." She offered a ghost of a handshake. "I see dead people." After a skittish pause, she burst out laughing.

Michael and I forced our lips into smiles. James scowled and slammed his hands into his pant pockets.

"Works every time," Dr. Tizzard said.

"I'm going to kill her," James muttered through clenched teeth.

"What did I miss?" I planted myself between her and James.

"We've only served appetizers so far. The main course will be herb roasted veal tenderloin with spring nettles and morel mushrooms." She giggled again.

"Cut it out," James said.

Her giggles fizzled. "Not a fan of comic relief, I see. Where were we?"

"Figuring out answers to questions that haven't been asked," Michael said.

James leaned against a wall, nostrils flaring. He crossed his arms over his chest and practiced deep breathing. I did the same whenever I was freaked. He adjusted his tie, jungle green eyes boring into mine. My heartbeat quickened, and I unlocked my gaze. I turned to the ME.

"We have to be sure to collect every possible piece of evidence," she was saying.

"The challenge is in not knowing what could be important later," Michael said to me.

"Were there signs of a struggle or another means of death?" I asked the ME. "Other than sodium azide?"

Dr. Tizzard turned to a clipboard on a shelf. "The amount of sodium azide in his stomach was enough to kill a grizzly bear." A chill tarried in the room, but Dr. Tizzard fanned herself with a thin file folder. "No signs of a struggle while he was alive. After expiration however, he was tossed around quite a bit, like a ping pong ball in a clothes dryer, probably thrown in the back of a car or trunk and flung out again. And again. Eventually ending up in the spot where ADA Zachary found him. The subject expired approximately eighteen hours prior to discovery."

"Any clues as to who was responsible?" I asked.

"Clues, you say? There is an astonishing amount of DNA evidence present on this body. It's complete chaos. The amount of contaminated evidence renders results inconclusive."

"Since this case is related to the Druby Valdez matter," James said and strutted around to face me. "We've requested the Valdez body be exhumed and an autopsy conducted."

"To see if sodium azide was involved with him as well?" I asked.

"To check for signs of foul play. We need to know whether to treat his death as a homicide."

He stood way too close. Licorice and lemon and some other delicious masculine scent crowded out the aseptic smell. It was intoxicating.

"Can sodium azide be found after so much time has passed?" Michael asked.

"It can be detected for years afterward," Dr. Tizzard said. "Decades, in fact."

James stepped back, toward the door. He transferred his attention to the ME. "What are you going to do about the DNA circus?"

"Well, once you leave, I'll review the evidence again to see if some piece appears with greater frequency."

"We'll get out of your way."

The three of us scrambled through the doorway, pushing and shoving our way out into the sterile corridor. We aimed ourselves toward the parking lot.

"Where did you get the angry pope photo?" James kept pace with me.

"I told you. From a co-worker." Michael opened the exit door.

We stepped outside.

"I wasn't talking to you."

"Chill, okay? I'll meet you at the car, Corrie, in case I slip and make a certain someone angry." Michael marched away.

"Now look what you did." I stopped and planted my hands on my hips.

He did the same and gazed down at me. "He's just mad that he wasn't with us last night. I told you not to tell him."

"And I told you I tell him everything." I took a deep breath. "About last night, did you get into trouble?"

"No. But if I'm found at another crime scene, uninvited, I'll be looking at possible suspension. Nice to know you care."

He smiled long enough for a frisky breeze to sweep around my hair. His smile whisked around my heart.

"It could have been worse," he said. "I could have been suspended, without a warning. I'm not worried. Delgado will send me an invite to anything related to this case."

"Why?" I banished the blush that threatened my cheeks.

"For letting her be the one to call it a homicide." James sauntered off.

"Where're you going?" I asked. A small packet of emptiness wormed its way into my heart.

"To meet Delgado. I showed her the photo with Root in pope gear and she got all excited. She's got a warrant to search his place."

"You're going to Rob's tonight?"

"I'm going now." James turned to me and stopped. "You okay?"

"Why wouldn't I be?"

"Finding a dead body under your tires and side-stepping a police interrogation aren't like flipping pancakes."

"You flip pancakes?" I doled out a grin.

He returned the favor. I shifted gears. I told James about Hilda's call.

"The dry cleaning stain may have pushed Root over the edge," James said.

He believed the pope photo wasn't enough for an arrest since Tom John was considered an unreliable witness who'd identified the pope rather than an impersonator. But because the DA's office was involved, and James argued that Rob was the only person close to Druby that owned the pope costume, a search warrant was possible. Rob's place would be ransacked for something more concrete, and he'd be taken to the station for questioning. "Be safe." James hurried off.

It was unsettling to be around a decent James. I dragged myself away and joined Michael in his car. He slouched down low in the driver's seat, rubbing his chin between his index finger and thumb.

"I remembered something," he said. "Tom John described the pope as tall. Whoever he saw that night stood above him in the dark, on a hill, about ten feet away. But Tom John was surprised, even at that distance, that the pope looked so big. Rob's a tall guy, right?"

"So are you. How does he know you weren't impersonating the pope?" I asked. "It's all part of Tom John's delusions. I mean, he's seen Big Foot. Maybe the Jolly Green Giant or oversize popes are also part of his repertoire. It's hard to take him seriously, Michael."

"Someone took him seriously. That's why he's dead."

"You're right. Wait a minute, I almost forgot." I dug inside my purse and pulled out the videotape. "I've got a surveillance tape, from across the street. It shows someone going into Billy's car. I meant to tell James so we could view it on high tech equipment today."

"We might still be able to. I'll check." Michael pulled out his phone from his pant pocket and wrote a text. "What's on the tape?"

"A camera caught the bottom half of someone, opening the car door, reaching in, grabbing the backpack, and running off. Which reminds me of something else." I dug in again and took out Arthur's list. "Take a look." I showed the paper to Michael. "Arthur's pinpointed three suspects: Rob, Alana, and Stefon. Rob's the obvious suspect. Alana is Bryce's assistant. She's a living, breathing, plastic surgery redo with an unnatural love of cross-body bags, but that doesn't make her a killer."

"And the last guy?"

"He's the accounting VP. I can't figure out why Stefon's on the list."

"Is Alana tall?" Michael asked.

"Amazonian. Stefon's a big dude too. Who'd you text?"

"Rita. She's at a security company in Irvine. I'm going to get us in to view the tape."

I told him about finding Winona in my office. Before Michael could react, his phone rang. He stepped out of the car to answer and his smile got all goofy. Annoyance buzzed around my head, like tiny gnats.

By the time Michael rejoined me, my hands were balled into fists.

"Who is she, Michael?"

"Who? Oh, Rita. Her dad owns Cal-Coast Security Systems in Irvine," Michael said. "Thought I'd call her about the surveillance tape. She's happy to help."

Did I expect to be the only female in Michael's life? He was attractive, eligible, kind, intelligent, sensitive, and yes, I did.

"Are you listening? You want to go home and I'll take a look?"

"Let's go." I marched toward my car.

When we got there, Michael knelt by the front tire on the passenger side. "We might be hanging out here a little longer."

"What do you mean?"

I joined him. A groan rolled out of my mouth. The bottom of the front tire sagged against the asphalt. I kicked it with my shoe. Peep toe wedges are not meant for kicking tires. My whole leg reverberated in pain, but I barely flinched.

"Are you all right?" Michael asked.

"Of course." If only I could faint at will.

"Your face is all red and sweaty, your right eye's twitchy, and your bottom lip is hanging at an odd angle.

If you want to scream, I'll plug my ears. Then I'll change your tire."

"I don't want to scream, and I don't have a spare." My voice sounded like it belonged to the Incredible Hulk. I took a deep breath. "You drive."

"Right," he said. We returned to his BMW.

"I've gotta make a call," I said. I phoned the main line at the Complex. No one picked up, so I tried Billy instead. He answered on the first ring. "I need to talk to Arthur."

"Why?" Billy asked.

"It's important, that's why."

"Is this about the surveillance tape?"

"No."

"The note?"

"No."

"Well, I don't know…"

"Now!"

"I have to see if he wants to talk to you."

"Fine. Call me back." I disconnected. "Why did he make that so difficult?"

"People take power trips at the most inopportune times."

We traveled in silence for a few minutes before Michael asked, "How did Arthur come up with the names on the list?"

"He doesn't like Rob. He probably doesn't like Alana, and the same goes for Stefon. It seems if you're not on Arthur's good side, you automatically become a murder suspect."

My cell phone rang. It was Arthur.

Chapter 50
Uncomfortable Encounters

I asked Arthur how he came up with the list of murder suspects.

"Rob's the obvious frontrunner, right?" Arthur said while once again chewing into the phone, if not chewing the phone itself. "The guy's an inferno and hates everyone. I'm surprised he hasn't killed anyone else. Alana's just plain freaky. I thought she'd make a super addition to the suspect list. And Stefon, he's obsessed with numbers. That's not normal."

"Isn't he an accountant?"

"I rest my case. Dealing with so much money on his salary makes him the prime suspect. But most importantly, he and Druby got into a fight the day Druby died."

"Do you know what they fought about?"

"Probably money. Or women. Or both. I heard Stefon tell Druby to stay away from her."

"From who?"

"Claire. Or maybe Winona. She gets around."

"What about the May twins? Do you think they were involved?"

"Not a chance."

I waited, but Arthur still chewed. I wondered if he chewed in his sleep.

"They were with me," he said. "So were Bryce and

Marshall. It was poker night. Solid alibis, all of us. No one left my place until after four in the morning. Bryce and Ben spent the night."

"What does Dom May do?"

"He does what needs to be done."

"Such as?"

"He arranges recreational activities for the staff. He's like a cruise director."

"Right." Totally vague. "We'll talk again soon." I disconnected.

"What happened?" Michael cut glances my way while he drove.

I shook my head. "I'm fighting the urge to roll my eyes."

"He was useless?"

"Pretty much, and I have a strong feeling the picture of Rob outfitted as the pope is going to lead nowhere too."

Ten minutes later, Michael pulled into the driveway of a white-washed, single-story, stucco coated warehouse on Mitchell, in an industrial section of Irvine. It sat among similar buildings, all with low maintenance plants and small strips of grass rolled out in front.

"Is your friend expecting only you?" I asked.

"I don't recall if I mentioned that my best friend, lawyer, amateur investigator, and Ninja warrior was tagging along."

"Convenient." How serious was he about this one?

"Convenient that I forgot or that you're all of those things?"

"That you know this person." I contemplated those old movies where the bashful lead character can't bring himself to tell the leading lady his true feelings. Should I say something to Michael? Like what? Can we be more than friends? Did I want to be? Or was I seeking stability in what turned out to be a hectic life?

I shadowed Michael to the building and grew grumpier with every step. He didn't mention me because I wasn't important in his scheme of things. Never mind that he spent most of his time with me. I trailed farther behind, dragging my leaden heels through the nearly deserted parking lot. I got no sympathy. I wouldn't be surprised if he forgot I even followed. Until he patiently held the door open for me.

"Where is everyone?" Michael asked.

The empty reception area smelled of trapped, stagnant paint. The miasma assaulted my nostrils. I opened my mouth to complain, and maybe tell Michael how I felt, when a lovely woman in dark sunglasses slid in through a side door. She carried a white cane with a wide, red stripe at the bottom.

"Michael."

She slid over to him and I viewed her through Michael's eyes. She wore a revealing, V-neck T-shirt in papery cotton that stretched across her ample chest and required no imagination as to what lied beneath.

Michael gave her a big hug. I grimaced. He never hugged me.

"I brought a friend along, Rita." Michael broke free. "This is Corrie."

"Hi," I said curtly.

Her grin faded faster than an Oregon sun tan. "Corrie," she said without a trace of enthusiasm. "I should have known you'd be here. He's mentioned you." Perfectly placed chestnut ringlets framed Rita's gamine features. The little button nose really got on my nerves.

"My memory's not as keen as yours," I said. "I don't recall Michael mentioning you."

"That's because I usually call her Professor Rice," Michael said. "Margarita Rice. She was my humanities professor at Stanford."

"Of course. The one who gave you the glowing recommendations."

"I couldn't have gotten my new job without her."

"I write very effective letters of recommendation," Rita said. "For those who tickle my soft spots." She tickled Michael under the chin with her index finger.

We chuckled, although mine sounded more like I choked on spicy sunflower seeds. "Are you still teaching at Stanford?" I asked.

"I devote my life to community service and to those less fortunate. Too many of us are chasing rainbows when the real satisfaction lays in lending a helping hand." For emphasis, she glided her hand to Michael's chest and rested her head on his shoulder. "Michael, you know what I'm talking about, don't you?" Her hand slid down to his stomach.

"Sure." Michael slammed his hand on hers to stop its downward journey. "And we fit perfectly into your plan. Because we need help."

"I'm all yours. Come in." She snapped around with her cane and led us through a door behind her.

We wound our way down a narrow hallway to a room housing monitors and technical equipment with thick wires. Michael handed her the surveillance tape, which she slid between her hands. But not before I noticed Michael's hand lingering in hers. She slipped the tape into one of the machines.

"Watch the screen, up there." Rita pointed her cane toward a larger monitor sitting in the middle. The cane shot upward and Michael and I ducked.

"It'll have to be rewound to—" I started to say when she pushed rewind.

"Tell me when to stop," she said.

"Now," I blurted as soon as the rapidly reversing images came to Billy's truck.

She stopped and hit play. We went back and forth several times, and Michael and I discussed what we saw in great detail. Sneakers, pants, part of a sweatshirt and gloves, all in basic black.

"The sneakers could help you figure out the identity." Rita fluffed her hair.

"The shoe brand?" Michael asked.

"No," I said. "The size."

"The brand is common. But as usual, size matters." She gazed toward Michael.

He reached into a pocket and pulled out a small candy roll. "Lifesaver?"

I longed to break Rita's cane over my knee. But the sturdy aluminum exterior could cause major bruising to my leg. I unclenched my teeth and took a deep breath.

"I'll get some stills of the shoe in comparison to the tire," she said. "And we'll determine an approximate size. I can't give you an instant answer, but get me the make and model of the truck and the front tire, if you want to speed things up. I want the rim width and overall diameter."

"Can't you zoom in more? I need to confirm what the intruder removed," I said in a huff.

"It's on full." Rita's lips bunched up. "Can't get

better than that."

"I think you can."

"Can't."

"Can!"

"Can we confirm it's a man?" Michael asked.

"Man or woman, it's a confident individual," Rita said. "I can tell by the swagger and straight back. Could be female."

"How do you know?"

"There's a barely detectable wiggle."

Rita demonstrated which made me want to kick her in the butt. "Men don't walk like that. Not the men I know, anyway." She sidled up to Michael and grabbed his bicep with her talons. "She holds the backpack using her arms. The hands are too small."

"Wait. You can see?" I asked.

"Of course," she replied. "Oh. You mean these?" She removed the glasses. "I just had minor cosmetic surgery on my eyes. They're extra sensitive. You thought…I'm not blind." She appeared insulted. She clamped her mouth shut and turned her back to me.

"Wow. That's amazing, Rita. I never would have noticed the wiggle on my own. Or the hands. It's a woman for sure." Michael looked at me and nodded to urge me to follow suit.

"Or an effeminate guy." I thought of Pat and crossed my arms over my chest. Rita kept her head turned away. "It's the cane. It helped round out the image. But even so, I thought you were a very capable blind person."

"That's a terrible thing you did." She faced me. "Jumping to the conclusion that a person must be handicapped. It's not always about looks, you know.

The crippled are so misunderstood."

"I think disabled might be a better word here," Michael said.

I exchanged glances with him. His expression pled with me to make amends. I chose silence.

"Rita," said Michael. "Corrie's had a rough day and a flat tire sent her over the edge—"

"I didn't jump to a conclusion," I said. "I plummeted. I'm sorry. I see why you've always been Michael's favorite professor."

Apologies and compliments have the incredible power of repairing almost anything. Besides, it was a good way to have the last word.

She put out a hand and patted my arm.

"What's next?" Michael asked. "Hold on." He pulled out his vibrating phone from his pant pocket. "It's a text from James. He wants us to go to the Newport police station."

Rita divided a glance between us, ending up with Michael. "Get me the information I requested and I'll get you the shoe size."

"Done."

Michael leaned to plant a kiss on her cheek, but she turned her mouth toward his at the last second. Too bad blindness didn't prevent her from viewing my killer expression. I turned away before Michael could see my face. We said our thanks and goodbyes. And left.

As soon as we entered the car I said, "Michael."

"I know. Rita's got issues. But she's the only fast lead I had for that tape."

"So she needed a cane for her cosmetic surgery as well?"

"She said she twisted her ankle rock climbing. And

somehow she borrowed a cane from the Braille Institute. Look, she loves attention. She'll get it wherever she can. That's why I thought she'd be eager to help."

"Well, she's clearly got the hots for you."

"Me and every male in this galaxy."

"Sorry, Michael."

"You know what this means?"

"Yes. I'm sleep deprived and—"

"It means there are two people involved: a small woman and a very tall male or female."

"You're right. We should make our own list of short and tall suspects. And we need to—"

Before I could finish, my cell phone rang. It was an unknown number.

Chapter 51
Dad Pops In

I answered my cell phone, pushed the mute button, and told Michael, "It's Francois."

"Who?"

"The chauffeur." I unmuted and said, "How are you?"

"Check your e-mail," he said.

I ended the call, but before I could stir, Fran rang again. "Yes?"

"You hung up," he said.

"I did."

Francois went quiet. Had I offended him? I must be stuck in insult mode.

"Are you there?" I asked.

He grunted. I'd clearly offended him.

"I thought we were done."

"Bon-bons? You like?" He pronounced the treat name perfectly. Like a native Frenchman.

"Uh, yes, but the American kind. With vanilla ice cream in the center. I like ice cream sandwiches better."

He snorted.

Did I insult him again? Ice cream sandwiches are the best.

"Bye." He disconnected. This time there was no question.

"I'd better look at my e-mail." I slid open my smart

phone. Arthur had written: *The CEO is paying a visit next Tuesday. Wrap this up ASAP. I'm going to bring bon bons when we take the 'copter to LA.*

Bon bons and LA aside, it was one thing when Michael gave me a deadline, but Arthur? What if I didn't solve it by Tuesday? Worry liquefied into cold beads of sweat that trickled down my breastbone. That was a lot of sweating in one California winter day. "Can you speed up?"

"Why?"

"We're on a tight schedule."

Michael gunned his BMW. It roared like a cornered lion. The forward surge plastered my back against the seat until we arrived minutes later.

"Gee," I said after he parked. "I didn't know you had it in you."

"I can when I want."

I followed Michael into the lobby of the brightly-lit station, my eyes fixed on my phone. I texted Billy to ask about his car specs for Rita. I should have paid attention to where I was going, but I didn't and collided head-on with James.

"Watch it, pumpkin." James gave me a not so gentle push back. "The division captain's questioning Root. A waste of time and effort, in my humble opinion."

"Since when—" I started.

"Since you—"

"Since we are on a tight schedule, let's go," Michael said.

Before we could budge, a clean shaven fellow approached us. By clean shaven, I mean the only hair from the neck up was in his nostrils and dark brows.

"We haven't had a homicide in Newport for five years," he said. "Why're you bringing us one now?"

"You're so Mayberry here," I replied. "You've got to keep up with the outside world."

"We try." He turned to me. "A housewife beat up her nanny this morning."

"How bourgeois," I said.

James introduced us to Lieutenant Yamaguchi.

"Corrie Locke? Montague Locke's kid?" he said. "I remember when you solved that NBA player case. Good thing because I like Ty Calvin. Your dad was legend. Are you picking up where he left off?"

Michael answered for me, "We're helping out a friend."

I stared down an empty hallway and a rumbling sounded in my ears, crammed out moments later by a clanging, like that of a rapidly approaching cable car. The white walls stretched and swayed before me. My head began to pound. Then I spotted him. His silvery hair still hung longish and wavy. The corners of his mouth curled slightly upwards, and he donned his usual square, wire rimmed glasses and ivory colored leather jacket. In his mid-fifties, he was as fit as a twenty-five-year-old. He moved across the room in his typical manner, long steady strides, chin level with the ground, hands clasped behind him. He turned a corner and vanished.

"Wait," I said.

"What?" Michael asked. He shadowed me and I darted down the corridor, nearly crashing into a uniformed officer.

"Sorry," I said.

"What's going on?" Michael caught up.

I raced down another hallway and stopped an approaching officer. “Did you see a man in a white leather jacket?”

“No,” he said.

“Are you sure?”

“I’m a cop. I don’t miss much. I’ve been delivering memos for the past ten minutes. I haven’t run into anyone out of a uniform until now.”

“Okay, thanks.” I swallowed hard and caught Michael’s patient eye. “Sorry. I thought I saw…”

Michael placed an arm around my shoulders and led me back to the others. “Sometimes we think we see those we’ve lost because we miss them so much. When Aunt Cece died, I thought it was her every time I came across anyone wearing braids. It got to be so I couldn’t go out that summer.”

“But I—”

“You brush your feelings aside, and this is what happens.”

Michael led me back to James who pretended nothing was amiss. “This is a pristine station,” he was saying. “I don’t see many like it.”

“And you won’t. We’ve got a power-cleaning crew that Martha Stewart would kill for.” Yamaguchi turned to me. “Root’s with the captain. Let’s go.”

We followed him down a dim hallway to the interrogation area and entered a cramped space with a two-way mirror. We observed a small room. Rob sat behind a long wooden table, large hands balled into fists. A brutish, hairless fellow with a pasty, puffy face glared at Rob. I wondered if head shaving was mandatory in this department.

“If yelling is an offense,” Rob was saying. “I’m

guilty, okay? Look, you want a real crime? I'll hand you one on a silver platter."

"What are you talking about?" asked the captain.

"Defacing private property. It's shameful. It goes on every single day in the parking lot of my office, completely unnoticed by the NBPD. I've seen it with my own eyes. It's the new girl. She's a vandal. She dented my car and she spit on a Porsche that was driving by. Her DNA is all over that car. You should be questioning her."

"Yikes," I said.

"Do you know who he's talking about?" Yamaguchi asked.

"What the hell?" James marched out and into the interrogation room. "Mr. Root, I'm ADA Zachary. How well did you know Druby Valdez?"

Rob sat back in his chair and assessed James. "I answered that question already when my place was ransacked today. Druby was a good kid. Irritating as hell, but decent. Nice suit. Versace?"

"Did you kill him?"

"Of course not. I yelled at him, but I yell at everyone. That's who I am."

"You hated him. He messed up your dry cleaning," James said.

"He ruined my favorite Tom Ford shirt!"

"Mr. Root," the captain said. "You're free to go." He turned to James. "Come with me."

They left the room and joined us moments later. The captain peered stonily at Michael and me until we practically fossilized. The lieutenant explained that we came courtesy of the ADA.

"We just wasted forty-five minutes, thanks to you,"

the captain said.

"But the pope costume…" I said.

"Root donated it to Newport Thrift Shop last Christmas. We confirmed the donation. This was a bum lead in a bum case."

"Last night a man was found dead in Aliso Niguel Park," James reminded him. "Root was a potential connection to another recent death in that same park."

"The deaths are linked," Michael said. "We just don't know how yet."

"Until you do," the captain said with a glower, "stay out of this station." He exited, followed by Yamaguchi.

"That's his way of saying 'I did you a big favor. You owe me.' I'll pay him back," James said. "Let's get out of here."

Minutes later, we entered the parking lot and I got an incoming text message. "What?"

"What?" Michael asked.

I showed him the text: *Back off, bitch.*

"Give me that." James snatched my phone and carried it into the police station to trace the unknown number that texted me.

"It's from a burner." I said to his back. I watched him disappear into the station.

"A burner?" Michael asked. "As in a stove?"

"As in an untraceable, temporary phone, purchased from outside of the area."

"I get it. As in disposable, like in diapers or razors. You know what our problem is? We have no theories. Until now." Michael stared at me earnestly. "Bryce killed Druby. And Paprika is his partner-in-crime."

"Maybe." A vague nervousness hit me. Why did I

see Dad in the station tonight? Were confusion and worry manifesting as hallucinations?

"Hey." Michael stared at his phone. "This is good stuff. James forwarded a text. It came in on your cell. It's from Billy. His car and tire specs. I'll send it to Rita."

"Please ask James when I'll have my phone back."

"You're not enjoying this?"

"We're on a strict schedule, remember? You want this case wrapped up. And so does Arthur. I need to keep my job, and I've a call to make."

"Who to?"

"Bryce."

"Why?"

"It's time we went out on a date."

Chapter 52
No Time for Goodnights

"You are not going out with a homicidal maniac," Michael said.

"That's *potential* homicidal maniac. It's going to be a set-up. You'll be there with James and a detective or two…besides, we have to test your theory. It's the only one we've got. It's not a real date—"

"Oh. Now I get it. It'll be faux, but real, but not a really real date. Makes perfect sense. In fact, take a fake gun, we'll do a faux death and beat him to it. Sheer genius."

"Michael—"

"No, really. This is funny. Lots of laughs. Lots of funny. You're taking my theory too seriously. "

"What're you two arguing about?" James stuck his head in Michael's open window.

"She." Michael pointed my way. "Wants to set-up a date with Bryce. Insane, right?"

"It's time we move in," I said.

James squinted at me. "Not a bad idea."

"What?" Michael said.

"She can do it. She can get information out of him."

"Because of the ring, he's our only lead." I looked at James. "What about the text?"

"Came from a burner."

"I called that one," I said.

"A deaf-mute could have called that one," James said and walked away. "Meet Bryce. I'll back you up."

"I can't believe it," Michael said. "Why doesn't anybody listen to me?"

"We're in the middle of a terrible, horrible thing," I said. "We have to take urgent, drastic measures."

He sank down low in his seat and looked straight ahead. Meanwhile, I left a voice message in my most sincere tone for Bryce, inviting him to dinner after work tomorrow and thanking him for the flowers.

"You'll be chillin' with the villain," said Michael. "And what about me?"

"It's not about you. According to Arthur, Bryce was with him on the night of Druby's death. So there's a chance he's innocent."

"You sure you don't, you know, have a thing for him?"

"Remember that time you fell out of the second story window of that abandoned warehouse and landed in the dumpster?"

"Yeah, I trash landed. That was because I'd used my body as a weapon. That was me in combat mode, trying to save you from that slick playboy hustler, when he pushed me out."

"That hustler was Dad's client and he didn't push you."

"Yes, he did. Right into that filthy garbage."

"I pushed you.

"You what?"

"After you accused me of having a thing for the guy."

"Well, did you?"

"Can you drive me home, please? I'll take care of my flat tire tomorrow."

Michael motored away in silence, but when we pulled onto the freeway, he said, "We're a team. We always have been and always will be. I'll come with you on this date. I'll just hover, close by. In case something bad goes down."

"Nothing bad will go down," I said. "Besides, if he recognizes you, it won't work. And if a female is involved, like you said, the best candidate is Paprika. My meeting with Bryce may spring her to action. You can keep an eye out for her."

"But what if—"

I placed my hand on Michael's arm. "Let's leave 'what ifs' alone. We'll plan carefully and leave nothing to chance."

Michael followed me inside my place, despite my assuring him that I was fully armed. "That's why you need me," he said. "If you're going to start shooting, I'll help you reload and tend to any wounds."

I hoped I didn't have to use any weaponry or get wounded. Or worse.

Michael's cell phone interrupted my thoughts.

"Hi Rita," he answered and made a face at me. He quietly listened and said, "Sorry I can't, but I'll phone first thing and we'll meet up. Thanks a mil." He disconnected. "She'll have the shoe size by nine tomorrow."

"And she wants you there in the morning?"

Michael's cheeks turned crimson, his gaze hit the floor. "She wanted me tonight."

I kept my mouth sealed, but my lips and tongue fought for freedom.

"She's high maintenance," Michael said. "But she'll get us what we need."

Before I could respond, my cell phone rang. I dug it out of my handbag. I'd barely answered when I heard a frantic Fo. "Yo, I need you. The clown's back. What do I do?"

"Fo, listen to me. Go into your bathroom and lock yourself inside until I get there."

He mumbled and disconnected.

"Why did you send him to the bathroom?" Michael asked.

"He's losing control. I tried to give him back some."

"That's genius. Especially if he really does need to use the bathroom. Let's go."

"Michael, you're recovering. It's been a long day. You should go home and rest."

"And how do you plan to get there?" He handed me his key. "You drive. I'll nap."

I didn't have the energy to argue. Or a car.

****

Fo's front gates swung open the moment we pulled up. We wound our way through the next pair of gates, up to the main house, and spotted Wiggins at the top of the fully lit driveway. We parked and got out.

"Mr. Fivie has locked himself upstairs, in the master loo. He's armed with a poker," Wiggins said.

"I'll—" I started.

"I'll need a high intensity flashlight," Michael said to Wiggins, and turned to me. "You talk to Fo. I'll examine the hole the gardener found."

"Okay," I said and raced into the house. It was a cozy crib, except you needed a compass to find your way around. I hustled up the stairs, made a few wrong turns, stopped and kneeled down to admire the polished, hand-honed, dark wood floors, and finally located the master bath. A scowling Fo looked small beside a carved stone fireplace. He sat sprawled on a lime green beanbag. He wielded a brass fireplace poker.

"Where were you? They're trying to get me and you don't even care." Fo twirled the poker through the air. "What am I paying you for?"

"Hold on." I removed the poker from his hand. "I haven't taken your money yet, remember? What happened?"

"It was the clown with the neon orange afro. Creeps me out. He showed up, all evil-like, in my bedroom."

"When?"

"An hour ago. AND a few nights ago, when I was sleeping. If he touches me, I'm gonna die. I know it."

"Did you call for help?"

"I called Wiggins," Fo said. A body shiver traveled from his head to his toes. "He couldn't find him. I'm tortured, man. Tortured. Can't rhyme, can't make music no more..."

"Did the clown wear a mask or makeup?" I tried to keep him focused.

"How do I know? It was dark. It was scary shit."

Michael barged in. Fo dove for cover behind the bidet.

"I hope I'm not interrupting anything because if I am," Michael said. "I can leave. I don't want to get in anyone's way..."

"What is it?" I asked.

"Can we step outside?"

A bulky guy wearing an oversize white T-shirt and plaid boxers rushed in, along with a cigarette puffing woman, toting waist-length, caramel colored hair, short shorts and platform wedges.

"Angel." She ran to Fo.

"Smiley?" I asked the man.

He nodded. He resembled a basset hound with his droopy face, sad eyes, and downturned lips.

"Did you see the clown?" I asked.

He shook his head. "I saw nothing and no one. Nowhere."

"No kidding." I turned to Michael. "Let's go."

We left the Fo gang and padded to the yard. Michael's flashlight led us to a hole in the immaculate lawn.

"Someone stuck a plastic pole in the grass and tied this twenty foot string to it," Michael said. He held out a long piece of twine. "It was used as an oversize compass, a center for a circle. That's what made the even diameter. I'm certain a blowtorch created the circle."

"Where did you find the pole and twine?" I asked.

"In the woodshed," Wiggins replied from the darkness. "Along with these items." He joined us and held up balloons, automotive emergency flares, and a helium tank.

"Those would explain the objects in the sky," Michael said. "The red flares were attached to the helium balloons and probably released close-by. As the balloons rose and popped, the objects disappeared, right before Fo's eyes, making him think he saw UFOs. Is there a blowtorch handy?"

"Not that I'm aware," Wiggins said. "But I found

this in Smiley's closet." Wiggins held out an orange afro wig.

"Why didn't you show these to us earlier?" I asked.

"I discovered them only minutes ago when I conducted an intensive, in-house, search and seizure operation."

"Let's see the shed," Michael told Wiggins. "And tell us about Smiley."

"A dolt."

"Adult?" I asked.

"Dolt, as in dunce or dimwit, who fancies himself a close friend of Mr. Fivie, but covets the very skin Fo inhabits. Envy is a great pain of mind."

"Hey," Michael said. "That's beautiful, man. The analysis, I mean."

"Thank you," Wiggins replied in his expressionless monotone.

We followed him to a garden shed resembling a mini log cabin, complete with windows and electricity. I half expected to find Daniel Boone chopping wood nearby. Wiggins unlocked the door and we stepped inside a dark room. He tapped the light switch, and two lanterns hanging from the redwood ceiling illuminated the Spartan interior.

"Is there a metal table on the premises?" I asked.

"I've not seen any," he said.

"Well, that doesn't mean there isn't one, does it?" Michael stormed off.

"Excuse me." I ran out after him. "Michael."

He stopped and hung his head.

"Don't be mad at me," I said. He was another one of my weak spots. Besides my stomach and desserts.

He inhaled. "I'm not mad." He exhaled. "Okay.

I'm mad. You and Bryce, whatever that is, it's bothering me. It shouldn't, but it is. I'll get over it, probably not tomorrow, but maybe in two weeks or two months…"

"Please."

He pressed his lips together and shot me a look. "I'm going to check out Wiggins' alibi. A maid said he helped her polish the silver during the abduction."

"Security detail and cutlery cleaner? Odd. What about the wig in Smiley's room?"

"I'll take a closer look at his alibi," Michael said. "Uh, it, we, he—Fo really has a nice lawn, doesn't he?"

With those parting words, he left. I rejoined Wiggins in the shed.

"Look here," he said when he saw me. He opened a knotty pine wall cabinet which revealed a row of high beam flashlights, awaiting orders on a shelf. He kneeled and unlocked a lower cabinet. A blow torch sat inside. "Astonishing, isn't it?"

I wouldn't be surprised if he opened the garage and discovered a flying saucer. Wiggins marched across the wide wood plank flooring to peer behind a bookcase holding gardening manuals. He squatted and pulled out a metal rod, about two feet in length, from behind the bookcase.

"My word."

"Perfect for prodding a drugged-out, unruly, hip-hop artist," I said.

"I daresay Smiley is behind this. He can't account for his whereabouts during the incidents. He claims to have fallen asleep. I saw someone lurking near here this morning. It could have been him. And there's the matter of the wig."

"Good point," I said. "Mr. Wiggins, would you please lead the way back to Fo?"

****

We entered the master suite where Fo sat perched on the bed, head between his hands. Flavia reclined by his side, now puffing an e-cigarette, and Smiley leaned against the opposite wall, bouncing his fist against his chin.

"I'm screwed," Fo said, eyes squeezed shut. "I'm gonna be like one of those celebrity legends that die young. Like Curt Cobain or Carole Lombard."

"You've heard of Carole Lombard?" I asked.

"Who? Shit." He looked at me. "All the excess meth in my blood is affecting my brain."

"We'll help you," Smiley said. "We'll get you fresh blood."

"So not a good idea," Flavia said. "People get killer diseases from other people's blood. Hospitals are infected with bacteria and germs—"

"I don't CARE about germs," Fo said. "The aliens—"

"I can handle clowns and turtles, but the alien crap? No. I don't want to be showering one day and beamed up to Mars or Jupiter by guys that got no—"

"You don't have to worry," I said. This was getting out of hand.

"Yeah, she does." Fo shot up, his head jutted forward. "I was tough shit before I was captured and used as a guinea pig for the aliens. Who knows what they did to my privates. Nothing's working right anymore."

"That is so true." Flavia's head bobbed up and down.

Michael ran in and pulled me aside. “There’s a stainless steel work table in one of the kitchen pantries, just the right size for Fo to lie on for prodding. And it’s on wheels. The maid said Wiggins borrowed it the night of the abduction. “

“He did?” I said.

“WHAT?” Fo demanded.

“Hey bro,” Michael said. “Is there a laptop I could use?”

Before Fo could reply, Flavia stood, patted her hair, ran her eyes over Michael, and said, “Out the door, past the Warhol Beethoven painting, make a quick right into the computer room.”

“Yo. How’s a laptop gonna help Me?” Fo asked, the last word spat out in one breath.

“I’m researching recent UFO sightings near here,” Michael replied.

Fo rolled his head around, like he was going to blow, wound down and said, “Cool.”

Michael raced out. Silence monopolized the room.

“I’m sick of standing around,” Smiley said. “We gotta do something. Fo can’t take any more of this.”

“Neither can I,” Flavia said.

“Guys, believe me. This is not a big deal.” I had an idea of how to trap the perp. “It’s an amateur at work. A novice. Probably just a prankster. And not a very intelligent one. There’s a logical explanation.”

“Yeah? Explain the frickin’ clown in my bedroom,” Fo said. “How come he didn’t trip no security alarm or show up on security cams? How’s that logical?”

“Not to mention the circular marks seared onto Mr. Fivie’s upper arm,” Wiggins agreed. “Hardly an amateur. No ordinary person could create such perfection."

The room went silent again. The dependable ticking of a grandfather clock in the outside hallway counted the seconds.

"Fo," I said. "Did you tell anyone about the bull's-eye? On your shoulder?"

"Yeah. You."

All eyes turned toward Wiggins. Michael chose that moment to burst into the room.

"Did I miss anything?" he asked.

Chapter 53
Late Night Arrest

"Don't be ludicrous," Wiggins said. "I only noticed the circular marks on Mr. Fivie's arm when he changed shirts this morning. Don't you remember?"

Fo's eyes orbited around their sockets. "Maybe."

"Say what?" Michael took a step toward Wiggins. "Well then, how do you explain the concentric tattoo you seared onto suspected spy Anton Faraday in Cambridge? When you were in F Branch of MI5."

"What the 'F'?" said Smiley.

"After that, you were transferred to T Branch, where you tortured Irish terrorists by branding them with a series of concentric circles, using electro-cautery branding. You're a branding connoisseur."

"What do you think I am?" Fo puffed out his chest and moved closer to Wiggins. "A cow?"

"Sounds painful," said Flavia. She raised a shoulder to her ear.

"Not nearly as painful as one might imagine," Wiggins said. "Done properly, surface nerves are killed, making the amount of pain minute. It's very humane really. Defects in others may be vastly improved through proper use of pain. Imbeciles."

Wiggins emitted a banshee cry, spun around, and performed a round-house kick from a standstill, pushing back all surrounding him. I ducked in the nick of time.

Smiley wasn't so lucky. Wiggins dove for the door. Before I could give chase, Michael took matters into his own hands. He knocked Wiggins over the head with a black crystal vase. Wiggins went down and the vase remained intact.

"Wow," Michael said. "That's some crystal."

"It's a Lalique," Flavia said, twirling a lock of hair.

Chapter 54
A Late Night Kiss

Michael and I awaited the arrival of the police, gave statements, and crawled home. It had been a very long day.

Wiggins had refused to talk, mainly because of a raging headache, but admitted to tormenting Fo. "Blatant idiots have no business accumulating such an obscene amount of money," Wiggins said before lapsing into a comatose state.

A maid had informed Michael that Wiggins had gone missing for almost an hour during the silver polishing orgy. Enough time to wheel the metal table to the shed and drag a drugged-out Fo over to mimic an alien abduction. A branding iron was found in a locked metal box, under Wiggins' bed, along with a cage housing a snapping turtle. He'd dummied up the security cameras so that they showed past, peaceful tapings.

Michael had called James from the kitchen. James had called *Thames House*, London, MI5 headquarters, and managed to persuade someone in B branch, also known as human resources, to cough-up background intel on Wiggins, which James e-mailed to Michael. Michael printed out the report from Fo's computer and handed it over to the police.

"I'm cool. You're cool. It's all cool." Fo opened

his arms wide and gave Michael and me a hefty embrace. He stuffed an envelope into the pocket of my jacket. “You earned it, woman.”

It was $5000 in cash, which I split with Michael. We headed home.

“We should make a run for it,” Michael said when we got to my pad. “To Costa Rica or Miami.”

“I’d say yes, but it’s not quite enough for us to retire on. Unless you’re a trust fund child and holding out on me.”

Michael followed me up the stairs and inside my place. “Corrie?”

“Yes?”

“Don’t.”

“It’ll be fine. Are you going to be able to sleep tonight?”

“If I say no, will that change things?”

“If I say I’ll keep a finger on the trigger, will that help?”

“What if I drop in later, unannounced?”

“Yell loudly and hope I hear you.”

He tapped my forehead with his lips. Some kiss. He might as well have used a hammer. He skipped down the stairs. I called after him, “Michael.”

“Yes?” His voice floated up from the street.

This was my chance to come clean. One shout-out under the moon and the stars to tell him how I felt. Really felt about him. About us. About how we were meant to be together, not in the same way, but better…

“You looking for me?” Michael stared down at me from my doorstep, his face aglow with a smile.

“Uh, yes, as a matter of fact.”

“What a coincidence.”

"Isn't it?"

"Funny, after all that's happened, I don't feel at all tired. Probably all the excitement. Is that what you wanted to say?"

"I…lo…lost an earring. If you find it, let me know."

"Sure. But you've got a pearl in each ear."

"Oh." My hand shot up to my ear. "Silly me."

He skipped back down the stairs. "Sweet dreams."

I closed my door and leaned my head against it. Fail. Fail. FAIL! I could wield a gun, find a kidnapped cat, and hunt down a fake alien, but break open the lock on my own heart? Fail.

Minutes after I dragged myself to bed, I received a text from Bryce:

Tomorrow 6:30 pm. Bernards on Balboa Island. For dinner. It's about time.

How arrogant, I thought and drifted off to sleep.

Chapter 55
Morning Breaks

The sun had barely unfolded its rays when I bolted upright on my airbed. I was carless. I'd foolishly left it in the ME's parking lot yesterday. How was I going to get to work? Maybe my frenemy James would take me. It was too early to call him, so I pulled on my sweats, managed fifty sit-ups, wolfed down blueberry toaster waffles, flipped onto my futon, and glanced out my living room window. My car sat in the driveway.

I raced downstairs. The flat was fixed. The note beneath my windshield read:

Your carriage, my lady, arrived courtesy of my buddy, Enrico. He owns a tow truck company in Anaheim. I'm pretty well connected. Love, Michael

"Thank you," I said to Michael and to the Universe for watching my back.

****

I arrived at work to find Caitlyn hovering in the doorway to my office.

"Don't tell Marshall I want a ring like Paprika's," she whispered. "Because I don't. I want a two carat, Tiffany diamond, square cut, white freaking eighteen carat, gold ring. He can afford it. Cheap bastard." She stormed out.

What to do about the sapphire on Paprika's finger? The ring was nearly identical to the one at Depuis, if not the exact same.

My cell phone chimed. I pulled it out and read a text from James.

Root donated pope-gear to thrift shop late December. The costume was purchased a week later by Stefon Bellendorf. I'm running a check on him.

"No way," I whispered. I heard a light rap on the door.

Veera poked in her head. "Can we talk?" Her long hair was braided in tiny cornrows all over her scalp in a sideways sort of spiral. Tightly braided strips flopped around her shoulders.

I scribbled a note and passed it to her. It read: *There's a listening device under my desk.*

"For real?" she said. "Having been in high level security and all, for the Chinese mafia, I should have checked first thing. You know who's responsible?"

I shook my head.

"Hold up." She exited.

She returned moments later and dragged in Winona by the arm. Winona smiled and twisted her hands together in front of her. Her hair had also been braided, but in a half-hearted attempt. Two zig-zag parts were bordered by three loose French braids that ended in stray pieces sprouting out of orange rubber bands.

"She spent the night at my place so I could keep an eye on her," Veera said. "We ended up braiding each other's hair. I lost interest after about thirty seconds." She turned to Winona and held my note up to her eyes. "What do you know about this?"

"It's Arthur," she whispered. "He puts them under the desks of all new employees."

The girl was a fount of information. I moved closer

to her. "You know anything about Druby getting into an argument with Stefon?" I whispered. "On the day he died?"

"I could use some hot tea," Winona said.

"Let's go." Veera whisked her toward the door.

A woman in a beige skirt-suit blocked the threshold to my office. "Winona? Are you okay?" Mandy asked. "I called last night, but you didn't answer."

"We had a slumber party at my place," Veera said.

"How fun." Mandy smiled.

"I'm Veera Bankhead, Corrie's executive legal assistant." Veera pushed Winona toward the doorway. "Excuse us. We're about to go into a meeting."

"Talk later," Winona said and Veera led her away.

"We should have lunch," I told Mandy and followed Veera out.

I passed a sharply dressed Rob Root on the way. He gave me the evil eye. "Don't even bother watching your back. I want you to see me coming."

"Good to know."

We made it to the kitchen and huddled in a corner.

"On the day Druby died," Winona said. "He and Stefon got into a big fight." She pulled a chamomile tea bag out of a cabinet. "I heard him telling Druby not to trust her. That she was greedy."

"Was he talking about you?" Veera asked.

"No." Winona shook her head. "It had to be Claire. She was high strung and nutty. I'm not like that."

"The hell you're not."

"Do you know where Paprika's sapphire came from?" I asked.

She poured hot water from a dispenser into a black

mug. She dropped the teabag in. “There are two schools of thought. According to Bryce, she’s two-timing him. The ring is from the other guy. According to Paprika, it’s from Bryce, but he doesn’t want anyone to know. Personally, I think he gave it to her after she got him good and drunk. Absinthe works every time.” Winona placed a hand on my arm. “Are you hoping he’ll get you one too? You should try absinthe.”

“I am not hoping,” I said.

“Although,” Veera added. “She wouldn’t turn it down if he did. But here’s the thing, Corrie. Winona was spying. It has something to do with that paper she took from your office. Only Winnie won’t tell me who she’s working for. I told her she’s gonna get in trouble. Big-time.”

“And I told her I won’t,” Winona said.

“Who’s protecting you?” I asked.

She clamped her lips.

“If you drop a word about the list to Marshall or anyone who works here, you’ll be sorry.”

She turned pensive a moment, and then perked up. “Not a word.” She pretend zipped her lips with her fingers.

I had no reason to trust her, but I had no time to do anything about it. We turned her loose.

“Keep an eye on her,” I said to Veera.

“The thing is, last night I might have dozed off and she might have got hold of my cell phone and might have text messaged somebody about the list.”

“Like who?”

“Okay, look. I was tired, see? That firecracker cleared my phone when I caught on, so I don’t know.”

“If I lose my job, so will you.”

"Gosh dang it. Let me see if I can fix things." She exited.

If I solved this Druby matter, things would get normal, right? I really had no choice at this point. I was waist deep in quicksand with no rope in sight. I called accounting to speak to Stefon.

"He should be here any minute," his assistant said.

"Ask him to call me, please." I disconnected.

I'd barely hunkered down to work when Bryce poked his handsomeness in.

"Looking forward to tonight," he said.

I forced a small smile. "Me too."

He exited. Was I looking forward too? He looked good, was interesting, and was a hot-shot executive. But did he play a pivotal role in the Druby case? I picked up my cell phone to text Michael, but I didn't have to. He'd sent me one.

Rita is still working on shoe.

And working on Michael, no doubt. I called him, not caring that he was with Rita. He answered before the first ring finished.

"Thank you," he whispered.

"For what?"

"Giving me a break from Rita."

I pictured Michael: disheveled hair, shirt ripped open, pants unzipped, barefoot, lipstick spotting his cheek. My temperature skyrocketed. "She's, well…are you okay?"

"I think so."

"Thank you, Michael. For taking care of my car."

"You're very welcome."

"You're very thoughtful."

"Shucks, it was just the gentlemanly thing to do.

Got to go. Rita's chasing this guy with a bat. Swollen foot, shades, and all."

"Is she going to get to the shoe or not?"

"I'll see what I can do."

We disconnected and I contemplated my next move. I closed my eyes and pictured Stefon. Tall, dark, curly hair, eyes the color of a moonless night. If he was to audition for a part in a movie, he'd easily win the role of the villain. "Where are you?" I whispered.

I decided to nose around the accounting department. I shot out of my chair, but before I could make it out the door, I ran smack into Arthur.

"Where do you think you're going, young lady?" Arthur leaned against the doorframe of my office.

"To find Stefon. I need questions answered."

He stopped leaning and spoke quietly. "Good. We've got to finish this business."

"Have you seen him?"

"Downstairs. In the screening room."

I pushed past him toward the back stairs.

Lesley stopped me at the top. "Where you off to?"

"To find Stefon. In the theater."

"I'll come along. I'm looking for the bastard. There's a client on hold for him."

We skipped down the staircase to the Complex home theater. We'd almost made it to the entrance when Caitlyn wedged herself between us and the door.

"Where's Marshall?" she said.

Lesley's eyes fluttered rapidly as if she was communicating in Morse code. She pursed her lips and spoke through clenched teeth. "He's upstairs with Arthur."

Caitlyn folded her arms across her chest. "Molly

saw him down here, with Clayton and Bryce." She turned to me and announced, none too quietly, "Clayton's wife, the former Bonnie Pearlman who, as everyone knows, is uber rich and uber pregnant, ran off with Ronnie Earl, this very morning. Arthur is so worried. We've got to pull ourselves together."

Arthur didn't appear worried. And Clayton—I took a deep breath, the kind where the chest rises skyward and the exhale is audible within ten yards. My objective was not to beam over his misfortune, beyond say, ten seconds.

"Is Stefon with them?" I asked.

Caitlyn stared at me, as if to say, "Are you kidding me?" She'd unveiled this drippingly juicy news and all I cared about was Stefon? Clearly, I lacked proper social skills.

"You'd probably get more dates if you asked better questions," she said. "Don't you effing get it? What goes around comes around. Haven't you heard that Justin Timberlake song?"

"Spreading nasty rumors is unprofessional," Lesley said. "Especially since you're the head of HR. And isn't this a rumor free zone? I read the employee handbook."

"What rumors? This is real life, Les…"

While they battled, I pulled open the heavy door and slipped into the darkened theater. No Stefon, but Bryce, Marshall, and Clayton stood near the stage. Each of Clayton's hands supported a side of his fat head, which he swayed from side-to-side, probably contemplating a way to cash in on the pre-nup he'd signed when he married his toilet paper heiress.

"Need something, Corrie?" Bryce asked.

"Sorry to interrupt," I said.

Clayton raised his head and eyed me.

"I'll come back later."

"We should talk," Marshall addressed me. "There's been a bump—"

"This is a lot bigger than a bump!" Clayton said. "I may never recover."

Marshall gazed at him a beat and said, "Okay, maybe a small explosion—"

"My world has crashed."

"Regarding the Earl deal, call Winona and tell her as far as we're concerned, it's still on. Tell her to do what she can to stall leaking the news. And be sure to…"

"Stroke her," I said. "I know."

"Well, that too, but keep this under wraps."

I looked at him. It was probably going to be a *Variety* headline tomorrow. *Bonnie and Ronnie Run From Keith-Ameripictures Deal.* I nodded and left. Lesley and Caitlyn were still arguing outside the entry.

"I never spread that rumor," Caitlyn was saying. "Everyone knew Winona had a thing for Jamaican taxi drivers."

"Freakin' A," Lesley said. "I've got a VP from CBS on hold for Marshall." She jetted inside. Caitlyn lunged in after her.

I jogged upstairs and left a voicemail for Winona. I was about to slide into my chair when I spied a note on the seat. It was from James. It said, *Sodium Azide killed Druby. Be at ME's office at noon.*

"Veera," I called.

She came bounding in.

"Did anyone enter my office while I was gone?"

"Not a soul. Why?"

"No reason."

How in the world did James leave a note for me here?

Chapter 56
Late Morning Jab

I believe in hunches. The small, sudden gusts of thought or feeling that dictate actions and words with solemn fierceness, refusing to go unheard. I nursed a strong hunch to call Charlie, the one with the plastered-on hair and magnifying eyeglasses. He answered on the first ring.

"How hard would it be to get my hands on sodium azide?" I asked.

"It's in airbags."

I could almost hear the continuing expansion of his already broad smile.

"And fungicides."

"I mean in pure form."

He was quiet. I expected him to ask why, but he didn't. "Any large chemical supply store."

"And how do you know this?"

"It's in one of my screenplays. Arthur didn't do it."

"Glad to hear it." I disconnected and read a text from Michael:

Going to Tizzard's office at noon. To meet James. Can you come?

I texted back "Yes," and looked up to find a sullen Clayton loitering at my threshold. He walked in and stopped by my desk.

"I hoped you'd hear it from me first. You're the

only one who understands my pain." He gave me the once over. "You look really hot today." He flipped back his curtain of starlit hair and sniffled. "Bonnie's running off with Ronnie emphasizes the broken state of our marriage. I tried to tell you." He dabbed at his eye with a knuckle.

I searched deep within me for a trace of pity. To my surprise, I came up with a bottle cap full. It had never occurred to Clayton that his womanizing might drive his wife away. I grabbed my purse. "I've got to run."

"What about dinner tonight? Or tomorrow? Strictly platonic, of course. I need to talk to a friend."

"We're not friends. Try Marshall." I brushed past him.

His hand shot out and his fingers locked around my forearm. My animal instincts took over. I elbowed him in the ribs.

"Ouch."

"Next time, I won't be so gentle," I said. "And I'll lower my aim. Front and center."

I darted toward the door and heard him say, "Ever think of taking the high road?"

"I get nosebleeds," I said and made my exit.

Chapter 57
Michael Goes Down

Usual weekday lunchtime traffic on OC freeways is sluggish and touchy. I huffed and puffed the whole drive, but no amount of lane changing or expletive-laced outbursts quickened my pace.

Nearly twenty minutes later, I maneuvered into a parking spot and observed Michael, pacing outside the entrance, eyes canvassing the lot. He saw me and hurried over.

"Where were you? You didn't call or text. Not even a smoke signal."

"Sorry," I said. "Traffic."

"That's it?"

"What did you expect?"

Michael looked like he didn't believe me. He handed me a stick-on name badge. "Here's your entry pass. And don't get into any tussles this time."

"Everything's under control." I stepped out and onto the smooth asphalt. "Where are my keys?" I rummaged around my seat. "They were here a minute ago."

"In your hand."

"Of course." I'd been clenching my keys. I tried a grin on for size, but it didn't fit.

Michael walked a few paces ahead of me. He looked over his shoulder. "I got the shoe specs from

Rita. It was a gnarly experience, but now we know. It's a man's size seven."

I jogged to keep up. "I've bought men's running shoes before. Women do that."

"Worthless clue, isn't it?"

"No, it tells us it was a small man or average size woman. What's the matter?"

"I could ask you the same."

"I'm trying to keep my job. And my sanity. What's with your attitude?"

"It's part of my survival gear. You know, like a battery operated chainsaw in a zombie apocalypse."

"Michael—"

"I'm scared, okay? This is insanity, and we're in deep. At first, I liked the adrenaline rush, but did you know an autopsy's going on inside?" He pointed to the lab. "On a real person. On Druby. On the body of a man that's been murdered. And we're stalking the killer."

"It's not too late for you to turn around."

"Stop."

We faced each other in a stare down, a storm brewing in and around his hazel eyes. He looked resolute, maybe even a little stubborn around the edges.

"We're going to see this through and come out standing," I said.

"What if I get tired of standing?"

"I'll bring you a lawn chair. We're not here for small victories or compromise. We're here to win. Total victory. We'll solve this."

"Let's get a move on," Michael said. "James is waiting."

I rushed alongside him. "Stefon bought the pope costume from the thrift store."

“What?”

“And Druby and Stefon argued the day Druby died.”

“The photos we found in your car.” Michael raked his fingers through his hair.

“What about them?”

“I gave them to Rita to blow up.”

“What do you have to do in return, Michael?”

“You know. Giggle and bat my eyelashes.” He turned down a hallway and frowned at me. “You, of all people, should understand that we upset those around us when crime fighting.”

“Michael…”

“Dr. Tizzard reviewed the coroner’s report for Druby. It was unsigned and marked ‘no autopsy.’ The coroner didn’t even check for fluid in the lungs,” Michael said. “Finding the body in the lake was enough. Homicide was overruled.”

“It’s never good to take the easy way out.”

“You should take your own advice.”

“What?”

“Aren’t you taking the easy, but guaranteed to be dangerous route, by meeting with Bryce?”

“That’s not fair.”

“There it is again.”

“What?”

“That industrial strength, disinfectant stench. It’s brutal on the nasal passages.”

We approached the Medical Examiner’s area and I held my breath. Michael opened the metal door and followed me inside. Dr. Tizzard stood hunched over a body while James leaned in across from her. Both were gowned and gloved. My eyes shot to the body. The cadaver was covered with sheets, except for the open—cut-open, that is—mid-section. We couldn't see much from our vantage point, but my imagination stood tall. Blood and slimy guts. I gulped and hovered near the entry. So did Michael.

"No obvious signs of sodium azide," Dr. Tizzard was saying. "But the insides tell a sad tale of an ancient wrong and a wayward love. It's like reading tea leaves." She broke into a smile.

"Cut the crazy," James said to her.

"What exactly is sodium azide?" Michael cleared his throat and asked.

James' eyes locked onto mine.

"Welcome back." Dr. Tizzard held up a mucky, surgical gloved hand. "Starting with the simple questions, I see." She giggled. "Sodium azide is colorless and odorless, a crystalline solid. Like salt. It's very soluble in water, but only slightly soluble in alcohol. And highly toxic."

"It's what killed Druby?" I asked.

"The subject expired from a combination of ventricular fibrillation, respiratory depression, acidosis, and circulatory collapse caused by the poison. Normally, a sodium azide victim suffers convulsions, loss of consciousness, lung collapse, and ultimately, death from respiratory failure."

"What do you mean 'normally?'" Michael asked.

"There is blunt force trauma on the back right side of the skull, indicating cranial cerebral injury. Inflammation is present, consistent with head trauma. He was struck on the back of the head with a heavy object that knocked him out, but didn't immediately kill him. I removed all the organs and weighed and examined them for injury and disease. When I peeled away the skull cap…”

This was where Michael went down. I didn’t even see it coming.

Chapter 58
Afternoon Misunderstandings

Smelling salts really do work. Michael revived quickly and was made to lie down in Dr. Tizzard's office on a hard as a steel beam, maroon leather sofa, his feet propped up on fluffy pillows. "To improve circulation and prevent another fainting spell," Dr. Tizzard explained.

Embarrassed and grumpier than ever, Michael mastered silence after that. His fall caused a "boo-boo" (Dr. Tizzard's words) on one side of his forehead where he cut it on his metal watchband when he hit the tile floor. She fixed him up with a bandage. Michael and I left shortly afterward with James on our heels.

"Why Balboa Island?" James asked after I told him where Bryce and I were meeting. Michael darted ahead of us to his car.

"His choice."

"No easy way on or off that place."

That did not sit well with me. "Well then, I'd better beef up my security detail. Make sure you make yourself useful."

"There's only one move I can't follow."

"What's that?"

"The slow, unskilled kind."

Scary, yet provocative. I gave myself a mental shake. "Did you check out the other suspects?" I asked.

"Stefon?"

James nodded. "Mostly clean. Arthur's got a sealed juvy record. I couldn't get details."

"How did the thrift store know that Stefon bought the pope costume?"

"He left a card in case they got another one in. He'd told them he collected costumes depicting religious authority figures."

To make sure Stefon wasn't easily forgotten. "James?"

"I like the way my name slides off your tongue."

He slowed his pace and so did I. My eyes flicked to his. I couldn't tell if he was serious. Until he grinned.

"Stefon fought with Druby the day of the drowning," I said. "But I don't think he did it."

He dropped the grin. "Who do you think did it?"

"I'm not sure."

"Francois Dupree has a history of assault and battery."

"So do most bodyguards."

James picked up speed. "Who else?"

"Can you check out Paprika Martino? And Benson and Dominic May?"

"Roger that," James said and strolled away. He took notes on his phone, then stopped and faced me. "We can do this. You and I. Michael's not as bright as he should be. If he was, he'd know that you—how you—never mind." He turned and stormed off.

I watched his back. I felt all fluttery inside and excited and conflicted and muddled. I could have used an icy shower and a mental blindfold. As I drifted away, I heard,

"Looking especially good today, Ms. Locke."

I turned around. A different James faced me. The wide smile was back. He gave me a slow, admiring once over. I was hiding behind a flawless makeup job, thanks to the high I got from finding my car in the driveway. Maybe I should glam-up more often.

"Looking somewhat sharp yourself, ADA Zachary," I said. What an understatement. I turned to leave when I suddenly remembered. "That note on my desk chair. How did you put it there?"

"I've got informants everywhere." He slipped into his car and drove away.

Privacy was now officially extinct.

I caught up to Michael who sat slumped in his car. He moaned. "I'm really sorry. I don't know what happened."

"Gaping guts happened." I placed my hand on his. "You did what many viewing such a scene might do."

"How come you didn't faint?"

"You beat me to it, that's all," I said. "And distracted me so I forgot about fainting. You've always been competitive."

A tiny smile lit up his face. Where James' grin was mischievous and troublesome, Michael's was kindly and good. Moments later, he turned serious again. "Ever been to an autopsy before?"

I shook my head. "To a morgue once, to view a dead body. I expected to be horrified. But instead I felt nothing. Indifferent. It made me wonder if I was capable of any deep feelings."

Michael surveyed me. "Did you have a delayed reaction later?"

"No. I guess I'm superficial. That could be why my relationships last only a few months before I'm off and running."

"That's not true. We've been best friends since junior high school."

"I meant deeper relationships."

Michael took back his hand and turned away. I immediately regretted my words.

"I'm sorry," I said. "You are my deepest relationship. And my dearest, I hope..." I swallowed my words.

Michael ripped off the bandage from his forehead, winced, and faced me. I detected a more somber tone when he spoke. "So Druby was knocked out before he was sent into the lake. Why?"

"When sodium azide is ingested, it mixes with stomach acid and forms a toxic gas. If Druby vomited, that would expose the killer to the toxin."

"Wow. How do you know that?"

"A little Internet research."

"You think we're dealing with a chemist?"

"Maybe," I said. "How does the sapphire fit in? There's a possibility some other guy bought it for Paprika."

"No. I've expanded my theory. I think Bryce had a thing for Claire. Claire liked Druby. Bryce is used to women liking him back. He got jealous and killed Druby, but not before taking his credit card as a souvenir. A final joke on Druby was purchasing a ring for Claire. She dies, and he gives it to Paprika."

"Not bad, Michael. But why wait so long before gifting the ring?"

"Haven't figured that out yet."

"Arthur claims Bryce was with him the night of Druby's death."

"Somebody's lying."

"Somebody usually is."

"What if Arthur got busy or drunk?"

"Or hungry."

"And didn't notice that Bryce left?"

At that moment, my cell phone rang. The number was unfamiliar. "This is Corrie," I answered.

"It's me. Stefon."

Chapter 59
Early Afternoon Goose Chase

"Are you at the office?" Stefon asked.

"No."

"Right answer." He spoke at a racehorse clip. "I was told not to talk to you." The roar of a jet drowned out most of his words. "To avoid all contact."

"Who told you?" I asked. "Arthur?"

"Bryce."

"Why?"

"He has information that could cost me my job. I don't want to lose it."

"What kind of information?"

"You've got to believe that although Druby and I argued on the day he—I had nothing to do with his drowning."

"He was poisoned."

Silence dominated.

"Are you there?" I asked.

"I've got to go."

"What about the pope costume?"

"What?"

"The one you bought at the thrift store. It belonged to Rob."

"I don't have any costumes."

"I'm having dinner with Bryce tonight."

The line went dead. I looked at Michael. "I have to

find Stefon."

"Bryce could make his move tonight. You know that, right?"

"Good. Then the case will be closed, and you can start work on Monday with a clear head."

"What about your safety? He's probably hatched a diabolical plan."

"Who do you think he is? *Doctor No*? This isn't about world domination. It's about the usual motives: greed, ambition, jealousy. Of course, there's also psychosis, sheer insanity, and any number of high octane disorders. But you and James will be steps away. So will a police detective. Plus, I've got plenty of hardware."

"Bryce could have gotten away with Druby's murder if it wasn't for you. Don't you think he's anticipating trouble tonight?"

"If it is him, he's not acting alone. He can't be. We have to find his partner."

"I don't want you to go."

"And I don't want to pay full price for a ruby red cashmere sweater at Bloomingdales. It's all about anticipation and preparation. Don't worry your pretty little head—"

"Haven't you been listening to me?"

"No, but I didn't think you noticed." For the second time in one day, Michael had yelled at me. I put a hand on his arm. It felt warm and safe. Like a soft blanket.

"What about my sanity?" he said. "Don't you care how I feel?"

"Very much. But all will be well. Trust me. For now, we should find Stefon. It sounded like he was at

John Wayne airport. Hope he's not leaving town. Let's go."

"No," Michael said with the stubbornness of four mules on a hot day. "Go back to your office. I'll find Stefon."

"What am I going to do at the office?"

"Act normal and keep your head. We need concrete evidence to take the killer down."

I kind of liked Michael's bossy side. It gave me the chance to relax.

"What does Stefon look like?" he asked.

I gave him a brief description while I pulled out a legal pad. I sketched out his outstanding features.

"That looks like Little Orphan Annie except with dark hair, bee sting lips, and bushy brows," Michael said.

"Think Drake with Orphan Annie hair."

"Recording star meets comic strip character. I should spot someone that unique looking in no time."

Chapter 60

Marshall Lectures Me About Gossiping and Bryce Nearly Cancels

I returned to work and sank into my desk chair. Francois marched in minutes later.

"Stefon?" he asked.

Our phone conversation was so brief, it wasn't worth mentioning. "We didn't really talk. Any idea of what I should do next?"

"You're the detective."

"Private investigator," I said. "Actually, I'm a lawyer who got mixed up in some chaos."

"To help Artie."

To help him find a killer or to help him hide the fact that he was the killer? "You're very loyal to Arthur."

Francois grunted.

"He's lucky to have you."

Fran swallowed a lump in his throat. "I'm lucky." His eyes roved over to the wall behind my desk and landed on the cleft from Michael's knife. Fran squinted.

"It was a deformed nail," I explained. "I was trying to hang up a picture."

He snorted and left.

Toward the end of the day, Marshall summoned me into his office. Familiar dread flooded my senses. I could never win with him.

As was customary, he ignored me when I entered. He labored over paperwork and thumbed through a stack of contracts. Then he scanned a graphic novel and clipped his fingernails. He brushed away my attempts at conversation and finally spoke when I turned to leave.

"There are rumors," he said.

"If they're only rumors, why should we be concerned?"

He gave me an upside-down smile, flimsy brows scrunched together. It was the kind of expression reserved for simpletons and lost kittens. "We need to keep a low profile and make sure we're unaffected by gossip."

I could work with "we."

"Of course." I didn't have the heart to remind him I'd started less than two weeks ago and hadn't much chance to raise my profile.

"When money's at issue, in this case, missing money, everyone is suspect."

That would make me a prime suspect since my paycheck was so low compared to Marshall's and probably compared to everyone else, but I maintained my composure. "What money is missing?"

"That's not important," he said. "Be careful what you say to people, you know what I mean?"

Marshall Law Rule Number Five: "Only the boss is allowed to gossip."

He dismissed me with a glance toward the door and I left, wondering about the latest rumors. If this was about money, Stefon had to be involved. I grabbed my cell phone. The screen displayed a missed call from Stefon.

I rang him, but was sent straight to voice mail each

time. I leaned back in my desk chair and contemplated my next move.

"It's you and me tonight, kiddo." Caitlyn stuck her head into my office. "We'll go to the Beach Ball. It's the premier spot to pick up guys." She left before I could open my mouth.

I darted out of the office and after her, but Bryce stopped me halfway.

"Our dinner reservation's at six-thirty. We'll take my car." He closed in with every word. "I'll show you my place afterward."

"What?" I took a giant step back. All office activity froze during his one-sided conversation. "Would you mind?" I waved toward my office.

He trailed me inside. "We'll enjoy the drive and the ferry together. Get to finally be friends."

"That sounds fun. But let's do separate cars." I had to take control. "I'm leaving a little earlier and running errands before dinner. You know, gotta get my work done before I can come outside and play."

"I'll drive you and wait. Impatiently."

I clasped my hands tightly together. "Here's the thing, I like driving myself. I thrive on alone time. I'm better company that way."

His reaction surprised and unnerved me. His face fell and his body drooped. Either he was vying for an Academy Award or he was sincere.

"I've been looking forward to tonight," he said. "I like to plan moments, down to the last detail."

That could explain the hair remains, the careful execution of Druby's death…

"I want to enjoy your company. Talk. Maybe laugh a little. Show you a good time. I feel safe with you," he said. “On second thought, let’s cancel tonight.”

“No. I mean, that’s not necessary. Like heaven, my errands can wait.” Bryce was our best lead right now. I needed to do this and I had to admit, I didn’t mind spending time with him. To put an end to the possibility that he was a suspect. Or find out otherwise. “You drive.”

He flashed a gorgeous smile and straightened. “So be it.” He left.

I waited a decent amount of time before racing out the door, down the stairs, into the parking lot, and across the street. I didn’t stop running until I reached the corner. About three industrial size buildings away. My feet, held hostage in black patent sandals, made me yearn for painkillers. The kind provided to elephants and whales. I slowed to a limp. A light sprinkling of mist dampened my skin.

I called Michael and babbled away. I started with Marshall and the missing money and ended with Bryce chauffeuring me. Michael remained silent. “Are you there?” I asked.

“Yes.”

“I’ll be carrying a gun and I’ll be wired.” I tried to reassure Michael. And myself.

“I’ll let James know,” Michael said, his voice low. “And I only found one tall, Orphan Annie-Drake look-alike at the airport, but she worked in the baggage check. Corrie…”

“I’m going back to the office now, but Michael? Everything will be all right.” I disconnected.

My phone rang again. It was Stefon. “I didn’t kill anyone,” Stefon said. “Uh sh o heh an ire…”

“Dammit,” I said.

His voice kept breaking up. The line went dead. I dialed and redialed without success. As I wound my way back to the Complex, the phone rang again. I quickly answered.

"Stall Bryce if he's early," James said. "I'm on my way to your parking lot to plant a tracking device on his car. Which one is it?"

I described Bryce's Mercedes while my insides fluttered with butterflies, bees, and hornets—a whole nest of flying insects. I ended the call and took a deep breath.

When I entered the lot, I strode to my trunk and opened it. I removed tonight's outfit, a small black satchel, and a pair of stilettos. It was show time.

Chapter 61
Pre-Dinner Surprises

I phoned Bryce from the office and told him I was running late. Then I changed into a black plisse trimmed cardigan with a deep V-neckline and matching flounce-hem, Jersey skirt. Perfect to hide all sorts of covert operations' paraphernalia, from the wire that would be strapped to my chest, to the gun holster circling my upper thigh. As the final touch, I wore my black belt with the star shaped buckle to house my secret weapon. My shuriken. A loaded Sig sat in a pocket of my satchel, which I'd emptied except for my wallet, lip gloss, and cellphone. I slipped the Sig into the holster and pulled out a mirror. I stifled a scream. Thanks to the late afternoon mist, my hair lay molded to my skull on the top, stiff and flat like that of a Roman soldier. I fluffed and loosened the best I could. I added fuchsia lipstick and peppermint gloss to plump my lips and divert attention from my hair disaster.

I heard a slight shuffle. My eyes cut to the doorway. James stepped in and closed the door behind him. How he located me without fanfare I couldn't fathom. "Are you going to wire me?" I whispered. My lips tingled from nerves and peppermint.

"No. I'm doubling up on tracking you. Here."

He handed me a flower hairpin with green crystals at one end, which easily slid onto my hair. I guessed the tracker was in the crystals. Clever, since it is forbidden for a man to touch a woman's hair on a date, lest he mess with careful styling and unleash a deadly tornado. Even a potential murderer knew that rule, I hoped, for his sake. I pulled back a chunk of hair from the front and secured it on top. No more flat-top for me. James was my hair-saver.

He asked about the rest of my arsenal, all in whisper mode. We leaned close together against the wall farthest from my desk.

"Remove the holster from your thigh," he said.

I must have made a face because he added, "If you don't, I will. He'll spot the bulge when you're in the car."

"I don't bulge," I said, but I released the strap. I did not want to waste energy. I had a long night ahead of me. I threw the holster and pistol into my desk drawer. James scrutinized my office. At least I had my throwing star. I lightly tensed my fingers and wrist in preparation. I'd spent the night before, practicing quick removal and target hitting on my war-torn dart board. My aim was solid.

"Cool belt," he said, eyes glued to my waist.

"Thanks." I tossed my head, threw back my shoulders and distracted him with my sultriest smile. "How do I look?"

His eyes roved over me and returned to my face. "Like a hand grenade masquerading as Audrey Hepburn."

"Why, thank you." Who doesn't like Audrey Hepburn?

James placed a shoe on my chair and stepped atop my desk. He examined my smoke detector, to confirm it didn't house a camera. Satisfied, he jumped down and stared at me a few more uncomfortable moments. "You look good enough to—"

"Explain how you got up here without being announced." My heart palpitated, machine-gun tempo.

"I told the receptionist I was a long lost boyfriend and wanted to surprise you."

"She fell for it?"

"I could have told her I was going to plant a pipe bomb under your seat and she would have sent me up. I can be charming when I want to be."

"I'll take your word for it."

"I'll be close by, and there's a tracking device under Bryce's front bumper." He squeezed my hand and held it, sending an odd, warm sensation up my arm. My tension melted and I immediately relaxed. He released my hand.

"How did you do that?" I asked.

"Do what?"

"Uh, locate Bryce's car so easily."

"You told me which one it was, remember?" He turned to leave. "Don't get soft on me."

"James," I called after him. "What about the names I gave you?"

"No priors," he said and disappeared out the door.

I could have sworn Paprika came with a record.

"No fair, you have all these hot guys around." Caitlyn slinked in moments later. "Who is he?"

"A friend."

"God knows I could use a hunky friend like that." She gave me a sour head to toe glance. "Why are you all dressed up?"

"I tried to tell you. I have a date."

"Even you?" Whimpers hit her and she turned to face the window. "Why doesn't Marshall want me?" she said between sobs. "WHY? I've been so freaking good to him…" She went silent and sucked in a wad of air. "Oh. My. God."

"What's wrong?" I asked.

I rose and moved closer to her. I followed her gaze out the window and into the parking lot. My office offered a limited view. Only a slice showed where a few lower level staff parked and where there sat a large rectangular, blue storage bin. Behind the bin, mostly hidden, stood a man in a dark suit. His head was slightly tilted and his lips moved. Whoever he spoke to stood out of our line of sight. He stroked the arm of his companion.

"Who's Rob talking to?" I asked. "I've never seen him smile before."

"It's…it's…"

I was about to turn away when the reason for Caitlyn's shock came into full view. I was speechless. Caitlyn's mouth hung wide open. I could have stuffed a tennis ball in it quite comfortably. "This is an unexpected twist," I said.

Chapter 62
A Knight in the Ocean

Rob had finally found solace. In Marshall. We spied them from my window, holding hands, wrapped in a warm embrace that sent them tumbling behind the bin and out of our view. They emerged a minute later, straightened their suits and walked away, separately.

"We can't tell anyone about this," Caitlyn said. "Mind-wipe."

Translation: she'd be the news source. I nodded.

"It makes perfect sense." Caitlyn's face was all aglow. "Marshall's obsession with my silk skirts. He makes a wicked croque monsieur. And his failure to be jealous, no matter how many times I sent myself flowers. Today, I have clarity." Caitlyn floated out of my office, chin held high.

Why would Marshall keep his feelings for Rob secret? If they made each other happy, maybe they'd both lighten up. And leave me alone. I shook thoughts of Marshall aside and kicked off my heels. I paced, wearing out the floor by my desk. I didn't like that Michael was mad at me. And was I crazy to spend time with Bryce tonight?

"I thought you'd never get here," I said when Bryce strode into my office.

****

We exited the Complex, amid long stares and loud

whispers. I felt slightly breathless as I made my way to the passenger side of Bryce's Mercedes.

"Over here," I heard him say.

I shifted my gaze over my shoulder. Bryce was headed toward the driveway. I hurried after him. "Where are you going?"

"I'm not taking my car to Balboa Island. It'll bottom out on the ferry."

"What?" I asked.

"I rented a car for tonight." He drifted down the street, away from all Complex eyes and security cams. A film of sweat spread across my skin. "You don't mind, do you?" he asked.

My throat had constricted. My legs moved forward, but my mind grew numb.

He opened the passenger door of a black, late model, Chevy Trailblazer with beefy tires. I could smell the testosterone in the air.

"Let's take my car," I said.

"Trust me. You'll be glad we didn't." He started the engine.

I sank onto the generic cloth seat and slurped up the new plastic odor. I buckled my seatbelt. Bryce was with Arthur the night of Druby's death, I reminded myself. A solid alibi.

He shifted, mashed his Gucci loafers on the gas and peeled out, cutting off an oncoming car and swerving to avoid a pedestrian in the crosswalk.

"These aren't exactly German-grade brakes." He drove the mid-size SUV like a Ferrari. The engine groaned in protest.

"Hey," I said. "I'll have a tough time eating dinner with cracked ribs."

He glanced at me with a tight-lipped smile. He slowed and the car took a nosedive. "Sorry. I'm a little wound-up. It's been a trying day."

Bryce reached across the gray plastic console and patted my thigh. I stiffened, glad that I'd removed the holster. I had James to thank for that. It was good to know he'd be nearby. The wind howled through the closed sun-roof and I slowed my breathing.

"Most women find me..." Bryce paused.

"Irresistible?" I offered. A vision of a shirtless James streaked through my mind.

"I was going to say 'enigmatic.' But I like irresistible. You find me irresistible?"

I swallowed. "I find you enigmatic."

"I'm really a pretty simple guy."

My white knuckled hand gripped the side handle as Bryce powered through a red lighted intersection. "The sapphire ring on Paprika's finger didn't come from a simple man."

He raised his chin slightly. "That ring is a sore spot."

"How so?"

"I thought I was the only man in her life. I wasn't. Paprika wears the ring to torture me. To flaunt that there's someone else that she could get serious with. My pump's not primed for serious." He turned and gave me a lingering look. Long enough where I had to snap the wheel counterclockwise to avoid oncoming traffic. "Sorry. I'm glad it's just you and me tonight. I haven't felt this comfortable in a long time."

So he said. Yet his loafer remained superglued to the gas pedal. "Is her other guy someone you know?" I asked.

"You like torturing me, don't you?"

We narrowly missed rear-ending a FedEx truck.

"If you don't want to talk about it…" I said.

"It's Stefon."

"What?" Again? Were there any good guys who worked at the Complex? I'd settle for a law abiding driver right now.

Bryce looked at me and breathed out a laugh. "Am I making you nervous?"

I unclenched my hands. I was sweating enough to form my own salt lake by my feet despite the chilly evening. "Should I be?"

"I'll make it up to you."

He grinned and skidded to a bumpy stop. We'd reached the end of a small side street that dumped us onto a floating dock. I scanned the surroundings for the boat that would take us across. I couldn't find it. The Chevy scuttled beneath a brightly lit, yellow overhead sign that read, *Auto Ferry*. In front of us sat an oversize red and white raft with an engine.

"What is that?" I asked. "I expected something…"

"Bigger?"

"More stable," I said. "Don't tell me that's the ferry."

"Okay. It'll be my little secret."

The Chevy's nose tilted up, and it bucked onto the ferry. I glanced behind us. Where was my tail?

Bryce ground the truck to a park and cut the motor. "We'll be fine. It's only a ten minute ride across," he said. "I'll take good care of you."

Part of me wanted to relax and enjoy the evening. But the other part was ready to clamp him in a headlock until the police arrived. What was a girl to do?

The cozy deck fit three cars, but there were only two onboard tonight: us and a VW bug in front. The ferry's engine burped and rumbled as it began its chug across the small bay.

"Check it out." Bryce opened his door.

I stepped outside. The cool night air lightly grazed my cheeks. My eyes followed Bryce to a booth that squatted along one side. He pulled out a bill to pay the nominal fare, and I shifted my gaze to the bay. Twinkling lights from neighboring crafts skimmed the rolling waves. A sleek modern vessel drifted toward us, about twenty feet away. Part baby yacht, part speed boat, it floated in a pool of brightness lit by recessed bulbs glowing along the bottom perimeter. The wash of lights danced merrily across the dark water.

I dropped into an empty bench-seat across from the booth and leaned over the side. Diesel exhaust choked the salt sprinkled air, seawater sprayed my face and hands. I heard the distant bellow of a foghorn.

Bryce slipped next to me and out of his sport coat. He placed it behind my shoulders.

"You're getting drenched," he said. "It's choppy tonight. Let's go upfront."

We joined the four others onboard. They stood, staring across the bay, mesmerized by the bevy of sparkling lights dotting a Ferris wheel and neighboring shops. The dark waves sizzled with streaks of madcap colors reflected in zig-zags on the murky surface. A dash of cold water sprayed my skin again.

"We should have brought galoshes and raincoats. This is getting to be like Niagara Falls." Bryce surveyed me. "Let's try the back. It won't be as wet." He reached for my hand and tugged me along behind him.

We stopped behind the Chevy. I turned my back to the waves and leaned against the red metal railing. The ferry was small, but we seemed very much alone.

"I liked the front," I said. "I could see the whole Ferris wheel."

"Pretty girl," he said. "There's nowhere else I want to be than right here."

I took in the warmth of his coat and the dancing lights reflected in the dark blue of his eyes. "I have to admit, Balboa Island is nice," I said.

"You're nice. I'm a lucky guy."

"You are?"

He moved closer. "I got to escape tonight. With you."

"Only because you were brave enough to say yes when I asked you out."

"Do you ask men out often?"

"Actually, you're my first."

"I'm flattered." He traced my cheek with his index finger.

"I hear wallpaper is making a comeback." Nervousness made me incoherent.

"Do you want to wallpaper my place?"

"Is there a Home Depot nearby?"

"I've got a better idea."

"I don't think you could top the wallpaper…"

"Why don't we help fund the Colombian economy later?" Bryce placed a hand lightly around my shoulder.

I'm a little slow in the more cosmopolitan aspects of life. When I think Colombia, I think coffee beans and rain forests. "I'm not into drugs, Bryce," I said.

"What are you into?"

"Making things right."

"Wrong can be right sometimes." He smiled and threaded the fingers of his hand through his hair. "Can't believe my hair. It's a mess. I've let it grow too long. No thanks to Paprika."

"She won't let you cut it?"

"She's the one who used to cut it."

"She's a hairdresser?" I asked. A chill trickled down my spine.

"That's how we met."

I could feel my sweat glands opening up again. "What about…?"

"What about what?"

He leaned toward me and kissed the side of my neck.

"What about Druby?" I asked. Might as well get it over with.

"What about him?" He shot me a frown. "He killed himself. Everyone knows that."

"Not everyone."

His blue eyes drilled into mine. "Tonight's about us, remember? Why are you grilling me?" He took a step backward. "Wait, I don't want to know. Did Art put you up to this? I'll call you a cab when we reach the other side." He turned away from me.

Putting him in a headlock didn't seem such a good idea anymore. "I jumped to a conclusion about you. I guessed that you were involved somehow in whatever happened to Druby. I guess I was wrong." That was a lot of uneducated guesswork for one evening. I placed my hand on his shoulder. "Is it too late?"

He faced me again. He took my hand and brought it to his lips. "Let's skip dinner and go to my place."

"How about mine?" I had no idea where I was

going with this. I was following my animal instincts, which led me to wrap my arms around his neck. I moved in closer.

"What will we do at your place?" he asked.

Good question. My hand reached downward, unbuckled his belt and yanked the smooth brown leather out of the loops in one quick jerk. "For starters…" I dropped the belt and returned my hand to his neck. "We'll get comfy."

"We can get comfy at my place too."

I planted little kisses on his cheek. His skin felt warm beneath my cold lips. "My bed is pretty comfortable."

"Bet mine is more."

"You'll have to see for yourself." I pictured my double size airbed, a full eight inches off the ground. An inflatable bed didn't exactly make the comfortable cut.

I pressed my lips to his and felt nothing except a chill. He tried to liven things up with some tongue action, but it only made me feel colder. This was uncharted territory. There were so many ways to lose myself. And my job. I pulled away and looked out over the water. A low fog hovered above the waves. "It's mistier out than when we first left."

Bryce's gaze scanned the water. He planted kisses on my neck. "Looks like someone spilled a boatload of dry ice."

"What?" I pulled back.

"The fog."

I studied him. "You said dry ice. I've never touched dry ice."

"Smart girls don't touch. You'd get a major burn."

"Right. Water ice is thirty-two degrees Fahrenheit. Dry ice is negative one hundred nine degrees. Water ice floats in water. Dry ice has greater density, so it doesn't float. You did it. You killed Druby."

He frowned. "That's ridiculous. Did you ask me out to make stray accusations?"

"And to see Balboa Island. You threw dry ice on the accelerator of Druby's car. After you parked it by the lake. The bag was left open, so it dissolved once it hit the water. Brilliant."

"I've had enough. Haven't you?" He pulled me close and I stiffened.

"Stop," I said, wriggling my wrists away.

His grip tightened. "You've put me in an awkward position," he spoke through clenched teeth. "But I like awkward positions. Maybe you do too."

In an instant he was behind me, a sturdy arm gripped my neck in a chokehold. The chokehold that I was supposed to give him. In one quick move, he tackled me to the ground, his chest pinned me to the wooden deck, flat on my belly. His hand lay firmly across my mouth. I writhed and bit hard into the flesh of his palm. He responded by pounding the back of my head with a steely fist. He rolled me off the ferry like a wagon wheel into the dark churning waters. Unlike a wagon wheel, I didn't float.

My clothes fluttered around me and I sank in slow motion, anchored by terror, regret, and helplessness. I was a speck in an opaque cosmos, about to be consumed. I had the swimming skills of a snail.

"Action cures helplessness. Inaction creates terror," Dad had once said.

Action, action, action, that one word echoed and

spun around my aching head. I shut my eyes and kicked out, my arms pumping water. I exhaled and propelled myself upward. My chest was about to burst. I fought to keep my mouth closed. Just when I lost all feeling in my legs, I pierced the surface, sucking in gobs of air between salty lips. I cried out for help. The rumble of the chugging engine and roar of the waves filled my ears and muffled my pleas.

The ferry rambled ahead about twenty yards, leaving behind a trail of toddling waves that pushed me away. My teeth chattered and I switched direction. I could swim to shore. Well, maybe I could float to shore, on my back, until I was spotted. Oh please, someone help.

I swallowed a mouthful of sea water. I coughed and sputtered. I couldn't die out here. The bay wasn't even that deep. Great Whites didn't hang out in small bays, right? I shuddered when I recalled the telescopic snout. And killer teeth. It was so dark and cold.

"Help," I cried.

This was a stupid way to try to kill me. Too simple for Druby's killers. They'd gotten sloppy. I dog-paddled toward shore, swept around by aimless waves. I can do this. If I could keep my job with all that had happened, I could swim a few hundred yards to shore, couldn't I? From the corner of a teary eye, I caught the outline of a vessel. The lights had dimmed, but I recognized the baby yacht-speed boat, resting nearby.

"Help." I waved an arm. "Help. Help!"

A shadowy figure hovered at the edge of the deck. He tumbled backwards into the water with a small splash.

Thank God. I churned seawater and waited

impatiently for my rescuer.

"Help," I called out again and again.

My eyes strained to catch swimming movement in the water, but the shifting waves between the boat and me sat empty. My chest tightened and squeezed all the breath out of me. I flailed my arms wildly. Where was my rescuer?

"Corrie!" A voice coasted over the waves behind me.

I turned around, toward a flashlight and caught the silhouette of a man in a suit, shore lights twinkling behind him. He stood tall in a small motorboat that rocked in the waves. He bent down, leaned over the side, and dangled a hand toward me.

"James," I called out, my mouth a depository for saltwater. I coughed and struggled toward him.

His hand stretched out. I extended mine. Not close enough. He was paddling water in large strokes with his other arm to reach me, but the waves pushed him back.

"You can do it," he said. "I've almost got you. Come on."

My fingers touched his and he caught my wrist in a strong, firm clasp. Suddenly his grip broke. I was yanked away, beneath the surface. Shock held me hostage. A sea creature gnawed at my ankle. It dragged me under in a savage vise. I felt no pain.

My eyes flew open. All was dark, except for a spot of brightness by my feet. A light. It was attached to something. A hand. A hand with a mounted scuba diving light on top of the wrist. My legs kicked out in fury. This was a human shark in scuba gear.

I still wore my heels and slammed a stiletto into the cheek of my captor. Even in slow motion, I made an impact. He released his hold and I rocketed upward.

I broke through the waves and gasped for air. James swam to me and hooked an arm under my shoulders, but before we could budge, I was yanked under again. Now I was pulled in two directions. Pain attacked me, exhausting my body and arresting my mind. James let go. I was jerked beneath. My attacker clutched an ankle in each hand. I kicked out wildly. James tore down through the water, Glock drawn. He fired a shot that burst out of a huge cylindrical bubble at the end of the barrel. He missed, but my assailant loosened his grip. It was enough for me to wrench away and upward. I heard the puff of another shot just before I surfaced, gasping.

****

James had steered the little motorboat toward the ferry and shifted into neutral not far from my thrashing arms. He'd been trying to pinpoint my location. That was when he heard my wails. He'd motored toward me and called Delgado. She'd hustled to the ferry and nabbed Bryce before he could exit. She'd detained all onboard for questioning.

"Good thing you wore that pin on your head," James said, panting between his words. "It saved your life. It led me to you."

Once he'd realized Bryce's Mercedes remained at the Complex, he tuned in to my tracker and discovered me near the ferry. When he arrived, he heard crackling sounds from my hairpin.

"It went haywire," he said.

James confiscated the small motorboat to follow the ferry. "I didn't expect to find you splashing around in the water."

My eyes stung and my ankles and calves ached from a steady dose of electrocuting pain. A ferry crewman brought us blankets. We wrapped ourselves in them and sat on a concrete wall to dry off and catch our breath. The yacht-speed boat had disappeared, but James alerted Harbor Patrol. I told him about Bryce pushing me in.

"Any ideas about the underwater attacker?" he asked.

I shook my head.

He stood and threw off the blanket. "Let's get you home."

"Are you kidding me? I need to talk to Bryce. Pronto."

"What for? We've got him. And we know his partner was the scuba diver with the underwater foot fetish. We'll get him too."

"James." Oh no, I thought, here it comes, and a stream of warm, angry tears poured down my cold, sticky face. "He tried to kill me."

"I know." His gaze darkened and he put his arms around me. I didn't resist when he pulled me close. Or when he stroked my wet hair. Or even when his warm lips lingered on my forehead. "You're safe now. I'll always keep you safe."

This was not the James I knew. I looked up at him. The five o'clock shadow and slicked back hair enhanced his absurdly handsome face. But his usual expression had gentled, which I found irresistible. Any harshness I'd felt toward him had leaked away into the ocean.

"James."

"Corrie."

"I…Michael—"

"He would never forgive me if I didn't keep you safe." He pushed me away.

I chucked him on the shoulder. For a moment, I thought he cared. "We're wasting time. Let's go."

We took a motorboat across the bay. I shivered the whole time and nearly threw up, but I made it.

Moments after we hit the landing, we hightailed it into a tourist shop and bought sweatshirts and pants, light blue for me and black for James. I also bought a pair of flip-flops. I'd had enough of my soaked heels. My raisin-like flesh gratefully slipped into the warmth of the dry clothes. I slid my shuriken into a pocket and looked in the mirror. My smeared eye makeup gave me the evil Satan worshipper look. I pulled back my hair into a high ponytail and cleaned away the drippy mascara.

I stepped back into the night. Delgado and her men stood scattered around Marine. Bryce leaned against a squad car. His SUV was double-parked nearby.

"Hey," I said.

A uniform grabbed my arm and dragged me over to Delgado.

"Delgado!" James soldiered over.

"Step away, Zachary." Delgado's face folded into a frown. Her eyes shot from James to me. "What's this mean?" She held my cell phone up to my eyes. I'd left it in my purse, in Bryce's car. I read a text from Michael:

Got photo enlargement. Sapphire ring on Mandy Keith's finger. Same as Depuis.

What? How did the ring jump from Paprika's finger to Mandy's?

"Let go of her," James said.

The cop on my arm glanced at Delgado. She nodded. The moment I was freed, I charged toward Bryce. I slugged him across the face with my fist. It felt so liberating.

In moments, two cops grasped my arms. It was worth it. Delgado and James arrived seconds later.

"What's the ring doing on Mandy's finger?" I asked Bryce.

"What ring?" Bryce raised a brow and narrowed his eyes, blood oozing from a nostril.

"You're just the Complex idiot, aren't you?" I said.

"You're the idiot."

"You tried to kill me."

"Hardly. You accused me of murder and tried to throw me overboard." His eyes cut to Delgado. "Like I told you. I had to defend myself. You just witnessed how violent she can be."

"You son of a..." James lunged forward, but Delgado's guys let go of me and intercepted him.

I took that opportunity to box Bryce's ears.

Delgado grabbed my arm and came around to face me. "You want to tell me what really happened?"

"What do you mean?" James said, shrugging himself loose from the cops. "He shoved her into the bay, while his goon waited on a boat dressed up in scuba gear. He dove in, grabbed her ankles and dragged her under to mimic a drowning. What part of conspiracy to commit murder don't you understand?"

"Bachman's got no priors," Delgado lowered her voice and turned her back to Bryce. "And no one on the ferry saw him push her in. We've got to look at all angles."

"Not when I'm around. I was the one who pulled her out."

Delgado shifted uncomfortably. "Look, it's obvious you've got a thing for her—"

"Don't mess with me, Delgado." His voice turned low and dangerous. "You're squandering an opportunity to solve a double murder in your own backyard."

"Where's Michael?" I asked, my heart raced to keep up with the unfurling events. The scene went silent.

Chapter 63
Missing Michael

Solving murders rarely comes easily, absent a live confessor or witness willing to talk. Hard evidence doesn't hurt either. So who was Druby's killer?

A few hours ago, NBPD had received an anonymous tip about Stefon. They'd paid a visit and found the pope costume in his condo, stuffed inside an antique blanket chest. His bank account was padded by nearly a million dollars, transferred yesterday. Bryce claimed Stefon regularly embezzled money from the Complex and Druby found out. That's why they'd argued the day Druby died. And that's why Stefon had killed him.

The missing Michael further confused matters.

"His car was parked over there when I saw him earlier." Delgado pointed to the street behind us.

"When was that?" James asked.

"Right before I got to Bachman," she said. "I can't hold him, you know. It's her word against his."

"Delgado," James said, gritting his teeth. "Who's in charge here?"

He stormed over to Bryce who now sat in the back of a squad car. James leaned in and spoke to him. I could only see James' profile. A moment later, Bryce head-butted James. Two cops intervened. James shook his head, as if to rid himself of Bryce cooties and rejoined us, smoothing back his hair.

"Now you have it. Battery on an officer of the court. Take him in. Come on," James said to me.

"Hold on," Delgado said. "Bring her to the station. You hear? Otherwise I have to cuff—"

"Where else are we going to go?" Bryce said.

I hurried after him. "We have no car."

James stopped and dropped his head. He turned to face me, lips turned inward. "Let's find one."

"I just did." I darted over to Bryce's Chevy. The key was in the ignition.

"I'll drive," James said.

I raced to the passenger side and landed on the seat. "How are we going to find Michael?"

"Same way I found you," James said, landing next to me. "I'm tracking him."

"You put a pin in his hair?"

"Funny. Although he could pull it off. It's in his keychain. It sends me updates every fifteen seconds." He dug in his pocket and opened his palm to reveal a small black box, the size of a smoke detector battery.

"I was wrong about you, James."

He raised his roguish brows, a grin lapped around his mouth. A wild sunflower hue rimmed the pupil of his green eyes. "Let's get Michael."

My gaze cut to a silver sports car sitting across the street.

"He's at Turtle Isle," James said. "Know anyone who lives there?"

"Arthur Keith. But wait." I pointed to the silver Porsche Boxster. "That's Paprika's car."

Chapter 64
Going Deeper into the Night

The tired wheels in my head creaked and groaned as we plowed our way toward Turtle Isle. "What's Paprika doing with Michael?" I asked.

"She was keeping tabs on Bryce," James replied. "And got sidetracked with Mikey."

"So why would Michael go with Paprika to Arthur's house?"

"We don't know if they're together."

"Assume they are."

"To get something from Arthur. Or spend quality time together. How would I know?"

Michael and Paprika were both looking for Arthur. Why?

James sped the entire time. He ignored stop lights, signs, and other cars. He even drove over a sidewalk to skip past vehicles that blocked our way. He was good at it too. No nicks, near misses, or close calls. We did a half spin once and lost the driver's side mirror to a telephone pole. But mishaps are to be expected when one is driving forty miles over the posted speed limit. I tried calling Michael. I got voice mail each time. Throughout this topsy-turvy excursion, I placed another call.

"I knew I'd hear from you again soon," Charlie said.

I asked him about Stefon.

"He's not a murderer."

"Who is?"

"I don't think…it…it can't be…it's not Arthur."

"I didn't say it was." Charlie wavered this time. "Tell me something useful."

In less than two minutes, Charlie provided pieces to the puzzle. He now suspected Arthur. Charlie carried incriminating information, which he offered surprisingly quickly.

"I don't want anyone else to get hurt. Things changed after Druby became Art's partner. One minute he'd say, 'Druby's the best thing that ever happened.' The next minute he'd complain that making Druby a partner was a big mistake. Art planned to end the deal after their first project."

"Thanks, Charlie."

"There's more," he said. "If Druby was fired for good cause…or died, Arthur would own all work product."

I let out a breath. It was Arthur all the time.

"You asked about Dom May."

"Yes?"

Charlie paused. "He's Art's drug dealer."

I'd finally moved off of square one.

Chapter 65
An Evening at Arthur's

Michael's empty car rested on the side of a road near Arthur's place. I called his phone again and again. Still no answer. I comforted myself with my latest mantra, "Michael can take care of himself. Michael can take care of himself." But I loved playing devil's advocate, so I countered with, "Really? Explain why he's at Arthur's house? Is Paprika with him? Did she kill Druby? Or was it Arthur? Or both? Did Michael bring his knife?"

"Can you talk to yourself more quietly? I can't concentrate," James said.

"Sorry."

James pulled onto Arthur's concrete driveway. How many Complex workers dropped by his place? Apparently, quite a few. The maid who opened the door experienced no problem ushering me inside.

Arthur lived at the northern tip of Turtle Isle, in a large, window-studded, Spanish style estate, steps away from the bay, complete with its own dock. Magnificent among the other homes, in the way Versailles outshone other palaces, Arthur had purchased the place shortly after receiving his multi-million dollar production deal. Was Michael here?

I waited alone, in a dimly lit, high-ceilinged entryway, next to a surreal oak staircase. Each individual piece of wood protruded from unevenly cut, dimensional sandstone walls, giving the appearance that each piece levitated. My eyes flicked to a thin beam of light outside a window. James quick-stepped around the front and conducted an exterior search with his penlight. I'd insisted on going in alone. Before we'd separated, he'd slipped a one-inch square, black box in my pocket. A voice transmitter. It seemed I wasn't the only one with an arsenal of spy stuff.

"I'll be listening the whole time," James had said. "I'll jump in if things get hairy. As will Delgado. She'll be here soon." He'd squeezed my arm and disappeared.

The maid returned and led me to a bright, spacious dining room where Arthur reigned on a mahogany armchair at one end of an elegant inlaid table. A white cloth napkin was tucked into his dress shirt and he savored a large piece of dark chocolate cake. Fran stood at attention, nearby.

"Hey, you're dressed super casual," Arthur said. "I like it. Did you find the killer?" He spoke between bites, completely unfazed by my visit.

"Yes."

"Stefon?" His mouth was full, but he sounded hopeful.

"I really admire Fran's loyalty to you." I approached Fran and looked up into red-tinged face. "But that's because, despite his criminal record, you hired him."

"Superior bodyguards have criminal records."

"Fran said that you understood. That's because you've been there yourself, haven't you, Arthur?"

He stopped chewing. "I don't know what you're talking about, young lady."

"Your juvy record was sealed years ago, so no one would know about your convictions for murder, rape, and assault." I asked about his juvenile record despite the fact neither James nor Charlie provided any details. I held my breath, hoping I'd made an impact.

"Actually, you're wrong. It was for theft. I stole a car. Can't seal juvy records for violent crimes. There's not much privacy when it comes to violence." He slowly wiped his mouth with a napkin.

"You got rid of Druby so you could obtain full rights to his picture book. He signed a document turning over work product to you if anything happened to him." I threw Charlie's tidbits at him. "You don't like to share, do you, Arthur?"

Arthur grinned like a Cheshire cat about to pounce on a mouse. I could almost see his ginger striped, snake-like tail snapping and twitching behind him. "That's a good story. Outrageous, but good."

"What's going on?" Mandy Keith entered. Her brows knitted together, and she looked quizzically from person to person.

"Our junior lawyer dropped by to tell me a story. A tall tale."

Her frown dissolved into a smile. "Nice to see you. Would you like some cake?"

"Did your boyfriend like the gelato?" Arthur asked me.

"Where is he, Arthur?" I said.

He blinked and raised his brows. "Who?"

"Michael. My boyfriend. Where is he?"

"What makes you think he's here? Having a juvy record doesn't make me a kidnapper."

"I know who killed Druby. He did it with a little

help from a cold-hearted female. You know all about it, Arthur."

"What?" Mandy asked.

"Got sodium azide?" My eyes cut from Arthur to Mandy. She'd gone pale.

"Where are you getting this offensive, yet intriguing information?" he asked.

"You hired me to hide the facts. Druby was poisoned. But you know that, don't you?"

"Poisoned?" Arthur scratched his head. "That's ridiculous and mean. Just plain cruel. Druby was my friend. I was going to drop him after our first project, but I changed my mind. I signed a deal giving him more if our outing was a success." He shoved his plate aside with the back of his hand. "This is getting boring…"

"Mrs. Keith," I said. "Your husband—"

"What about him?" She moved closer to Arthur. "You find me boring too, Art?"

"Mandy," Arthur said, nonplussed.

"How do I know she's not just another ho?" She pitched her head toward me. A .38 Special, snub-nose revolver pointed in my direction. "And what's this about giving Valdez more?"

"What are you doing?" He shot up, cake crumbs tumbling down his shirt.

"Protecting my best interests, sweetheart," she answered without taking her eyes from me. "Fran, drop all your weapons on the floor behind you, one at a time." Fran didn't budge. "Now."

He obliged and dropped a revolver, two knifes, brass knuckles, a manriki chrome chain and nunchuks. Mandy moved closer and smacked him across the face. He barely flinched, but a dark red smear appeared on his cheek.

"That's in case you're hiding anything else. Next time I won't be so gentle. Well?"

Fran removed another knife from a sleeve and dropped it. Mandy turned to me. "Why wasn't Paprika arrested? She's obviously guilty."

"How do you know she wasn't?" I asked.

"Because I have her. And your boyfriend. If she'd been arrested, you wouldn't be here, and I wouldn't be so determined to shoot you dead."

"With your husband and Fran as witnesses?" I hoped for an opportunity.

"Mandy, what are you doing?" Arthur's full attention was on his gun wielding wife.

"Shut your mouth." She waved her gun around.

"Or what? You're going to shoot me?"

"I've no choice. You and Paprika will be responsible for the murder of Druby and the lake derelict, and your latest ho here, along with her jealous boyfriend. I'll be in shock, after you kill everyone tonight. I'll need intensive psychiatric treatment to recover. Probably in Paris or Milan."

"This isn't happening," Arthur said.

"Where is Bryce?" she asked me.

"The police have him," I said.

"Good. He'll have an alibi."

"It's just a matter of time before he cuts a deal for himself."

"Never."

"Who was the scuba diver?"

"Dom May did the menial tasks."

"How'd you get Dom to do your dirty work?" Arthur asked.

"He's a drug dealer, you ass. He's already dirty. We told him you were planning to replace him. If he worked for us, he'd keep his lucrative job. This economy is tough on everyone." Her gaze fixed on me. "How did you know I was the mastermind?"

"I didn't," I replied. "I thought it was Arthur."

"Ha. The only thing that buffoon is good at is gorging himself."

"How does the sapphire fit in?"

"It was a gift. From me. To me. Druby received an outrageous advance from my stupid husband, and I wanted it back. I copied the credit card information from Druby's wallet when he was here for the holiday party. I made the purchase flawlessly, using messengers. No one was the wiser."

"That was the time you spilled the merlot all over Druby's pants," Arthur said.

"If only you exercised such cleverness in picking our film projects."

"Dom broke into my place looking for the photo. The one showing you wearing the sapphire," I said.

"You suspected Paprika. It was brilliant of me. Giving her a faux trinket made her appear, if not guilty, connected somehow."

"Faux?" I asked.

"Her ring's a fake. I ordered it and had Bryce gift it to her. A ruse to steer attention away from me. It clearly worked. If it wasn't for that damn photo. That was Druby's fault too."

"You told me the ring was a family heirloom." Arthur tried to catch up to the rapidly unfolding facts.

"What did you expect me to say? My boyfriend bought it? You should never have made that Mexican your partner."

"Who stole money from the Complex?" I asked.

"Nothing was stolen, it was rechanneled. So Bryce and I could fund our own undertaking. A successful one. Studio money was wasted on mediocre projects that went nowhere."

"Bryce?" Arthur said, faintly.

"How are you going to survive this massacre?" I asked Mandy.

"Don't worry about lil' ol' me."

"Why Bryce?" Arthur asked.

"It's obvious. He looks phenomenal, and we love each other."

"Bryce only loves Bryce."

"You don't know him like I do."

"You're the one who doesn't know him," I said. "He came on to me like a fly on cowhide." That did not evoke a very attractive image.

"That was the plan. You'd fall for him, and he'd keep tabs on you, become your confidante. It was strictly business."

"That's not what he said in bed."

"Shut up." She fired her gun.

I threw myself down on the hard marble, and Arthur ducked. She shot again and shattered the mirror behind Arthur's head. The odor of sulfur infiltrated the room, like a hundred matches had been lighted. Fran stood, unflinching.

I slowly rose. Where was James? "I want to see Michael."

"You're in no position to make last requests."

"Yeah, well, what about me?" Arthur straightened up, a fist on each side of his waistline. "You wouldn't have any of this." He waved his hands around the room. "If it wasn't for me."

"This?" She waved the gun. "We have no equity in this dump, and we're behind on the mortgage, thanks to your unsurpassed knack for picking losers. If the banks weren't run by morons, we'd have been foreclosed on by now."

"Why did you kill him, Mandy?" Arthur shook his head. "Poor Druby."

"You killed him by making him your partner over my objections. He had no right to our profits. That peon was a freeloader. Bryce understood."

"I thought Bryce was with you on poker night," I told Arthur.

"He was." Arthur looked at Mandy questioningly.

"You came to the kitchen to make your cholesterol-loaded BLT. I told you Bryce was sleeping in the guestroom. But he was out, baiting the blockhead. He told Druby you needed help for a new project. Druby expected you at the lake. Bryce poisoned him, knocked him out, and sent the car into the water. We made it look like he'd drowned by suicide. It was the perfect murder."

"But Bryce was here at breakfast," Arthur said.

"So was Dom. They came back, stupid. I let them in."

"Where did you get the poison?" I asked.

"On the Internet, where else? I worked as a chemical engineer with injectable pharmaceuticals before this gig. Working with poison was a natural progression."

"Some would say unnatural," I said. Panic hit me. Where was Michael? "You poisoned Michael."

"Antifreeze is hardly a poison. Dom followed him after you met with that detective. If your boyfriend wasn't such a snoop, we'd have left him alone."

"You tried to kill him."

"If I wanted him dead, he would be. It was a warning. It's one thing to kill a low-life, but you or your boyfriend—there would have been more of a probe. Now you leave me no choice."

"Bryce tried to kill me on the ferry."

"Only as a last resort. You got too close."

"Why kill Tom John?"

"He talked too much. Dom dressed like the derelict, went to the library, and e-mailed you to meet him at the lake. We gave you a second chance. You should have backed-off. It's all your fault. We wouldn't be here now if it wasn't for you. It'll feel so good to get rid of such a colossal troublemaker." She raised her pistol and aimed at me.

"Here I am!" Winona barged into the room and tripped to a stop.

"You're going to get yourself killed," Arthur said.

"Actually, she's not," Mandy said. "She'll be my witness."

"Don't believe her, Winona," I said. "She can't risk leaving any witnesses."

"Shoot her," Mandy said.

Winona reached into her handbag, rummaged around and said, "I found it." She pulled out a pistol and pointed it upward. She shot a few bullets into the ceiling.

Mandy turned and fired. The air was split by a clang that scattered all other sounds. Winona yelped and crumpled. Fran and I lunged forward.

"Freeze!" Mandy aimed at us.

"Why did you shoot her?" Arthur asked, folding into a chair.

"She failed me for the last time."

"Don't criticize her!" I said, following Marshall Law Rule Number Three—Take control by acting like a lunatic. "All she ever wanted was your friendship."

"In the present tense, please," Winona said, fluttering her eyes. A puddle of blood gathered near her shoulder.

"You don't get it, do you?" Mandy said. "Bryce, Dom, Winona—they're on my team."

It was so tempting to reach into my pocket. To the shuriken. I prayed she'd keep talking, so I could make a move. I didn't have to. Fran made one for me.

He charged toward Mandy. The air split again and Fran keeled over, a well of blood springing from his side.

"Frannie." Arthur started toward Fran's motionless body. "He needs help."

"Don't move." Mandy pointed the pistol at Arthur.

"Billy was right. He knew you did it from the start," I said.

"How could that clod know? Dom practically tapped him on the shoulder before knocking him out in San Pedro."

"Why did Dom hit Billy at the dock?" Arthur's eyes were glued to Fran.

"To kill the ass, why else? We had no idea he was so hard-headed. He wouldn't leave the suicide theory alone." She turned to me. "Go stand by Art."

"No," I heard myself say.

"What?" Arthur and Mandy asked in unison.

"'So be it,'" I said. "That's what Bryce said. After he killed Druby. Tom John heard him."

"Who cares?" Mandy said. "Move."

"Tell me first if Michael's okay." I fixed my gaze on the entry. "Michael."

The moment Mandy's eyes followed my stare, I reached my right hand inside my pocket and wrenched out the shuriken. I hurled the blade toward Mandy, barely taking aim. The clap of her pistol rang out. I dove and hit the hard marble floor for the second time, landing on my hands and stomach. I felt certain I cracked a rib, the pain was so monumental. I wasn't sure which slammed the ground first, me or the pistol when she dropped it. I raised my head. The bullet had smashed through a window accompanied by the off key, melodic clink of breaking glass. Arthur watched in fascination, astonishment playing around his open mouth. Fran sprang to life, slid over, and clasped the pistol, his face creased in pain. The shuriken had struck Mandy squarely in the forearm.

"Call an ambulance," she said, staring at her arm. "I'm bleeding."

"Call 9-1-1." I jumped to my feet and turned to Arthur. "Press napkins against Fran's wound." I yanked the shuriken out of a frantic Mandy, wiped it clean on her skirt, and shoved it back into my pocket. I grabbed the gun from Fran, worried that he'd pass out. Blood gushed out of his middle section like water from a broken hydrant. Arthur moved at light speed to stop-up Fran's wound.

I pointed the gun squarely at Mandy. "Where's Michael?"

She tipped back her head and opened her mouth,

her body shook with laughter. I slapped Mandy across the cheek; my palm stung from the heat of the blow. Her hysterics evaporated and she stared at me in shock. So did a fascinated Arthur. I was surprised he didn't grab a bucket of buttered popcorn, with all the theatrics.

"Where's Michael?" I repeated.

"I'm hurt, Artie," Mandy cried.

"Where's Pokey?" Arthur asked.

I looked at him.

"Pokita. The maid. Mandy locks her in her room every night. So she doesn't wander around the house."

If I wasn't already horrified, this would have pushed me over.

"Pokey's illegal," Arthur said. "So she doesn't complain."

"You're a superlative ass, Arthur," Mandy said.

"Where's her room?" I demanded. "Better yet, go check, Arthur."

I traded spots with Arthur and a panting, bloody-lipped James appeared. Dirt spattered his torn sweatshirt and a sleeve was ripped at the seam. Detective Delgado, accompanied by assorted men in black, hot-footed inside behind him, guns cocked and ready.

"Finally," I said.

"Looks like I missed all the fun," James said.

I lowered my gun. "Were you taking a nappie-poo?"

"Yeah. With that guy." James pointed to a big, handcuffed fellow with a swollen eye and lip, held by one of the officers.

"The pool man? Petey's in on this?" Arthur gaped at Mandy.

"I told him not to let anyone but Winona inside. Grazie, Pietro," Mandy said.

"Let's find Michael. Come on, Arthur," I commanded and told Delgado, "Beat the answers out of her. Just beat her." At that moment, I was all for police brutality. I left before I beat Mandy up myself.

Arthur scrambled and the ambulance arrived. He paled and wiped his forehead on a sleeve. "Hope Frannie's okay. This way."

He led James and me and a couple of uniformed cops down a narrow, winding staircase to a tiny, dark room. A cheap plastic dinette set posed in the center and a small kitchen veered off to one side. Arthur tramped down a short hallway leading to a closed door. "Here."

I tried the doorknob. It was locked. "Open it."

"I don't have the key."

I pounded my fist against the closed door, shouting Michael's name. There was no response.

"Stand back," one of the uniforms said and aimed at the doorknob. He shot enough times to blow a hole large enough for a toy poodle to jump through. My ears throbbed from the discharge. The stink of sulfur infiltrated my nostrils once again. I was certain I'd lost most of my hearing on the spot and possibly blown an eardrum.

The cops kicked open the door and we stormed in. The room sat empty, except for a few sticks of plastic furniture.

"Where else?" I asked Arthur.

Arthur hurried away. We ran after him, upstairs, racing past the stretcher loading Fran into an ambulance. Winona limped behind him. Arthur led us out a back door, to the dock. “That’s the only other place she’d stash them,” he said. He hurried toward his yacht.

Chapter 66
The End of the Day

With the help of Pietro the pool man, Mandy hid Michael, Paprika, and Pokey in the wood paneled master suite of Arthur's yacht. Although she'd duct taped their hands, feet, and mouths, it took Michael all of twenty minutes to do a Houdini impression and escape. It took another minute for him to free the other two with the small, but trusty blade he'd taped to his lower back.

While they plotted freedom from the confines of their windowless room, Pokey tried the doorknob.

"You must come," she'd said to them.

"Pokey, can't you see we're trying to figure out the fastest way out of here?" Michael had said.

That's when Pokey opened the door. The lock was broken. This realization came when we bounded down the stairwell leading to their luxurious cell.

When Paprika had learned of my "date" with Bryce, she'd sped to Bernard's only to find Michael blocking her from barging into the cafe. He said her body jolted from spasms of anger as he held her back. But not because of my monopolizing Bryce. Her rage stemmed from a visit to a jeweler. Paprika had the sapphire ring appraised. The value? $295.00. She'd expected the real deal from Bryce.

"I'm going to kill him," Paprika had said.

"No." Michael had sat on a chair so he could meet her, eye-to-eye. "I saw the ring. The actual gem. On Mandy's finger."

Paprika's fury escalated.

"It was like there was an earthquake happening," Michael said. "Right beneath her feet. She shook all over."

She suspected Mandy, (of course, she suspected all females), but Paprika assumed Bryce bought Mandy the sapphire, leaving the fake for Paprika. To be tossed over for such a "swamp donkey" was beyond her comprehension. She insisted on paying Mandy a visit. Although Paprika maintained she didn't kill Druby, Michael accompanied her to prevent another potential murder. Michael wrote me a text telling me to go to Arthur's house, but accidentally sent it to his mother. She'd noticed it after she and Michael's dad finished hot-tubbing. She'd texted him back, requesting the address. After Michael didn't respond, she tried James. But he was in the midst of his own scuffle. I was next in line. By that time, I texted her that the party was over.

Mandy spotted Michael and Paprika, just before they reached the front door. She'd tricked them into believing Arthur had switched rings, and Bryce didn't know. She'd told them Arthur was on the yacht. Pokey was added later as a hostage, after she'd let me in without asking Mandy's permission. Detective Delgado had dragged Bryce to the scene, hoping to get a confession. She had him cuffed and leaning against an unmarked squad car. Once the captive trio was liberated, Paprika spotted Bryce. She launched toward him with such ferocity, she knocked him to the ground, exerted superhuman strength to uproot a nearby baby boulder and clobbered him, resulting in a cracked skull (said he) and a chipped front tooth (it was in plain sight), which put Bryce in hysterics. Paprika disappeared after that.

Michael gave me what was possibly the longest and tightest hug of my life. We'd still be hugging if Detective Delgado hadn't forcefully extricated us, so that we could give our statements to the police and be done with the whole thing.

"I can't believe Billy predicted it was Mandy," I said. "I'm glad you're safe, Michael."

"Not half as much as me," he said.

"And I won't say I told you so."

"About what?"

"The convenience of keeping a knife on your person."

"I'll never leave home without it again."

"Hey," James said. "I'm coming over tomorrow, Corrie, and confiscating all of your weapons."

"What are you going to do? Sell them on eBay?"

"You don't need them anymore."

"Fine." I shrugged. "But you'll never find the rocket launcher."

Chapter 67
Finale

Veera called early the next morning to tell me she'd retrieved the missing text message sent by Winona.

"I got me this new text saver app. And there it was. Winona contacted Mandy Keith and gave her the names on that list of yours. What do you make of that?"

"Veera, you just solved Druby's murder."

"For real? I knew I was good."

"Except that Mandy confessed last night."

"Well, it's good to know that if she hadn't, we would have kicked her butt today, anyhow."

"True story. And I was wrong. Winona was Mandy's informant, not Marshall's. But, Veera? Thanks. I couldn't have done it without you. You were a big help and a great friend."

"Well, I'm responsible for you, remember?"

That night, Ty made good on his promise to get Michael and me courtside seats at the Staples Center for his big game. And Ty's mojo was back. His team won 122-86.

Minutes after the game ended, Center security approached us and handed me a small, robin's egg blue jewelry box.

"What's that?" Michael asked.

"A Tiffany box. Earrings maybe." I used my keen

sleuthing skills and shook the box. “Maybe a watch.”

The attached note read,

It’s about time. Thanks again. Ty.

I opened the box and stopped breathing.

“Is that a…?” Michael’s mouth hung open.

“Ke…ke…key.” A small note was folded inside. “Oh, dear God. It’s the key to a new BMW coupe, courtesy of Ty.”

A high-pitched screech pierced the air, causing a small stampede from those sitting closest to us. Only one lone celebrity a few seats away remained. He turned his black shades toward me and held a finger to his lips. The scream that had been gurgling in my throat for so long had finally escaped.

****

Michael and I spent the day reliving yesterday’s events. Bryce had fingered Stefon, so he and Mandy could escape.

“Bryce had this cold streak in him,” Paprika had confided to Michael. “The ring came as an enormous surprise. We’d been together two years and he gave me flowers once. And they weren’t even roses. They were tulips or daffodils or some other silly bulb. When Alana told me he was with the woman lawyer at the new office, I showed up to see for myself. Bryce surprised me with the ring. I knew it was a bribe, but I’m a very accepting person with a weakness for shiny, sparkly things.”

That explained her sudden arrival at the new, improved Complex.

Bryce sent Dom a regular stream of business, so he was only too happy to do his bidding. Harbor Patrol found the rented yacht-speed boat empty, but Delgado nabbed Dom early this morning, hiding out in the Complex 2.

I'd underestimated Bryce's skills. He'd convinced Arthur and Stefon to set up a subsidiary, and deposited money from the Complex for future projects. He later made it seem that Stefon had embezzled funds by depositing a portion in his personal bank account.

"I loaned Bryce money and gave him my account number," Stefon explained at the police station. "To repay me. I trusted him. I thought we were friends. But he took Complex money and put it in my account so I couldn't talk while he and Mandy funneled out funds."

Stefon had argued with Druby about Mandy on the day of Druby's death. She'd pressured Druby to bow out of his partnership with Arthur. "He didn't mind the harassment," a shaken Stefon recalled. "Dru said he'd do his best to help her. He was willing to make it an eighty-twenty partnership. After a while, he said five percent would be enough, but she wanted it all. I told him to go to Arthur about it, but he wouldn't."

And Claire? How did she fit in?

"After Druby died, Claire collapsed. She loved him. She came to me for help. But what could I do? What could anyone do? I didn't think she'd kill herself."

****

Hilda broke down when Michael and I stopped to see her late last night, to let her know her son had not committed suicide, and that those responsible for his death were caught.

"It means so much to me," she had said. "I knew he wouldn't hurt himself. He couldn't. My boy."

****

Dad wasn't around to guide me in solving Druby's death, but our time together fueled my fire and helped me to help others. The small role I played in bringing about justice would have made him proud. Even Mom was okay with it.

"Maybe they'll promote you to senior attorney now," she said. "And give you a raise. Be sure and ask for one. But no more investigating. You are not your father."

"Right," I said. I'd hang up my shingle tomorrow. It would be a part-time gig. Maybe.

I was happy. I'd found Michael, safe and unharmed. I still had my job. Arthur had called this morning to tell me Fran would be okay. How would I repay Francois for saving my life? And how would I make it up to James for being there when I'd needed him? "Oh, James. Oh, Michael." I closed my eyes. Life was simply too complex. But one thing overpowered all other emotions: gratitude. Yes, I was grateful and happy. Happy to put all that happened behind me. Just happy.

Even Rob came around. He'd sent me a text:

I forgive you.

Rob and his boyfriend had dressed up as the pope every Halloween. After they broke up, Rob donated the costume to the thrift shop. Mandy sent Dom to buy it back under Stefon's name. He hid it in Stefon's condo and tipped off the cops, anonymously, yesterday afternoon. Stefon was part of Mandy's Plan B. In case the suicide theory didn't work, Stefon would be blamed.

And Billy had called. "You did good," he said. "Real good. I told you Druby wouldn't do that to himself."

"You were right, Billy. He was lucky to have you for his friend. You were right about a lot of things."

"I want to ask you something." Billy hesitated. "My dad skipped out on me when I was nine. I heard he's living in Pasadena. You think you can track him down?"

"I don't find missing persons."

"No. You just find missing cats."

"Where'd you hear that?"

"I read all about it. 'Ty Calvin Finds His Loud-Mouth Cat.' In the *National Chatterer.*"

What did I tell you?

A word about the author…

Lida Sideris, like her heroine (Corrie Locke), hails from Southern California and worked as an entertainment attorney for a film studio. She has written numerous magazine and newspaper articles, a poem or two, and a teleplay. She shares her home with one husband, two sons, and an assortment of dogs and chickens.

Visit her website at:
www.lidasideris.com

Thank you for purchasing
this publication of The Wild Rose Press, Inc.

If you enjoyed the story, we would appreciate your letting others know by leaving a review.

For other wonderful stories,
please visit our on-line bookstore at
www.thewildrosepress.com.

For questions or more information
contact us at
info@thewildrosepress.com.

The Wild Rose Press, Inc.
www.thewildrosepress.com

Stay current with The Wild Rose Press, Inc.

Like us on Facebook

https://www.facebook.com/TheWildRosePress

And Follow us on Twitter
https://twitter.com/WildRosePress